The Colony Chronicles

Scott Pauker

Smithson International
Los Angeles

The Colony Chronicles
Scott Pauker

Smithson International
910 E. Walnut Avenue
Burbank, CA 91501
www.smithsoninternational.com

ISBN-13: 978-0-9856749-8-4
ISBN-10: 0985674989
Printed in the United States of America

Cover Design by Haig Simonian
Special thanks to Christopher Langton, founder of the Langton Ant.

First Edition: June 2012
10 9 8 7 6 5 4 3 2 1

May we be guided by the wisdom and kindness
of a boy who touched our minds and our hearts.

"May the stars watch over us."
-Evan Lee Burns, 1997-2011

The author would like to acknowledge the following for their enduring patience, kind words, and strong support:

Brandon Andrew Pauker, Brielle Alysse Pauker
Bonnie Pauker, Gregory J. Schwartzman
Jesse Amarillas, Kerry Burns, Elizabeth Winter
Cori Cohan, Deborah de Cuir

The Colony Chronicles

I

I call him Father; he calls me Son. Our relationship is one of parent and child, although I've never seen another parent interact with a child. To the colonists he is known as Antboy, a Beast, but to me he is Father, and to him I am Son.

Father saved me when I was just a baby. He told me that I was the first human born since the settlement of the Colony and that I was a month premature. Father explained that the Council was afraid of my coloring and it could not allow me to introduce this perceived inferiority or any genetic defects that I contained into the Colony. The Council unanimously agreed that I was to be deselected due to my yellowish pigmentation which Father calls "jaundice".

Father said that I was selected for destruction because the HSI code, the Human Survival Initiative, required male babies to be deselected if they posed a genetic risk to future human reproduction. Any irregularity in male new-borns was to be reported to the Council and a vote was to

1

be made as to whether the infant should be retained or destroyed. As the first born on our man-made satellite planet, a world that orbits the sun, about four hundred thousand miles closer than the earth does, I was also the first to be deselected.

Father was opposed to the vote but could not voice his opinion because he was prohibited from interfering with the affairs of the Council. It is forbidden for him to directly affect the outcome of any of the Council's decisions. He is only supposed to offer interpretations of the HSI code and advise that things run according to it. Stringent rules had been imposed by HSI when it launched our synthetic satellite planet, rules deemed necessary in the quest to secure the survival of the human race.

The assignment of my deselection was to be delegated to one of the Council members, but Father volunteered to complete the destruction duties himself. He left the Council meeting, and at an appointed time he proceeded to Dome Seventeen where I had been left, hungry, wailing. Even though he was very afraid of what would happen if he were caught, he knew that I had to be saved. He hid me in a blanket and hurried quickly back to his dome, the Dome of Maintenance.

He spent the rest of that day reworking the dome so that he could feed me nutrients from the food generators. To prevent me from being discovered, he created a secure space beneath the floor, our Alcove enmeshed in metal, to hide me. Often we hide together when the Scouts roam our district. Since the Council believes that I was destroyed, Father has sternly warned me that I can never safely leave our dome. Petrified, though, I know that I will, I must.

"Shhh, Atum," whispers Father harshly, sternly scolding me.

"But Father, the Scouts have been gone for hours," I reply.

"It doesn't matter, son. This hiding place is not fool-proof."

"You always told me it was."

"I know I did. I told you that so you wouldn't be afraid. When you were younger, you would fall asleep easier, and completely, when you felt safe. I wanted you to feel secure and rest well, especially during the times when we needed to spend several days and nights hiding here."

"So, our Alcove is not safe? You said they couldn't sense us through the metal panels."

"That's true, they can't. All right, Atum. You're right. They can't hear us, but that doesn't change the fact that I'm tired and I think we should both rest. We've spoken enough for tonight. Besides, you need to remember that our voices may cause vibrations outside of this chamber, and we both know how sensitive they are to vibrations."

"But you told me that if we keep our voices very low, below the level of a single decibel, then they can't detect the vibration, and that we're safe to talk. Tell me again how you saved me." Father often tells me the story of how he saved me. I'm always comforted by his recount of my rescue.

"All right, I will, but if I leave out a few parts, it's because I'm tired."

"No problem, as long as you promise not to cry this time."

"That's a deal." Yet Antboy vividly and indelibly remembered every intimate detail of that day, choosing to share only certain things with Atum. He carefully omitted most of

3

the events surrounding Atum's birth. Burying this knowledge, he chose to never divulge the identity of Atum's mother, Lavender. Antboy's true and only love, Lavender, had been callously ordered to scorn him, and then was directed to mercilessly abandon Atum. There was no alternative for Antboy; he could never reveal the specific details and circumstances surrounding Atum's birth and his rescue, neither to Atum nor to Lavender. Such a revelation could prove calamitous.

Lavender ultimately came to Antboy, having scrubbed away her wretched state of punishment, to regrettably end what they had unfortunately begun. Between her stammering sobs of grief, Lavender informed Antboy that she was prohibited from visiting him again.

Antboy immediately experienced an utterly precise, wrenching pain. Attempting to ease the intolerable ache, to console them both, he involuntarily, carelessly, and effortlessly leaned toward Lavender, kissing her passionately and deeply.

At length they embraced, and the intimate moments that followed reflected eternally in the mirror of their shattered love. Yet, Antboy's stomach filled with butterflies and he was weak in the knees, and anxious. He recognized and completely understood that Lavender would adhere to Siren's momentous pronouncement. To insure her safety, and to safeguard the welfare of her unborn child, Lavender chose to obey Siren's implicit command. From that dreadful day forward, she vowed to permanently renounce her love for Antboy.

Aware of the grim ramifications that would befall Lavender if their relationship continued, Antboy also knew he would be held severely accountable if he persisted. Realizing that this was to be their final intimate moment, he was absolutely powerless, destined to be forever solitary, having loved but for a brief time. Tormented, Antboy had never encountered such great pain, and he suffered loneliness while still in Lavender's momentary presence.

As Lavender caressed his distressed face, tears streamed down hers. Cuddling for hours, neither wanted to break the soothing comfort of their closing embrace. Then, an abrupt convulsion was felt, and they were startled and shocked to hear the sound of gushing water.

Their eyes sought the source and in seconds Antboy was carrying Lavender, calming her, telling her not to worry, insisting that she would be fine, begging her to relax, instructing her to inhale and exhale deeply, and reassuring her. These were the gentle words that flew from Antboy's mouth when he swiftly discovered that Lavender's water had broken, a month premature.

Weaving through the elaborate and convoluted tunnel system toward the Dome of Birth, he transported her for hours, praying that he would have the strength and speed to get her the proper care she so desperately needed. Forgetting completely about the circumstances of their parting, and the finality and necessity of her decision, he persevered. He thought only about her safety and the birth of her child.

Eventually he delivered her to the colonists. He was irately greeted by a swarm of their white tunics, and as they overtook him, they pelted him with some hardened objects, and cast insults. Although the pain from these hurled items distressed him, the harm was superficial, incomparable to the profound hurt that enveloped his heart. Knowing that the external bruising would undeniably heal, Antboy feared his internal wounds were forever. He felt his heart rip, a tear

5

so sudden, yet eternally deep, perhaps the only mechanism with valves that Antboy possessed no power to fix.

When Antboy awoke the next day, he thought only of Lavender. He repeated the arduous trek to the Dome of Birth, longing to see Lavender during her recovery. She was alone, resting, and there was no sign of her baby. He approached cautiously, and went to her side. She looked so peaceful, so serene in her gown, and so empty. Where was the baby? He knelt down and held her hand and her sweet lips formed a weak smile. She struggled to keep her lids open and then he heard shouting. Three sentries were pointing at him and in the commotion he was ushered out of the dome.

His frustration was transfixed on one point, one action. He sought Siren. He would convince her to put an end to his exclusion from the colony of females and he needed her to end his ban. Siren had to understand that he desired but one thing, Lavender.

He approached the Dome of Gathering determinedly and his stride exuded confidence. Just before reaching the entrance, he was overtaken by the same three women, those who had tended to Lavender and had hurriedly run to catch up to him. Before he could attempt to bypass them and enter the dome, they rushed past him and crossed the threshold. He was suddenly met with a closed door. He knocked, and knocked. He pounded on the door, thumping and banging it with both hands. Realizing he could manipulate the entry panel to the right of the door, he attempted to circumvent the barrier. Soon it opened.

Upon entering, he was greeted with a silence as deafening as the torrential eruption of a long dormant volcano. The colonists sat calmly and just stared at him. No one moved. No one tried to defend herself or attack him. But without movement there was power, for they acted as an ocean whose motion was in uniformity, and he was but a ship at the mercy of this ocean. With their synchronization they could crush him and swallow him whole. He was afraid. Although the ocean was momentarily calm, he knew it might eventually swell up and smother him. So he treaded the waters very carefully, since he still had plenty of work to do and was unprepared to succumb to the currents. Thus, he bowed.

He bowed his body down to the ground, in supplication, and with his movement he begged, pleaded for just a moment of their attention and consideration. He was prostrate, sitting on his shins, his forehead touching the ground, arms outstretched in front of his head, his eyes averted from direct visual contact with the females, the mandatory position of a loyal, subservient male. He was signaled to remain prone to the ground and to edge slowly toward the circle. Crawling over to the circle, he patiently waited until the ocean parted briefly.

He was admitted into their ring, and in the center was the baby. He looked at the newborn, wrapped in a white blanket, head to toe, except a small opening for it to breathe. It looked like a boy, but he was not certain, for all he could see were the eyes and the face. But from the eyes he knew that this infant, almost a month premature, was certainly Lavender's. He also noticed that its skin color was slightly yellow. Recognizing that it was not yet his turn to speak, he remained silent.

They were discussing the child and then they began to pass the infant throughout the circle. Every female held and then surveyed the baby, and grunted. When the newborn finally made its way to Siren, she asked some form of question and made sweeping motions with her hands and then she rose, the baby held high over her head.

Antboy was pleased. He saw the power of the life-providing females, the respect for human life that he had wanted to see in this new human order. Slowly, the women began to rise. Some remained seated. Those that sat were shaking their heads, disapproving of something. Those that stood, started speaking, and pointing, while holding their Codex up high, and they said, "The color is bad. It is poison."

Then the seated women joined them, each holding her precious book, her Codex, aloft, and Siren said, "The time has come. This male must be deselected. Who will do it?" Two women approached Siren, volunteering for the task.

Antboy quickly rose, but the ocean began to swell and he knew he must stay low to the floor of the dome. Rapidly, he hunched again, sat and spoke, "My Queen."

"Yes, Beast. What is it? Why are you here? You are not welcome here," Siren stated.

"Yes, I know. What is wrong with the child?" He asked.

"It is sick. It cannot be allowed to breed. It must be deselected. That is the law." A chorus of solemn agreement could be heard.

Afraid for the child, he needed to do something, and asked, "Is there no other way?"

In unison, the waves crashed down upon the surf, with a defiant "Nah!"

And so he offered, "I will do it. I will do it. Today, I will do this job." Antboy held out his arms to take the child.

Siren waved him off, stating that it was too soon. She expressed that he must deselect the child when the moon is directly below them, for that is the time of utter darkness, and it must only happen then. She pointed upward and with her hands cupped she looked to be in prayer to the moon.

He was ordered to go to Dome Seventeen when the moon was least visible and take the baby far from the Colony to be destroyed.

The women began to rub each other's stomachs and to pray, prayers for their unborn children not to meet the same fate. In unison they chanted. Siren pointed to one of her helpers to show him where the deselected child would await him. From the doorway, Siren's assistant indicated the direction of a dome where Antboy would later retrieve the boy.

As he turned to look at the expectant mothers, he saw Siren's belly, the biggest by far. He also noticed something dangling from Siren's neck. He spotted her mindlessly fingering a shiny object that hung from a string, placed securely within the cleavage of her bosom. As she twirled the object between her fingers, he recognized its shape to be that of the key that he had placed around Lavender's neck the day before. Siren had taken this trinket from Lavender when she was most vulnerable, perhaps even unconscious.

Symbolic of Siren's control over the Colony, the key, which perhaps Siren didn't understand was a key, since no keys graced the planet, represented both freedom and imprisonment. She now held the key to the future. A key that closed doors and opened possibilities, and she took it without permission, he knew that for certain. Siren must have confiscated Antboy's gift to Lavender as punishment for her trespasses outside of the colony's boundaries, specifically for her reconnoiters with him, the Beast.

This piece of metal, dangling from her neck, seemed to give Siren a sense of control and comfort, for now she compulsively, repetitively spun the key between her thumb and forefinger. She had single-handedly taken away Lavender's world, her baby, her love, and the key to her freedom. Thereby, Siren severely destroyed Lavender, as an austere lesson for all to obey the sacred code.

As he stared at Siren, and the others, they no longer acknowledged him. The colonists displayed an uncanny ability to remove him from the room, even when he was physically present. To them he no longer existed; he was but a Beast, a male that had no place in the Colony.

As he waited for the terrible moment when he was to destroy the child, he felt empty, vacant and alone, and in despair, for he did not know what to do. He felt pity, shame and compassion for what had befallen Lavender, and he alone was to blame. If he had concealed his love for her, she would not have visited him as frequently during those first weeks and months of the colony's settlement. Had he withheld his love and suppressed his expectation of her daily visits, they would not have grown close. Instead, he held back nothing. He even tread into terrible territory and probed her about the Codex and its laws about males. It was Antboy's reaction to what she shared with him that compelled her to approach Siren. He should never have displayed his shock.

When Antboy learned what would befall the males due to be imminently born into the Colony, he could no longer make eye contact with Lavender. She quietly endured his rejection, and then, to appease him and earn back his love and respect, Lavender made the grave mistake of approaching Siren. She questioned Siren's interpretation of the Codex with regard to male births, and hoped to have an open discussion.

Unfortunately, Siren viewed Lavender's request as ridiculous, labeling it as insubordination, tantamount to treason. Siren made it clear that she was not beholden to anyone to explain her interpretation of the Codex, and she made that evident by punishing Lavender. Siren decided that Lavender's boldness needed severe repercussions. Lavender would serve as an example for anyone that felt the desire to question authority. Siren's irrevocable edict caused great suffering and deep anguish for both Lavender and Antboy.

Siren's response caused Lavender severe distress and trauma, which pushed her baby too early into the world. Siren and the colonists blamed Antboy for the sickly child. He had brought upon Lavender a shame and humiliation and tragedy that he could not reverse.

To them, it was fitting that he be given the responsibility of deselecting the child, because on this satellite, not far from earth, he was considered nothing more than a beast. He dreaded that they would no longer permit him near Lavender, nor any colonist for fear that he would poison another child. His fears were realized. Siren soon banished Antboy from their affairs, deeming it an appropriate measure for his interference.

With heavy, broken, and trammeled heart, he returned to his home to wait for the fateful hour, and he trembled with anticipation and despair. He prayed that Lavender would not blame him for carrying out Siren's order; his only fear was that she would no longer love him.

He waited and waited. The sands of time fell one by one through the hourglass until the time arrived. He had no plan, no idea how he was going to do what he had to do, how he would find the strength to commit this most horrific act now deigned in the best interests of their new human order. It was too late to question the underlying theories and principles behind the Colony. He had no alternative but to accept things as they were. To try to affect any form of

11

change, he would surely bring ruin upon the Colony, himself, and above all, Lavender.

Penitently, he left his home, the Dome of Maintenance, bearing the gait of a condemned man who walks the longest path to his death. But it was worse, for he was to commit the murder of an innocent child, an unspeakable crime against humanity. Every step he took was mechanical at best, one foot after another. He was no longer in his own body. Instead he hovered above himself, pulling the strings like a puppeteer, wrenching his body step by step to the chosen spot at the designated hour. It was only by these means that he propelled forward, one heartbeat at a time. The pounding in his chest grew louder and thunderous until he was certain that the entire planet was pulsing with the blood that swiftly moved through his arteries.

II

Antboy could just make out the obscure silhouette of Dome Seventeen. His hazy vision faded into blackness with circling, buzzing, bits of gray-white lights and he felt himself falling, fainting. Yet he kept walking, and repressed his thoughts, for he had a duty to fulfill. His countenance assumed the demeanor of a murderer, a deviant psychotic. The muscles in his face pulled tight against his cheekbones, and he drew gaunt, his jaw clenched, his teeth ground tightly against each other. He was resolute and determined.

Entering the dome, he caught a glimpse of a woman in a flowing gown, her head veiled, holding the baby to her chest. As he approached, he saw that the gown was pulled down her shoulder and the baby was nestled between her arm and her breast, feeding. When his footsteps were heard, she hurriedly placed the baby in his cradle and turned away, gliding out the back entrance. In his heart he knew who nursed the child, although he was not certain. He detected the subtle scent of Lavender, who had come to bid her son farewell, but she would not stay to greet the reaper.

For a brief moment through the hardened stillness, their eyes locked but a second, yet eternally, and the tear running down her cheek spoke to the hidden tear in his eye and then she was gone. Yet the tear in his eye remained and it wandered from his eyelid, down to his cheekbone, and proceeded to travel toward his chin, and then it clung there, grasping tightly to his skin. It would not let go, for if it did then he would have cried, and he could not cry now, not now, when he needed to be so strong.

Instead, the baby was crying, wailing, in fact. As Antboy leaned over the child, his tear trickled, falling slowly, and time and space were motionless as the teardrop descended from his chin toward the child below. It fell into the eye of the child, and the child stopped crying, and looked up at him. It was then that he glimpsed, and truly saw, the powerful, green eyes that were Lavender's. He lifted the child up, who was no longer afraid, and he ran from the dome, into the night, to commit the horrendous act that was his destiny, an act that defied the Codex, the law of this female order.

He saved the child. And he called him Atum. And Atum never cried again, after that day. He hid the child and cared for the child and he never told Lavender, for if he were found out, tragedy would befall both Lavender and Atum. So she never knew, could never know, that her baby, her boy, her son, was alive and well. Yet, Antboy's choice tortured him; he witnessed what became of Lavender, but could do nothing to intervene.

The next morning, Lavender was relegated to Worker status. She had conceived badly, and her role shifted. No longer was she to bear children. Instead, she was to perform jobs necessary for the Colony and the expectant Mothers.

That same morning Atum needed her milk. He needed her food, for his body was failing and her nourishment was the only thing that could save him. But how was Antboy to obtain her food, the nutrients in her body that would maintain and nourish Atum, without revealing his sinister secret? He stayed up that night and knew there was no other choice than to go to Siren. In the early hours before dawn, he arrived at the entrance to the dome where Siren resided, now designated as the Dome of the Queen. He bowed down low to the two females that stood watch, their bellies small, their frames petite, their status diminished. He waited.

He waited for Siren to stir and rise, but every moment lasted an eternity, for he worried about little Atum. He had positioned Atum securely within a blanket, propped in a recess restricting movement making it virtually impossible for him to roll over and suffocate. But still he was concerned and grew anxious, especially since he was the child's sole guardian. Instinct replaced logic, and his protective, innate programming to protect this child dominated his thoughts and actions. He weighed the risk of Atum starving versus the danger of leaving Atum unattended and he chose to depart.

He worried that Siren would see through his deceptive reasoning, his irrational rationalization of what he was about to propose. But he had no choice; he had to try.

So he came bearing a gift. He knew no other way into her good graces than to come with a present. His offering needed to demonstrate his reverence for her power and beauty. He stopped at the Dome of Birth, designed to hold many new babies but as yet vacant, and he found a small, unused baby blanket, made of an unbleached, off-white material.

He perceived that Siren wanted to stand out, to be somewhat different, and her necklace, her stolen necklace, showed her desire to be unique. Yet all the clothing worn by the colonists was, as designed, colorless, and devoid of individual style.

Hastily, he could think of only one way to symbolize his respect for her as leader. He pierced his wrist and let the blood accumulate in a bowl. Then he cut his leg behind his knee and secured even more blood. He squeezed even more from his armpit. When he felt he had enough, he took his index finger and began to draw upon the blanket spread out on the floor of the nursery. He drew the symbols that represented this society. He drew a circular dome and spirals of hands, each holding the other, forming a united circle. Then he drew what he hoped she would respond to, a picture of herself. He drew the profile of a beautiful feminine face, flowing locks of hair, a full bosom, and a baby, a newborn clutched to the breast of this gracious, powerful leader. He sketched several women holding their infants outstretched for Queen Siren to nurse. She was smiling, smiling benevolently on her clan, with an expression so confident and proud, that it symbolized a foreshadowing of great glory, prosperity, and fertility, which would befall this world. If given a brief audience with Siren, he was satisfied that he would obtain what Atum desperately needed, the sacred fluid that only Lavender herself, the first to birth, could provide.

When he was finally allowed to squat in front of her, he felt her thoughts probe him. He began to explain the purpose for his visit. His hand and body movements were controlled and direct. He motioned that the deed was done and his words, simplistic and detached, were deliberately circuitous. His object was to lead her to draw certain conclusions and issue certain commands that she would believe were her own doing. He needed her to unwittingly make decisions and act according to his desires, without comprehending that her actions had been manipulated. He knew that this was his only hope. Or he could go directly to Lavender and tell her what he had done, which would risk everything. So he was strategic in his approach.

"My Queen, I am here to thank you."

"For what, Beast?"

"Thank you for the task. I want to be needed and to obey the law. The poison is gone."

"Good. That job was yours; you were needed for that single job, but nothing else."

"I have a gift for you."

"I want nothing from you."

"Then, my Queen, may I now leave?" With that he made an almost imperceptible movement to crawl away.

"No."

"Then, my Queen, how may I be of service to you?"

"You have nothing I want." She was greeted by silence. Then she was quiet for a few moments also. "Show me this gift, Beast," she commanded.

He bent his head deeply to the ground and held out the blanket that he had fashioned into what could be worn as a scarf. She took the scarf while he remained with his head bent low, eyes and forehead pressed to the floor. He could feel the energy that now pulsated from the heat of her cheeks, and he sensed that she was proud of her present. His eyes strained to catch a glimpse of her face, and he gathered that it was working, for he spied that she was blushing, and her smile was pleasant, and strong.

"You are smart for a Beast. What is it you want?"

"Nothing, my Queen. Shall this gift bring you everlasting fertility! May I leave now?"

"You will leave when I tell you to leave." She grew terribly frustrated. It was she that would decide when he was to go. "Sit up straight!" She demanded.

He quickly shifted position to sit upon his knees, kneeling on his knuckles and looking up at her now radiant face.

"You are a seer, Beast. From the Codex, it is said you see the future. Perhaps you understand dreams. This is the reason for the gift, yah?"

"Yes, my Queen. That is why I am here."

"Do you have anything else to share with me?"

"Only that it is time to gather the food, your Majesty."

"What food?"

"The food that will feed the children." He motioned to the Mothers on the scarf.

"The food is not yet ready and it is too soon. No more children have arrived."

"Lavender's food must not be wasted. Others will need this food later. It must be taken and stored safely for a possible shortage. In time it will be too late."

Her eyes grew wide, and her expression displayed apt concern. Within moments, one of the sentries ran inside in response to Siren's shout. An order was issued and suddenly Lavender was brusquely seated before the Queen, her gown improperly and unwillingly jerked above her head. Antboy saw her manifest elegance, her supple unblemished skin and ample bosom, so enticing, so smooth, so soft. The sentry was fashioning some type of bottle, and she was wrapping a plastic material around and about it, perhaps carved from one of the domes itself. A small hole was poked into the tip of this bottle, and then she placed it upon Lavender's nipple and areola, but Lavender was startled and drew away. The sentry again placed it on Lavender's breast, but as she drew back again, Siren barked out, "Move not." Then Lavender stood still.

The bottle formed suction between Lavender's nipple and the plastic cover and the sentry began to gently tug at the nipple, cupping her breast underneath and massaging. A few drops fell into the bottle but much more began to sprout from Lavender's other nipple and then dribbled down her bosom, a translucent white, watery thin fluid. Siren's eyes grew angry at this waste and she screamed for the other sentry to enter. Siren commanded her to fashion another bottle, demonstrating for the sentry to form her mouth in the shape of a circle and to make sucking motions, until the second bottle was ready. The sentry placed her lips around the whole of Lavender's nipple and began to suck, at first gently and then harder, until her mouth was filled with the fluid and she spat it into the first bottle. Then she did so again. Lavender's fury was deeply inscribed on her furrowed brow, and her oppressive stare pierced Antboy's eyes, face, torso, heart, and he knew that she suffered and was violated.

Although he was to blame for her situation, and he felt terrible for her misery, Lavender's milk was all that mattered to him now. His protective, parental instincts had surfaced; he had no choice but to restrain his desire for her love. At that moment, communicated by her mute expression, he was wordlessly told that her love had dissipated as suddenly as her milk had expressed.

He offered to take the milk to the Dome of Nursing, and Siren agreed. Lavender threw daggers of condemnation from her fiery pupils, but they were deflected by his defensive armor of hardened determination. Holding the warm bottles, he crawled, then walked, then ran as fast as his legs could carry him, back to the miracle, the sleeping little boy whose hungry body was crowned by his heavenly, placid little face.

"You did it, Father. This time you didn't cry."

"Well, Atum. Now that you're thirteen, I have a lot to be thankful for."

"Tell me more about the ants. I promise I'll go to sleep as soon as you tell me."

"Why can't you sleep, son? What's on your mind?"

"So many things, I don't know where to start. I'm afraid every time you leave our home. And you're leaving again in a few months to go to the Endeavors. I have a lot of questions and there's way too much that I still don't understand."

"You know enough, and you've absorbed plenty, a great multitude of things, so please stop worrying. Eventually I will teach you everything I know. I promise. Will you promise to study the disks when I'm gone?"

"Yes, I promise. This time I will, I really will."

"Good," says Antboy as he gently rubs Atum's forehead.

"You told me that owning metal is against the law, but our hiding chamber is completely encased in metal, and the disk reader too. We can get in loads of trouble, can't we?"

"We can get in tremendous trouble. It's imperative that we always conceal this space. I violated the law to protect you. I broke it to build our Alcove."

"I still don't understand why we're here, so far from where you used to live, where you were born?"

"Actually, we were never supposed to be here, so far from home. This was not the solution. Instead, this is a distortion, a hypothetical irregularity. My home, my planet was badly broken. After my conversation with Hiawatha, I spent years trying to find answers. My theories and calculations were designed to fix things, and I truly thought that they did. Now I sometimes I wonder if there is a solution."

"He taught you a lot of important things, didn't he?"

"You mean, *she* taught me a lot of things. There are no male ants after mating, remember? Yes, she, and the others opened my eyes."

III

"Well, during those long, humid and rainy summers, I spent most of my time tromping around in the mud. Sometimes I would sit on the stoop and watch the earth literally dry out. If it dried enough, I knew I could run around the woods with my friends, or play baseball and football. Sitting there, I would watch the ants poke up through the drying mud, to then dig out their chambers. If they stayed down inside their caverns, then I knew it was going to rain again, and that's when I would go inside to watch cartoons, play video games, read adventure stories, and draw colorful pictures of ants."

"The paintings with all the colors you've described?"

"Yes, Atum, all the colors."

"Tell me about "green" again, and "yellow", and "red". I want to remember them, especially since it's totally dark in here right now."

"Well, red is the color of your blood. And green is the color of your eyes, and yellow is like the color of the sun, where we get all of our energy. Come closer, Atum, it's cold, and we are long overdue for bed. Close your eyes."

After a few moments, just when it appears that I've drifted off, my head upon Father's chest, rising and falling with his every inhale and exhale, and my steady breathing in sync with his heartbeat, I rise slightly and say, "Go on."

"Well, you know that this wasn't the first time I spoke to the ants."

"Yes, Father, you told me you disliked the nickname that the neighbors and some of the mean kids called you."

"That's right."

"But you knew that the ants were smart, and honest, and told you important things."

"Yes, the ants were highly intelligent and they shared important things with me. When people in the neighborhood saw me huddling over anthills, they at first considered it to be very odd, but eventually they no longer thought it was such a spectacle. They would just say, "Look at Antboy." I quietly detested, but outwardly accepted the nickname Antboy."

"I bet they thought you were very strange, Father."

"Well, they did, and now I truly am, Atum. I'm considered very bizarre here, and there's no one like me. But back then I just wanted to be a regular kid. So, mainly out of boredom, on those summer mornings, I would sit there, and watch the earth dry out, waiting to see if the ants would surface, to begin the tedious and monotonous job of carrying out the earth. If I saw them, I could forecast that it wouldn't rain and I was always right. Neighbors would wait to hear what I predicted, and then they would call their friends and make or change their plans. It was rumored I would become a meteorologist."

"What's that?"

"Basically, someone that used to tell us if it would be hot, cold, wet, or dry. It's hard to explain, especially when we don't get that type of weather here. So, I sat and watched the ants until I saw the signs I needed. If it was going to be dry, then I could roam and explore for hours."

"Tell me more about that one day, when you were eleven, the one with Hiawatha."

"Okay, well, it was like any other early morning, when the dew and the previous night's rain formed puddles, and muddy ground. It was very cloudy, but then the sun surprisingly peaked through, and before long it was exceptionally dazzling, yet radiating a dreadfully dry heat. Then I saw an ant push her head out, and look around, left, right, back, and forth. She began to rapidly go in and out of that small hole, dragging chunk after chunk of earth with her.

"It didn't look like there were any other ants around, so I thought it might be a fluke, maybe an autonomous ant on a suicidal mission, waiting for the pounding rains to wash her away. So I waited awhile, and then watched as she dragged corpses back to the hole and dropped them downward. Sometimes she would bring crumbs of earth out, and pile them on the sides of the hole, making a mound, and other times she would search around for her dead brethren and carry them up the slope of the mound to drop them down below.

"Why do you do that?" I asked.

"Why do you do that?" She asked.

"What?" I replied.

"What?" She replied.

"Why do you always search for dead ants and retrieve them?" I asked.

"Why do you care?" She retorted.

"I just do. I've always wondered."

24

"Well, you wonder too much. You wouldn't understand."

"Try me. I think about all types of strange things."

"Fine, then I'll appease your curiosity. Every ant is very important to our colony, and species. We recover all of our dead, just like you. Humans respect their dead. We're no different."

"I think you're very different. You put your dead in piles, in mounds. We bury them."

"True, but that's because we're already buried when we're alive. Since we live inside the earth, we don't need to cover our dead with dirt. If we did, we couldn't absorb their knowledge."

"What do you mean, 'absorb their knowledge'?"

"Every antling is born with the knowledge of its entire species, millions of years worth of data. Sometimes ants, in their short life spans, have very unique experiences, so we try to absorb every bit of new information."

"And you can do that, after they're dead?"

"Yes, by gathering all of our dead together, we hold a ceremony and absorb their wisdom. Often nothing original is gained, but even if it takes a thousand years to absorb something novel, while preserving everything from the past, it's worth it."

"So, when you gather, you absorb the old knowledge again and perhaps some new facts?"

"Yes."

"I guess it's similar to backing up on a computer. Making sure not to lose any data."

"You certainly are fond of your computers these days. Sure, it's like that, but not quite."

"How's it different?"

"When we gather our dead and absorb their knowledge, it's for the benefit of our entire species, to support and justify our roles at this place and time in our evolution. You back up your computers to make sure your personal data is not lost. But your backup is incomplete. No one makes sure that the knowledge of your whole species throughout the ages, your wisdom, your logic, your humanity, is saved. We fully back up our species. Every day, we do so in totality. We transmit details through our genes, and particulars are passed on intact to our youth, at birth. Your young are born helpless and ignorant. Even as your generations progress, your children are still born without survival instincts and essential knowledge."

"I guess you're right."

"You 'guess', which means you still have doubts. You make no effort to learn from the older species, those that were here before you. It's because you think you're nearly invincible. Well, I have news for you. We ants have seen countless numbers of species, both larger and smaller than yours, disappear completely from earth. Will you listen to what I have to say, or would you rather leave me alone so I can continue my job?"

"I'll listen."

"Please stop being so dubious. Your youth do not have a homogenous transfer of information like ours do. Few of you know how to grow food, dig wells, or build bridges. When it rains, you prefer to go to the mall or stay indoors, rather than collect precious rainwater like your ancestors did."

"Not me, I prefer to be outside, even when it rains. Though I usually get reprimanded if I go inside dripping wet."

"Well, then I'm truly grateful that you're not splashing through the puddles today. It makes my job, much, much easier, and faster. You would have ruined most of the work I needed to do. Anyway, I'm going to finish here pretty soon. Do you have any other queries before I go?"

Father stops speaking, certain that I'm sleeping soundly, but I'm not. Reaching up through the tangle of my light slumber I plead, "Don't stop. Please tell me the rest." Struggling against sleep, I incessantly want more. Tonight I want as much as I can get, since Father will leave our home soon, especially as the Endeavors draw near. "Tell me again what you asked her. Tell me again what she said."

"You've heard it all before," Father firmly states, but he knows that I haven't.

"That day, Father. I want to know everything. Please tell me," I implore him.

This sun of Antboy, though not his son, appeared radiant and glowing, in the dark, confined space. Atum was ready to learn that which he previously could only vaguely recall through the subconscious of prior dreams. He had never been able to remain awake during the next part of Antboy's recurring story, falling fast asleep before the story was fully revealed. But this night, Atum would not sleep, and he intended to remember everything Father would tell him.

Father looked at Atum and smiled, relieved. Atum would soon know what had been held sacred for so long. He was the son Antboy never had the privilege of conceiving, yet somehow, they were as close as kin, and even looked alike, the same shape of eyes, and nose. But no child had Antboy ever created. He prayed that Atum learn nothing about his mother and her reign, Queen Lavender the Loving, as she was known to the Colony. There were some things Atum just didn't need to know.

Surprisingly, Atum no longer appeared to be a child. His transition had not been apparent to Antboy, until that exact moment. No matter how tired and concerned about the

Scouts' return he was, Antboy recognized that this was Atum's absolute moment of transformation. He was both eager and ready for this knowledge.

"Ok, Atum, tonight you shall know the full story, but if I'm going to tell it, you must remain awake, to hear it all. Events are approaching rapidly, Atum, and you may soon need to utilize all that I've taught you. I asked the ant, who informed me she was called Hiawatha, the only question that came to my mind: "How do we back up humankind?""

"How do you think?" retorted Hiawatha.

"By recording all our knowledge on a computer and then backing up that computer?"

"It sounds simple enough. But that assumes you will always have the power, the energy to power that computer. And what if your species is wiped out, what good will knowledge on a computer do if there is no one around to access it?"

"So, are you talking about backing up not only information but also people?"

"Precisely. Any thoughts on that concept?"

"Yes. How about building a space city, or human settlements on the moon, or on Mars?"

"Great idea, why haven't you done that?"

"We're working on that."

"No, you're not. Space travel and space settlements aren't in your near future. You went to the moon more than forty years ago. You're a long way from major advancements distant from this planet earth. There are still energy needs in space, in addition to oxygen, food, and water requirements. You haven't figured out how to replenish those supplies when they run out. If your species survives long enough, you will probably get there. But no matter what, regardless of the promise of space, you need to know more about where you're from, where you're going, and how to get there. Use your brain, Antboy. How can you back up right now, or in the very near future?"

"I sat there, and watched her diligently gather pieces of earth and deceased ants, tossing both down the slope of the growing mound. I got on my hands and knees, and peered into the hole, trying to find the best angle to look within. I heard some snickering from a neighbor's window. There I was again, hunching over, hands and knees in the mud, mumbling aloud, staring at the ground, a spectacle. Then, the sun cast a particularly strong beam toward me. The hole was briefly illuminated, and I could clearly see the intersection of several caverns, which looked like a system of miniaturized mining tunnels. I could see an ant running here, running there, each one carrying something, just within my line of vision."

"Well, Antboy? No answer yet? You look puzzled."

Puzzlement wasn't the feeling I had; it was more like frustration. My face was visibly contorted as I began to formulate the backup plan. "Down in the earth," I sputtered.

"Well, yes, sort of," responded Hiawatha.

"What do you mean?"

"Not just in the earth; in the mantle."

"The mantle?"

"Yes, the mantle."

"I just read about the mantle in school."

"What do you remember?"

"Well, I learned that earth's crust, where we live, only comprises one percent of the planet's entire volume. The core is fifteen percent and, let's see, the remaining eighty-four percent is the mantle. But the only part that's suitable for human life is the crust, where we live."

"Interesting recollection that you have, but you're ninety-eight percent wrong if you think that only one percent of the earth, the crust, is suitable for human life. Although don't feel bad, because it's what you were taught and it's what you've been led to believe."

"But I don't see how we can live that far underground. There isn't any oxygen, food, water, and the closer we get to the core, the hotter things get, and it's already very hot up here."

"It seems like you have it all figured out. Why don't you go play with Tommy, now? He's been watching you for a while, standing over there holding his football."

"I don't want to play with Tommy. I want to talk to you."

"Well, it's going to rain soon, and then I will have to go. So I'm hoping you can put some pieces of logic together and figure things out quickly, for your sake, not ours. We ants will survive. We live not only here on the crust, but also in the upper and lower mantle, and in the outer and inner core. When we sense something way out there, in space, or here within the earth, whether a meteor, or an earthquake, we go where we need to, but where will you go? How will you prevent ending up like dinosaurs?"

"I don't know. Is it preventable?"

"It's completely preventable. The dinosaurs couldn't live underground. You can. You have the technology to do it. Some of you need to do it. This way, if a cataclysmic event happens up here, on the crust, you still have ample human specimens living below. And eventually, you will live above, in space."

"So, what do we do? Dig a hole, about a hundred miles deep?"

"Yes, dig a hole, but it only needs to be about three to six miles deep, drilled where the earth's crust is thinnest, at the bottom of an ocean. Go to an area where two tectonic plates meet, an ocean and a mountain range, for example. Eventually, by drilling and a process called subduction, you'll be pulled down and trade places with other matter getting pulled up through convection. You travel in a compartment made of tungsten carbide, which melts at six thousand degrees Fahrenheit. It can go all the way through the upper mantle to the lower mantle, but not as far as the outer core, where it will melt since it's about seven thousand degrees Fahrenheit there. Use something your scientists call cobalt sixty as a heat source to allow the tungsten vehicle to push itself through. There are patches of the mantle where temperatures are moderate, and life can and does exist. There's plenty of oxygen. Almost half the weight of the elements there is oxygen. There's also plenty of silica and magnesium. Unfortunately, finding water is tricky, but hydrogen can be found since it's the most abundant element in the universe. You seek out rich reservoirs of hydrogen trapped in the mantle, expose it to oxygen, and water forms. Or bring honey."

"Honey?"

"Yes, honey. Honey is hygroscopic. It's a substance that has the ability to absorb and attract molecules from the surrounding environment. Hydrogen in the mantle escapes upward, because it's the lightest element, but the honey will make it stick and trap it. Honey, in a place where oxygen is abundant, attracts the lightweight hydrogen, which then combines with oxygen. Water then appears as droplets on the honey."

"So, let me get this straight. We go to the bottom of the ocean. Then we find a boundary between two tectonic plates where convection and subduction occur. We drill several miles down. We travel in this tungsten carbide vehicle, heated by cobalt sixty, and bring bee colonies to create honey?"

"Exactly."

"What about food?"

"There's plenty of food down there, trust me. Just make sure that the food you discover doesn't eat you first. Hahahaha."

"That's not funny. It doesn't sound very appealing. I prefer the space colonization idea."

"Of course you do. Though you won't understand much about space until you figure out what's truly inside your own planet. One day, if you can actually study the core, you will understand how to travel through space. Eventually you'll comprehend that the layers of space are on top of each other. Then you'll pierce far into the universe, if your species lives that long."

"Is our species in that much jeopardy?"

"Definitely. You've figured out a multitude of ways to eradicate yourselves. Once you're gone, you're gone, and can't come back. So, you need to focus on solving real problems, though there are many. Unfortunately, you're an utterly unfocused species. Make sure to start preserving your bees. You'll need a lot of bees, and their honey, which will provide you food and attract water."

"It sounds too risky, very dangerous, and deadly."

"Do you think I'm telling you it isn't? Haven't you seen ants die en masse in the thousands, even millions at times? We make necessary sacrifices for the survival of our colonies and for our thousands of different species. You weren't alive at the inception of the space age, but initially humans sent up monkeys. Other mammals died first, then humans, in the world's quest to orbit the earth, to land on the moon, even to go up in a shuttle and perform basic experiments. Nothing is foolproof until it's tested, and even then, nothing is certain or completely predictable."

"This whole idea would need lots of testing and money, over many years," argues Antboy.

"Of course. At best, colonization of the mantle might yield a failure and fatality rate exceeding ninety-nine percent. Yet, even with less than a one percent success rate, shouldn't new frontiers be crossed, studied? Many will perish, until you get it right, but the ones that die will be heroes. Those who may not have a solid future here on the crust, and are willing to risk their lives, will be remembered as heroes for their courage," counters Hiawatha.

"Heroes?"

"Yes, of course, heroes. One day, their names will be remembered as those that pioneered the underground colonies. For several more decades, perhaps even a century or two, those aboveground will retain their comforts, until there are none more to have."

Antboy asks, "What do you mean 'none more'?"

"During the course of ordinary planetary changes, it's commonplace for a planet to undergo periodic shifts from life below to life above, and back, alternating cyclically over epochs. Your current crisis on the crust warrants urgent attention. The earth has shifted slightly, caused by the turmoil of your extractions. She has no choice now; it makes sense for her to throw you off."

"What? What do you mean?"

"You've taken too much metal from earth. You've mined too much, shifted too much metal, and then you created metal machines that need oil, the earth's blood, and you took too much of that. Without its blood, a planet cannot keep the tectonic plates well oiled, and they will collide over and over, as you've seen them do in the past few years.

Massive earthquakes are ravaging your fragile world more frequently because those plates grind into each other rather than glide through pockets of oil. Quakes will cause oceans to overflow onto the land. The metal and oil you've removed have also lessened the mass of the earth, so it's lighter, and it rotates just a smidgen closer to the sun. But a smidgen is a lot, and every smidgen adds up, causing more glaciers to melt, leading to more water and less land on the surface.

"About six centuries ago, the planet was the perfect distance from the sun to sustain life on the crust, but now the scale has tipped, and it's out of balance. Basically, you're in a tough spot, because you can't really put back the metal and the oil and pretend everything's all right. Much of it has been burned up and sent into the atmosphere and cannot be recovered.

"And now there are additional issues. Beyond puncturing the crust like Swiss cheese to constantly extract the earth's guts, there are many other human practices that are extinguishing what was once a perfect balance. The forests you cut down, the oceans you overfish, the air you pollute, and the pesticides and various chemicals you disburse throughout the land have all deeply disturbed the balance.

"The crust, where one hundred percent of you live, is about to crack and peel off, like an amphibian's dry skin, because its natural oils are depleted, extracted beyond replenishment. The planet can survive without her one percent crust. The crust serves no other purpose than as an external, thin layer that insulates earth's most precious assets, her mantle and her core. Earth can shed her skin, her crust, and grow new crust, just as long as the rest of her volume, the mantle and core, remain pristine and relatively unexploited.

"The hardiest species' will adapt. Beetles and ants won't have problems, but the crust will become unlivable for your species and you may not fare so well. It's just too late to fix these problems; now you have to back up. If you have an old computer that might soon break, you back up. I advise that you work on digging a really deep hole, and get in it, and you better save those bees. The rain is coming. Bye."

"Wait a minute. How do I save the bees?"

"I have no idea. One of our deceased ants knew that it was necessary and we absorbed it. That's all I know."

"That's all you know?"

"Yes. I just know, through the vibrations of the earth, that you need to do something relatively soon."

"Well, how do we make this deep hole?"

"Make a really big drill. Work like us, the ants, night and day, and you can drill a hole deep enough. Hop to it, there's no time to be wasted. You better get with the program."

Antboy and Hiawatha stare silently at each other.

"Atum, a few drops fell from the sky, and Hiawatha looked up at me, with pleading eyes. She wanted to return to her home below, and I was selfishly keeping her. Yet there was no way I could let her go right away. Puddles were forming, and she was standing on the top of the mound waiting for me to speak or waiting to be released. This part is sad," adds Antboy.

"I know. You told me how sad that day was for you," responds Atum.

"I was selfish, but I needed to know as much as I could, rain or no rain. I was not going to let Hiawatha go, until she told me more about the mantle, so I kept asking her stuff."

"Hiawatha, tell me what the mantle is like, and then I promise you can go."

"Fine, but I won't repeat myself, because I need to get underground quickly. The pressure in the mantle has been much greater than here at the crust for billions of years. The mantle is made up of about one-fifth silicon, one-fifth magnesium, and almost one-half oxygen. So silicon dioxide, is formed, which is called silica, as well as magnesium dioxide, called magnesia. The pressure has been extraordinary for a very long time so there's an abundance of sand, quartz, crystal, plastic, and glass, which are formed from silica. There's plenty of light because there's a large magnitude of magnesia, which accumulates in deposits of white powder. Magnesia spontaneously reacts to heat and burns bright. This light reflects off the silica providing an incandescent, mystical quality of reflection that encompasses a variation of colors throughout the spectrum. Just be careful. Like honey, magnesia is hygroscopic, but dangerously so for you. It attracts water to form magnesium hydroxide, which, even if inhaled, will cause an extreme laxative effect, and can drain you of all your liquids. So, never get too close to any bodies of white liquid, resembling milk, and especially don't let any of it touch your skin."

"You mean if I breathe too much in, or touch it, I can die?"

"Yes. You'll basically crap yourself to death. Non-stop diarrhea. Magnesium is barely absorbed by your intestinal tract. Instead the magnesium draws water from the surrounding tissues through osmosis. It not only softens the feces until it is completely liquid, but also causes excretions of a much higher volume of feces. This continues until the body loses most of its water, leaving one to die completely dehydrated and desiccated. Avoid white pools of liquid and you'll be fine. Listen, kid, I have to go. I'm dancing around here, trying to avoid these drops, but one of them will kill me." Antboy and Hiawatha again stare silently at each other.

Father explains, "Atum, I reached down to pick up Hiawatha, but she refused, stubbornly hoping to return posthaste to her cavern below."

"Ok, Hiawatha, just tell me anything more I need to know, please," pleads Antboy.

Hiawatha rolls her eyes, "Fine. Everything there is relative to here. It's unbearably hot in some regions, where you'll be immediately incinerated. In others, there are patches of moderate temperatures, which can be measured and mapped from above. Imagine going down a shaft, an elevator shaft, where there are various levels of departure. The tungsten carbide capsule you create to lower into the mantle will withstand this heat, and protect you from it, so that you can get to the appropriate level that can support life. As a precautionary measure you'll need to initially wear a suit of thin tungsten, just like a spacesuit, which will protect you from high temperatures. It needs to be carefully designed to preserve and recycle your internal water.

"The mantle is a world within a world and we ants long to return there. Looking upward from the crust, here where you live, you see the stars and planets at night. Similarly, looking upward from the mantle, you can see the bottom of the tectonic plates as the sky. Upon that sky are patterns of light reflected from the multitude of crystalline structures, which appear to be constellations. There is ample life among the hundreds of thousands of miles of silica tunnels, comprised of plastics, that connect to thousands of miles of sandy, quartz beaches, that border oceans, not of water, but of glass and crystal. Goodbye Antboy."

"What? Wait! Goodbye, Hiawatha," I grumbled, wanting to know more, but it was too late.

"I had held her up too long, son. As she turned vertical to go into her hole, a droplet of rainwater fell upon her, and she was swept away. In the torrential downpour that followed, I looked for her around that muddy area for hours, hoping the neighbors mistook the water dripping down my face as raindrops, rather than the salty taste of fresh tears, bitterness rolling down my cheeks, reminding me of my selfishness."

"Oh, Father, I feel sad for her. Please tell me about the bees. What happened?" I ask.

"I didn't get to the bees for almost two decades. There were great changes, swift and indomitable, that altered my course. After my research and findings were stolen, I turned from saving toward hunting. I joined the Army and served in two wars. Goodnight Atum."

"Please, please, tell me about the Army."

"Not tonight, but soon, very soon, son. We both must sleep now."

IV

Father has lived what seems like several lifetimes, his experience belies his years, and he says he feels older than forty-five. He is a careful and meticulous man and his system of beliefs is strong. He doesn't waver from what he believes is right for our world and the world he left behind, the world he stares at every night before bed. Father refuses to lose hope. He is stubborn and persistent in his belief that he can change things. He says that I represent hope for mankind.

Father tells me that my green eyes are the color of grass, of which he attempts to describe and I attempt to imagine. He says their beauty reminds him of the purity of true love and that if he stares into them for too long he becomes hypnotized by their depth and power and hope for the future, for life, for love, and for the return of green grass. He named me Atum.

Father is firmly against the destruction of human life. His research and writings focused on preserving life but his analysis was misinterpreted and misconstrued when it was translated into the HSI code, the Codex. His theories and ideas were strictly hypothetical but his original documents were modified and his pure theory was put into a literal code, leaving no room for interpretation or variation. Although Father's work had been dedicated to the preservation of life, circumstances of the world called for his theories to be put into solid form in a most distressful fashion. His research and premature conclusions were judged by others to be the necessary solutions to the problems threatening human survival. But Father knew that his work was rough, unfinished, solely theoretical, and could not possibly comprise a practical, workable model.

Unfortunately, his theories were set in stone by others, with no possibility for gray areas or interpretations, and clearly delineated so that no alterations or deviations could be made. While the preservation of human life was at its core, the Human Survival Initiative adopted a radical philosophy, condoning and even requiring death in certain circumstances. Even though Father sought only to preserve life, not destroy it, he feels he has done more harm than good.

Father says that since I'm now thirteen years old he must continue telling me why we're here. He tells me it's important that I know about our past so that I can truly understand human nature and learn equally from our triumphs and failures. At times I dream about the things he tells me. The vision that he paints for me seems unreal but I strive to understand, to comprehend, and to remember that which I will never experience. He says that his memories must become a part of my knowledge so that one day I can teach the children of our world the story of their history.

On earth, six-dozen females, ages twenty to twenty-two years old, boarded the shuttle with Father to settle our Colony. They had been exposed to limited knowledge during their sterile foster upbringing, separated from society, denied the majority of its products, and stripped of worldly technology. Chosen in their infancy, these girls were taught the HSI code, as it was being developed in its infancy. They had been programmed to universally adopt, enthusiastically accept, and fully support the developing HSI code as it was compiled within the Codex.

Retrieved from orphanages, the colonists were raised from infancy, held essentially captive, in compounds sanctioned by the International Coalition. As infants, involuntary orphans, they were selected, four per nation, by the eighteen countries that had ratified the HSI code. They were chosen through extensive genetic searches and testing, rescued from seemingly random orphanages. Retrieving them made no news splash due to the everlasting barrage of hourly media dissemination.

Unknowingly isolated from outside contact since birth, they were given no knowledge of the world beyond their walls. They had been fed, housed, and instructed in basic essentials throughout the twenty-year span since HSI's initialization. Their information had been limited to vital hygiene, health care, prenatal care, labor and delivery, childcare, nutrition, and key survival techniques. In their late teen years, they were taught specific insemination methods, which were to be scheduled every eighteen months upon settlement of the Colony.

All seventy-two women, four from each HSI member country of the International Coalition, had been given fertility treatments and inseminated prior to Departure Day. They were initially assigned nine vials and given specific instructions. The first was used during the primary insemination on earth, and the remaining eight were to be utilized upon colonization of the satellite planet, every year and a half. Each woman was responsible for the care of her own vials, and was instructed on proper care and handling to preserve the seed, the lifeblood of the society. They were to be administered every eighteen months, until all vials were exhausted. Future provisions for further conception were to be revealed in the HSI code. As a result of the fertility treatments, the women were informed that they would conceive between one and six children from each vial.

Father strictly prohibits me from making the journey outside but I'm allowed to roam freely within our dome. I've had no desire, until recently, to explore the world outside our dome. It's safe here, yet I want to see the things Father has described. I'm afraid to tell him about my plan to leave the dome for fear that he'll prevent me. Soon I'll venture out, but for the moment I put aside my desire to explore. As soon as Father awakens, I ask him to again tell me the story beginning with the day, that one, special day that he heard a very important speech, when he was nearly twelve, a year and a half younger than I am now.

I sit and eagerly listen as Father describes the afternoon that changed his life, and the events that followed. It was the day he overheard Queen Elizabeth and he recalls every word.

"As I stand before you I know that this will be one of the last speeches I give as your Queen. My time is drawing near to step down and let the youthful energy again infuse the leadership of this tribe. Our state of affairs meeting tonight is unusual in that I face tens of thousands of my fellow colonists. Throughout my career I have never called a meeting with the entire tribe, it seemed self-serving and needlessly risky, to gather the whole colony in one place. Nevertheless, due to the continued demands of the Youth Council, tonight I have gone against my best judgment to deliver my address, to everyone in the settlement, all assembled here today.

"Friends, family, tribesmen, we come together today to celebrate and discuss our accomplishments and successes of the past, and to make plans for our future. Who among us has not thrived and prospered in recent times? Who among us has not seen their children also bloom and flourish in this period of plenty? Who among us has not been provided ample food and adequate shelter? If you truly disapprove of what has been accomplished, stand now and be heard. Come now, I cannot hear you. Is there even one dissatisfied party in attendance? By your deafening and unified silence, resounding and echoing throughout our chamber, it is clear that you approve of our sustained peace and prosperity.

"I commend those of you who have continued to provide us with an abundant variety of food. You have risked your lives to secure our future. At peril you continue to amaze us all with your ingenuity and perseverance in obtaining our necessities and indulgences. I extol those that in times of battle have carried many times their own weight in bringing the dead or wounded back to our village. I praise the strategies employed in waging battle against the evil men that would sooner see us crushed and destroyed than to even offer us a scrap of bread in times of famine. I laud those warriors who, when necessary, have entered evil men's homes and upon being discovered, and having no weapons at their disposal, have had to rely on their own resourcefulness to fight back. I congratulate the mothers that have borne our children. I applaud the decision-makers among our tribe who have thoroughly contemplated the causes and effects of each one of our actions. I acclaim the children that we have raised, and those not yet conceived that will fulfill our destiny and continue our race, carrying our seeds of wisdom and cooperation into the future. I thank you all.

"Take a moment to marvel at your accomplishments and revel in the moment. I am proud to see you hug one another and I can see a mass of limbs jumping, dancing, trampling, and applauding. Take a few moments, but then please settle down. I must have silence to continue.

"Thank you for giving me this unheralded opportunity to humbly serve you as spiritual leader. I only hope that the scribes will record me as a fair and generous leader, one that always put the needs of the village before my own. I have birthed many children and I hope, for the continued and prosperous procreation of our race, that our tradition of strong fertility is upheld. We have strength in numbers. Let no one that ever holds my position tell you differently, or restrict this emphasis on fertility which is the key to our evolution and strength.

"As your leader, your Queen Elizabeth, I now bid you to… wait, what is that awful noise?! I think it might be, oh, no! Run, run quickly, run fast; it's a flood, take cover, save your selves. Float to the top, try to get some air from above, oh no, it's too late, all gone, can't breathe, such a traged…"

Father explains to me that three children are squatting on the cement sidewalk, and two of them are giggling hysterically as one boy pours boiling water over the anthill into which Father has been peering. Thousands of ants bubble out of the hidden cavern, dead instantly. Still others swim momentarily before the hot liquid squelches their attempts. Father explains that he had tried, to no avail, to stop the kids from their contemptible act of torture and cruelty. He failed to stop them, and soon he was alone, sitting and crying for Queen Elizabeth, especially for what those three cruel children had done to her colony. Wonderfully, fantastically, he had heard every word of the ant's speech, this powerful, wise, regal Queen Elizabeth.

Father says he became confused and disoriented by what he heard that day. The speech indelibly resounds in his memory and in his ears, throughout the day and into the night, repetitively, for weeks. He attempts to return to his normal patterns of attending school, visiting friends, and conversing with his parents. But he couldn't shake the profound impact of that moment, unable to move forward in his daily routines, and his guilt about the ant tragedy overwhelms him. Television no longer holds his interest. He completely abandons his extensive stamp and baseball card collections. His complex science experiments, which had won him almost every award the state could offer a boy of eleven years, come to a complete halt. Test tubes, beakers, and projectile motion configurations begin to collect dust in his room. His computer games, which had been taken apart and are in various stages of reconfiguration, sit untouched on various shelves. Teachers send his work home. Although he effortlessly and perfectly completes all assignments, having consistently studied several grade levels above his age, to the amazement of visiting professors from the local university, his interest in the curriculum is lackluster. Prior to Queen Elizabeth's speech, and the massacre that followed, he had been attentive. But ever since that tragic day, he feels as if he's a foreigner, a visitor, even a critic within the community.

For weeks he spends time on a roller coaster of emotions riding anger upward, rounding the bend on frustration, heading downward on depression, and finally coming to a complete stop at peace, hands and feet intact. The decision is made. He gathers materials, and resolves to preserve life at every level, starting first with the smallest creatures, the highly organized, yet persecuted society, the ants.

He refuses access to his room for several days, feigning nausea and fatigue, and his parents begin to worry, never having seen their nearly twelve-year-old son so isolated and sick. Doctors are sent for but to no avail; no diagnosis is made and no prognosis is evident. He is constantly building, designing, molding, mounting, and revising. He creates prototypes and destroys them. His schoolwork is sent for but he lets it pile up for days, weeks, and then in a burst of frenzy and energy he completes the mounting assignments in a couple of hours. Food is brought to him but he requires that it be left outside his door on a tray, and at odd hours he opens the door to satiate his hunger and thirst.

Soon a psychiatrist knocks at his door and he unbolts the locks that he had fashioned to prevent entry. Without awaiting a greeting from the unwelcome intruder, he menacingly stares into the psychiatrist's analytical eyes. Then, he defiantly states that he is not only saner than the shrink himself, but also anyone with whom the doctor will ever come into contact. He grabs the tray of food that the psychologist had been holding for him, and he dismissively closes the door to ingest his food and resume his work.

Two months pass, and he is very pale but quite healthy and sound. Friends no longer visit. Even his parents have settled into an almost complacent acceptance of their child's condition. It is on a June day, just prior to the school year's end, when he quietly leaves his room, his house, his neighborhood, his city, his state, with a covered structure on wheels that he pulls behind him. Tucked away in his pocket is almost a year of allowance money. Tacked to the front of the refrigerator is a brief note informing his parents that he will return in a few days. He asks them not to worry. He walks through the sweltering heat to the bus station. After two hours the daily bus arrives, the bus that will take him to the Patent Office, in his great nation's Capitol.

V

The journey is long, dusty, and bumpy as the bus treks across the country, and he is alone in the rear seat. But as an only child, he was used to being alone. Although his parents appreciated the family unit that they had created, mother, father, and son often retreated into their own worlds of creative self-discovery. Accustomed to entertaining himself, he seldom relied on others to keep him company. When alone, he sometimes passed the time by competing against himself in Monopoly and various card games, and he always won. On the long bus ride, though, there were no games to play. He had nothing but time, which provided him an opportune occasion to think.

Reflecting on his home life, his childhood, his upbringing, he has no doubt that he needed to leave. He was the product of two geniuses, two psychiatrists. He sometimes debated whether his parents chose to have a child as a social experiment or whether there was a true desire to nurture. He could never figure it out, but it didn't matter, because he knew they loved him regardless, and he loved them. But at the dinner table during their evening meal, he often felt that his parents thought of him as a patient that they were trying to perfect rather than a child who needed emotional guidance and parental understanding. Accordingly, they neither supported nor condemned any of his accomplishments or misdeeds. Instead, they wanted to make sure he understood the reasons and motivations for his actions so that he could master his impulses and live rationally.

Strange as their love might be, mechanically displayed every night after yoga by a solitary kiss and hug, he grew up in a caring, loving home. But that love, though, was focused on teaching him how to live life without depending on anyone, even on them. Self-reliant at a very early age, he even remembered administering his own eye drops. He was neither neglected nor cuddled, but instead was analyzed and evaluated. For Antboy, something was missing, and he felt somewhat stunted. That is, until he heard the ants speak, and then he was inspired.

He was a confident child. Since his earliest recollections he approached every task, chore, assignment, or project knowing that he would perform exceptionally well. In fact, he often undertook difficult projects, challenging and pushing himself to his limit. Some childhood acquaintances and school administrators felt ego was behind his success. But that was far from the truth. His belief in himself stemmed from the self-reliance that he mastered. His parents' obsessive desire to teach him how to fend for himself deepened his yearning to be free and willful and attempt anything and everything that he set his mind to. At an early age he sought independence, realizing that he needed to believe in himself so as not to be dependent on others.

Although his classmates and teachers often remarked that he was cute, dappled in freckles, which surrounded intelligent, piercing blue eyes, contrasting his thick, wavy auburn hair, his actions and movements revealed more than his good looks. He was a gentle genius. A little smaller than his peers, probably due to his accelerated advancement in school, he was never picked on, however, and it was probably his assuredness that made him seem untouchable. Relied upon to help others with their assignments, he always accommodated them because he loved to teach, to help. He was compassionate toward anyone that needed a helping hand. Though he rarely revealed himself emotionally to his parents or friends, he was always reliable and was highly regarded in the circles that he entered.

Determined and sometimes stubborn, he seldom changed course once he set off in a particular direction and he was compulsive in his desire to complete every project that he attempted. He viewed his ambitious nature as strength and he considered his current obsessions, whatever they were momentarily, to be his mission, his compass, his calling. He always proceeded onward, consistently motivated, toward his destination, unstoppable, indefatigable.

The bus finally arrives at the Capitol, after nearly two days of nonstop discomfort. Wheeling his creation almost two miles, according to his tattered map, he finally arrives at a stark white edifice fronted by seven tall ivory pillars, atop approximately fifty daunting steps. Step by step he ascends the stairs to the Patent Office and, profusely sweating from the humidity outside, he exhaustedly enters the building. The entrance opens into a large room, a waiting area, with chairs lined along three walls. He pulls a number from a dispenser, and gratefully sits in one of the few vacant seats, nearest to a loud window fan. Straight ahead is a long, very thin counter, which runs the length of the entire building, and behind this barrier are aisles and aisles of files, and clerks are shuffling papers, bustling in various directions.

Neither an inventor nor an administrator notices him. When one of the clerks calls his number, he is summarily and gruffly dismissed as a prankster. But he is prepared for this possibility and he waits patiently, settling in for the long haul, pulling out both a stack of pre-packed peanut butter and jelly sandwiches and the book whose title itself is the year he was born, Orwell's *1984*. Most of the constantly rotating workers assume he's the child of one of the many applicants, the countless rejected and dejected and deluded inventors with defective devices.

He leaves the Patent Office to find a pay phone and make a necessary phone call, a call to his parents to notify them that he's safe. When his mother answers the phone, she is hysterical, and he hears chaos erupting in what was normally a relatively placid home. It sounds like there is an entire team fruitlessly positioned there, frantically dedicated to finding him. He realizes that he should have checked in sooner than the forty-eight hours it took for the bus to arrive at the Capitol. He hears someone shouting to trace the call. Before hanging up, he quickly explains to his sobbing mother, and the missing persons team that is quietly yet attentively listening, that he will be gone for about a week. He assures her that he's fine, not to worry, reminding her that he's always been very self-sufficient.

As Antboy stares at the receiver, which he leaves off the hook, dangling from the public pay phone, he is distressed for his parents. At this precise moment, they cannot understand that he has elected to dedicate himself to a higher purpose. As always, though, they will methodically reach deep within to seek meaning. They will consider the psychological ramifications of controlling his decisions and, after conducting the appropriate analysis, they will hopefully rationalize his actions, and ultimately accept his decision.

He returns to the Patent Office just before it is due to close. He situates himself in a corner of the waiting area, behind a heap of oblong metal and splintered wood, amidst some abandoned architectural blueprints of someone's futile failure, among refuse awaiting removal by the late night janitor. For three consecutive mornings, he's unquestionably the first in line. He peeks his head above the desk, waving his number when it's called, and thrice he is ridiculed and refused.

Taking a different approach to complete his objective, he heads to a local hardware store and spends the rest of his allowance on materials. He finds an abandoned office in a partially unused building adjacent to the Patent Office and sets up camp. He builds two more prototypes, dome-like creations with gears, levers, ventilation shafts, a series of drilled holes, retractable floors, and a variety of hidden features including tubes and pulleys.

Walking a block away to avoid harassment by the Patent Office clerks, he hosts a lemonade stand next to a display that highlights his three completed structures. In each featured dome, he has set up an entire ant community. Dazzling onlookers, he periodically demonstrates the intricacies and complexities of his creation.

He prices each contraption at double his materials' cost to insure that the proceeds from every sale will fund the construction of two more structures. He sells these three showpiece structures to thirsty passersby upon completion of their lemonade purchases. Each customer refers two more, and business booms. Throughout the second night he's so busy building that he barely sleeps. He's determined, focused, and undeniably intense.

"Father," I interrupt, "weren't you scared, being all alone, far away from home?"

"Atum, I didn't even think about it at the time. Nothing could have stopped me from trying everything possible to save the ants. When I look back now, it's as though I was never actually that boy. It's like I'm speaking about someone else, who was within my body, guiding me. Sometimes I wonder if the boy I speak of, who was afraid of nothing, could really be me, the man whose every move is monitored by our Queen, Queen Lavender." And with that he stops, suddenly stunned by the heartrending realization that his life has so drastically changed. "Atum, give me a moment, I need some time alone."

Father leaves the dome, and I hear whispers down the hall. I put my ear to the door but, as usual, I cannot make out the words. At times I hear him addressing someone named Lucy Lips, or something like that. I think Father consults with her once in a while, or maybe he's conversing with himself, as he's known to do. After several attempts, I give up trying to decipher what he's saying and I return to my seat hoping he'll soon resume his story.

When Father returns he seems composed but somewhat distant, less animated, and he continues his story telling it as if he were talking about someone else. I think he truly has disassociated from his childhood and the early years when he was first called Antboy. It's no wonder, for Father has experienced several traumatic changes in his lifespan. Nevertheless, his story captivates me entirely and he resumes speaking about his boyhood, right when he is perched on the sidewalk, thirty-three years ago, selling his ant sanctuaries.

While driving by the lunchtime rush that was swarming the boy's lemonade stand, a distracted Detective patrolling the boulevard observes him mechanically, and glides over to the side of the road to park his patrol vehicle. Without recognizing the underage status of the city's newest vendor, he nonchalantly asks the boy for his identification and business permit. When the boy explains that he has neither, the Detective commences writing a citation, completes it, and issues it. Then he embarrassedly chuckles, finally realizing that he had just cited an adolescent for operating without a license, rather than for truancy. Antboy is told to gather his stuff, and then the Detective opens the rear door, motioning for the boy to get into the car.

As Antboy settles into the back seat, he notices a few pieces of the Detective's dog-eared literature on the dashboard, Huxley, Vonnegut, and Bradbury. Surmising that the Detective may become a potential ally, or at the very least believing that this erudite man could be open to new ideas, Antboy demonstrates the comprehensive systems of his ant sanctuaries. Then he shares the difficulties he's had with the Patent Office.

His story is met with no visible response; the Detective is impressed, albeit speechless, and he ponders the child prodigy's invention. The young man asks to be taken to the Patent Office. The Detective surveys the boy's structures, which were packed tightly into the squad car, and he acquiesces, choosing to drive one block to the building. The Detective helps him unload. While visibly displaying his badge, he sits close to the boy at the Patent Office, and peruses the domed structures. Less than five minutes pass before a supervisor appears, readily offering to assist them.

The Detective emphatically states that neither of them will leave until the child's creation is submitted for review.

Relaying the conceptual framework of the lad's invention, the Detective convinces the supervisor to accept the device and analyze it. He signs a stack of paperwork on behalf of the youngster. A multitude of documents are stamped "pending", and the unlikely pair is bureaucratically told to return the next afternoon.

The Detective and the youth walk to the empty office in the adjacent building where Antboy had been manufacturing his ant structures. They retrieve the boy's sparse, essential belongings, and then they drive to the Detective's home. Upon his arrival, the youngster is directed to the telephone to call his parents, and then the Detective gets on the line to reassure them that he is safe and sound. It is agreed that Antboy will remain under the Detective's supervision until his parents can complete the two-day journey.

After a brief introduction to the Detective's family, tired Antboy is led to a guest bedroom where he takes a solid nap. Meanwhile, the Detective relates the events of the day to his astonished wife and three children. When the rested boy later joins the Detective's family in the entertainment room, they are polite and hospitable at first, warm and welcoming during the evening meal, and eventually relaxed and enthralled a few hours later while listening to the lad's tale of his most unusual journey.

The family settles in for the evening but the boy cannot sleep. Neither can the Detective. They both sit in the living room, pensively, wordlessly, each having retreated into his respective thoughts. The Detective is puzzled which is an unusual feeling for someone so highly decorated. He is an analytical professional who had encountered a variety of law enforcement issues in the Capitol, yet today had been unique. Confused by the mysterious appearance on this very ordinary day of this exceedingly extraordinary youth, he's perplexed and solely proffers minimal small talk. Initially they discuss trivial things, which do not evolve into meaningful conversation.

Eventually, the curious Detective engages the child in discussing the interesting, domed structures that he had displayed on his rickety lemonade stand. The boy responds passionately and explicitly explains the various components of his invention. The Detective is truly enthralled by the youngster, this protector of the ants, and he ambitiously sees beyond these ants into something much greater, much more vast in scope, possibly thinking too deeply, probably not. But the specific vision, the actual focus of what the Detective perceives is ambiguous, cloudy, yet evolves into clarity while conversing with the lad.

The young man's arrival is not accidental, of that he is certain, and he hopes that some purpose will be revealed soon. From his professional and personal experience, all answers to all questions are within reach, if one looks, and seeks. Regardless of the outcome of this intensely driven child's self proclaimed mission, to patent his invention, he is relieved that the boy is here with him tonight, in his home, with his family. Often he's called in too late to protect life's victims. In this case, however, he was timely. The youth needed both his guidance and his dutiful, paternal presence. Taking advantage of a brief lull in their conversation, he dons his fatherly cap and convinces the lad that they both must rest, to replenish their energy for the day ahead.

VI

Just before six a.m. there is an abrupt, booming knock at the door. The sleepy, surly Detective peers through his peephole and is taken aback to find two men in dark suits, flashing official credentials on his doorstep. The men ask the Detective to wake the boy, and emphatically request that the Detective and boy accompany them in their car. A few minutes later, Antboy and the Detective are hastily seated in a vehicle, which departs suddenly, along with two others simultaneously, forming what appears to be a security escort.

They arrive at the Patent Office just after seven o'clock, an hour and a half before the doors officially open for business. Yet the supervisor is already there, the one they met with the day before, sweating profusely, and he leads them to a room toward the back of the building. Then he brings coffee, juice, and donuts to the two suited men, the boy, and the Detective, who all readily scarf down the food and beverages. After a few minutes of eating and drinking pleasantries, they are surprised when a high-ranking military officer, a general, appears flanked by two colonels, and greets them. Kind, yet commanding, decisive eyes, set atop a tall, muscular and broad-shouldered frame, decorated by multiple medals declaring his powerful rank, face the child, search him, speak to him, in a paternal, protective manner.

"Let me cut to the chase, son. I'm hereby rejecting your patent application under the powers provided to me by our government. What you've created is no longer your property. This isn't the first time our country has had to step in like this but it's the first time in my extensive military career that I've encountered an invention of this magnitude. You're obviously aware that the self-contained apparatus you've created has solved certain fundamental problems regarding water purification, waste removal, oxygenation, conservation and replenishment of natural resources, elemental accumulation and recombination, fertility, and food production, and that's just what has been discovered after only a few hours of study. We cannot grant a patent that would allow mass-production of this technology without proper control. It's too important to the survival of the entire—."

"General?" Interrupts an officer who bursts into the room.

The General looks up, visibly irritated by the interruption. "Yes, what is it, Major?"

"Sir, there is a phone call for you, sir."

"Take a message, can't you see I'm busy?"

"Sir, yes, but it's quite urgent, though. It's the National Security Adviser. He says he must speak with you right away, sir."

"Excuse me a moment. We'll resume this discussion in a few minutes. I'll be right back." The General gets up and heads out the door to the adjoining office. His voice, though hushed and barely audible, has a tone of urgency, which the Detective and youth subtly sense as they strain to perceive a few overheard words on one end of the terse, private conversation.

The General returns hastily, yet authoritatively, to the table, quickly regaining his military posture, calm and controlled. "Let's see. Where were we? Yes, we were discussing the scope and magnitude of your invention, weren't we, son?"

"Yes, sir. We were. You just told us that my sanctuary has solved all of the major problems affecting the survival of ants. I have worked so long to provide a safe environment for ants, and I was sure I had, but then it seemed that no one would take the time to look at my ant domes. Sir, you are the only one who sees and understands the importance of protecting the ants."

"The ants? Ants? I'm not sure I understand."

"Sir? What don't you understand?"

"Your purpose here, with this structure. Ah, I see. Did you design it strictly for the ants?"

"Of course it's for the ants, sir, what else would it be for?"

"Well. I guess, nothing. Now that I look at it, there couldn't be any other purpose for these sanctuaries, could there?"

"No, sir. Does this mean that the ants will be saved?"

"Well, uh, the ants saved? So, your main purpose for this invention is to save ants, correct?"

"Yes, sir. I have dedicated myself to this purpose. We must preserve life at every level, and even the smallest creatures, the ants, should be saved."

"Ok, son. I get it. It all makes sense to me now. Your trip here to the Patent Office and your design of this structure is definitely going to help the ants. Let me see. What if we were to take this back to our laboratory and rework this thing so that it would get patent approval, to be used for the preservation of ants, would that make you happy, son?"

"Very happy, sir. When would it be ready?"

"Hmm. I imagine they could start on it early next week and probably have it ready within the month. In the meantime, we'll need to contact your parents because it'll be necessary to keep you here for a while, while we work out all the details. I'll arrange for you to stay at our intelligence headquarters under adult supervision until your parents arrive. Would that work for you, son?"

"That's fine, sir, as long as I can continue working on my project. Could you please tell my parents that I'll be home soon, safe and sound, and that they don't need to visit right now?"

"I'll make the call first thing. So, son, you don't miss your home, your parents?"

"Not right now, sir. I love them very much, of course, but presently the most important thing is this undertaking. I know they want me to be happy, and at this moment I am. I just hope they understand why I had to leave and why I'm here and that I want to stay for a little while longer. There's so much more ant research that I need to do."

"Well, son, with a little persuading on my part, I'm sure they'll understand. Actually, besides me, there may be quite a few officials who will actively encourage you to continue with your brilliant research. My file here shows that you've broken many state records on your intelligence exams, and I see that both of your parents are psychiatrists. Is this correct, son?"

"Yes, sir, it is. I always seem to test well. I guess it comes naturally for me. But school has never held my interest. The formal process of attending school has never excited me, but my current exploration of this project is fascinating. My parents are often very involved in their own research and we seem to be in separate worlds most of the time."

"Son, have you ever heard of independent study?"

"I've heard it mentioned before, sir, but I don't know how it works."

"There are programs that will permit you to complete your compulsory schooling in an alternative setting. You can continue with your investigations that you seem so passionate about while complying with the mandatory coursework requirements. Does this interest you?"

"Absolutely, sir. I would love the opportunity. When could it start?"

"Son, let me begin working on it. I'll sort through and plan the details. Obviously, we'll need your parents' permission, which I believe is something I can handle personally, and expediently. By the next time we meet, I'll probably have some paperwork that will place you in a different custodial situation. Do you understand what I mean by that, son?"

"Not really, sir. What does that mean?"

"It means that instead of your parents making decisions for you until the age of eighteen, it may be me, as guardian, or another representative doing this. Does this concern you?"

"I don't think so, sir. As my guardian, you wouldn't allow any harm to come to me, right?"

"Of course not. I will look out for your best interests. It's in my best interest and that of our nation to look out for its people, its citizens, especially those that can help the country. Boys and men have placed their faith in our government for centuries and have grown up defending it, and that is because our country provides for its citizens, and protects their liberties. So, take pride in our great nation. Are we in agreement, son? If your parents approve, will you accept that I make decisions on your behalf?"

"Yes, sir. I will."

"Well, son, I must leave immediately. My men will remain to see you to your quarters, situated in the scientific research wing of our intelligence headquarters. You'll be based there while we await your parents. Thank you, Detective, for your help in this matter. Goodbye."

As the lumbering General strides toward the back door, the Detective stands upright, at attention, and impulsively says, "General, sir, can I have a word with you?"

The General brusquely motions for him to draw near. "That depends, Detective, about what?"

"Sir, I'm a little concerned about this situation, especially the child's well-being. After all, sir, I'm the one who found him, and now that you've taken over he will be separated from-" asserts the Detective, who is cut off by the General.

"Are you questioning my authority in this matter, Detective?"

"No, sir, I'm not, it's just that-"

"It's just what, Detective? What part of this discussion do you oppose? Do you understand that the government has jurisdiction here, and is acting on behalf of its citizens? Are you denying this boy his rights, Detective?"

"No, sir. It's just the opposite. I'm trying to protect his rights."

"Well, so am I. And the youngster and I are in agreement about what is right for him. It's settled, Detective, and again, thank you for your cooperation. I will see to it that you are given the appropriate pay grade increase for acting in the best interests of your country." With that, the General dismissively marches out, saluting his officers, the Detective, and the boy, and they each return his salute.

Blatantly disregarding the lowly status of his rank, the Detective had broken protocol and voiced concern, which went unheeded. Trembling slightly with obvious anxiety about the child's well being, he recognizes that the General's decision, or command, is final. The Detective, though in struggle, suppresses his outward resistance by surrendering to the situation, and does nothing more than give the lad his telephone number and address, advising Antboy to contact him at any time.

He looks deeply into the boy's eyes for just a moment and is mesmerized by their strength, their power, and their brilliance. Suddenly saddened by the mandatory departure of this young man who is so kind, even-tempered, so well mannered, polite, and so brilliant, the forlorn Detective blinks back tears, which begin to well in the recesses of his downcast, concerned eyes. After an emotional farewell, the compassionate Detective heads toward the welcoming comfort of his grateful family. The officers escort the youngster to a military vehicle, which makes the fifty-five minute journey to intelligence headquarters.

VII

"Father?"

"Yes, Atum."

"So, you thought the domes were to be strictly used for ant preservation? You had no idea that they could be used for humans, like they are here?"

"No, at that time I didn't. At that time I didn't know much at all. When the General took that telephone call in the middle of our first discussion, I made certain assumptions, which he led me to believe. Right then I thought it was all about the ants. I was turning twelve, and I was naïve, and easily manipulated, perhaps necessarily so in those circumstances. Atum, you must always think for yourself. Realize that those in power can manipulate others to fulfill their own selfish desires to retain and gain power. Do you understand what I'm saying and why I'm discussing these events?"

"Yes, I think I do. But I want to know what happened at the intelligence headquarters?"

Father responds to my request, and weaves his captivating story and as it unfolds, in my mind, I become him. I'm the child he talks about. I am Antboy, and I see him and I see myself and I see the boy.

The intelligence community is quite sterile yet stimulating for Antboy. He's given access to certain laboratories and scientific studies and he avidly observes. As he witnesses experiments conducted on animals, including humans, he quickly realizes that he must be very cautious. He must never reveal that he has the ability to hear and understand the language of ants. Not wanting to be the subject of any experiments, he quietly vows to hide his ability, share it with no one, and rarely use it from that day forward.

About a week passes, and while reading some scientific journals in his simple, sparsely decorated quarters, he receives an update about his parents. They have been informed that he's in the secure hands of military headquarters and they're relieved and comforted that he's safe. The General had requested that Antboy be given a few weeks to recuperate from his journey, and they agreed to postpone their visit. They'll arrive in three weeks to celebrate his twelfth birthday, and to review and discuss the paperwork that the General wishes them to sign. They miss him dearly and look forward to seeing him.

Nearly a week later he is shown the prototype of his creation and he's quite astounded and impressed by the decoratively colorful and aesthetically pleasing modifications that have been made. He notices that certain features have been removed, but these changes do not significantly alter the sanctuary, still providing protection for the vulnerable creatures that he hopes will proliferate. Confused yet excited by the new device, he awaits the final changes, which will be made by the end of the following week. The project manager tells him that when everything is finalized there will be a meeting of about twenty important people in the Presentation Hall where some type of 'unveiling' will take place. Dozens of scientists will work in constant cyclical shifts for a week straight in preparation for the presentation. In anticipation, Antboy brims with excitement.

On the morning of the unveiling, he awakes early and eager. He paces his room and the hallway relentlessly, obsessively, until he is finally alerted that the meeting is about to take place. Two men in military uniform escort him to an elevator that goes down two floors to the main level and then just continues downward subterraneously, seeming to spiral around in a circular sequence for several minutes. What sounds like large bolts clank open and then Antboy is guided down a long hallway, brightly lit by virtually pure incandescent white light, until he's in front of a steel door. One military man accesses the fortified entry by using his palm print, a retinal scan, a card swipe, and finally pin code procedures. The gateway opens.

They enter what appears to be a banquet hall containing oval dinner tables dressed with pristine tablecloths beneath formal silverware and china. Tuxedoed waiters are bustling, and a large projection screen hangs above an elevated stage. There are two platforms atop the stage, each with a burgundy tablecloth covering two bulky items. A far cry from the prediction of twenty attendees, the room is at capacity, and Antboy estimates at least two hundred present. Tables display the ethnic flags of its specific guests, and various dialects can be heard overlapping, competing, and echoing throughout the stately banquet hall.

Antboy is seated at a table toward the front and center of the room. He's visibly surprised and greatly pleased to see the General enter and sit next to him, who warmly greets him with a firm pat on the back and a monumental grin. Once the guests are served platters of rare roast beef au jus, creamy garlic mashed potatoes, and steamed, buttered asparagus, the presentation begins.

A rather rotund, ugly man ascends the dais and walks deliberately away from the podium, drawing very little attention from the guests, who seem only to notice the plates in front of them. He speaks in a soft and monotonous voice, standing several feet away from the microphone. Minimally, nearly mutely, he announces that an invention is about to be unveiled that will preserve and provide sanctuary to ant colonies, insuring their continued survival by protecting their environment. He points to his left as the creation is unveiled and there is brief, lukewarm yet polite, scattered applause throughout the hall. The audience continues eating and drinking boisterously, some even raucously and uninterruptedly carrying on loud conversations, rudely distracting and diverting attention from the production as in a sideshow.

Antboy is asked to stand and take credit for his accomplishment. Additionally, an older, balding, miniscule man rises, donning a pair of horn-rimmed spectacles, a Financier, the audience is told, that is going to spearhead the production, distribution, marketing, and sales of this new product. The Financier, perceptibly shaking with eager anticipation for the entrepreneurial project ahead, approaches Antboy and offers him his small, clammy hand that juts forward from his scrawny, almost emaciated torso. Antboy sizes up the man whose size matches his own adolescent frame, and he searches for eyes that he can trust. The man's eyes, beady and brown, yet twinkling with intelligence and business savvy, yield signs of mutual respect and a sense of kindness and understanding. Even so, Antboy suspects that this man may have a whole set of hidden agendas that belong to the world of commerce, a world he cannot possibly understand.

The speaker indicates that Antboy and the Financier should leave the hall immediately, so that they can begin initial discussions regarding operations. Noticeably skeptical, Antboy approaches the man's outstretched hand with a delayed, uncertain motion indicating his obvious trepidation. As they grip hands, the Financier says, "I look forward to working with you."

The Financier is greeted only by Antboy's respectful silence, and a slight nod of tentative assent. Then Antboy walks back to rejoin the General at his table. Preparing to leave, Antboy indicates to the Financier that he will join him momentarily, and turns back nervously, suddenly whispering to the General, "Sir, I'm about to leave with the Financier. What I'm wondering is, well, how can I put this, um, when will I see you again?"

"Son, sooner than you would expect. Of course, I'll be watching out for you in the days and years ahead. You've done a tremendous job for the whole world, I mean, the ants, and I have the utmost faith and confidence that you'll continue to serve your country in many ways. Whether as inventor, soldier, lawyer, accountant, engineer, scientist, teacher, doctor, or wherever your talents are needed, please remember that your country comes first.

"It looks like the paperwork is nearly finalized. Your parents have spoken with me on several occasions and I have reassured them of your safety and happiness. They plan to allow you to become a ward of the state, with reciprocal visiting rights. I would rather call you a benefactor *to* our country than a "ward" *of* it. You will be granted ample accommodations and many scientific resources shall be at your disposal. You will achieve great things. Remember that you can directly contact me at any time."

With this the General hands Antboy a card with a few jumbled letters and numbers and a telephone number. This man of power and great stature, in full military regalia, who had so subtly suppressed his feelings just moments before, is profoundly and visibly emotional, even slightly distraught. He salutes Antboy and then, as they are about to part, he bends down and hugs him tightly, his eyes overflowing with paternal tears. Gutturally clearing his throat, he coughs phlegm, then sputters authoritatively, "Go save the ants, son, while we save the world."

Awaiting their imminent departure, the heavyset speaker feigns patience and casually saunters toward the second veiled platform. The hall begins to buzz with the sensations of anticipation and nervous energy. Then he charges the podium and eagerly seizes the microphone. He emphatically bellows that time is of the essence. While passing through the exit door, Antboy glances back just when it is closing, to spot the second item as it is being unveiled. He squints to discern the invention, just a moment too late, because the door is pulled shut from the inside.

Locked out of the banquet hall, he and the Financier stand in the bright hallway listening to the deafening applause from within. They walk toward the bolted steel elevator. Two guards lead them into the lift, which goes around in its circuitous route, then steadily upward for quite some time until they exit the main floor.

Before parting, Antboy again sizes up the Financier and looks deeply into his face. He sees a man who he believes to be a proponent of the invention, an honest man ready to do business with the world. Antboy feels comfortable that the Financier will do justice to this project. They agree to meet the next day in the late afternoon so that each of them can get some solid rest, and sort out his thoughts about how to bring the Ant Sanctuary to the world.

VIII

Day one is very productive and the Financier mainly focuses on getting the required approval from Antboy for certain specifications necessary to proceed with mass-production. Roles for each are defined and discussed. Antboy conveys that his main concern is to personally maintain a large number of sanctuaries for extensive research, while the Financier shares his goal of personally maintaining a large bottom line. They strike a profit-sharing agreement and mutually determine that Antboy will neither be involved with operations nor virtually any mundane part of the company. The Financier will handle all aspects of the daily necessities.

Antboy wistfully asks to be specifically given a large, very huge home, with multiple floors and wings, in order to set up hundreds, perhaps thousands of sanctuaries, prefera-bly with little to no adult supervision. The Financier agrees to secure Antboy a residence meeting these specifications within the surrounding ninety miles, complying with the guidelines and restrictions placed upon the boy's designation as a ward of the state. The Financier shows Antboy the governmental ward documents, which detail his regimented housing arrangements and educational requirements. Antboy must reside with two domestic adults at all times, who will alternate as cook, housekeeper, driver, and nanny in addition to a live-in tutor, who will help meet compulsory education laws, plus two military personnel who will function as security and maintenance.

During the following week, as arrangements are made for production of the ant sanctuaries and procurement of the mansion, a more relaxed Antboy returns to the Detective and his family. He is again welcomed warmly into their home. He integrates himself into their daily routines, socializing with the Detective's three children and the other neighborhood kids. For a few days he attends school with the Detective's kids, even substituting for one of their teachers when an unforeseen emergency calls her away from school.

His parents are due to arrive in two days to celebrate his twelfth birthday. He is worried about their upcoming visit. Will they understand and accept why he chooses to be here rather than in the comfort and security of his childhood home? Will they assert their parental rights and deny him this incredible opportunity for research and discovery and learning that he hopes will define the rest of his childhood? Will they try to revoke their approval of his status as a ward of the state? The General, under the pretense of national security, could probably impose certain inexorable governmental powers to block their attempts, but it would be much easier if they acquiesced to their son's wishes and helped him to achieve his goals.

Anxiety dissolves into reality when the day arrives for their visit. He awakes to the Detective's famous whole grain chocolate chip pancakes topped with twelve birthday candles. After breakfast, he goes out to the front yard to play kickball with the neighborhood kids. Although he rarely joins group sports, he focuses, applies himself, and is quite good.

As soon as his parents spot him getting ready to boot the ball, they ask the taxicab driver to let them out a few houses away from where he's playing. They remain undetected, observing their son in a rare moment of mindless boyhood play. It is a moment that they will never forget, and will cherish forever. Antboy's mother is extremely relieved to see her son looking healthy and energetic, happy and playing outside, a dramatic change from when he had quarantined himself in his room. Sobbing uncontrollably, she holds her husband tightly, tears of joy streaming down her face. As she composes herself, wiping tears from her makeup-smudged face, she calls out to her boy, her only child, her most perfect creation. Antboy looks up from his game and runs full-sprint to his parents and hugs them both. His father picks him up and swings him around and his mother squeezes and hugs and cuddles him.

Overwhelmed by their affection, he's surprised at the unexpected, uncommon emotional outburst from not only his usually undemonstrative mother but also his quite reserved father. Although his parents generally exhibit firm control over their feelings, he never doubted their love for him, and he's both comforted by their affection, and somewhat overcome with relief. He had never expected, nor could he have predicted, such a loving reaction from both parents. Rather than analyze this moment, though, as they had methodically compelled him to do in every circumstance from his earliest years, Antboy wants only to remember this moment and to appreciate, to relish, and to savor it as a lasting memory of his love for his parents and their enduring love for him.

They spend the remainder of his birthday together and his parents inquire about his welfare and future plans. His foremost concern is to ask them for their forgiveness. He apologizes for not discussing his invention with them and realizes he should have asked permission before venturing on his cross-country journey. An Ant Sanctuary, he explains, is what he has invented. A dome that his government has chosen to enthusiastically support in his attempt to provide safety and security for the world's smallest creatures. Excitedly, he continues to tell them that his creation will soon be sold worldwide to ant lovers, through his new company, and that he'll be given ample facilities to continue his true love, his research.

They are thrilled, although not surprised by his intelligent invention, and nearly gloat at the success of their son. By the end of that remarkable day, they appear visibly relieved that he looks so animated, which they had not witnessed in ages. It is late evening when they part, and mother, father, and son try to withhold tears, but they just flow, not out of sadness, but from acceptance and understanding. They are all, surprisingly, emotionally drained. Later that evening, after reflecting upon the marvelous events of that momentous day, now indelibly etched in memory, Antboy falls exhaustedly into bed and looks at the wall calendar, and waits.

IX

Nine days later, Antboy hears news. The Financier, with ample help from the General, has acquired and prepared the home that will house Antboy, the team of five, and his ant sanctuaries. He is sending a car in the morning to pick up Antboy and his belongings and bring him to his new home.

The next morning he quickly packs his sparse belongings and dutifully promises to keep in touch with the Detective's family. They extract a pledge from him: to invite them over as soon as he gets settled. Waving goodbye from a black van with government plates, he's driven toward spacious mansions that dot the countryside. The drive is calming, shaded by oak trees, with sprawling homes built from stone, covered with climbing ivy, and acres of manicured land.

As they enter a remote portion of the woodland area, they turn on Oak Tree Lane. They proceed slowly to a house at the very end of the block, waiting momentarily for a gate at the property boundary to swing open. The serpentine driveway continues to escalate for almost twice the length of a city block until the house is visible, a house with an address of, simply, One Oak Tree Lane.

Antboy is solemnly greeted. An obscenely tall gentleman with slick black hair, in full formal attire, greets him with a heavy bow, perhaps dramatically obsequious. Then, in a swift movement, he simultaneously holds open the door, grabs Antboy's sole bag, swinging it upon his shoulder, and offers a hand to the boy. Two military personnel stand attentively, hands resting readily on guns holstered at their side, their serious faces awaiting communication from a single cordless earpiece in each man's left ear. Antboy is introduced to a graying, middle-aged woman, with kind, intelligent eyes who will serve as cook and general house-keeper. As he offers her his hand she rejects it, instead draping him with an uncomfortable, unenthusiastic, imper-sonal hug. A hand obtrusively approaches his chest, jutting from a red-haired, freckle faced, geeky-smiled mid-twenties lad wearing uneven, scratched spectacles claiming to be a masters student at the local university. He conveys how thrilled he is to be working as Antboy's tutor.

Antboy is stunned, astounded at the magnitude of the magnificent mansion and palatial grounds that lie before him. The Financier explains that the home has approximately twenty-six rooms, depending on how one counted these rooms, including eight full or partial bathrooms, almost tripling Antboy's expectations, allowing enough space to set up several thousand sanctuaries. With the exception of the resident living quarters and certain common areas including the library, dining room, kitchen, and entertainment rooms, he is permitted to do what he wishes with the remaining half of the property.

Before dismissing the staff, the Financier explains that they are all due in the dining hall at five o'clock for a 'family' meeting where roles will be discussed and any other issues resolved. As the Financier escorts Antboy to the master quarters, he explains that at least two armed military personnel will be present at all times, and that they will be rotated regularly. Mistaking Antboy's unresponsive demeanor to the security detail as concern, rather than the pure indifference that it reflected, the Financier hastily explains that this number can be quickly increased one hundredfold should the security status of the country change. He adds that a force of such size can be logistically positioned to arrive within fourteen to eighteen minutes.

Antboy is rendered speechless. He realizes that he has created an essentially revolutionary product to conserve and preserve his precious ants. However, he didn't know, until then, what an important emphasis the nation was placing on the continuation of his project. At that moment, looking upon the majestic setting where he would live and conduct his research, he changed his view of the government full spectrum. From the inimitable contempt he originally experienced at the Patent Office, his opinion reached the absolute opposite pole, immense respect. The administration's priority to protect the earth's smallest creatures, his beloved ants, tactically dissolved all shreds of criticism remaining within him.

It's noon, and he realizes he has about five hours remaining until the meeting, so he decides to explore and familiarize himself with his surroundings. In the main entrance, there is a grand portrait of, as he reads the plaque, a former Governor, who had resided there for eight years some time ago. He discovers that the house has three floors, plus an unfinished basement that runs the length of the mansion. The basement is filthy, insect infested, and obviously untrammeled during the last few decades making it a suitable place to set up his sanctuaries under a variety of controlled and uncontrolled conditions. The top floor has an enormously large room where he imagines setting up a massive train set, punching bag, and huge Tinker Toys that he can use to simulate structural modifications to his invention on a much grander scale than previously envisioned. He will also need to set up a bank of computers to be integrated with an immense customizable online library, with enough disk space and memory, to run complex data input and perform interpretive laboratory analysis. With these facilities he will be able to observe more than four thousand five hundred ant species and document the life cycle of almost every known species of ant discovered around the world. More than satisfied with his accommodations, he resolves, with the full backing of his new parent and guardian, the government, to completely research and fully authenticate the lives and workings of ants.

To him, the ants are by far a most perfect society. Who could question the beautiful perfection of the ants, social insects living in organized colonies? Having witnessed and been traumatized by the horror and cruelty stemming from his own friends, who mercilessly killed, without feeling, the defenseless, harmless ants, in front of his home just months before on that fateful summer day, he ardently, inwardly renews his vow to protect and uphold these creatures' rights to life.

With just over two hours until the family meeting, he goes to the library where he finds a sheaf of paper and pencil. With the first words he will etch into a journal, he is determined to remark frankly upon everything he has studied and learned since his manifestation as Antboy, the familiar moniker he overheard whispered peevishly among the staff during his earlier, initial exploration of the grounds.

Neither offended nor comforted by the nickname with which he has been anointed, he sincerely hopes to insure the survival of his beloved ants.

Antboy writes down all that he has learned. In ant colonies there are females that are winged and those that are not. The wingless females are infertile workers and operate mainly for defense of the colony, foraging for food, and tending the babies. The winged female becomes a queen and founds a colony when she lands from the nuptial flight in which she has become inseminated by one or more males, has lost her wings, and has found a protected place or excavated a chamber. Males die after mating; their only purpose is to procreate and once this has been completed, they die.

The queen lays eggs that develop into larvae, then pupae, and then adults. In some species the queens start their new colonies alone, in others they leave with workers from the old nest. Queens starting on their own do not have a lot of food to begin with, which is why the first workers are normally smaller than they are in a big nest. When times are hard the young queen must eat her eggs to stay alive, but as soon as the first non-winged females, the workers, are born, she's out of trouble. These workers begin foraging and hunting for food and tending the brood. Then the queen has only one job left, to lay more eggs.

"Father?"

"Yes, Atum. What is it?"

"You really love the ants, don't you?"

"Yes, Atum, I do. I pray that one day you may also witness the beauty and perfection of an ant. One day soon, I hope."

"Father?"

"Yes?"

"Have you ever loved anything as much as the ants?"

"Well, yes I did. Only once did I experience something that compared with my love for the ants. Only once. But that was long ago and didn't last very long."

"What was it, Father? What was it? Please tell me, you must tell me."

"Atum?"

"Yes, Father?"

"You must promise never to tell a soul. Do you promise?"

"Yes, I promise."

"It was Lavender that I loved. My love for her surpassed my love for the ants."

"Lavender? Queen Lavender? How could you love her, Father, how?"

"Atum, it's very difficult to explain. Lavender was not always Queen of this Colony. She was not the original Queen, who made me the outcast I am today; that was Queen Siren, the first Queen. After three birthing seasons, Siren was succeeded by Queen Iris, who ruled for two seasons until she succumbed to an insurrection led by Queen Blue. Lavender eventually overthrew Queen Blue during her third term. At one time Lavender was a friend, a very close friend, and she actually defied the ruling Queen, Siren, and was truly punished, severely chastised for her disloyalty. It was at that time that I loved her and I believe she deeply loved me. However, I don't even know her anymore, and to her I no longer exist.

"It's as if that time and our love never occurred. It's still in the distant recesses of my memory, although she may have completely erased it from hers. You cannot understand how I felt. It was a feeling that transcended all my concerns, all my fears, and I felt safe and whole. But that time was never meant to last, not here, not ever, not in this world where we live as ants, a place where females rule, and men are virtually irrelevant. What I felt was taboo. You must never feel that for anyone here on our colony, ever.

"One day you will leave here. You will travel to the world below and I pray that you will feel the love for a woman as I have, however brief that was. I hope that your love will last forever, and that you will be able to create a child, as I have not. You must live to tread on the planet below, and when that happens, then I will not have struggled in vain. It's too late for me, Atum. I will never again experience what Lavender and I shared in the earliest days of this colony, thirteen years ago. I will never recover from the severe loss of that love. My emotions, my mind, and my spirit were much less vulnerable when I truly loved only the ants. That's why you must listen, and understand all that I must tell you. You must know everything there is to know. So, please listen, and let me continue uninterrupted for a while."

Father glances toward a collection of journals at the far side of the dome. Over the years he has referred to his writings as his most valuable possession. "There is so much to tell you," Father cajoles me into listening to his tale.

X

Interrupted by the tinkling of a bell, a dinner bell, Antboy closes his journal entry, and leaves the library, trotting downstairs to the main dining room for the first meeting at his new home, the Governor's Mansion. He is warmly greeted by the Financier, who is trailed by several dozen large cartons, which he explains house the first delivery of Ant Sanctuaries that the boy will use for his research and study.

"Ahead of schedule!" proclaims the excited Financier, seeking Antboy's gentle nod of approval.

The meeting starts with Antboy introducing himself. He briefly tells them a little about his birthplace, family background, interests, and a few tidbits about his academic influences. But when he enthusiastically explains, in length and in great detail, what he'll be doing throughout the house with his Ant Sanctuaries, the staff stares at him nervously, perplexed. Realizing that he just instilled anxiety among his companions, he quickly adds that the ants within these structures will be unable, under any circumstances, to escape their environmentally controlled domiciles. This admission slightly eases the team's consternation. Discussion then proceeds around the table. Staff members briefly state their backgrounds and current responsibilities.

The Financier emphasizes that although Antboy is virtually in charge of the house there are certain conditions over which the five adults technically retain control and power. Antboy shall be fed regularly and punctually. If he does not partake of adequate and recommended sustenance then any adult has immediate executive privilege to contact the Financier who will then take necessary and appropriate action. The tutor will ensure that Antboy meets all minimum compulsory educational requirements, unless more is deemed necessary, and if these requirements are not met, the Financier is to be alerted. All rooms will need to be accessible for weekly cleaning, and no exceptions will be allowed. Irregularities or concerns, with regard to any matters, must be instantly reported to the Financier. The security team will be rotated properly and one member of the team will accompany Antboy on all excursions away from the grounds. If Antboy violates this security protocol whatsoever, by leaving the grounds unattended, security will contact the General who will address the security breach. The senior security officer explains that there is an evacuation route consisting of tunnels located below the basement level, which will only be disclosed in the event of a natural disaster, national crisis, or security breach. The officer warns each of the housemates, while staring sternly at Antboy, that they are never to attempt accessing these tunnels without official military escort. He reiterates that the conditions of the tunnels are dangerous and primitive.

After casual review of the meeting agenda set before the housemates, which posts the weekly cleaning, meal, and educational schedules, Antboy appears amenable, realizing he will have ample time for his research. Surmising that as long as he generally follows the house rules, he figures he can maneuver the situation to best suit his needs, especially once he is trusted and a routine is established.

In due time, he will need to explore the tunnels below the Governor's Mansion. He smiles, forming a mischievous grin, and everyone takes this as a cue to smile, shake hands, exchange welcomes, and partake in their first meal together. Once the dessert plates are cleared, the Financier dismisses everyone but Antboy. They're alone in the main dining hall.

"We're in full production at the factory and our first worldwide orders will be shipped within two weeks. Am I to assume you will want the remainder of your sanctuaries at the same time these first shipments leave the warehouse?"

"Yes, definitely."

"How many?"

"Two thousand."

The Financier cringes visibly but had already prepared for this practical necessity. After all, Antboy is obviously not in this for profit. If the only drag on the bottom line is this initial bulk request, the impact on profitability could be minimal and quickly contained. "Done. We can pack five hundred domes per truck so I will arrange four trucks, all long haul eighteen-wheelers. I will also hire an additional ten-man team, supplementing the drivers, to set up everything upon delivery. When these trucks and men arrive, you'll need to be very precise and clear as to your requirements and exact layout specifications. Can you be ready for delivery within two weeks?"

"Yes, definitely. How about the ants? When will they be here and how will they be handled?"

"A separate truck will be carrying your initial request for eight hundred species. Four leading specialists will see you through the entire initialization process. They'll arrive two days after the Sanctuaries."

"I need females. Please make sure that the population is almost completely strong females. Males are pretty much irrelevant, so only a small male minority is needed. Some of the females need to be Queens, others will assume that role later."

"Of course, just as you told me last month, and I've communicated every detail to our suppliers. I feel everything will go as smoothly as can be expected, considering our unusual and unique logistics."

Antboy definitively stands up and confidently shakes the Financier's hand. "Well, until next time," Antboy says, satisfied. "Until next time," the Financier replies, relieved.

Closing the door behind the Financier, Antboy requests a level, tape measure, and other tools of precision to be retrieved, and he fervently heads to a wing of empty rooms. For nearly two weeks he takes only short breaks, allowing himself to be distracted only briefly from measuring, sketching, and blueprinting solely to partake of the minimum fluids, solids, hygiene, and education expected of him.

One morning, Antboy wakes to a very loud, thunderous rumbling. His housemates, panicked and startled at the trembling earth, rush downstairs to the main floor, pajama-clad, crusty-eyed, and reeking of odoriferous sleep. The tutor is fervently gesticulating, generously genuflecting, and they huddle together in genuine prayer, asking for protection from this unholy, unheard of earthquake. The front door opens and a security man yells, "The trucks are here!"

Sheepishly, they return to their respective rooms to freshen up and prepare for the day of chaos ahead. Soon, the scent of strong coffee permeates the premises. Antboy quickly starts delegating assignments from a weathered yellow legal pad, feverishly adding notes as rapidly as he crosses others off. He asks the tutor to paste specific diagrams on the doors of ten selected rooms scattered throughout the mansion, which display the exact measurements of each particular room in addition to his sanctuary setup specifications. The diagrams precisely pinpoint his planned layout and he insists that they must be followed to the letter.

The next fourteen hours are exhausting and stressful, yet certainly productive. Men, in blue and gray uniforms, carrying space-age like dome shaped structures, each a solid color, baby blue, gamma green, orbit orange, radiant red, trek here and there throughout the palatial grounds.

Antboy stands on a step stool barking orders into an old megaphone he managed to find in the deep recesses of the garage. He watches the clock mechanically and, so that everything moves swiftly and at maximum efficiency, he coordinates meal breaks in separate shifts. He asks the housekeeper to place an order for eight pizzas and enough sodas for everyone, which arrives just before the first planned lunch shift. Dinner is fried chicken, corn, mashed potatoes and buttermilk biscuits with honey, and the order arrives promptly.

When the last truck rumbles down the driveway and departs Oak Tree Lane, after completion of the entire dome setup, the housemates, except Antboy who is indefatigably energized, haul their weary bodies upstairs and somehow stumble to their respective quarters. Alone, Antboy visits each room that houses sanctuaries. He checks every setup against his diagram, makes a few adjustments, finds two rooms completely backwards, and fixes them. Hearing a distant clock chime two in the morning, he calculates that the ant deliveries will arrive in thirty hours, and he retires immediately to get much needed rest.

He dreams that night, his first in quite some time. He is on a mountaintop standing before billions of assembled ants, as far as his eyes can see. They are bowing to him and he is smiling. Then the ants hold sticks, then swords, and then wave guns and hurl bombs. Antboy is flying, driving, swimming, running, and crying. He is covered in crude oil, on fire, and jumps in a lake and begins to drown. He sees the ants laughing, but they pull him out and begin to overwhelm him. They are in his mouth, ears, nose, and lungs. He can no longer breathe. "Ahhhhhhhhhh!" He awakes, curled in a ball in the middle of his bed, shuddering and shivering, dripping from sticky perspiration, reminiscent of sweat he had only previously encountered on occasional humid summer nights.

He walks outside and stares up at the stars and moon to calm down, convincing himself that dreams and nightmares come and go as they please, without a basis in reality. He doesn't return to his bedroom, instead he visits the library to continue documenting his research.

After the Queen lands from her nuptial flight, having been inseminated by her now-dead suitors, each male dying after procreation, she finds a protected place or chamber and starts to lay eggs, from which larvae emerge. During the larval phase the ants grow, so they have to be constantly fed. The Queen may search for food outside the nest or regurgitate her liquefied wing musculature, since she will never fly again. In this initial period the Queen is responsible for all colony tasks, not only feeding the larvae, but also maintaining the nest and defending the colony.

After the first workers are born, which are the ants that do not give birth, the Queen no longer needs to perform maintenance and colony development. She restricts herself only to egg laying and grooming, while the workers do all the other tasks, even feeding the Queen. The colony enters a growing phase, not only in population but also in nest size. Additionally, the area over which the workers forage for food is increased. After a few years, colonies may house millions of individuals living together at a given time, with only one Queen.

After a growing period of a few years, the colony produces its first generation of sexuals. The sexuals produced by colonies of a given region will fly on the same day and at the same time, increasing their chance to meet and fertilize in the nuptial flight. The cycle is completed with an impregnated Queen for each colony, and the death of the fertilizing males. Should a colony witness the death of her Queen, who may live up to twenty years, the colony is only able to survive a few months, since Queens are seldom replaced and workers are unable to reproduce.

Antboy speculates that ants and their form of society may be superior to mammalian structure, including humans, yet it's still too soon to tell. But inwardly he feels this to be true. The ant is bred for survival and its sole purpose is for the continuation of its species. There is no selfish ant. Like humans, ants contain a head, a brain, eyes, a digestive tract, a nervous system, a stomach, a large intestine, 'legs and arms', a gut, and an anus. Humans can't stand ants because they are nuisances to their lifestyles and, of course, ants dislike humans because they murder them without thought.

Over the years, when he hears news reports of bombs dropping sometimes here, sometimes there, Antboy often wonders who would survive if the really big bombs dropped, ants or humans? He's certain ants would survive, but who would believe ant species to be superior in their societal structure and survivalist philosophies to humans? After all, could the world ever accept the superiority of a female-dominated society, where males are essential strictly for purposes of breeding? Antboy chuckles generously at such an implausible notion.

Father and Atum stare at each other solemnly.
"Who could have known?" Father said.
"You knew, Father. You knew."

XI

Antboy spends the bulk of the next day, excusing himself from formal meals and his tutor, preparing proper environments within the Sanctuaries for the various species that will arrive the next morning. From his research, Antboy has learned that ants are generally omnivorous, but some need specialty food. They build a nest either underground, or aboveground in trees and houses where they live and bring their food. Fungus-growing ants cut leaves, Leafcutter Ants (species *Atta)*, and bring them home to their nest to fertilize the fungus gardens they build. Harvester Ants (*Messor*) frequently visit grass fields to harvest and store grass seeds. Specialized workers crack the seeds for other ants to eat. Many ants eat the sweet fluid excreted by aphids. Some species keep and protect aphids, even in their own nests. Honeypot Ants (*Myrmecystus*) feed certain workers with enormous quantities of honeydew, using them as living containers to store food. These worker ants' bodies become so big they cannot move anymore. The nests of the

Army (*Darylus*), or Driver Ants, are built out of the clustered bodies of millions of workers hanging down from low branches or logs. In this cluster the Queen and her offspring, the brood, are enclosed.

After the nesting phase is completed the nomadic phase starts. The whole colony moves with the Queen and brood protected by huge soldiers who kill everything that comes their way. In areas where Army, or Driver Ants have already passed through, no living insects will be found. Even young birds that are unable to fly, lizards and other small animals are killed if they cannot get away. After forays and attacks against other species of ants, Amazon Ants (*Polyergus*) bring back unconsumed young ants to serve as worker slaves once they've matured.

Antboy discovered that nesting takes on a great variety of forms in ant colonies. For each of his domes, he designed alternative internal setups with several levels to accommodate the differing needs of varying ant species. What might initially be an inconspicuous cave when a colony is founded will develop into an accommodation that is steadily being enlarged in the course of a colony's life cycle. What looks like a complete mess at first sight, truly has a perfect system. It is the nest where the food is brought, the brood is protected, and the Queen is housed in a microclimate that is just right for the ants. Nests may even contain sub-nests of smaller ants for added protection and insulation. Workers are constantly busy regulating the nest climate. Eggs, larvae, and pupae are transported through corridors into areas of the nest that correspond to their climatic needs. Ventilation shafts are opened or closed according to the weather. When it becomes too warm, ants together with their brood move to the lower areas of the nest. With colder weather, the brood is taken into the top chambers to utilize the warmth of the sun. Soldiers guard the nest entrance and control the incoming workers carrying their prey. As soon as these incoming workers have handed the food over to other specialized workers, they again run towards the exit to retrieve more food. Different workers are responsible for nest hygiene and they transport pupae covers, foraged insects, and dead ants to dry spots far from the nest.

Antboy had extensively studied food and predation among ants, and he incorporated his findings into the Sanctuary designs. He meticulously reviews his notes and checks the directions that he will give to the scientists when they arrive in a couple of hours. They were already provided lists of food requirements per ant species and are due to show up with ample stock.

Insects, spiders, and worms contribute protein to the ants' diet and are captured alive or collected when they are already dead. Killed prey is taken to the nest at once, and if it's too big, it's cut up on the spot. The biggest hunters in the ant kingdom are the Army or Driver Ants. They are involved in the removal of dead vertebrates like birds or mice. They're called the health police of the forest since infestation of pests is considerably lower in areas with these ants, compared to those without.

Ants go through both stationary and nomadic stages. During their stationary stage they stay in a nest that is made up of their own bodies while the Queen is fully engaged in laying eggs. These nests hang on low branches or between trees standing close together. At dawn the workers spread into all directions and kill every living thing that cannot escape. Big soldiers with mighty mandibles patrol the area. Bumpy terrain is surmounted by bridges, which are formed out of the ants' bodies. Big spiders that would kill a single ant without any problem, are killed by large soldier ants, cut up and transported back to the nest. When food in the surrounding area is running short, ants start their nomadic phase. The Queen finishes laying eggs, and then the whole colony migrates toward a new hunting area.

Antboy unwittingly drifts off while reading his notes, sitting in the library at his grand mahogany desk. Rising three hours later, he wipes drool from his journal and he realizes that the scientists had already arrived and have begun the colonization process. Fortunately, at this stage, they are more skilled in the setup than Antboy. They started without him, but followed his exacting specifications.

He simply observes and occasionally supervises. He watches, sometimes offering constructive, corrective advice. Food sources are integrated into each sanctuary as well as nesting materials appropriate for each species to be colonized. With minimal criticism, he allows the appropriate species of Queens, female workers, and short-lived males to be introduced into the sanctuaries scattered among the various floors, rooms, basement, and rear courtyard of the former Governor's Mansion. When the last scientist leaves and Antboy is alone with his sanctuaries, he is overwhelmed yet relieved by his critique of the day's accomplishment.

A study of such magnitude had never been conducted before, and Antboy is eager and excited. Famished, he sits down to enjoy the first of his three peanut butter and jelly sandwiches before he takes a tour of duty and observes the foundation of the various colonies. He realizes that some domes will provide success among species that will thrive, while others will be complete and outright failures.

He will witness young females of various species digging a founding chamber under a stone, tree bark, or other protected place. At times she'll leave the chamber to search for food, returning to take care of the brood until the first workers have grown up. The Queen is considerably larger than the first workers because she greatly increases her fat substances during the larvae state. Her shed wing muscles, eggs, and some young larvae will serve as the Queen's own natural food reserves.

As the months roll by, Antboy watches, listens, and records significant events in each sanctuary throughout the grounds using a ledger attached to each dome. There is incredible order in colonies and immense adaptability, which makes survival of each species nearly certain. Their proliferation is conditioned on the female being the dominant gender in ant colonies, and the provider of food, shelter, and babies while the male is used solely to provide the seeds of life. Being extinguished immediately after their sole job is complete, males, due to their brief life spans, drain little resources from colonies.

On the eve of his thirteenth birthday, as he is about to fall asleep, Antboy hears the ants talk for the first time since his arrival at the Governor's Mansion.

"We are grateful to you, oh Antboy, for you have done us an immense service here in your home and throughout the world. You have provided us shelter and food and you have made up for the Great Flood that you failed to stop when you were a younger boy. The Great Flood was very devastating to our species and we thank you for compensating for the great losses to our western colonists. You are now a part of our history and no young ant will ever reach adulthood without learning how to pray and show homage to you, Antboy. Let us say together, Antboy, Boy of Ants, we thank you, we need you, we love you."

"I need to know something," interjects Antboy.

"Antboy, Boy of Ants, what do you need to know?"

"In your colonies, females dominate and rule. Why are males killed right after they perform their reproductive functions?"

"Antboy, Boy of Ants, males are only needed in our society for their reproductive role. Our society is based on cooperation, which fuels the continuation of thousands of our species. Females are the carriers of our future generations, and therefore rule our society. Males are very important to our society but have a limited role. After their duty has been fulfilled they are killed before they become aggressive as all males do. If allowed to live, males become counterproductive and sometimes harm our colony for their own selfish needs. Look to your society and you will understand why ant colonies limit the male contribution strictly to reproduction."

"I have looked at my people, but your form of society will not work for humans."

"Antboy, Boy of Ants, it must work and it will. It is the only order that can work. Look at your failures as a civilization, as a culture. We may be small but our species' are much older than yours and we have watched you evolve for thousands of years and learned from your mistakes. We will always provide for our colony, to forever survive and prosper. We do not kill our own species or steal from each other. We live in harmony. Each member of our colony serves a purpose for our continued survival. Study us and learn."

"I intend to, especially since the government is very supportive of my research."

"Antboy, Boy of Ants, what is a 'government'?"

"Father?"

"Yes?"

"What did you say?"

"What did I say about what?"

"What did you tell the ants about government?"

"I didn't tell them anything."

"Why?"

"Because, I didn't know how to answer the question. I didn't really understand what a government was at the time, or how to explain its functions. I was just a boy, a boy about to turn thirteen. All I knew was that the government was supporting my life and had provided me with the means to continue my research. And that's all I cared about."

"Do you know what it is now? Do you know what a government does?"

"I certainly know what it is now. And on the day of my eighteenth birthday I learned what powers a government can enforce. My life as I knew it changed radically that day. From the moment I met the General, the government has played an inextricable role in my life, eventually leading me right here, to this launched satellite world. Does that explain the meaning of government?"

"No, Father. I still don't understand what it is."

"Let me put things more simply. A government is a small administration of people that sets and controls the laws of a geographical region in which a larger group of inhabitants resides. Each locale has laws that affect the education, transportation, food, communication, health care, commerce, armed forces, and land of the populace that resides within its realm. The leaders rule and make decisions that affect the lives of the masses in their constituency.

"Governments support themselves by establishing and enforcing taxation systems. They can also borrow, print, and issue currency. Taxes, which require a person to give up part of one's property, must be paid to the government. Residents that do not pay their taxes risk seizure of property or loss of liberty.

"Some governments are formed by elections where people vote and choose between various contenders who want to lead the country. Voters are given certain information about the candidates that want to rule them. Then they cast a ballot by making marks on pieces of paper, which are counted. In certain distinct geographical areas, or countries, arguments over which nominee received the most pieces of paper occur. Sometimes the person that gets to rule the population is not the one who garnered the most pieces of paper. At other times regimes are formed without popular consent, when certain factions seize the power of a particular country, or region, by force or other means.

"The majority of people are afraid to live without an organized and established system and feel safer in this type of societal structure; they have fewer decisions to make and they pay for their sense of freedom and security. By giving up some of their assets, citizens generally believe they will be protected, or at minimum, not persecuted. The leaders of most governments are men, unlike the female led society that rules our world."

From my blank stare, Father knows he just confused me. I'm more interested in something Father has yet to explain.

"Atum, I understand it's hard for you to visualize the concept of government."

"The ants, how do you speak to the ants? How do you understand them and how do they speak to you? Do their mouths move? Do they even have mouths?"

"I can't explain to you why or how I'm able to communicate with ants. Possibly stress that I endured caused something to burst within my brain, or perhaps an epiphany I may have experienced altered my chemical composition. I really don't know. I must have been indelibly affected. I had never conceived of such a thing, but there I was, hearing the ants speak.

"No one but you has ever known about this ability that I possess. I've always feared reprisal from those that, due to their ignorance, would have labeled me a freak and possibly caused me harm. But every year, around the anniversary of my birth, often on the eve, some form of extrasensory channel opens and I hear the ants speak. I've always attributed this to some type of solar alignment that only occurs around that date, the date I was given life, the day I should appreciate life, in every shape, in every form. And, Atum, I don't know if their mouths move and they speak aloud, or whether their speech just forms within the confines of my mind, impressed into my consciousness. The words are just there, and I've never questioned how they get there. I hear them, then I speak and somehow the ants hear me and respond."

"Every year around your birthday?"

"Every year. But my thirteenth birthday was the last one that I celebrated with a party."

XII

The birthday morning arrives like any other day. Antboy heads downstairs and is surprised to find the main dining hall decorated with balloons and party hats. He can't help but laugh because he hasn't a clue how anyone knew. He's told that the party begins sharply at one o'clock, which means he only has a few hours to get his research and schoolwork done. Entering the kitchen, he receives a brief Happy Birthday salutation from the caterers who are extremely busy making preparations for the affair.

The clock strikes one o'clock and first the Financier arrives, then the Detective and his family, the General with his military escort, the tutor, housekeeper, and finally the butler file in and the party begins. Everyone shakes Antboy's hand. There's music, games, and an enormous heaping of various foods, followed by an exquisite chocolate cake. Everyone files out promptly at four o'clock except the General, who stays behind to walk the premises with Antboy.

Proudly exhibiting his research and journals along the way, Antboy commences his house tour with the still unkempt yet vastly improved sprawling basement. He continues his labyrinthine journey, with the General patiently in tow, all the way up to the third story of the house. The General seems pleased with Antboy's progress and asks, "Are you happy here, son?"

Antboy replies formally and gratefully, respectful of the General's rank, "I'm extremely happy here, sir." They adjourn to Antboy's favorite sitting room, with a magnificent view of the grounds, several large, comfortable leather recliners beckoning, and a fireplace gracing half a wall.

"How is the research going, son?"

"Very well, sir. The ants are establishing their colonies throughout the sanctuaries and I'm recording their activities in great detail. Recently, though, I've expanded my aim for the project. Since our sanctuaries are going to preserve ant species worldwide, and I'm thankful that there has been such international support, I've changed my focus from preserving the ants to understanding the ants. There's just so much to learn from them. My new direction will be vastly different from what I'd originally intended."

"Sounds very interesting, son. What is the basis for this new focus, this new direction?"

"I'm comparing human society to the structure of ant colonies. My initial hypothesis, sir, is that ant colonies are far superior in structure to human societies and that ants have a greater chance of continued survival than do humans. Of course, at this early stage in my research, there is no data available yet to validate this hypothesis and I still have years of work ahead."

"Ah, that's very fascinating, most remarkable indeed. I had no idea that your young mind would have leaned in that direction. Intriguing, amazing. Do you realize the magnitude and scope of your accomplishments already, son?"

"Yes, ants today are more preserved and safer in the world than ever before, sir."

"Ah, yes, the ants, yes the ants, well so I've heard the same news. Actually, you've done more with your Sanctuary than even we can predict at this point. Of course only the history books will show the true outcome, if there remain any history books. You've seen the news? The news doesn't look good for us in the long run, son."

"I rarely see the news with all of my work and when I do, I don't really understand it. It seems so foreign and strange when I hear what people are doing to each other, that I prefer to stick to the ants, sir."

"Well, I certainly understand why you prefer the ants. If I could stick with ants I would, but I have to leave that job to you while I work with mankind. I've worked with many scientists over the years and they all share one commonality. Do you know what that is?"

"What, sir?"

"They never want to draw a conclusion until all the facts are in. They always want to hedge their opinions until every single 'i' is dotted and each 't' crossed when, for the most part, they knew all along, at the outset, exactly what their research would prove. The whole founding reason these scientists got started in the first place was due to a hunch, an instinct, or a type of intellectual revelation. Are you willing to give me your gut feeling on this?"

"Absolutely, sir. My initial conclusion is that human societies should be modeled after ant colonies. The research may prove me wrong, but I doubt it."

"Very bold, son. I'm proud to have made your acquaintance. You're quite a fellow."

"Thank you, sir."

"I'm sure you have no idea at this point, son, and I'm sure we're years away, but what is your prediction on how long it will take for you to complete your research?"

"Sir, I'm giving myself about five more years until I'll have accurate data and detailed research. Enough evidence for me, or anyone for that matter, to draw a definitive conclusion."

"Well, I figured about as much. Let's see, son, today you're thirteen, so I guess that puts your estimated completion date right around your eighteenth birthday, the date you're able to vote and also serve your country. Don't get me wrong, you already are serving your country, after all, whether through your scientific research or my military expertise we both serve our country but eighteen is a whole different story. At eighteen you can walk out of here and live your life any way you see fit and you officially become a man in the eyes of our country."

"Yes, sir."

"Well, as you know, I came here today to wish you Happy Birthday, son. I honestly don't know if I can make any more birthdays due to the distance and security risk both to you and me. But you know how to reach me, so never hesitate, and I mean never. As for the research, keep up the work. I look forward to getting updates from time to time, and then seeing your findings upon completion. Very importantly, please call your parents today because they can't directly reach you here. They called me yesterday to remind me. They would appreciate hearing from you, as any parent would. Would you do that for me and on every birthday going forward?"

"Yes, sir, I'll call them just as soon as you leave."

The General gets up from his recliner and heads toward the door, hesitates, and then turns around with his arms widened to give Antboy a hug, surprised to find the boy, standing like a man, in full military salute. A tear gently slips from the General's eye, falling mercifully upon one of his many tarnished medals of valor, and he returns this gesture of honor with a long, strong, patriotic salute. As the General walks out of the mansion's magnificent foyer, Antboy continues to stare out the window at his disappearing visage. While the military vehicles rumble down the lane, he is dimly, yet painfully aware of a weary feeling of loneliness.

After a brief conversation with his parents, who are more than grateful for his call, Antboy returns to the sitting room and restlessly waits for his housemates to retire to their quarters and settle into slumber. Ready for something different, unusual and perhaps exciting, he decides on an adventure, a nocturnal birthday quest, and sets out to explore the forbidden tunnels.

Descending to the basement, he approaches an immense metal door at the far corner of the room and lifts four separate latches. Then he pushes and shoves and forces the door until it opens just about two feet, into a tunnel. He follows this tunnel, dimly illuminated along the decaying ceiling by a row of emergency lights, until it branches sharply, widening into a vaulted, rock encrusted cavern. In the distance can be heard a running stream and he descends yet further into the cavern, toward the beckoning water.

He reaches a point where the tunnel intersects yet another tunnel, and he sees a stream. He spots something in the shadows just to the right of this underground body of rushing water. It's a thin railroad track although much too narrow to serve a locomotive, instead supporting a line of four separated go-cart apparatuses with push-sticks.

He steps into the leading go-cart, and lowers himself into the first of six seats. He heaves up and down on the push-stick until the go-cart glides effortlessly along the track. It proceeds, adjacent to the stream, persistently continuing through the dimly lit tunnel, with the cold air nipping at his earlobes. Time elapses, silently, darkly, for perhaps forty-five minutes until the ground begins to rise and the go-cart, unable to defy gravity, finally slows and then halts.

Antboy pulls himself up and out of the vehicle. Looking for an exit from the dank enclosure, he spots a rusting, damp wrought-iron ladder on the far side of the track and he climbs slowly, yet steadily upward, careful to avoid the imminent danger of rusty lacerations. As he progresses, his goal becomes the round metal cover, possibly a manhole, several feet ahead. In moments he angles his shoulder and pushes it into the stubborn lid, then again, until it budges. Minutes later he extracts himself from the manhole, and he sits to the side of the dislodged disk, his eyes adjusting slowly to the natural light of the moon. He believes he's in a park, a vast expanse with scattered buildings. He vaguely recognizes, then absolutely identifies the place from history books. He realizes he's in the center of the nation's Capitol.

Overwhelmed by this vision, surrounded by grand, intimidating buildings, memorials and statues, he sits down to catch his breath, his pounding heart throbbing thunderously. There isn't a soul to be found at this time of night. He walks hesitantly toward a structure with a stoic man in a large chair. As he draws closer he is awed by its magnitude, beauty, power.

The distinguished man, larger than the greatest giant in the most fantastic animated cartoon Antboy has ever seen, sits with his hands placed on his chair, or throne, as it appears. Antboy climbs the steep, marble stairs slowly ascending onward and upward, until he finally reaches, then involuntarily kneels, at the feet of one of the most powerful leaders to ever grace the free world. He was a prominent man whose nation fought its greatest and worst battles leading to the largest loss of life his country had ever seen, all for an internal war, a civil conflict, an epic campaign within its own borders.

Due to the condensation of Antboy's breath, a smoky veil exhaled from his mouth clouds his view of the worthy leader, who, through this haze, now seems alive. Antboy waves away his misty exhalations, trying to get a focused view of the eminent man who begins speaking directly to him, in warning.

He informs Antboy about the dangers that lie ahead, explaining that even though notable leaders have tried to save the world, no one has been successful in rescuing humans from themselves and their own devices, greed, and selfishness. He cautions that errant behavior, unless checked, will lead to the downfall of this great planet. He counsels Antboy to think beyond today and plan for tomorrow, by preparing and building a brighter future for the living and those yet to be born.

Listening to the renowned man's tale, Antboy climbs every stone and marble column that he can get a footing on. He listens for hours, indelibly inspired, growing resolute from the advice that this great man shares. Saluting him reverently, Antboy departs, promising to do his part.

Then he meanders over to a long, tall, marble partition that spans perhaps a tenth of a mile. He traces his fingers over the engraved names in the wall and he reads name after name after name on panel after panel after panel. He's not sure what the wall represents. He runs to its point of origination and learns it's the War Memorial, the one he had studied in school some time ago. A war his country supposedly neither won nor lost, but by reading the countless rows of names he is certain that it lost many soldiers. He cannot fathom why people wage war. He feels that there must be some very important reasons for these decisions but he just cannot understand them, no matter how hard he tries.

Tracing as many panels of names as possible before he must leave this park, he decides not to risk this journey again until his next birthday. He traces random names along various panels and he cries for each of these men that gave their young lives for his freedom, his future, and for the continuation of his way of life. Rather than accept that these lives could have been lost in vain, he feels that each man, in turn, truly believed that he died for a higher purpose. Their dedication and ultimate sacrifice reenergize Antboy to return home immediately, stealthily, and proceed with his work.

Preservation, not destruction, is his true aim. He vows to remain focused on his research, to suppress any distractions that can cause him to be derailed, to postpone even his own boyhood curiosities.

Before returning to the manhole and go-cart, he decides to seek out the General's five-and-a-half-sided building, at least to catch a glimpse of the structure, the massive fortress that represents the protection and security of his country at its highest and most elegant level. Fruitlessly attempting to walk the entire perimeter, he is stunned by the daunting architecture and superior scope of the enormous compound.

Satisfied with his limited progress, he notices the sun begin to peek her curious head above the horizon. Due to the light slowly piercing the darkness, he realizes he must leave, and he urgently sprints back to the manhole, the sunlight of dawn now his enemy. From his vantage point, about to descend the ladder, he briefly salutes the Capitol. He must return to his mission, and shut himself away for another year before exploring again.

When he returns home, Antboy falls into the thickest of deep sleeps and he dreams dreams that are no dreams at all. He sees men on horseback and they are swinging blades at people, chopping, severing limbs and bodies, and mutilating them. Then they are on foot, burning homes, stabbing others, and tossing bodies into the fire. They are ripping the clothes off women and raping them in front of their helpless children. The men get back on their horses and ride off to a distant city where monuments and statues are erected in their names. Now the horses have turned into ships carrying men and weapons to distant shores where the helpless natives know not what will befall them when these foreigners set foot upon their land. Flags are planted upon the usurped lands, a claim established for a distant kingdom. Proud are the conquerors, the murderers, who have taken lives and liberty from the innocent inhabitants of this occupied land.

The vanquishers establish settlements in their new territory, yet they are fearful. So terrified are these invaders that they know no other way to calm their apprehension than to murder others, and to take from the weak. They are afraid that other men will come and do to them what they have done to the rightful residents of their subjugated land. Their fears are warranted because on the horizon other ships can be seen and as they grow closer it is obvious that the recent conquerors will meet the same fate that they ravaged upon the helpless. They plead for their lives to be spared but the enemy does not understand their words and is frightened by the color of their skin and no mercy is shown them. This cycle repeats and each group is worried about the next invaders who will come and murder them to gain temporary and false power by claiming their land. New monuments and statues are erected and time passes, until on the horizon can be seen men with guns and weapons of mass destruction who inviolably attack.

Antboy sees in his dreams what he witnessed in reality, monuments to war and death, not life. They represent death in the name of peace, murder justified for the common good. He is confused, deeply perplexed. His dreams show nothing but men killing other men. The reasons for the killings are muddled, and he spots few women in combat. He sees nearly no countries led by women, nor does he witness women wielding weapons, nor observe women leading other women against each other.

The battlefield blurs and a voice on a television is announcing cities and times, populations and predicted casualties. A map of the world is displayed on the screen and the announcer is somber as the time for his city draws near. Warnings to take shelter, preferably underground are repeated. Antboy's city is mentioned on the broadcast and it is displayed on the screen with twenty-seven minutes to impact listed.

He tries to change the channel but there is only one channel on the air. Panic overtakes him. He's unable to breathe, choking and shaking. His shaking grows perceptibly stronger, just seconds to impact, a piercing bright light approaches rapidly, burning into his retina, his eyes are on fire, and he screams, a horrific scream that deeply frightens the housekeeper, who, having been worried about his health, being three in the afternoon, had just opened the shades, allowing a magnificent bright light to enter his dream.

XIII

"Father, did something like this happen to you every year on your birthday?"

"Every year, Atum. And to this day, my birthday signals great change, enormous change heralded for some reason because it's the anniversary of my birth. After my subterranean, forbidden journey to the Capitol, and the startling dreams that followed, I confined myself to observing the founding of colonies for many months."

"Then what did you do?"

"Well, I already told you that I had spoken to Hiawatha, that sage ant, when I turned eleven, but most of what she had told me made no sense at the time. And a year later, I had heard Queen Elizabeth's speech, which left me crushed but determined. So, I began to think, to ponder, and to really learn about the world that year. My dreams showed a disturbed world, a man-made world where people might man-make their own extinction. I knew that I needed to get a better understanding of the world, to truly connect with

109

the world, and to educate myself. So I turned on the television, and focused on history channels and world news and my vision of the world was shaped by the images in front of my eyes, images of violence, destruction, fear, political confrontations, corporate power struggles, and general disregard for human life. I was afraid of these images and terrified about the future."

"What did you see, Father? What could have possibly terrified you? I can't imagine anyone braver than you. These things must have been very scary."

"They were. And I've told you about some of them, some of the history of humans, and I've tried to teach you the history of our people, and our world not far from here."

"I know. You've taught me so much over the years, and you always tell me that one day I'll visit the world you left, but earth seems so far away."

"Son, we are four hundred thousand miles away from earth and the moon is about two hundred fifty thousand miles from earth, so we aren't much further. When we first went to the moon, sixty years ago, it took three days each way. From our further orbital position here, we can probably be back on earth in just over a day, but this structure isn't programmed to return for another twelve years. HSI determined that twenty-five years defined a generation, and they wanted us to complete a generation here.

Always remember that the spherical satellite planet that we live within, is a man-made spaceship, technologically designed and constructed in the shape of our metal ball which circles the sun, its gravity set to equal earth's, rotating and revolving around the sun in nearly the same pattern and period as the earth. The earth orbits slightly closer than it used to, about ninety two million miles from the sun, and our satellite sphere is just a half percent closer to the sun. We get all our energy from the sun, so we're completely solar powered. As long as the sun doesn't send a tremendous flare, this colony can sustain itself."

"Father, I hope what you tell me about returning there comes true, and that we can return soon. I'm afraid here, afraid of the Workers and the Mothers, and terrified of Queen Lavender."

"Atum, then you must listen carefully. Listen to what I'm going to tell you now. It's what I learned from the television, during those months. And believe me, I wasn't just seated passively in front of that television. Somehow the images on television, with a little help from my omniscient friends, the ants, transported me throughout the history of mankind."

From his seat in front of the television, Antboy looks out of the window to the world, and he doesn't just peer out, he moves the curtains, slides open the window, pops out the screen, climbs out head first, and enmeshes himself fully inside, outside, throughout every facet, reasonable and unreasonable, superfluous and superficial, supernatural and horrible, by flying everywhere. Flying everywhere, with wings, but whose wings?

Wings lift him higher, ever higher, far, far away, and with each birthday he flies even deeper and further to the far reaches of the known world. And he sees and understands everything: different cultures and civilizations, governments and people of every shade and shape, size and system, belief and foundation, and every religion and stratification. He sees completely thanks to his wings, but whose wings? The wings look unusual and so thin and what is that, that movement? It's something on his back and it tickles him as he flies, and it's black, and beautiful. She is an ant; a giant winged ant.

The graceful, beautiful ant is quiescent, intensely quiet, seldom speaking during this flight throughout the wilderness that is humankind. "You must see with your own eyes," says the coal black, beautiful, graceful ant with the shiny and sparkly, pretty eyes.

It is all too cold, and somewhat difficult for Antboy to get used to his nakedness. Unencumbered and pure, he flies through time and space, feeling vulnerable, protected from the elements only by his thin layer of hair and the keen instincts of the ant that carries him. He struggles with his uncertainty. Has he actually left the confines of his own home or is he merely transfixed by some unusual images appearing on the television?

He relaxes slightly and opens his eyes and ears wider and deeper than ever before, and begins to comprehend. He understands that the ants have seen it all. Their species' have witnessed the entire evolution of man, whereas television, a product of man, only emulates man's history; it cannot truly interpret it. He realizes that only through an outside perspective, a view from a separate species, such as the ants, can humanity be truly known. As he flies, carried along by this ant, he joins the collective consciousness of living things. He sees images that are, in fact, memories permanently embedded into ant genetic code; sights that no human has ever witnessed, and observations that ants have carried with them since mankind's origins.

The visions do not follow proper time and speed and everything is in accelerated motion. He sees a baby born in a cave, and it is a painful experience for him because he can do nothing for the poor woman's pain. Her shrieks and yelps are quelled only by biting into a stick that the other women continue to shove into her howling mouth. Soon it is over, and while the screams fade into infrequent moans, there is relief and appreciation on the woman's face as she begins to nurse her child. The other women clean up quickly and one stays behind to care for the woman and infant.

A group of men outside are using rocks and tree limbs to bludgeon and then carve up a bloodied animal. They are naked and covered in hair. They mainly move on all four limbs, on occasion awkwardly standing on just two. And this is the dawn of man.

This same group migrates from one place to another, finding shelter in caves and in trees. Large animals freely roam the area. Mankind does not dominate its environment; it lives at the mercy of the elements and predators. One man playfully dances around with the pelt of a recent kill on his back and around his waist. The other men grunt at him and everyone begins to pull at the pelt until it's ripped in several pieces. Each man in turn begins to jump around with a piece of the pelt around his body. Then they hunt again and more animals are killed and more pelts are gathered until the entire tribe, both men and women enjoy the fur and leather that covers their bodies. They feel superior to the other animals. They believe they are better off because they wear the skin of their prey. None of the other animals wear the skin of another, so man is warmer and more protected from the elements than he had been previously.

Antboy travels to the mountains and valleys, deserts and forests, vast stretches of forbidding terrain that cover all the continents. He views tribes of diverse colors and sizes, and he notices different features of the face and body. Each region has its own distinctive genetic characteristics which enhance that tribe's ability to adapt and survive. But in each snapshot vision he sees a creature, man, attempting to control and dominate his environment, protected by clothing and now shoes and hats made from dead animals.

Some tribes find shelter not in caves but under the protection of large fallen trees. Members of these tribes begin to gather rocks and start to smash other, smaller trees, until they also fall. They dismantle these trees with the rocks and create pieces that they lean together and drape pelts over. These structures prevent entrance from both invasive animals and the intrusive elements and man again feels confident and superior.

Man has mastered his environment; he begins to no longer fear the world around him and he starts to lay plans. Tactics that involve protection against other neighboring tribes of people who look and sound differently. Strategies that involve sharpening rocks and sticks and using large, heavy bones from their predators that have now become their prey. Campaigns that involve seeking the best territory for their tribes.

Man realizes that when resources such as water and food become scarce his tribe becomes weak. He fears that stronger, more populated and better-armed tribes will take from his weaker tribe. He is afraid that he will face the same fate as his prey. Fear of strangers that appear unfamiliar and different, and fear of death, causes one tribe to kill another. Man notices only what it has achieved, not what it has lost.

Due to his thumbs, feet, thinning layer of hair and various other physical characteristics and emotional attributes, man is unique. Fear of his inferiority spurs man's desire to destroy and dominate the animals around him, even to kill and enslave his own species.

Man then decides he should walk on two legs instead of four. He had previously walked on four and stood on two to see higher and further. Determining to use only two, he is no longer able to outrun his predators. However, with his opposable thumbs, he holds things to kill the predators and builds things that protect him from the forces of nature. Man makes things to cover and warm his body, causing less need for hair, which thins and even disappears completely from parts of his anatomy.

Due to his reduced ability to live off the land without protection, man keeps trying to improve his quality of living. He finally feels superior to his environment, but can no longer survive without conveniences. He makes homes from trees. Yet man does not realize that by killing the trees he also destroys the shelter for the animals and plants that he needs for nourishment. He does not consider this.

Originally all the women worked together and had specific tasks that were natural to their physiology. The men also worked together according to their anatomical skills. Then differentiation of tasks evolved. Responsibilities were divided among distinct people, who only worked on a defined aspect of the society. Due to specialization of duties, each member of the tribe knew and performed only their specialty, yet depended on others to fulfill different precise tasks for the entire group's survival. As a result of his reliance on others to properly complete their specific duties, man lost the ability to be solitary and self-sufficient.

This lack of independence allowed certain groups within each tribe to take control and run the tribe. Members of the tribe were encouraged to give up their individual power to these self-proclaimed leaders. Those holding the power began to form rules that seemed unnatural, but could not be disputed, since these rulers were both influential and dominant. Rules such as restricting rights of women, reducing privileges of men without property, enslaving people of color, limitations on religious beliefs and countless other laws were imposed.

People were afraid and supported these groups by giving them part of their daily resources. Those in control soon required more resources, thereby gaining in strength and power, and they started to dominate the trade of many items necessary for survival. They formed the initial governments that began ruling the varied lands of the world.

And then metals were found. Metals contained powers that mankind could not fathom, and so began the decline of humans. Before metals were found, tribes prayed to the heavens and elements to continue providing them the protection that they sought. But populations soon believed that metals were more powerful than the heavens and elements and were divine in nature. People began to build from these metals and pray to them and create trade and commerce with values represented by metals. Metals became something that everyone sought.

The groups in control, the governments, controlled these metals and assigned them values. By doing so, they restricted the tribes of the world who were now forced to accept precious metals as compensation for their labors. Thereby, money was created and man was enslaved. Money was more important than trees and grass and water and animals. Natural laws were soon broken in pursuit of precious metals. Humanity turned its thoughts away from survival and toward accumulating more metal. Man's vision became blinded by this lust, this greed, this depravity, and he forgot from whence he came. For metals were dangerous, and poisoned the blood of any that touched them. Metals carried a curse, an incurable virus that invaded the veins of the beholder and would not let go.

Mankind did not fear metal; instead it revered the strength of metal. The durability of metal far outlasted any substance that had heretofore been discovered. Man could have turned away, but he was entranced and hypnotized. Acquiring something that will outlast him was intoxicating. Molding something that will stand, long after the sculptor turns to ashes and dust in the ground, was irresistible. Ultimate respect was afforded to the ownership of metal, because metal far outlasted mere human life. Metal was not biological in nature, and so did not grow or thrive without human intervention. In fact, metal seemed to have come from a different world, from the deep reaches of the universe at the inception of the planet.

Humanity tinkered with something very strong, and turned myopic, unable to see the impact of its actions. Metal did not die, and did not bleed. Man did not perceive what he had created: monstrous creations that he relied upon to survive and to kill. Mankind placed stock in metals, no longer believing in the power of his own flesh and blood.

From swords to guns to trains to forks to knives to electricity to autos to semiconductors to wiring to planes to cables to bombs to buildings to telecommunications to computers, were metals used. Dependency spread and intensified and people began to rely on the conveniences afforded by metals. Reliance turned into expectation, and expectation fueled desire.

Humans had elevated themselves, no longer wanting to fall prey to other predators. But dependence on metals positioned humans on a precarious precipice, with a steep drop to annihilation. Due to disuse, many people lost their innate survival instincts and were at risk of perishing.

As Antboy flies overhead, he sees men, women, and children flourishing for a while and then decaying, rotting from the inside out. The infection is deepening, and he sees that in a world of plenty, plenty are unnecessarily dying, of disease, starvation, war.

From his vantage point, he sees that it is too late to turn back the hands of time, and that certain things appear irreversible. Society can no longer live without the automobile, plane, phone, computer, and television. Humanity feels unsafe without arsenals of bombs and weapons, becoming prey, an actual victim to its addiction to technology.

The winged, ebony ant says, "Well, now you have seen, and now you know. Farewell." Off she flies, into the distance, and in the silence, Antboy ponders.

XIV

I listen intently. Father explains that when he was my age the television was his window to the world. I try to picture what a television looks like and how it functions. Father explains that it is a box-like structure with pictures of people, places, and things, images that one can look at and perceive. He says it is similar to the disk reader that he brought to our planet.

I can imagine Father's shock and fear, when his insulation was pierced by the images on television and he was thrust upon the social order of the human world.

"Atum, we better take a break for a moment and return to what must be done around here. I'll tell you more while we do our repairs."

Father rises and we walk to our dome's main panel to begin the necessary dome maintenance and make sure it functions as he designed it. While we perform the diagnostics on the panel I feel very close to Father. Proudly and quite regularly, he teaches me a little bit at a time about the

119

specific technical aspects of the dome. Each dome recovers molecules from space outside the satellite planet and breaks them down, decomposing them and converting them into pure elements, which are then recombined into different molecules. He shows me that our water, comprised of hydrogen and oxygen atoms, comes from the recombination of hydrogen and carbon dioxide gases that are extracted from either prolific patches of space, or the moon's dust. Never far away, the moon's water laden frozen dust is mined by our unmanned drones, which frequently traverse the commute from the satellite planet to the moon.

Pointing to a sequence of dots adjacent to certain letters, he explains that they measure the amount of calcium, magnesium, nitrogen, carbon and other elements that our dome has accumulated. These elements are filtered from compounds that enter the intake valve from outside our satellite planet, through the use of penetrating probes and compression chambers, and later recombine based on each dome's measured demand.

Our home is the Dome of Maintenance, remotely located at the colony's extreme outer fringe. Here, compounds are separated into raw elements and then recombined into different compounds, which make food, water, air, and other basic needed materials. These materials are distributed, as needed, by exact request per dome, through a network of tubular shafts that connect to each dome of the colony. Whatever each dome needs to survive is first extracted from outside our satellite, then passes through our dome, the Dome of Maintenance, and is distributed throughout the colony by shafts, to eventually return to our dome as waste material. To complete the circuit, waste products are then recycled. They enter the compression and extraction chambers of our dome and are decomposed and recombined into other usable compounds, which are then redistributed.

Our domes are essentially the same structures he designed for the ants, except reconfigured for human use. Without his ingenuity, there'd be no water for us to drink, air to breathe, food to eat, or clothes to wear. Because Father has provided us the means to use and reuse and recombine what space itself provides us, in addition to what our own bodies create as waste, we're able to function and survive here without concern about depletion of resources. Father's innovation has allowed every member of the colony to live here without fear. Few of us are aware of the petrifying limitation of scarcity that exists right outside our satellite.

He never imagined his invention would be used this far from the earth's surface, nor that it would ever house humans. In fact, ants were the sole reason he invented his sanctuary. But the General and his scientists quickly realized its vital importance. Earth's persistent problems of increased pollution, declining fertility, diminishing resources, hazardous exposure to disease, and the risk of mass calamity perilously threatened the human race. Father's sanctuary uniquely solved these imminent dangers.

Clandestine plans were formulated over two decades to modify his creation and utilize it here. Tested only on the ants he studied for years, Father's structure had been altered by the government, evolving its purely theoretical implications into the practical necessity to house and support us. This was done without Father's participation. Nor was Father included in the planning stages to launch our satellite 'planet'. He was also excluded from the process of compiling the Codex, the book of laws based upon Father's research. This has always troubled Father.

Next to the maintenance manual, which we are using for our dome repairs is the Codex. It is spread open to a detailed map of the colony. I have memorized the map. I study it during those rare nights when my sleep is fitful while Father's is blissful, and even then it is usually hidden. Father infrequently leaves the Codex out, only doing so when he is unusually careless, because he is prohibited from possessing one. Even I am not privy to where he conceals it. But one night, when Father was forgetful, I completely memorized the colony's map.

As we finish the last steps in the maintenance routine I again test my memory. The Dome of the Queen is located in the absolute center of the colony. Surrounding the Queen's dome are four other domes: the Dome of Fertility, the Dome of Study, the Dome of Gathering, and the Dome of Council. The next several layers of domes surrounding these are the Domes of Mothers, each housing four fertility-ranked Mothers. Mothers move upward or downward within these Domes depending on changes in fertility status, which is calculated every equinox during a nocturnal ritual of gratitude. On the outskirts of the planet are the Domes of Workers. When Mothers fall in fertility rank they shift to a ring of domes closer to the Worker village and when they rise in ranking they move closer to the Dome of the Queen. Between the Domes of Mothers and the Domes of Workers, are located the Dome of Birth, Dome of Nursing, and a dense cluster, the Domes of Girls. There are four remote domes, larger and far heavier than the others, which are located at the four magnetic poles of this scientifically constructed life support system. These four outermost domes including our home, the Dome of Maintenance, together form the perfect balance and weight necessary to stabilize our satellite planet and to keep our synthesized life structure in orbit.

Markings on the map show that our dome is near the transport shuttle that brought Father and the original colonists here. The obscure, hidden route to the original docking platform is sketched so faintly, that it is indiscernible to me. The Dome of Endeavors, on the opposing pole, plus those at the other poles, the Dome of Darkness, the Dome of Beasts, and ours, the Dome of Maintenance are visibly marked "restricted" on the map.

Father notices my continued glances at the Codex and he frowns ever so slightly, casually closing it with the back of his palm. He points toward the planet below, which he stares at every night. He explains that he alone, out of all the colonists, has true memories from earth, the true home of the human race, where his wisdom was formed, and to where we must return.

A loud, piercing whistle alerts us of unexpected visitors, and thrusts us into a brief moment of utter panic. Father shoots me a look of warning. His alarm system is rarely activated and from prior experience I know I must move swiftly. I quietly, quickly pull up the one floorboard that hides the handle to the secure space that Father built when he first rescued me. I'm barely below ground, in our Alcove, when the Queen's Scouts enter our dome brazenly, as is their custom.

Father is unaware that I've fashioned, from previous times in hiding, a thin rudimentary scope, allowing me to see and hear, and I cautiously push it upward, very slightly through the floorboard, yet unrecognizable to the naked eye. What I see I've seen before. Father is prostrate, assuming the required subservient position in which he has instructed me, for any males that do not adhere to this posture face grave punishment.

"Beast, your presence is required at tomorrow's Council meeting. We will begin the Endeavors in three days. The Queen must discuss the event and settle all issues so that everything is in order. Arrive at the Dome of Council at dawn tomorrow morning." Without awaiting a response they turn and leave suddenly.

Father stares at the door for a few moments to make sure they are really gone. Walking hesitantly to our hiding place, Father begins to noticeably shake and shudder. Seeing him this way concerns me and makes me nervous.

He pulls up the floorboard and signals for me to come aboveground. After he secures the hidden space, Father is reticent, reluctant to continue his story. He subtly avoids my bewildered, questioning stare, and instead resumes his daily tasks in a routine, somewhat mundane manner. But it's obvious that something is distinctly altered in his demeanor and he seems visibly distant, absorbed in his thoughts.

"What's wrong, Father?" I try to elicit some form of response.

"Nothing, nothing," he replies noncommittally.

"But Father, I know something's wrong. I heard them. What's happening?"

"Atum, I must leave early in the morning. I'll be home periodically but gone for most of the next three days. You are not to leave our sanctuary. Do you hear me? You are never to leave this place without my permission."

"I know, Father. You've made that very clear. But you know I want to leave."

"Yes, I do. How could you not? But you must never yield to your curiosity. It could lead you somewhere that allows no return. Don't put your life in jeopardy. One day we'll be free. We may not be permitted to roam this land, but we will gain our liberty when we return to our homeland. For now you must remain nonexistent, you must remain 'dead' as the Queen thinks you are."

"Do you really have to go to the Endeavors, Father? Must you attend?"

"Yes. I wish it were otherwise. Imagine trying to argue with those Scouts, impossible. A perfect reason to have me killed. Then, most certainly, a doomed fate would befall you. As expected, we're out of seed. More than thirteen years have passed since we arrived and the seed is gone; now the Queen has decided to proceed with the first Endeavors. I've no choice; Lavender has summoned me to witness this event, as prophesied in the Codex, an event of great significance. I must go. I will prepare all night and I will leave before dawn. Atum, stay awake with me while I prepare."

"Yes, Father, of course."

XV

"Atum, I retired after ten years of military service, and when I returned to civilian life the General and I communicated extensively. Four years later, when I was thirty-two, he was very persuasive. He explained that it was necessary for me to lead this colony, a temporary, experimental settlement based upon my theories.

"Though I was designated to found this colony, I was swiftly banned to its perimeter, which came as no surprise to the ruling females here. My fate had been foretold and prescribed in the Codex when it was devised on earth. Before we ever boarded that shuttle, my future had been predetermined.

"The General, and others I had innocently trusted, concocted and described my limited role in great detail in one of the earliest chapters of the Codex, Renewal: 4.3 - 4.6. The societal structure of our colony was encoded in that book, set in symbols and pictures, which only the females had been taught to decipher. I was neither allowed a copy of the Codex, nor was I taught how to decode its language.

"During their pre-launch indoctrination on earth, the female colonists were taught the Codex, but I was excluded. It's considered blasphemy, punishable by starvation, for males to possess a copy. After rescuing you as an infant, on a night you slept deeply, I dared to steal one.

"Atum, it was just a theory, my theory. They had no right, neither to steal my work, nor to create this monstrosity, this distortion, this Codex. What horrors I've created, what horrors they've contrived, oh please forgive me!" Father's voice cracks as he pleads with an invisible force, holding his arms outstretched high above his head, and then his utterance trails off as he shuffles away to a remote part of our sanctuary and sobs sorrowfully.

I walk toward Father to comfort him. While I gently rub my hand on his trembling back to soothe him, I vividly remember a particular night when I heard Father crying uncontrollably, weeping as he does when he remembers certain things from his past. His pain especially reemerges when he recalls how he was manipulated, so many times betrayed. I specifically recall that frightening night. He was in a state of terror, barely conscious. I awoke to hear him moaning, panic stricken. He was reliving a time of deep loss and loneliness, the moment they had stolen his work, his theories, a time when his ideas became the property of others, who later warped them, creating our world and the Codex that guides it.

That night I asked, "Father, what's wrong?" And he pleaded, "Atum, how could they?" His words at first are unintelligible, then somewhat halting, then they rush at me profusely in a torrent of confused emotion and I try to calm him down so that I can understand him. I ask him what he's remembering. From his semiconscious state, he tells me that he's revisiting a time on his eighteenth birthday, when he was bawling. Father speaks and I close my eyes; I see him, and I am one with him. I see he is alone, all alone, cold, wounded, abandoned, sitting wretchedly in the park, the park he had traveled to on each of his successive birthdays, the park in the nation's Capitol.

Antboy is wailing and his tears are an endless well of emotion, from years of solitude, emptiness and sorrow. His mind is a mass of turbulent emotional chaos. What's left, what exists after so much has been taken? None of his work remains, not his beloved ants, nor his sense of determination and focus. Focus, he must concentrate, and find a central point in which to believe, but so much is lost and he feels empty. He should've predicted that they would take everything, all that he'd produced and studied and hypothesized. But now his research is gone, stolen. How could he *not* have realized that they would eventually take everything? How naive and innocent and stupid he felt. He made copies of nothing, not a thing that he could use to reproduce the evidence of his work, or to support the findings behind his theories, and today, on his eighteenth birthday, it's missing, all taken, completely vanished. He should have known, but how could he have? How could he perceive that strangers, cowards, would come, surreptitiously, under the thickness and concealment of night, and take all his documents, research and most importantly, his findings?

He has zilch left, except memories. Disjointed, confused remembrances of a solitary, pedantic, philosophical, deprived life. His social interaction limited to a few house servants, his beloved ants, and specters of military and government officials. His thoughts are rapid, panicked, his vision blurred. What now? Where should he go? He has no clothing, no money, no home, no direction, and no friends. Extreme fear, overwhelming anxiety overtakes him. He sits motionless, pulse racing, blood draining from his face, unable to catch his breath, his scantily clad body oblivious to the park's cold earth and the dampness of the glistening grass beneath him, mindless of the approaching dawn. He repeats aloud, calm down, be still, compose yourself, you can do it, gather your thoughts, make a plan, start with the first step, move to the second. Then his mind is again racing, panic takes hold and he can no longer see, he falls forward and his head nearly strikes the marble edge of a soldier's statue.

As he lies prone in the damp earth of the park, he remembers, explicitly recollects an indelible image of a recent revelation, a conversation from the first morning hours of his birthday. The dialogue that triggered his conclusion, the absolute, ultimate goal of his research, and the last entry he wrote in his ledger. Thinking about his conclusive journal entry, he tries to slow his heart rate, and he tries to remember, to slow down his thoughts, and recall his first actions of the day, the morning of his eighteenth birthday.

He had risen at his usual seven o'clock and, after munching on a quick breakfast bar downstairs, he returned to his room to resume his latest study, the ritual of procreation and death of the male after insemination of the female. He was making entries in his latest volume when a voice interrupted him, as usual, on the anniversary of his birth, the annual ritual of great philosophical thought and deep change, a conversation with the ants.

"Oh, Antboy, do you not see?"

"See what?" Antboy asked the ant that stared up at him.

"You have seen so much yet now you are blind. One must blur one's vision somewhat to see the whole picture. The depth of your vision is limited. Step back and look."

"Look at what? What do you have to show me?" Antboy asked the ant staring up at him.

"I can only show you that which you have already seen, that which you already know. To my sisters, I am Joseph. I am the only male ant chosen to survive in my colony. I explain the dreams of the Queen and her descendants and in doing so I am allowed to live. Our colony is one of many that has established this ritual."

"After procreation, male ants die. I didn't know any males survived the mating ritual."

"Well, that's true and general observations follow this pattern. But one male is always chosen to interpret the dreams, the visions of the females. And it is this balanced perspective, female dreams analyzed by a solitary male, which has allowed our species to flourish and maintain the course that evolution has chosen for us. Every species follows a different course of evolution and it is necessary to evaluate the progress of a species. Some species do not establish the correct balances and eventually cease to exist. Our species was one of the earliest on this planet and we continue to survive as we adapt and evolve."

"Yes, I know. And it continues to intrigue me. But why are you sharing this with me?"

"You are a seer. You will help determine the fate of your people. Haven't you read what you've written? Aren't your volumes enough to show you the way and lead you?"

"How can I be a seer? I'm no seer. I've spent very little time among my people. I live apart from them and study them as one does a textbook. My life is consumed with your species; I'm entranced in my work. I barely interact with anyone and my experiences are purely vicarious, mostly dependent on media like television and newspapers. What I write is pure theory and supposition. My theories are just that: theory. Based on empirical data mainly derived from my studies of ants. I'm not sure anymore if I believe my theories, even if I've proven them true."

"Do not doubt yourself ever again. You must believe what you see, what you know to be true. Things went wrong during early human development when man first exerted physical superiority over woman. The order of the world, the world of your species, was established, established in direct contradiction to the way things were supposed to evolve. Your thinking is inherently wrong for a species. No species can concentrate on the annihilation of its own species so wholly as humans. No species distrusts itself so completely as yours. Your studies, your research speaks to you. It speaks for you. You are the only one to understand what you have seen. You are sage, and a visionary. The time has come to save your people, to prevent your species' extinction. You must take the necessary steps to preserve your work, your life, and your sanity. Never doubt yourself."

With this, Joseph suddenly trots off and Antboy is left alone, sitting on the floor beside the bed, his manuals and journals spread along the ground. Perturbed and irritated, somehow he's perceptibly relieved. Reassured that, at least according to an ant called Joseph, he's been on the right path. He laughs again and again, at himself, at the world, at his ants, and as he recollects his conversation with Joseph, he refreshes his mind and is rejuvenated.

Closing his eyes, he thinks of all that he has witnessed on television and read in magazines and newspapers from his cloistered fortress, his secluded captivity. The results of his detailed experiments, spanning five years, whir through his mind. Joseph's words dramatically but emphatically reverberate, "*...take the necessary steps to preserve your work...*" He hurriedly grabs an unused journal, swiping aside the others and performs some calculations, then several more, plotting them into graphs, which he overlays, determining their intersection, and then he abruptly stops, and ponders briefly.

Frantically he writes words that spew onto the paper like the spume of a fire-hose. Paternal society has failed. The ravages of man are evident on every channel, newspaper, and city block. He has studied, tested, observed, and documented many species of ants that clearly differentiated male and female roles in synergistic efficiency. Their maternal society benefitted each species, allowing ants to avoid extinction and flourish for millions of years. His conclusion is transformative: *Mankind must reorganize to a female dominated society, patterned after ants.*

XVI

Antboy vaguely hears a rumbling sound approaching from outside the mansion, growing louder and closer, reminiscent of the thundering arrival of his sanctuaries some five years prior. Without explicit permission, visitors were not welcome at the old Governor's Mansion. Deliveries were rare, he realized. So what could this be, a security breech?

Trying to remain calm, but growing steadily alarmed with the rapid approach of the near deafening noise, he slams shut his journal, rushes to the spiral staircase, and winds down toward the main floor. Reaching the ground floor, he disbelievingly sees the towering mahogany front door visibly buckle and then splinter. Finally it flies off its hinges and a small regiment of military personnel appears.

"What do you want?" Antboy shouts. Deaf ears and mute voices refrain from response and he is dismissively ignored, roughly grabbed, and immediately escorted to the living room where two armed guards shout at him to be seated and silent.

Furious and frustrated, Antboy screams, "Why are you here?" No response. A moment later, "Take me to the General, I must see the General, he knows me!" Still there is no response.

An eternity of fifteen minutes elapses, ticking away like hours, compounded by his intense anticipation and anxiety. Antboy listens closely to the rattling and movement on the floors above and he realizes that they've come for his work. He quickly bolts between the two guards and stumbles along the slippery hardwood floor grabbing the first rail of the banister, his feet barely upon the stairs. He's tackled, and then, while he's prone upon the staircase, one of the invaders rolls him over. Taking his assault rifle, he backhands Antboy, adeptly pounding the cold metal into his exposed, vulnerable cheekbone.

The pain is sharp and he instinctively raises his hands to protect his face, now surprised to feel the warm, sticky squirt of blood that drips down his chin and neck. The anger and pain vibrate across his face and the guard momentarily recoils at the fury emanating from his injured opponent. Repositioning a few steps back, the intruder firmly commands him to rise and return to the living room. Antboy sways and hobbles a few slow steps away from the stairway, slowly regaining his balance. While shuffling toward the living room, with an assault rifle now jutting into his spinal cord, he hears the pounding of heavy boots upon the staircase. He glances back to see three men carrying boxes from the steps to the door, overflowing with his volumes of work.

"Stop, you can't take that!" He yells and instantly grabs his head protectively, falling involuntarily to the ground, the aggressor having just smashed the rifle between his shoulder blades. He looks up at the stoic sentry whose face begins to turn into little black and white dots and then all turns black but he fights it, struggling to regain consciousness. He tries to get up, leaning all his upper body weight on one elbow, waiting again to be beaten, in utter disbelief, but he isn't struck. The trespasser is gone. He hears the rumbling away of trucks, and everything dissipates except for his rage, violent wrath.

He rises after several agonizing attempts, painfully ascends the stairs, and begins to explore the mess throughout the house. He neither acknowledges nor perceives his housemates, who are stunned and in shock, vaguely lingering in the periphery of his awareness. Overturned furniture, smashed chairs, broken vases, and toppled ant sanctuaries litter his path room by room. He limps down to the first floor, clutching the banister, and screams, shouting to be left alone.

Deception. Has this all been deceit, the whole thing, from day one? His research, incomplete and incomprehensible in its current state, was carted off in used produce boxes to be taken who knows where to be read by who knows whom after all these years, these productive, powerful, enlightening years. What would come of his work?

Hours pass while Antboy lays slumped at the foot of the stairs, frozen in disbelief, a helpless shell of a person, the meaning of his existence now in jeopardy. Nothing is left, not one thing, neither thoughts, nor desires, not plans, nor choices, and no reason to live. His purpose is now in vain, and he feels emptiness, a severe void.

He notices not the trail of ants that climb his legs, sees neither the army that darkens his arms, nor hears their words as they gather in his hair, his nose, his ears, his mouth, and he can no longer breathe. He is being smothered and his lungs are no longer working. The ants gnaw him, searing, stinging bites and his breath becomes rapid and shallow. He rolls, sliding along the ornate carpet to rid himself of these beings, these friends turned enemies, destroyers, determined to suffocate him.

His pulse quickens, and rapid, hyperventilating asphyxiation overtakes Antboy. As darkness begins to cloud his brain, he is on a roller coaster which goes up, curves around and around, loops and loops, speeds up and makes a sharp descent and then goes up, curves around and around, loops and loops, speeds up and makes a sharp descent *I love you. I've always loved you so why are you doing this to me?* and then goes up, curves around and around, loops and loops, speeds up and makes a sharp descent *Please, please don't, I can't breathe, I can no longer breathe.* and then goes up, curves around and around, loops and loops, speeds up and makes a sharp descent *Where am I? Where have you taken me?* and then goes up, curves around and around, loops and loops, speeds up and makes a sharp descent *Please, please let me go. I have so much more to accomplish.* and then goes up, curves around and around, loops and loops, speeds up and makes a sharp descent *I can't take it anymore; I think I'm dying.* and then goes up, curves around and around, loops and loops, speeds up and makes a sharp descent *Why are my arms and legs sitting in the seat next to me?* and then goes up, curves around and around, loops and loops, speeds up and makes a sharp descent *Please don't leave me here. I'll do anything, just please get me off this thing. Please save me!* and then makes an even sharper descent, the sharpest plunge in the history of roller coasters, in the annals of mankind, and then the roller coaster comes to a complete stop.

He collapses on the adjacent seat. With a sucking noise he is able to wriggle his arms and legs back on his body, some of them in the wrong sockets but at least somewhat functional. He flops out of the roller coaster and then he descends, falling, plummeting, and it is getting hot, searing hot, scalding, burning, scorching, then boiling and his skin is sizzling and blistering, beginning to melt. *So much pain, please remove the pain, please help me, it hurts so much, oh please.* The white of his bones can be seen coming through his flesh and he is in agony. *Why can't the pain just stop?* Shock does not kick in to stop the pain, and the hurt grows, worsens; his bones are hot and his hair is on fire. *Put out the fire!* He reaches up to put out the fire and his ears rip off his head, and his eyeballs hurt and swell. *Please stay in the sockets, oh please. Why am I here? What did I do to you?* His nose fries, and his face bubbles. He is still falling toward the fire below. *When will I be there? Put me in the fire and finish this torture, please.* His right eye has fallen out, and he whimpers, nearly giving up. *But I was good and I shouldn't be punished.*

He sees a ledge, he reaches for it and he holds onto it. The melted, deformed mess of his body hangs from the ledge and he looks up with the remainder of his one eye. He grows angry, bitter, maddened, irate, incensed, infuriated, enraged, and indignant. He does not belong here and that is that, no way, no how. He did what was necessary for the ants. If this is the thanks he gets, then they never deserved his help, and they can fend for themselves. He wants to go back, body intact, deserving life. He vows to write an angry letter and that will be the end of it. He writes very impressive letters, and he's already composing one in his head to the General. As he signs and dates it, he is flying, soaring faster, upward, ascending through the caves, inside earth and within the ocean, into the sky, throughout the clouds where his skin regenerates, skyward beyond the atmosphere, into space, and he sees a pair of hands over him.

They are beckoning him, holding him, forgiving him. Wings are placed on his back and he spreads them, gliding, warm, and completely content. Then he realizes that something is in his mouth, and he bolts upright. A final impulse to fight back and to survive emanates. He reaches deep inside his spirit and pulls out a frightening death-defying scream that rises from his abdomen through his chest, within his lungs, and he clears his throat of the determined, obstinate, smothering ants. He quickly swipes them from his face and his arms and legs. As their stinging nibbles sharply cause him to reel in pain, he rips his clothing into shreds. He is retching, violently vomiting blood. He again rolls on the carpet to rid himself of the scathing intensity of the biting parasites that persistently attach themselves to his every particle. He runs, his clothes trailing in tatters, sprinting into the kitchen, grabbing a knife to cut the obstinate beasts from his skin.

Taking a long kitchen match, he lights it and burns the remaining ants off his unprotected body in various places, screaming for everyone to run for their lives. Horrified, his stunned, cowering housemates grab what they can, and bolt out the door. Then he takes the flame to the living room and sets the draperies on fire, then goes to his study and throughout each of the upper levels spreading fire. Hurdling down the stairs and out the front door, he is barely clad, panting, numb, and oblivious to the smell of burning embers from the torched, abandoned mansion.

Wandering aimlessly throughout the darkness, he inadvertently stumbles upon an opening to the underground portal of tunnels, which house the rail system that he takes annually to the nation's Capitol. Having nowhere to go, he descends into the tunnel and hand pumps the ancient underground shuttle to the sprawling, historic, nostalgic park, where he goes every year on his birthday to philoso-phize, fantasize, and spiritualize.

He reaches the end of the track, dismounts, and climbs the sharp, rusty ladder, which meets the circular piece of metal on the roof of the tunnel. Pushing upward to dislodge the manhole disk, which rolls in a small circle until it falls heavily a few feet away, he carefully lifts himself from the passageway. Exposed to the harsh nighttime chill, he immediately begins shivering, pressing the remaining shreds of clothing close to his body. He quickly finds shelter near the base of a soldier's statue, and begins to rock himself for warmth, to ward off the frigid, bitter cold wind.

He is in immense pain, utterly unbearable. He tries to shift his focus away from his bruised body, vastly covered by scrapes, bites, and burns, and turns his attention to other parts of the park. He vaguely sees a shadow, an outline that is approaching rapidly from the distance, but there are too many legs for it to be human. He wants to hide, to run, but he cannot move because he is paralyzed with pain and fear. The shadow draws nearer until it is no longer a silhouette but instead it is a face set upon six legs, a most beautiful female countenance. She reaches down with her outstretched, pointed forearm and caresses his cheek.

"Who are you?"

"I am Hypatia, a name your people gave to a philosopher who met with a terrible fate."

"Today I met a terrible fate. I ache so badly. Why were you named Hypatia?"

"I was named in tribute to Hypatia. I come from a family of influential thinkers and in every generation one of us is named Hypatia, to honor her for her contributions and her sacrifice. Hypatia was killed by an angry mob in what you call the early fifth century a.d. She was born to a mathematician named Theon. She taught at the Library of Alexandria, the greatest library the world has ever known, specifically in mathematics and natural philosophy. Hypatia contributed greatly to these fields. She traveled widely and corresponded with people throughout the Mediterranean. She believed that one must preserve one's right to think, for even to think wrongly is better than not to think at all. Unfortunately her life was cut short and she died violently by those who chose not to think. She was dragged to her death by a very angry mob who pulled her from her classroom into the street where they peeled her to death with oyster shells."

"This is a terribly horrid story. Why are you telling me this?"

"My obligation is to uphold the integrity and purpose of Hypatia. Not long after her death, a similar angry mob burnt down the Library of Alexandria. More knowledge was lost in that one event than in any other incident in the history of the world. The printing press had yet to be invented. Therefore, a multitude of unrecoverable, original documents of the world's knowledge and history disappeared forever in that fire, information that has never been recovered.

"Hypatia's death represents this waste of knowledge at the hands of people who persecute free thinkers, who would rather destroy than create. Soon after Hypatia was killed and the Library of Alexandria was destroyed, the world entered a period of darkness for almost a thousand years. Few contributions to learning were recorded during this subsequent dark period. Human history during this period of almost a thousand years is grim, filled with chaos and war. Hypatia and the keepers of knowledge did not adhere to the formal religious dogma of the time and were thereby destroyed by those who no longer valued the right to think for themselves. I am Hypatia; I am here to protect the world's most important intelligence. I am here to protect you in your time of weakness, so that I may protect the wisdom that you have gained. One must learn to understand oneself and accept one's purpose. Do you know who you are and your purpose?"

"No, not anymore. I no longer know who I am. I don't know if I ever knew who I was. I used to have a purpose, a mission, but now I am completely lost."

"You are not lost. You are just not sure of your next step. One cannot know at all times in which direction one will proceed. It is necessary to sometimes lose focus in order to better understand the picture. As in art, purpose sometimes becomes clear and understood if one steps backward and loses focus. Your vision will soon be clear."

"I don't understand, what do you know about me?"

"You have the vision. You are a seeker and you aim to change the world for the better. It is your mission and purpose. I have always been with you and I always will. I am man, woman, animal, bird, fish, tree, plant, water, fire, wind, rain, earth, sun, moon, past, present, future, I am you, you are me, and we are one. You know not what you have already accomplished and achieved, yet you are on the right path. Never doubt yourself; your destiny is one of greatness."

"What am I supposed to do now?"

"You will soon know. There will be times that you will not know why you do the things that you do but these things are all part of the greater picture. Pieces in a puzzle may not seem to fit or may appear to have no place but they are necessary to the completion of the puzzle. Your entire life is a mystery and may not be comprehensible until it is complete. The journey that you take will never reveal the puzzle in its entirety. The enigma is solved only when your life is over. Because of this, you will never know why you do the things you do, but you are a visionary and you must trust yourself. You will only find what you are looking for when you no longer seek."

"I don't want to find anything anymore. My research, my life's work is gone. I failed."

"You cannot fail because you have already succeeded. It is your duty, your responsibility to tread forward. You will always move forward. Even if you feel you are standing still, your every breath is a heartbeat toward the future. We are all links in a chain and the chain exists because of its links. When a chain is damaged, one can put the links of the chain in a different pattern, reconfiguring the chain so that it is stronger and has a better chance of remaining intact.

"One can only pursue the trail that lies ahead and must adhere to it because there is none other to follow. Your path might go along a different route than you had originally planned but you will always be proceeding in the right direction; there is no wrong course. Each person has a unique destiny, but we are all meant to do the things that we do. The choices that you will make in the future will be made because you have the courage to make them. Do not concern yourself with what is right and wrong, just know that your fate is to alter the order that has been established. The planet is in grave jeopardy and peril; you must resume dedicating your life to new ideas. Your mission is to accomplish good. You will not fail because you have already succeeded."

While covering him with a blanket to bring warmth to his shivering limbs, Hypatia caresses his cheek and wipes away his still moist tears. His eyelids lose the ability to fight their heaviness and his eyes flutter. Whether real or imagined, he thinks he sees her moving away from him, partially walking and somewhat crawling. As she travels further away, she melts into the distance shrinking smaller and diminishing. Then she disappears completely, perhaps digging into an anthill right next to his left temple. Clutching the blanket Hypatia left him, Antboy uses it periodically to wipe away his tears and muffle his sobbing cries of desperation.

XVII

"Father, please don't cry. Please, Father," I interrupt, pleading with him to calm down.

Father recovers slowly, admitting to me in halting, stiff words that he was entirely naive.

"What do we do now Father?"

"Atum, I won't sleep tonight and I'm sorry, neither will you. Tomorrow, I'll try to convince Queen Lavender and the Council to postpone the Endeavors, or to consider another ritual, which can replace them. Tonight I'll draw up partial plans to show them and then I'll tell you the remainder of what you'll need to know in case I don't return."

"What do you mean, 'in case you don't return'?"

"I mean exactly what I just said. No matter how remote that chance may be. I've told you about our past and about how things came to be the way they are but there are a few things, for your own safety, that I've kept from you. You must know everything in its entirety especially now that the Endeavors draw so near. Promise me you will listen closely."

"I promise, Father."

"What do you think I did when I awoke in the park, cold and hungry, stinging from the ant bites and cuts and burns?"

I shook my head signaling that I didn't know, and waited for Father to tell me.

"I limped toward the General's building, the structure that loomed a few, painful miles from the park. I went to the only person I could, the one individual I knew who might be able to help. I believed the General would be able to set things right. He had been there during those critical turning points in my life, for six years. The General had always shown me compassion and I figured he could grasp the situation. I hoped he would fix my dilemma. After the deceit that had shaken the foundation of my consciousness, all I wanted was to reach that massive edifice."

Father describes the sunlight as streaming and glimmering on the early morning dew. As he walks toward the military fortress, several taxis zoom by, perilously hugging corners along one-way streets in the heart of the nation's Capitol. He begins to jog and then sprint, the cool air invigorating his oft-neglected lungs. As he runs more rapidly, his adrenaline kicking in, he is soon free of the past, empty, void, and vacant. He arrives at the building quickly, but he cannot find an entrance, just brick and steel, without hinges or openings.

Searching for a way inside, he hears a loud whirring motor, and he turns around to find four men in sanitation uniforms hanging from a garbage truck, which steadily and rapidly approaches him. He's stealthily whisked onto the truck and ushered into its rusty metal interior. He's thrown an olive green sanitation uniform and told to quickly change.

"Who are you?" Antboy asks, repeatedly scratching himself while pulling on the uniform, his recent wounds itching from the gruff cloth of the starched outfit.

A slim man whose patch reads 'Bill Sherman, Waste Management Enterprises' responds, "The General sent us to find you, after he got word of the fire at the mansion. We spotted you running from the park."

The truck winds its way through the streets of the Capitol, passing the National Museum of Art, and then circles through alleys and into an unmarked garage at the base of a nondescript brick building lacking signage. The vehicle curves around and downward until there's no light at all except for the beam from the front headlamps. The pathway levels out and just as Antboy expects it to stop, the truck continues on a flat course for ten minutes and again descends in a diving spiral for a while until stopping. A rollup steel grated gate cranks open and they enter what looks like a massive dumbwaiter. Loud pulleys and wheels squeal as the vehicle climbs approximately two floors.

An amplified voice commands the passengers to exit the vehicle and proceed to the red door at the corner of the cramped elevator compartment. The uniformed men singly approach the entrance and look upward, their irises scanned by an orange beam angling downward from the top of the entry. The door separates horizontally into two interlocking parts and recedes into the wall.

They proceed forward to a dingy, ivory colored, barren, square room. Within seconds, several beams are emitted from various points on each wall, scanning each man's face, locking focus and traveling from the forehead down the nose and over the mouth. A high-pitched frequency pierces the stillness for a few seconds and then a portion of the floor retracts.

Dimly lit steps appear, sloping perilously downward. The men step carefully, assisting Antboy down the treacherous stairs. The staircase, somewhat damp and moss-laden, descends and curves steeply. At the bottom of the stairwell lies a narrow arched tunnel whose walls hold rustic bronze sconces, which light the walkway.

Barely visible at the end of the corridor, an orange door with black letters warns: DO NOT ENTER-Hazardous Waste Site. The lead sanitation man, the driver of the truck, inserts a key into the door and shoves hard to push it open. Bright light pierces the dimly lit tunnel. Shielding their eyes, they proceed down a hallway with offices, and conference rooms marked by names and titles engraved on shiny gold plaques beside each door.

The waste management team escorts Antboy to a conference room at the end of the corridor where a secretary offers them beverages, muffins, and a selection of cold cuts, cheeses, and breads. The men busily prepare sandwiches and motion for Antboy to help himself. He politely declines, instead pouring some ice water to quench his dire thirst. He quickly drinks up and pours more, now noticing the glass is imprinted with an image of the building.

So he made it. The clandestine, circuitous route, which circumvented various security protocols and paperwork trails, had led him inside the most powerful military headquarters in the world. His research is probably here, somewhere within these walls. To be studied, completed, or abandoned, he may never know. For the time being, he wants only a warm bed and some time to think. Waiting patiently for the men to finish their meals, he inadvertently and peacefully drifts off, meditating on the uncertainty of his life, and on the protection of the steel girders that support this fortress of security.

The telephone rings in the conference room and one of the men, with scruffy beard and balding head, picks up the phone, answering gruffly, "Yes?" He nods a few times and says, "Ok, uh-huh, ok, he's here, right now, yes sir." Standing abruptly, he says, "The General will see you tomorrow. He wants you to get some rest and I am to take you to your quarters. Come with me."

Antboy follows him down a series of intersecting corridors, right here, left there, until they reach a large brass elevator. The man inserts a key in a slot just to the right of the lift, which activates the motor and then the compartment opens. After the doors close the man inserts his key into one of the unmarked slots where buttons displaying numbers would normally be found, a security measure designed to effectively prohibit approved visitors from reaching unapproved destinations. When the doors open, a distinguished gentleman replete with thinning, matted hair, a mustache with twirled, graying edges, wearing a black tuxedo with tails, greets them warmly, announcing he is the Concierge. Antboy departs, and the elevator closes, taking his escort away.

"Welcome, bonjour, bonjour. Pleaz follow me and I will show you to your zweet." The Concierge whispers something into a bellman's ear, prompting him to run down the hallway.

"We function as any five-star hotel zo pleaz make yourself at home. In your room you will find zee map of zee facility. At your disposal eez a library, complete weez internet access, a fitness center with zee full indoor heated pool, a cafeteria open twenty-four hours or you may order zee room service, and an entertainment room with a movie library and, zee, how do you say, ah, oui, zee billyoords. Zere may already be zee itinerary waiting for you in your zweet but I do not track zeez zings. I'm not in zee loop as to which guests are here at Chateau Pentagonne zo I never pry into zee nature of zee business here. In fact, I am zupposed to ask nuzzing, zee nuzzing, know nuzzing and I ask you to respect zis by keeping your personal business personal. Whenever you are scheduled to leave zee hotel facilities for any of your business you will be provided an escort who will accompany you to your destination. I am at your service for any accommodations zat you may need zo please do not 'esitate to ring for zee Concierge if you need me. I was told to provide a varied selection of clozing and undergarments zo please let me know if zee wardrobe eez not suitable or if you require any additional items. Well, 'ere it eez and 'ere eez your card key. Au revoir." With this and a grand sweeping flourish, the Concierge bows gracefully as Antboy enters the suite.

Majestic. Fatigued as he is, everything is grand, and stately, in the three-room suite. He falls heavily into a leather chair, resting his feet on a Victorian ottoman. Just as darkness tries to overtake him he fights off lethargy and runs a warm bath. Settling into the soothing water, he succumbs to the darkness, and many hours pass, comforting, peaceful hours.

Waterlogged and exhausted, rising a little unsteadily, his equilibrium off kilter, he grabs a white velour robe that hangs on the knob next to the bathroom door. Stumbling over to the bed he falls face down onto the comforter and sleeps, unable to move, as if in a coma. He welcomes the deep, dreamless and healing slumber.

XVIII

Complete unawareness, no knowledge of this room, no memory of this foreign place, where is he? Unsure of how long he has slept, fragments of yesterday or today or last week return to him slowly and steadily until he begins to focus, to surround himself with the most recent, traumatic events. He concentrates and then vividly remembers, struggling to get up. Realizing that he must get dressed, he gains control and familiarizes himself with his surroundings.

Slowly rising, he approaches the closet and scans the various articles of clothing that have been provided. He spots something tranquil, a cream colored pair of linen pants and a white bulky pullover shirt made from a hemp-like material.

Food is on his mind and is essential. After investigating his new environs he will venture to the cafeteria. Leaving his suite, marked only by the letter K, he steps across a note in front of his door. Opening the folded paper, he reads the entry just below the letterhead that says: 3:45pm-Meeting at Central Command. The wall clock shows it is 10:15am.

Proceeding down the hallway, he looks left, right, left again, and then he heads right and turns right at the first corridor. A few steps later, he sees a portly, bearded, bespectacled man standing in a doorway waving frantically at him, and beckoning him to rush over.

The man holds out a small lab coat, ushers him into an adjoining room, pushes Antboy's arms through the sleeves and says, "Good, good, we thought maybe your flight was delayed due to heightened security conditions. Come this way, right in here. We must start immediately. Stage Two begins precisely at 10:30. There's no time for introductions; I will catch you up with yesterday's data toward the end of the procedure.

"Shh, quiet, there must be complete silence in the ante-room. Remember that the diagnostic work from last month's trials showed that any ambient noise can disturb the cerebral neurons and irrevocably trap a recurring echo which can be detrimental to the development of..." A gaunt, graying scientist motions for silence by drawing an imaginary slit across his throat.

Antboy and three men, assumed to be scientists by their clipboards, lab coats, and stopwatches, stare through a fiberglass window at eighteen girls, aligned, six rows of three, unmoving, in recumbent positions of rest. The lead scientist, the eldest, and decisive head of this crew, motions back to the laboratory and whispers into a recorder, "Stage Two begins now."

Dilated and barely open, the children's eyes begin to flutter and blink, adjusting to the bright sunlight that has just entered from the skylight above. Appearing to be about six years old, of varying heights and different ethnicities, each rises instantly and simultaneously, stretching their arms and bodies toward the sunlight above. Distinctly featured, and with skin of contrasting shades, the girls display a prism of sparkling and glittering colors from their eyes of varied shape.

They attentively face upward, outstretched, holding extended motionless poses. During the thirty-minute interval when the sunlight enters their domain, they are entirely immobile and transfixed. And then, when the skylight slams shut, they suddenly return to structured sedentary, stationary repose.

"Assemble the remaining three groups, with one hour separation breaks. We must document the synchronization of all seventy-two girls before sundown," the scientist directs.

The head scientist leads them into a small conference room, where four chairs face a multimedia station connected to a television screen. "The results speak for themselves, gentlemen," he proudly states. "We still have a long way to go before we complete this stage, but it's evident that we're on the right track. Our small team, the four of us, has been assembled to see this project to its completion and your specialties are necessary for each of the next stages."

"Who else knows about this?" Inquires the younger, short scientist, while pinching a pimple.

"Good question. Honestly, I'm not sure. But right now the classification of this project is on a need-to-know basis. It has also been highly classified as the foremost scientific project on the table and has been given the green light as urgent. Gentlemen, there are many things about this project that we are not privy to. This should not affect our work; we're here strictly for the advancement of science, and the preservation of the species."

The portly, bearded, bespectacled scientist interjects, "I know this may sound stupid. But what I'm wondering is whether this project is legal? Have we been granted proper governmental approval? There have been ongoing debates for years."

"Gentlemen, I have been given orders from the highest level of our government to assemble you today. We have witnessed day one of Stage Two and your expertise in this field, theoretical as it may be, will probably land our names in the history books. New HSI code has just been ratified giving full governmental approval for the completion of this goal. We are no longer operating in the basements and closets of the medical community as pariahs and quacks. We are right here in the nation's Capitol operating in the most secure place in the world, military headquarters. Which brings me to another point."

He sighs and frowns before continuing. "We are under lock and key. We will be watched constantly." He motions to cameras placed in discreet locations throughout the room. A deep breath is followed by a forced and tightly wound smile. "Our work belongs to others."

With this, the serious scientist sits down and somberly takes a drink of water, with trembling hands, awaiting their reactions. Antboy avoids eye contact with the scientists. He is inexpressive and his face is implacable. He wants to leave, but he is frozen in his seat. He wants to know more. He has so many questions yet he can't show emotion; he can't respond in any way or they will know he's a fake. Maybe he can ask the General about this program. What purpose does it serve? So many questions to ask, but right now his main concern is how to leave undetected without compromising himself as the inadvertent impostor he is.

The large, bearded scientist begins cleaning his glasses, adding, "I want to know more specifics about this HSI, this Human Survival Initiative. I remember reading approximately six years ago a little blurb about it. From my understanding, certain events surrounding a boy's invention brought about a global meeting. Some type of code was established that allowed certain inalienable and unilateral powers to be granted to the International Coalition.

"A code, the HSI, was established to provide for the survival of the human race. I believe I read that each of the races was to be preserved and provided for under HSI. Essentially, HSI levels the playing field for human survival, bypassing politics and global governmental positioning that clutter the race for world dominance. The initiative provides that certain actions be taken to effectively insure the continued existence of humans, despite no imminent threat. Circumventing the potential effects of global nuclear war and other natural or unnatural cataclysmic disasters, HSI aims for our species to survive.

"I thought this news was just a bunch of liberal media hogwash. I didn't think anyone was taking this seriously. Now, don't get me wrong..." and with this he looks around the room at the various cameras, "I love my country. I am free and safe here. Our society, representing less than five percent of the world's population, lives a lifestyle that some people cannot even conceive in their wildest dreams. I love my life and feel very fortunate for what I have. I will serve my nation as well as it has served me. My views are rhetorical at best. Justification is unnecessary for me to do my job here, but I question the motives of this clandestine HSI. Our work here is related to the survival of the human race, yet we're operating secretly. If our project is sanctioned internationally, why do we need to work in this covert manner?"

The lead scientist responds, "Gentlemen, scientific advances will always occur in secrecy. Or else, others will beat us to the punch and we can't afford that. We're advancing human life by our work. The government's funding and participation in this project is necessary. Otherwise, we have nothing. However, its involvement in our experimental research comes with certain rules, and the government's goals are unknown and ambiguous. Sometimes bad things come out of good intentions and other times the reverse is true.

"What you know about HSI, I know about HSI. We have all read about the precursor steps for HSI that were unveiled at the inception of this initiative. Six years ago, a miracle structure, a sanctuary that will insure the survival of the human race, supporting human life in the harshest of environments was revealed."

He continues, whispering almost inaudibly, "There are some rumors I've heard that I'll share with you, but after today we will discuss nothing other than our scientific progress. Apparently a lot of this HSI is based on the philosophy and research of some genius boy that the government recruited just before the unveiling of the sanctuary that we read about. This is strictly hearsay, and I have no direct confirmation of this, but I've heard that he also advanced a theory postulating the need for a female-dominated society."

"You've got to be kidding," almost in unison the two scientists respond, and Antboy nods in feigned disapproval and pretend shock. Aghast, the large scientist exclaims, "Men have ruled this world since the beginning of time, and protected their women! Men have died for this right!"

155

"Gentlemen, I understand what you are saying and agree with you. Theoretically, though, from a purely scientific standpoint let's consider societal structure, and the need to insure the survival of our species. Women conceive life, bear children and are the caregivers for the young. They live longer than men. They outnumber men. Women use more of their brains than men do. One man can fertilize many women but each fertile woman can provide life."

"That doesn't prove that a female-dominated society is superior," interrupts the young scientist.

"True, but we must appreciate the insane and brilliant reasoning of this child prodigy. Heaven help us if our government takes it seriously. However, with regard to populating the earth, man is obsolete, and completely unnecessary. Seed can be frozen for years. Women do not need a man to conceive, birth, or rear children. In an assumed, hypothetical world of limited resources, men are a burden. It's that simple and farfetched. There are other species that live in this manner, the ants, for example. And they flourish. So there you have it, and I'm sure we'll see a Twilight Zone episode about it one day, and we'll sit and laugh, but now that I know what I know," and he continues in hushed tones, "I will always wonder. Especially since every subject in our scientific study is female."

A door is opened and a very lean, wiry man in a lab coat interrupts with, "I'm so sorry. There were so many security checks at the airport, what with all the heightened security around the Capitol. Please bring me up to speed; don't leave out a thing."

The head scientist exclaims, "Who the?" And all turn toward Antboy, the impostor. "Oh my Lord, we have a security breach!"

With this, Antboy bolts for the door, toppling the desk and chair nearest him, and frantically sprints first left, then right, then right again through several corridors, searching for his suite, where is K, where is K, and there it finally is. He made a complete circle.

Evading him, eluding his fingers, his card key finally makes contact with the door. He inserts it and the green light appears, the handle turns and a deafening click is heard. Hours seem to pass in the process, and then he is inside. He bolts the door and falls down to the ground, head between his knees, shaking, hyperventilating. About to pass out, he crawls toward the bathroom and props himself up on the cloudy taupe marble sink and ushers cold water toward his face, his head, his mouth. He takes several slow, deep breathes, then the black fog lifts and he calms down realizing no one had followed him.

Startled by a knock at the door, he suppresses a scream. There is another knock, and a few moments later a loud thump. "Bonjour, bonjour. I'm zo zorry if you are zleeping. I didn't mean to disturb you. Your ezcort will be here in little over two hours. Pleaz ring room zervice, or Concierge, if you need anyzing. Security may knock also, zey are looking for someone. Au revoir, au revoir." Light, jaunty, almost fluffy steps can be heard down the hallway as he departs.

Antboy calms himself, recalling memories of his youth, remembering evenings of downward dog and cobra, chair position and warrior poses, as he and his mother and father performed their yoga practice, along the cool hardwood floor of their living room. As he centers his focus, he holds these poses, and his mind and body revert and relax, the repetitive motion pacifying him.

He waits for the escort that will take him to his 3:45 meeting with the General at Central Command. He no longer worries that security might instead knock on his door and whisk him off to a maximum-security prison for trespassing and compromising national security. He waits and sure enough the knock comes. He opens the door to find two policemen in military fatigues staring at him. "Please come with us, sir," one of the men commands.

"Where are you taking me?" Antboy inquires.

"The General is expecting you at Central Command," says one of them, noticing a prolonged sigh of relief escaping Antboy as they round the corner toward the main elevators. They pass an armed security team canvassing one of the neighboring hallways, demanding entrance into each room in the region of Suites E-H.

XIX

Father reminds me that he considers honesty to be a person's most important characteristic. He regrets that the General was only as honest as his duty would allow. Father tells me that there should never be a higher sense of duty than pure honesty to one's fellow man. Without truth we cannot trust, and without trust fear exists. Fear drives man to destroy that which he does not understand, namely other cultures and other governments, denying the common bond that unites humanity. "Stay true, Atum, and you won't fail, because you'll have nothing to hide."

"Father, I am going to leave the dome," The courage within me could not be contained.

"Please, Atum, you mustn't. I beg you. You don't know their power, or what they can do."

"Father, I can't lie to you. I was going to, but after what others have done, how they have deceived you, I won't. You're right; truth is necessary. I feel better now. When you leave for the meeting with the Queen, I will leave here for a little while. Father, I must. If anyone can understand how it feels to explore and understand and seek knowledge, *you* must. You'll see; I'll be fine. You've always said I'm wise beyond my years."

"You must be careful! Please reconsider. I pray that you do not leave here, but I cannot stop you. You obviously know it takes hours just to get to the Dome of Council and meetings are quite long. I'll be gone for nearly a full day. Can't you wait until you're older before you venture out? At least until the Endeavors are over?"

"I can't. I thought I could wait. I want to know more about where we live, and I want to see things with my own eyes, not just listen to your stories. I've tried to suppress my desire because I wanted to listen to you. You've told me that things will be better for me when we return to your home planet, but twelve more years is too long. I've wanted to sneak out and explore for a long time, but I didn't want to upset you. I can't control my curiosity any longer."

"Atum, I refuse to give you the fatherly advice that the General gave to me when I saw him, just after I turned eighteen. He cut me loose by telling me the truth that day. He told me I was the captain of my own ship, master of my heart, and the creator of my own destiny, all of which I learned to be true. I will not tell you those things, at this time, because you're younger than I was, and you're not ready for what you'll find outside of our home.

"The only father that I trusted was not my father, just as I am not yours. Though we're not blood, you're as much my son as any son I could have wished for. I realize that there are times when I will guide you, and counsel you, as the General did with me, but then you will make your own decisions, regardless of what I say. But I figured I had more time with you before that was going to happen."

"I know, Father. I'm sorry. I think I'm at what you would call a crossroads."

"Yes, it is a defining moment, one that I didn't see coming so soon. I was also at a turning point in my life when I sought the guidance of the only father figure I knew. I desired to leave the enclosure that had protected me. That's when I had my most truthful and revealing, yet still misleading, experience with the General. Truth sometimes hurts more than lies. He told me the truth, the General, but what he did not reveal, or chose not to tell, was a lie by omission."

After a few moments, I join Father in his ritual of staring mechanically, meditatively at earth. I know we'll talk all night since he is compelled to finish his story before he departs tomorrow for the Queen's Council. Soon he resumes.

The path to the General is directly into the heart of military headquarters. Antboy is impressed as he approaches the General's workplace, a large compound of interconnected offices, buzzing with military personnel, computers humming, large projection screens showing flattened versions of the world with red and green dots scattered throughout. Central Command is an active military complex in an actively militant world. He's escorted through several rooms until he's told that the General will be there shortly and that he should proceed through the door ahead marked 'Military Antiquities'.

The door opens to a room with vaulted, draped ceilings, in grand museum style. In the middle sits a cannon from the Civil War, and weapons ranging from hatchets, knives, bayonets, to rifles, handguns, grenades, and missile launchers dot the walls, categorized by year and war. Wax molds of military officers are clad in original uniforms of the day, and scenes of battle are depicted in photographs, litho-graphs, oils, and drawings, which hang chronologically.

He reaches to touch one of the more modern guns, and he's excited, yet frightened by the adrenaline rush that pulses through his brain. He's oblivious to the sound of heavy footsteps behind him and startled by a large hand on his shoulder.

"Well, well, look what the cat dragged in. Let me get a good look at you, son." The General takes a step back and is visibly shocked by the worn, bruised look of Antboy. "Whoa, you look like death warmed over."

Antboy shrugs back tears, and wants to hug the General, but is tormented by the thought of trusting again in this paternal figure.

"By the look of things, the confiscation didn't go over too well. Sorry for any problems that it has caused you; there really wasn't any other way."

Antboy is angry, utterly enraged, and feels deceived. He wants an explanation and an apology. "You could have told me they were coming, sir."

"No, I couldn't."

"Why?"

"Fundamental tactical military maneuvers: Never let them know you're coming. Basic principles and I'm alive today because of this philosophy."

Antboy sadly reflects upon the General's response for a moment and scans the room, perusing the military memora-bilia. "It wasn't a military exercise. I was almost killed, sir."

"Under no circumstances would you have been killed. My orders were that if any harm came to you, the perpetrator would be subject to a court martial. The story I got was that you resisted and the officer used appropriate force to accomplish the objective. It looks like you've been through a bit more than what I was told."

"Sir, why was there an 'objective'? Don't you think you could have made a phone call and asked me, or informed me, before you stole all of my work?"

"Son, I'm sorry, I truly am. No, I couldn't have made a call. The entire mission would have been jeopardized."

"Sir, what 'mission'? The ant colony studies that I conducted over the past six years?"

"Whoa! Come on! At this point you damn well know that this has gone way above and beyond ants. We couldn't risk the possibility that your research and findings fell into private hands, free and clear of the government once you turned eighteen. The operation was to eliminate all evidence that your studies ever took place, and to recover all of your records. Do you really think for one moment that the past few years of your life have been funded by this great nation strictly due to your tremendous charm and wonderful wit? Your mind, your philosophies are truly revolutionary in a world where the only thing that might save the human race is a revolution. But a rebellion in the wrong hands, especially with the conclusive documentation of your tested theories, could be very damaging to our country, and to the International Coalition."

"What am I supposed to do now, sir?"

"Son, since I met you, I've been in charge of you, and I've had the responsibility of protecting you and your work. I care for you, and I look at you as the son I never had. I want you to have a good life. You have been valuable to your country, actually indispensable to this nation, and to my career personally. We discussed things years ago, but now that you're eighteen, you're free to pursue your own path. What are you considering?"

163

"I don't know, sir. Can I leave here freely?"

"What do you think, that you're some type of prisoner? Son, we hold no prisoners here. Everyone is free to leave these premises. This is not a jail or holding cell."

"What about the scientists working on the HSI project?"

The General sighs deeply and replies a bit angrily, "That's different, son. What the hell do you know about that anyway? That information has been classified to uphold the safety of the nation. Even this conversation breaches the national security restrictions on the project. Admittedly, there are times when we need to hold people for the benefits of defense and for the sake of public welfare and protection. How did you learn about the program?"

Antboy replies stiffly, "I stumbled onto something earlier, actually I got pulled into it."

"So you're the one. Give me a minute." He pulls out a handheld radio and yells, "Shut down Fake Scientist! I've located and have in custody the infiltrator. Immediately post four armed guards at the compromised location and stand by for further breached security procedures. Terminate, I repeat, terminate." He turns to face Antboy, "Well, well. You never cease to amaze me. I'm sure you have a long list of questions for me now."

"Sir, I do."

"To answer you briefly and to put this matter to an immediate and definitive end, I am not at liberty to discuss this, nor do I have all the answers that you seek."

"Does this have anything to do with my research and my theories?"

"Again, I am not free to discuss this and I will answer no more questions, do you understand? Are we clear?"

"We're clear that you will not discuss this with me but I'm clearly going to continue seeking answers. Sir, you protected me, yet you deceived me."

"I am a general, what do you expect? I use deception in order to protect and to destroy. I obliterate that which threatens our way of life. I seek sovereignty over both the land and ideologies of our enemies; those that want us destroyed, I instead seek to annihilate. This is how I protect our country. When I was eighteen I joined the Army and I've been serving ever since.

"You may not understand or believe this, but I am a pacifist. The greatest military leaders are indeed peacekeepers. Nations never benefit from prolonged combat. Therefore, the most notable countries in history wage warfare when it serves their purposes, but decisive, expedient campaigns insure victory. Peace is my mission; unfortunately we must win many battles before we can live in tranquility. Look around you. Constant conflicts abound and the world is perpetually at war. Our enemies are intolerant of differing beliefs and ideologies, and there is an endless economic struggle for control of limited resources. Today, I cannot tell you who will be victorious in this confrontation."

"Sir, who are we fighting?"

"Son, our government is under attack from all sectors, domestic and abroad, and terrorist groups abound. We're hated and despised because of our military might, political systems, and freedoms. We're condemned for our diversity of religious beliefs yet some even hate us for our lack of fundamentalist orthodoxy. Our economic systems and territorial positions are under attack from extremists. There will never be a time when there's a perfect balance in worldwide power. I do what I have to do for my country. I don't make all the decisions, but I'm involved in many of them. I will continue to serve until the day I die."

Antboy breathes deeply, and responds, "Until yesterday, I always imagined, over the years I spent at the mansion, that I was serving my country. Though sometimes I briefly flirted with the idea of returning home and having an ordinary kid's life. What kept me from doing that was my belief that I was doing something good for people. Sir, have I served my country?"

"Son, you've served the human race. You've thought about how to sustain and preserve life and you've proven how to do it. For this your country will benefit. But your motives have been purely philanthropic and your goal was not to benefit your nation, instead it was to benefit life itself. And you have put the pieces in place for this to happen. But in certain ways, no, I would say you have not served your country. Look around you at these walls and these halls and see the faces of the men that have served their nation. Some have died and many lived in the service of their homeland.

"Let me make one thing very clear. Let's say you are in a bread line, in a time of famine, and you reach the front of the line and then they announce there is only one loaf of bread left. If this loaf is the only food that your wife and two children will have to eat for an entire week do you feel bad enough for the person behind you to give them your loaf knowing that your family will starve and theirs will not? It's a ridiculous question because you will obviously feed your own family and fate will take care of the other one. When there is only so much to go around, you take care of your own. Currently, there is only so much to go around: water, food, land, energy, and clean air. So we take care of our own. Our own country, that is.

"Great minds like yours help us, though. We need thinkers, philosophers, scientists, and innovators such as you to assist humanity. So your sanctuaries and societal research will serve our nation and by this you have served your country well. But so have I, in the trenches and on the battlefields and in Central Command. You have used your mind for science, while I have used mine to make war and ensure peace."

"Sir, when I leave here I have nowhere to go, no home to return to."

"Son, you need a new home, a new path."

"Sir, what about the armed forces? It seems like an honorable life. Do you think I'm cut out for the military?"

"No one is necessarily cut out for the military. You can make the military work for you. You can participate and innovate and find the right niche for yourself. Not everyone holds a gun and shoots people. Some of the greatest thinkers the world has ever known have served in the armed forces. It's not about death, it's about life."

Suddenly I stand up and interrupt Father at this most crucial point in his retelling of his dialogue with the General, his mentor, nearly a father to Father. A sense of panic overtakes me and I cannot hide it any longer. "Father, I need to find my mother. That's why I must leave. I'm sorry. I just have to."

"I know you do. It's natural that you want to find your mother. But even if you can locate her, you will never be able to talk to her and let her know that she's your mother. It's forbidden for Mothers to have contact with their male sons. At birth, you were a deselected male. But all surviving males are isolated and have lived as Beasts in horrific conditions. The only time Mothers will see them will be at the Endeavors. Even then, Mothers won't be able to distinguish which ones they birthed. You will gain nothing by finding or contacting your mother; instead you will risk everything."

I do not respond. We just stare at each other. There is nothing he can do to stop me; I am overwhelmed with an uncontrollable need to know who she is, to see her face.

"You must also understand that you'll never know your true biological father. Fourteen years after my conversation with the General at Central Command, was Departure Day. The females aboard the shuttle were impregnated through artificial insemination three months prior to departing earth. Anonymous donors, representing top genetic specimens, had been selected by each HSI participating nation of the International Coalition, eighteen nations in all. For a full year prior to insemination, fertility drugs were regularly administered to insure conception and, if successful, multiple births. Atum, I need you to understand that it's impossible for you to find your father, and it's best for you to never pursue meeting your mother, either."

Ignoring Father's solemn warning I ask, "Father, what did the General say next?"

"He didn't say anything."

"Nothing?"

Father sits for a while and ponders. It seems like it pains him to continue. He closes his eyes and I know that he's back in the antiquities room with the General.

The General says nothing of importance, but in nothingness he says everything. "I was born in North Carolina, son. I was the eldest of four children and my mother was a saint. When my father lost his job at the mill, he began to drink, heavily. Although he found various jobs over the years that sustained our family, he never lost his drinking. He was a mean drunk. Mama would whimper quietly after he beat her and make up all sorts of excuses about it being her fault and that Papa was a good man and that times were tough supporting a whole family, us being always hungry and always wanting, and her sometimes complaining about needing more.

"When I got toward Papa's height I would defend Mama and that's when Papa started in on me. He beat me up pretty badly but as long as I protected Mama and my younger brothers and sister I could handle his severe beatings. I never could take on Papa. Mama always said that when I turned eighteen, I should head for the door and never look back. So, that's what I did, and I joined the military. I knew that I wanted to learn how to fight and how to defend, so that no one could ever hurt me, or my loved ones again. The military built my self-esteem and turned me from a scared little boy into a man. I've overcome the deficiencies and inherent weaknesses of my genetics. It was the discipline that I learned that saved me. I needed to break away. At times we all need to escape."

The General and Antboy part with hug, handshake and salute, intermingled physically, yet undeniably emotional.

"Atum, I joined the Army the next day. I felt the necessity to help my country, and to serve in a different capacity than I had. My scientific work had been stolen and so had my innocence. I knew too much, I thought too much, and the only thing I wanted to do was to escape. Only later did I learn that the General, of course, knew right where I was.

"There really was no escaping, there couldn't be. The General wanted me to be part of every aspect of his plan, and he planted the seeds that sprouted into my military career. He knew that a strategic military background was necessary for me to lead the final stage of HSI, which began fourteen years later on Departure Day. It's very late, son, and I have a long day ahead. Let's perform our practice now and settle down."

Antboy notices Atum's disappointment, but he knew that Atum regularly grew quite irritable whenever he was deprived of sleep. They square off to begin their evening ritual of Shakthura, designed to quiet the mind, relax the body, and pacify the soul.

It was a ritual that Antboy learned in captivity many years earlier, not unlike the captivity he currently faced. Promulgated by the uniform he wore in the military, he had been detained, and then taught renewal. He experienced spiritual pedagogical rebirth inspired by his captors, who had instructed him that mankind wears no specific uniform.

Shakthura had been taught throughout generations among certain tribal peoples of earth. Allowing Antboy to truly understand that life stemmed from his being, his very presence, it was this practice that melded meditative and physical elements, contributing to resigned, inner peace. By learning to protect his body with the defensive and aggressive postures of Shakthura, Antboy also learned to guard his mind from the dangerous influences of worldly passions.

As their minds unwind during Shakthura's final stage of deep breathing, Atum eventually rises and retreats to his bed. While Antboy covers Atum, he strokes the boy's hair and detects his scent. It is a scent reminiscent of the woman who left Atum to die, but who then came back covertly, briefly. A cloaked woman with her face veiled, claiming to be a representative from the Council sent to verify that Antboy was carrying out the proclamation, was indeed Atum's mother. Even though the disguised Lavender held Atum for so long, tears streaming, she had no choice but to leave him, thereby respecting the law.

As soon as Lavender departed Dome Seventeen, Antboy retrieved Atum, the wailing deselected baby, who cried unattended and alone. With that impulsive decision, he had deceived the colony by pretending to destroy Atum, but instead had rescued him. That is all Atum needs to know.

Knowing that his mother came back to hold him, and then left Atum to die, regretfully, does not change anything. The first to bear a deselected child, Lavender eventually hardened, becoming strong and determined, transforming into a completely different person. If he tells Atum about his mother, he will admit lifelong deception. Yet through his continued deceit, Antboy believes he is protecting Atum.

As Antboy looks lovingly at Atum he remembers the scent, so vivid and so tragic. Sitting by Atum's bed, transfixed by the memories of the smell of lavender, he cannot rise. He is entranced by the fragrance, the aroma of life and death, reminding him of the bitterness of his past.

Atum, please don't go, he wishes silently.

XX

During the initial weeks of the colony's settlement, Antboy was in charge of everything. That changed overnight, and he realized how he had been used; he had become a pawn in a much larger agenda. Control was wrested from him and his role was distorted.

Antboy had been briefed shortly before Departure Day, strictly provided with limited information, scanty at best. He was severely warned by HSI and the International Coalition not to contaminate the Colony. By unanimous vote, he was restricted from informing these pioneering females about anything beyond what they had already been taught. He was ordered to set up the initial colony, then to solely observe it, and document his findings, as he had done during the years at the Governor's Mansion.

The day before boarding, the women were assembled and placed into a hypnotic dreamlike trance. They were given certain instructions that would be triggered by the word 'awake'. As they slept on the shuttle, each held a copy of the HSI code. Lavender was one of only four passengers from his country, and she was the only one to awake during the original shuttle launch to their satellite planet. She was disoriented and he briefly comforted her. Then she began to read the HSI code, as she had been instructed. The rest remained unconscious, until he gave the command to awake, as were his orders.

Upon arrival and docking, Antboy was supposed to exit the craft unattended, and prepare the sanctuaries for habitation, before issuing the awake command. However, he was accompanied by Lavender, who was alert and restive, and she watched carefully as he readied the controls and adjusted the many switches and levers that would activate the sanctuaries. He appreciated Lavender's company.

There were approximately two hundred domes within the interior of the satellite planet. Atmospherically sheltered tunnels connected them, to allow protected and oxygenated travel throughout the colony. Some domes were much larger than he had thought architecturally feasible, able to accommodate almost five hundred inhabitants, while others were quite small, to house four. His calculations predicted that the colony, based on extrapolation of birth projections, would reach an estimated population of ten thousand within twenty-five years. At that point, the entire satellite was engineered to return to earth. Other contingencies would be revealed in the Codex in the event that earth had become uninhabitable during their absence.

It was integral to the survival of the colony that certain steps be followed to insure that each woman properly departed the aircraft. No breach could occur between the shuttle door and the connecting tunnel. The shuttle had been configured with a proboscis that would fit into the enclave allowing the connection to last almost fifteen minutes before destabilization. Upon destabilization, a breach could occur and oxygen might leak faster than replenishment, jeopardizing their lives. After departure, the connection was to be terminated and the tunnel sealed, to keep the shuttle and connecting tunnel hidden. Antboy was advised to take extreme precautions, and to be discreet, using the awake command only when departure was imminent.

Antboy would usher the women in a circuitous route, creating maximum confusion, to one of the central domes, the Dome of Gathering, where temporary living quarters had been prepared. This indirect, almost meandering route to the center would obfuscate the exact location of the shuttle and its tunnel keeping them hidden and remote, to be later sealed clandestinely by Antboy.

The only problem was Lavender, who was wide awake. Antboy gave her very specific instructions to help during departure. He hoped she would be too engulfed with these responsibilities to memorize the path from the shuttle dock to the center of the colony. His plan worked. The geographic disorientation he choreographed bewildered everyone. However, by believing he could readily confound Lavender he clearly underestimated her intelligence, perception, and drive. This was the first of many miscalculations that he made concerning Lavender.

XXI

In just a few hours, Antboy would make his way through the many tunnels that separated him from Queen Lavender's council chambers, the Dome of Council. The Queen had announced that the Colony was ready to participate in the first Endeavors, which would commence in three days, and that preparations were to be made without delay.

He was horrified when he heard the Queen's announcement. However, it had been more than thirteen years since the colony was settled and the women had followed the procedures as dictated by HSI, eight separate inseminations, to be administered every nine months after the prior delivery. The colony had administered its eighth and final vials eighteen months before, and it had been nine months since the last birthing ritual. The seed was gone, and the point of maximum fertility was nigh.

The first Endeavors would take place in three days, and every eighteen months thereafter. The children born from the first vials were nearly thirteen and a half, of age to participate in the Endeavors. Entrants at the first Endeavors would be the male children born from the first vials. Female children born from the first vials would receive the victors once the champions were announced. The second Endeavors would include the victorious first vial males, and additionally those males born from the second vials. Future Endeavors would subsequently continue in this pattern, but would exclude females with poor conception rates, who would be relegated to Worker status. All Mothers and Workers were to be present at the Dome of Endeavors to cheer on their favorite contenders.

Atum, the first born on the colony, and the first deselected, was the oldest child by little over a month. He would not participate in the Endeavors because they thought him dead. Antboy had vehemently opposed Atum's death sentence. Yet he recanted opposition to that sentence, instead volunteering to carry it out.

Lavender outwardly supported deselection, but inwardly mourned, appearing at Dome Seventeen where Antboy was to deselect Atum. On that inescapable day, Antboy saved Atum. But his alleged death altered Lavender forever and estranged her from Antboy. Although Lavender hid her resentment of Atum's believed death, she was irrevocably infused with everlasting hatred for Antboy.

Atum's deselection jettisoned Lavender to the Worker category. The classification of Worker was the polar opposite of Queen. The Queen was selected as the most fertile, who gave birth to the highest number of healthy female babies in each Birthing Season.

Yet now Lavender was Queen. She had turned the agony of her child's deselection into strength. She was determined to learn, to seek information, as much knowledge as she could gain from perpetual study of the Codex. Eventually she gained control of the entire colony.

As Queen, her scent was evident at every Council meeting and the aroma disturbed Antboy. It reminded him of the months that he was in love, months that were distant but distinct in his memory, when the colony was first being settled, during the brief time when he directed everything.

At the time of initial settlement, the expectant mothers were compliant and mainly read the HSI code, primarily preparing for their births. Meanwhile, Lavender followed Antboy everywhere. She showed surprising interest in the technical aspects of dome maintenance. He was glad to have her as a companion and thought it very practical that he had an apprentice in case he was later unavailable to perform certain technical duties.

Antboy had been specifically instructed to speak nothing of earth, where Lavender and the others had been strategically and scientifically sequestered. Invariably intending to obey this order, Antboy soon found himself lonely and violated that command. He often spoke to her of his military career, his childhood fascination with and research on ants, and the reasons for founding the colony. When he was around Lavender he felt whole. She was the final piece in the unfinished puzzle of his life, and the fit was comfortable.

Then there was the kiss. The kiss that transcended the boundaries of space and time and it lasted but a few moments, yet resounded in his universe and orbited his galaxy eternally. They shuddered and twitched passionately for hours and held each other close, terrifyingly near, for they knew that what took place was unalterable. He was unable to deny the kiss as he stared into her mesmerizing green eyes, and the moment was unexpected and precipitous, poised on the eve of uncertainty. They could not have known that their supernatural kiss would be followed soon after by Atum's birth and deselection.

Atum's prescribed death led to the death of their mutual love. From the moment of Atum's deselection, Lavender withheld all emotion and affection from Antboy, and appeared detached. Thereafter it was as if their passion had never existed.

Attempting to fulfill her undisclosed private agenda, Lavender requested more than just general knowledge from Antboy. She sourced him for specific information in a straightforward and aloof manner. He gave her everything, and held back nothing. She asked precise questions about the functioning of the domes and he supplied the answers. She pursued him on topics of military history, strategy, and techniques, and he wanted nothing more than to please her with his knowledge. However, less than a year after she dutifully abandoned Atum, Lavender refused to speak to Antboy. There was nothing more she wished to extract from him. She had used him up.

Oh, how love is blind, and blind he was. *Atum, don't go.*

After a few hours of unsettled sleep he wakes to see Atum fully dressed and preparing their meal. Atum seems rejuvenated and his pinkish color betrays his anticipation and excitement. It's too late. Atum's mind is made up. Antboy knows that when he leaves for the Council meeting, that Atum will leave their dome too. *Atum, don't go.*

They sit in silence and finish their morning meal. They banter and speak of nonsensical topics unrelated to anything of importance. But Antboy and Atum know that they speak of trivial things so that they can prolong saying goodbye, which can no longer be avoided. "Goodbye, Atum. I will be back very late tonight. Please review the disks."

"Of course, Father, when have I ever forgotten?"

They hug, and hug once more, this time an embrace considerably extended. Then Antboy departs their dome, making an immediate left, to hide in the shadows. Moments later the door opens, and Atum leaves stealthily, skirting the perimeter of the dim tunnels as he heads toward the main artery of the settlement, the Village. Antboy helplessly watches Atum wander away.

Antboy can only pray that Atum has listened closely over the years to his meticulous instructions. At this juncture, it is vital that Atum heed the tales of survival techniques and military strategy that Antboy had gained in his country's service, their relevance having been conscientiously conveyed to Atum since birth. He had prayed this day would never come but he knew it couldn't be avoided forever. That's why he had painstakingly prepared Atum on a variety of important topics regarding how to survive in enemy territory, even if captured. Atum had listened intently, mentally and physically preparing throughout adolescence.

Atum's footsteps can no longer be heard, leaving Antboy in the silent shadows near their dome, in the outer reaches of the colony's maintenance region. He begins walking toward the interior of the colony, which usually takes nearly four hours to reach. For Council meetings he makes this trek, and he enjoys the labyrinthine walk, which gives him time to think.

He had decided in the early days of the settlement, that it would be best for him to reside near the shuttle's original docking station. This territory was on the edge of the colony and housed the main generators, which sustained each dome's equilibrium. Segregated from the colony, Antboy moved surreptitiously through this district. Rarely was anyone found wandering in this isolated area for it provided little interest to the colonists. As a precaution, he had taken great measures to prevent Atum's detection, by sealing off every portion of their dome, the Dome of Maintenance, where sound could possibly vent.

But Inspection Day was always a concern. Fortunately, he was privy to the schedule. In fact, he was required to monitor the system to allow access to every inch of the colony from its hidden recesses, deep into its bowels, and up its towering peaks. Forewarned is forearmed, Antboy believed, and Atum hid in the Alcove during the active hours of inspection. Like a military assault team, the Scouts, in alert formation, scoured the colony and reported back to the Queen.

As a Worker, Lavender had been avidly against Inspection Day, petitioning to abolish the proclamation, claiming it violated the colonists' rights. However, Lavender never terminated this very invasive act when she ascended the throne to become Queen. In fact, she ordered more stringent inspections than any prior Queen had required.

From the start, Lavender had wanted a lot of things to change, but she instead maintained her duty to the oaths she swore to uphold, and relished her new authority, and was revered. In fact, at the outset, during the very first meeting of the colonists, thirteen years earlier, the night after their arrival, it was obvious that Lavender's voice and her hands would be heard and respected.

XXII

On earth, the initial colonists had been taught a complex phonetic language of which Antboy had neither familiarity nor basis for comparison or derivation. Additionally, the women had developed forms of communication that utilized multiple senses and perceptions. Sign language and pictures were used along with certain guttural sounds, touch, various scents, and body movement. Although it was not difficult for the colonists to learn his one-dimensional oratory, it was challenging for him to pick up the subtleties of their language. That first meeting, the night after their arrival, was thorny for him to lead.

The women were engaged in various conversations, signaling each other with hand and body movements that expressed both words and emotions. As he sat and watched, it seemed like multiple conversations were taking place simultaneously between women adjacent and across from each other. While the entire Dome of Gathering was brimming with the excitement of these women, it appeared that each woman was intertwined in various conversations, a skill Antboy did not possess. He was, at most, able to engage in one conversation at a time and then, when finished, he could participate in another.

Sitting cross-legged on the floor, he realized he had never been present at an assembly of such a multitude of women. Even though they all turned to him to guide the meeting, he began to feel ill at ease, an intruder in the new society. But he knew there was a lot of work ahead to properly prepare the colony for survival so he shed his sense of insecurity and proceeded.

He noticed that they instinctually formed a circle and sat quietly. Then he perceived an almost indiscernible movement from one woman, whose hands were at her side, palms upward, toward the ceiling. Mechanically, each woman followed suit and interlaced her fingers with those of her neighbors to the right and left. The circle closed with him just outside the perimeter, which seemed appropriate. He was impressed with the sense of community and common bond that was evident at that first gathering.

The woman who had initiated the joining of the circle began a repetitive chant of discordant grunts and sounds that each woman repeated together. In its harmony the synchronicity was mellifluous. Upon finishing their methodical chanting, they dropped their hands to their sides and motioned for him to edge slightly back inside the circle.

He began by introducing himself. He asked them how they slept by clasping both hands, tilting his head to the right, and placing his hands underneath one ear, eyes closed. The circle responded together with general nods of approval, replying, "Yah."

As he surveyed the group he was pleased that the women had not seated themselves in a particular order. It was very important that they successfully integrate during the initial phase of establishing the order of the society. He had been concerned that they might naturally congregate with those of their own skin color but no such segregation was evident.

So many shades of skin and hair color, so many scents, hairstyles, eye colors, varieties in facial features, and body shapes bombarded his senses. All he saw was beauty, radiant beauty among all present. The women were about one trimester through their pregnancies, the life within already alive in their faces, and the increased blood flow of each woman brought a tingling sensation of energy throughout the dome. The presence of their energy was almost tangible in form. To Antboy, the most beautiful was Lavender. At first, when he made eye contact, she averted her eyes, and later, when she looked at him, he averted his.

The naming began, as prescribed by HSI code. He studied each woman, and then allocated seventy-two names based on the association that came to his mind. Coral, Iris, Catherine, Isis, Ivory, Ruby, Siren, Lola, Anna, Zara, Carmen, Lucy, Paula, Olivia, Florence, Isabella, Valentina, Eleanor, Sekhmet, Angel, Eve, Leslie, Blue, Medusa, Sarah, Ethica, Elizabeth, Diana, Lily, Layla, Constance, Edith, Rose, Grace, Amelia, Cactus, Aida, Olga, Maria, Fatima, Christina, Ariel, Hannah, Chelsea, Lea, Sofia, Jade, Anastasia, Europa, Eden, Alice, Bonnie, Victoria, Reina, Aurora, Dora, Summer, Ginger, Alejandra, Violet, Dolores, Brielle, Indira, Sheila, Rachel, Lavender, Jasmine, Rebecca, Asia, Venus, Amber, and Sage rolled off his tongue as he pointed to each.

They looked at him in puzzlement. He repeated the names again, and a few women tried to pronounce their given names. Most just stared blankly at him. The woman he named Siren, who had initiated the circle chanting, motioned for him to continue. He thanked Siren and asked to see her HSI book, which he opened to the first page. Each woman opened her own copy.

He was utterly confused at what he saw. The pages were filled with strange hieroglyphics, odd symbols, pictures, various charts, and diagrams, few of which he recognized, none of which he entirely understood. The women became animated as they flipped the pages and discussed certain topics among themselves. He tried to follow what they were saying and reading, but to no avail. Growing concerned that he couldn't comprehend the information that they were deciphering and absorbing, he decided he needed an interpreter. He selected Lavender and signaled to her that they would need to meet at the conclusion of the assembly.

He then asked for silence by placing his forefinger over his lips and saying, "Shhh, shhh, shhh." All turned their heads to him and made eye contact, but they continued conversing among themselves, motioning for him to proceed even while they chatted. He again said, "Shhh, shhh, shhh," and a few began to mimic him and then everyone was in turn saying, "Shhh, shhh, shhh," with their forefingers over their lips and some started to giggle. They soon resumed their chatter, while still holding their attention on him.

He was flabbergasted but did not want to scare them by forcefully calling order. So he continued by holding up the Codex and asked them to read through it, showing them that they should flip through each page and, with their index finger, should read each line of the Codex, concluding on the last page. The women signaled assent by copying him, and soon after Coral said, "Done, Done." Then she pointed toward the ground and around at the women in the circle and back to the Codex. She flipped quickly through all the pages, letting her hand touch each page, and put the Codex down and said, "Done." He moved his hands over the pages of Siren's opened book and realized that the letters, symbols, and pictures all had raised print. Feeling the HSI code with his fingers, looking not at the Codex, but at the circle of women he asked, "Done?"

"Yah," they said in unison, also moving their hands over each page, showing him their celerity by touching and turning page after page, flipping through the Codex rapidly. They each stared at him with anxious, quizzical looks, and he was aware that they were attempting to read his reaction. Having never encountered such heightened perceptive acumen, he attempted to conceal his shock. Not only the style of the HSI code, indecipherable to him in its current form, but also the fact that the women had apparently finished reading the entire book so quickly, alarmed him.

Although he tried to obscure his reaction, his face betrayed his true emotion. They suddenly mistook his distress for hostility. Though he forced his face into a tight smile, it was too late. Soon surrounded by angry faces, the circle quickly broke away. He was evidently no longer welcome in their company; he was an intruder. Siren approached.

She was by far the largest woman present, perhaps carrying twice as many babies as most of her companions, and it looked uncomfortable for her to move swiftly. Suddenly, she stared at him, eye to eye, and she pointed downward, toward the ground. He didn't understand what she wanted him to look at. He again looked at the floor and then he shrugged his shoulders and raised his hands, facing upward, to show her that he didn't comprehend what she wanted.

Almost imperceptibly she flicked her head and two slim women approached. They quickly swept their feet along the ground in an arc behind his right and left calves, knocking him to the ground, dropping him to a supplicant position.

185

Siren began stamping her right foot one-one, one-two, one-one, one-two and each woman repeated after her. She said, "Yah," and pointed to him on the ground. She repeated, "Yah," and pointed, on and on.

He realized he was being publicly humiliated, but he calmly swallowed his anger. Although he knew he could rise and knock her down, there were too many of them, and he would be easily overcome.

Then his brain began spinning frantically, frenziedly. He rapidly realized that his position as a supplicant was proper and necessary. He had been sent not to lead them, but to serve them. He would lead only by following, through submission. He would hold no power in this new world, a world run by women, designed to thrive by HSI.

He bent deeper into his submissive position and Siren began encircling his outstretched, prostrate body. Emitting various grunts and sounds she conveyed an overall sense of condescension and dismay at his very presence. By a rustling of emotionless stark, sterile white tunics, a tossing of hair, and sighs of impatience throughout the general assembly it was obvious that she held the view of the majority. Siren began to squeal a hellish deafening high-pitched scream and the women followed suit. Their feet stamped feverishly and the blood curdling lust for his deliverance was layered thick throughout the dome.

He was scared, actually terrified that he would not even survive the night. He was a foreigner to them. Somehow, by leading the meeting, he had instilled an inner fear in them, that manifested in Siren's very aggressive stance, which permeated the incited mob. His inability to communicate was a great impediment and he felt that any movement or sound from him might be detrimental to his survival. So he did the only thing he could do. From his peripheral vision he scanned for Lavender. It was not hard to catch sight of her for all he had to do was to look for verdant green eyes. Searching the eyes, brown, blue, hazel, until he spied the color of lush grass, he spoke to her, through his eyes, and pleaded for his life.

Lavender stepped forward and the mob quieted. Facing Lavender, Siren displayed utter contempt. Harsh, sharp dialect transpired and they faced off, the other women encircling the two, heads turned to witness the internal struggle. Antboy, conversant in the ways of his beloved ants, fancied that he could understand their language and he contorted slightly to peek underneath the underarm of his right, outstretched arm. What he glimpsed, he imagined correctly, was Lavender's attempt to save him.

"This person is important to us, your Majesty," Lavender explained.

"Why? How is this piece of rubbish of any use to us? It is nothing more than a Beast. It cannot even communicate with us, and yet it wants to rule us. I despise it and besides, it smells badly," and with this Siren spat two times on the floor and held her nose signaling putrefaction.

"It knows how these domes work and we may need it to survive. It also was the one who delivered us here and the Codex strictly forbids us to harm it," Lavender defended him.

"You may be right. For now, I will go against my instincts and spare him. In the future, we must follow our instincts, and trust them, for we are superior to this Beast. Do not forget this. If it ever interferes again it must be destroyed, for the Codex says that it must not meddle. If it wants to live, it must obey. Is this agreed?"

"Yah," Lavender and the women replied in unison.

"Tomorrow, you will go to it and you must begin to learn its language. Teach it very little but learn as much as you can about these," and Siren swept her hands overhead at the dome enclosing them. "Tell it to live very far from us, as far as possible," said Siren as she pushed outward and away with her arms.

With this, Lavender approached Antboy and gently placed her hand on his elbow, helping him to rise. She pointed to the door and said urgently, "Go! Go far, very far! Tomorrow." And she motioned with her hands and fingers that she would locate him, and travel to him the next day. As he left the dome, he looked back to see her waving her hands overhead as if to signal that he should go very, very far away, to the furthest reaches of the colony. And so he did. And so ended the first and last meeting he led.

He scrambled toward the outer edge of the colony and reached the point of their initial arrival. He made his home in the dome that was closest to the secreted path to the docked shuttle, the Dome of Maintenance. The dome was spacious and sparsely furnished with scattered tables, and thin layers of foam for sleeping. So this was to be home, away and isolated. Time for reflection, time for study, time to document and journalize the evolution of this new society.

They had already chosen a leader. He didn't imagine that this would happen so fast. It seemed like there was no election, only common assent. Had Siren planned this or had she just assumed responsibility and a leadership role, accepted by all parties? Perhaps these females did not associate leadership and power as something worth arguing or competing for. Somehow Siren acted with the unvoiced, unanimous support of everyone present to take the lead of those assembled. He had never witnessed a group elect a leader in such a smooth, flawless manner and it was most unsettling.

Had there been men present, a power struggle would have certainly ensued, with victory going to the contender that held the most influence, dominated by strong alliances and backed by raw physical might. Leadership and power were sought, revered, and preserved and that was the way men governed.

Perhaps these colonists uniformly desired not to assume the responsibility, bestowing it naturally upon one who apparently did, Siren. Or they innately and instinctively believed that the goodwill of the group would be maintained, with fair treatment accorded to all, by their tacit and unanimous selection of Queen Siren.

The bare essence of a fleeting thought of the fate that Lavender had just saved him from, cast spasmodic shivers throughout his muscles, his tendons, his nerves, and his skin. In their presence, he would forever feel humiliation because of that forced position of humble servitude.

Nevertheless, this was a second chance. Nature had been defied in the rearing of these women, the launch of the planet, the construction of the colony's life supporting domes, and in the fertilization process. Truly an unnatural man-made experiment where failure meant death, and death was not an option. Failure had already plagued the world they had just left. He vowed to suppress his humiliation if it meant that their colony would flourish. He would bow to them, bend to their will, and watch, wait, learn, and listen.

Lavender would help him. He needed her, and she was smart enough to know that she needed him. They all needed him, at least for now.

XXIII

Lavender came to him the next day with HSI's book, the Codex. When she arrived Antboy bowed low to the ground, but she hissed and pulled him upward. She pointed to herself and then to him and then to the floor and she wagged her finger, shook her head, and said, "Nuh, Nuh."

He would not need to display this contemptible, degrading respect when in her presence alone. For this he was relieved. They sat upon the mat in the center of the dome, cross-legged, and began to communicate awkwardly.

Although Lavender was extremely patient with Antboy, he struggled to communicate for weeks. Understanding her was much easier than actually responding to her. He was by no means a language aficionado. In fact, he had only learned one additional language, Latin, to his native tongue, and that was solely because it was essential to his scientific studies. He used his hands and arms in wide sweeping motions to communicate very simple concepts. He sounded out words too slowly and often too loudly for her to understand. She often placed her hands upon his own and showed him much easier and more direct methods of speaking, and her tones were hushed and controlled.

The communication methods that she innately seemed to possess depended upon body movement, subtle changes in expression, as well as differing angles at which she tilted her head and the volume with which she spoke. These actions were foreign to Antboy. In conjunction, they seemed like senses of perception with which he was not equipped.

From Lavender, Antboy learned that the colonists were able to communicate without words or signals. When Lavender noticed that he did not respond to her expressions and body movements, she placed more emphasis on verbal language interspersed with sign language. She hoped that he would eventually expand his ability to grasp the intricacies of their constantly evolving and ever developing language. In the meantime she instead directed her attention to learning his language.

Antboy's language befuddled her. It made no sense and, although Lavender's linguistic ability far exceeded his, she disliked conversing in it. She relied on his language only when absolutely necessary during those five months, and instead invested time in teaching him. Within a month, their communication gaps were sufficiently filled, but then Antboy struggled internally.

There was so much he wanted to share with her about himself and his world, but he knew that this would invalidate HSI's objective, and jeopardize the natural formation of this new female order. So he imparted some things and withheld others. They spent most of their wakeful hours together. Each sundown she left him to return at dawn the next day, for nearly half a year.

191

Lavender was the only colonist to see him as anything other than the Beast. In fact, Siren would not allow Lavender to enter any dome until she scrubbed herself thoroughly to remove any traces of the Beast. He was looked upon as an aberration, a pariah cast out to the edge of the colony, an unwelcome and foreign species, and Siren hoped he would fade away into oblivion.

The other women shunned Lavender, so when she was not with Antboy, she spent her time in the Village alone caressing her stomach in anticipation of the baby to come. Each evening the women took comfort from each other by massaging their swelling bodies and taking part in ritualistic chanting and dancing that eased their conditions, but Lavender was not called to participate. Day after day, bellies continued to swell and the women busily prepared the Dome of Nursing for the new generation.

At mealtimes the largest women, as they were believed to carry more babies, were served first and their allotment of vitamins, minerals, and nutrients were always the largest portions and the most freshly generated from the dome's processors. When Siren held the evening assembly, the slighter women were the ones that moved to make room for the larger women, who in turn sat closest to Siren. When any form of manual labor was necessary, the colonists relied on the smaller women, deemed less important due to their portended lack of proclivity to produce multiple children. Their more agile and diminutive frames were looked upon as reflections of weakness in genetics, designed to serve others instead of birth babies. Lavender, one of the more petite, often spent her evenings catering to the more fully emerging and endowed housemates.

At the beginning of each evening assembly at the Dome of Gathering, the colonists turned their attention to the

Codex. Certain things were clearly established and needed little or no explanation while other notions needed further interpretation. They mulled over a multitude of concepts and politely discussed and respectfully debated until a harmonious accord prevailed.

Antboy, although not allowed to attend, was curious about these meetings, the Codex and the development of their society. Lavender responded to his queries with patience, explaining the happenings of the new colony. She anticipated their meetings, arriving as early as permitted, and returning to the Village just prior to Siren's newly imposed curfew. Looking forward to their time together, Antboy regularly rose early to wash himself and to prepare the meals that they would share.

For Antboy, Lavender was more than just another one of the colonists. He trusted her implicitly. Her chestnut, luminescent hair fell in smooth waves upon her tiny, curved shoulders. Her eyes were warm and radiant with life and energy, reflecting the life she carried within her burgeoning womb. Her regal nose was dignified in its noble, aristocratic perch overlooking a vibrant, confident smile. She was more slender than most of the other colonists, and although not far along, her body looked like it carried no more than a single child.

From the moment he witnessed her awaken on their shuttle, Antboy felt something for Lavender that was strange and unfamiliar to him, and she stirred a sensation in him that could not be satiated. His eyes sparkled and his cheeks turned warm and his insides tingled when he first laid eyes on her. But it was the scent that emanated from her hair, her body, even from her white linen chemise wafting in tempestuous waves that mesmerized and controlled him.

Around her, he was no longer himself. Simply watching her distracted him entirely. In fact, he no longer knew who he was in her presence and he grew lost in the green, luxurious forest of her eyes, swallowed up in her voluptuous beauty, unable to suppress the tingling throughout his skin. Often he was speechless, a mute in love. He was unable to focus his attention on simple tasks when she drew near, for his desire was piqued, and he felt different than ever before.

But control was his only option; he had to exhibit control. He struggled with his inner desires, yet he knew that reason needed to prevail over passion, for otherwise the results could be disastrous for the colony. Restraint was necessary so he turned his mind to the past, to the discipline that guided his childhood, but in her company he agonized, for he felt giddy and somewhat silly.

Lavender also treaded upon the unfamiliar and peculiar path of unquenchable yearning. Confused by her pangs of longing for Antboy, she sought an explanation in the Codex, but none could be found. In fact, the Codex forbade relationships with Beasts, and she learned that their sole purpose was to provide the seeds of life, to be extracted at prescribed times, so that the society would thrive and grow.

But her emotions were undeniable, and they grew within her like the baby she carried. Antboy identified with her child, and respected her body, and patiently caressed her blooming stomach, now just two months shy of delivery. He imagined helping her care for the child but he knew that no such thing would occur, for he was an outcast in this society, a spectacle at best, superfluous.

Neither of them had ever experienced these feelings. Both were confused, and delighted, purely delighted to spend each successive day together. Even though they knew it was forbidden and impossible for them to share a future, they fantasized, enjoying each moment, allowing their love to deepen.

She was confused, deeply confused by what she felt, but in her confusion she began to grow restless when she was away from him, and she longed for his touch, his smell, his voice, and his attention. Similarly, Antboy paced like a caged animal when he awaited her daily arrival, and especially on the Day of the Spirit, every seventh day, he missed her sorely.

For on this day, Siren forbade colonists from leaving their domes for any reason, and none were to partake of fluids or food. Each woman was to care for her nest, and perform her mantra. There were times during the day of the Spirit that each woman meditated. Often they spent time in various stretching positions bringing blood and energy to key points within the body. Some danced and others chanted to achieve deeper, inner peace. A few spent intimate moments alone reaching ever deeper, inner sensual awareness, and exploring the depths of their bodies.

The women looked forward to this day, a day of rest, a day of self-satisfaction and meditation, a day of healing, thought, sensuality. On this day, though, Lavender was sad, for she knew that she would neither catch a glimpse of Antboy's brown, slightly graying hair, nor run her fingers through his curly arm hair, nor attempt to caress the now deepening wrinkles on his broad forehead, nor massage his knotted, tense shoulders, nor feel the press of his lips over her smooth, soft, swelling body. The morning after the Day of the Spirit, they embraced wholeheartedly and pressed close, for long periods, before they began the day's agenda.

Having overcome the majority of their communication barriers, they soon turned their attention to the functioning of the domes. Lavender was deeply impressed with his intelligence and technical skills. He was surprised at what a quick study she was. They efficiently reviewed the main elements guiding the colony's life support systems, the domes, and she learned proper operational maintenance procedures.

Lavender reported to Siren that she was learning much about the Beast's ways and the technical aspects of the sanctuary's ecological system. Lavender estimated that she would finish just before the birthing season began. When Siren asked about her progress, she prevaricated and reported that it was slow, for there was much to learn. Although she had already completed the Queen's primary assignment to learn his language and to understand the functioning of the dome technology, she still reported daily to his dome. At dawn she was always alert and at his door.

What Antboy most wanted to learn was the language of the Codex and how Siren, the colony's self-appointed Queen, interpreted and applied the HSI code. He felt the pages of the Codex but it seemed like nonsense and he became extremely frustrated.

How could HSI turn his philosophies and studies into a manual that he could not even comprehend? And how could the colonists understand these words? They had no formal study of language and the pictures and symbols seemed so primitive. Maybe that was it. Maybe the concepts and thoughts behind the raised symbols and pictures were based on a very primitive form of understanding, derived from pure instincts for survival and societal order.

Did these women have instincts that were so naturally part of every human, yet had been obliterated from sense and perception due to generations of neglect, apathy, and atrophy? Yes, he realized, they did. He felt betrayed and useless. How could he help the colony thrive if he had no idea what rules had been established?

He realized that the Codex provided guidelines for the colony to set up a societal order. HSI had designed it to achieve great success in preserving the species, to flourish and to remain on course. But what course? How could he know if they got off track and, if so, in what instance would he be allowed to interfere to keep the colony on target? Why was he even here? To pilot the shuttle, set up the domes, and teach them how to maintain them? Probably that was it. He should be grateful that they've even let him live, although as a pariah on the outskirts of the new world. What was he to them but a Beast? He was nothing more, and somewhat less.

Antboy wanted to crack the language of the Codex so he turned to Lavender for help. He asked her to help him comprehend the raised symbols and pictures scattered throughout the HSI code. He struggled and struggled but still there was nothing; he just couldn't understand. His fingers and hands told him nothing as they passed over the pages, and even the pictures seemed disjointed and foreign. Lavender ardently tried to develop his sense of touch, but to no avail.

"You must help me to understand this," Antboy pleads in their shared vocabulary, as he holds up the Codex. He wants Lavender to try to explain things to him.

"I will," she replies kindly, her lively, generous green eyes searching his face for understanding.

Then Lavender explains what she knows, and what she has learned from the other colonists who have studied the Codex, every night since their arrival, nearly five months earlier. Initially, what she explains, sounds like a presentation of his notes on ant research. Although he had assumed that the new female order would mirror the successful structure of the ants, the parallels are eerily, even deliberately and disturbingly familiar.

The Codex correlates the ants' societal system almost exactly to the projected order of the new society, in a cold, rationalized, matter-of-fact manner. The woman bearing the greatest quantity of female children will be Queen. As the provider of most life, she represents the strongest genes of the settlers and, by design, should guide the colony to great breeding success.

It was expected that Siren would bear the largest litter and be Queen, for she was the most voluminous and voluptuous of the group. Following each subsequent birthing season new numbers are to be tallied. The accumulated number of healthy female children born from a single Mother will determine if a new Queen should reign.

Below the Queen in hierarchal order are first, Mothers, then female children called Breeders, followed by Workers, and finally male children, Beasts. The society's labor-intensive duties will be relegated to Workers, those females that bear few or no female children, or bear children with genetic weaknesses. Workers will also care for and groom Breeders, instructing them in the ways of the colony.

Once deemed a Worker, one remains a Worker. Workers are no longer eligible to carry the seeds of life. Their uteruses are surgically removed, forever banned from the process of fertilization. Approximately twenty percent of the society will be placed in this category. This insures that the workload of the colony will burden not the child bearers, but instead those that are infertile.

Once the first birthing season concludes, permanent living arrangements are to be established. The Queen is to choose a select group of Mothers to sit on her Council. Each

Council Mother is assigned a dome, which she will share with three Mothers of similar fertility rank. Workers are prohibited from living in the same domes as Mothers and will reside in the Worker Village, in relative proximity to the Queen and the Mothers. Their lives are to be comprised of toil and duty, loyalty to the colony demanded at all times, self-sacrifice, if necessary, for the greater good of the society. Their responsibilities are considered essential to the colony, and the tasks they perform are necessary components to the proper functioning of the colony as a whole.

Siren instills in each colonist a sense of service to the community. She emphasizes that each segment of the society, Queen, Council Mothers, other Mothers, and Workers, have certain roles that contribute equally to the magnitude of the success of the settlement. A skilled orator, the prospective Queen Siren reinforces that the colony's continued existence depends on no one person alone. Instead, she espouses that triumphant survival is enmeshed in the symbiosis and synergy of each person's contributions, combined with every segment's active participation.

But when Lavender explains to Antboy exactly how the male children fit into this order, he is certain that she has misunderstood the Codex. He adamantly and emphatically argues that this part of the HSI code had definitely been misinterpreted in translation. It could not be, would not be, and should not be.

Males are considered Beasts, like him. Upon reaching the age of maturity, between thirteen and fourteen years of age, these males will be called upon for their life fluids, their seed. They are bred to breed, that is, if they are lucky enough to survive the colony's harsh, degrading conditions, and live long enough to vie for victory in the Endeavors.

His denial morphs into anger and he kicks and throws objects that come within his range of motion until he crumples in pain and frustration, like a heap of rubbish on the floor. In his agony he cannot clear his head of the picture that she has painted, so he sends Lavender away. She is perplexed, even hurt, by his sudden mood change and irate demeanor. She goes back to the probable Queen Siren to review this part of the Codex with her.

XXIV

When Lavender returns the day after Antboy's outburst, it's obvious she'd been crying for some time. Her eyes are completely bloodshot and her face is flushed a crimson red. Nervously, she goes intermittently to the dome's entrance to check if she had been followed. She can't hold her concentration long enough to tell him what happened. She can't even look him in the eye. She mentions that she has just violated the Queen's newly imposed writ banning her from visiting Antboy, and she cannot stay long.

She's overcome with panic. When she proceeds to again check the door, Antboy holds her shoulders and brings her close to him. Lavender sobs on his collarbone, and her anxiety sends spasms throughout her body causing painful abdominal twitches, which alarm her. She caresses her expanded, expectant stomach.

Antboy knows that Lavender is due in little more than a month, and she appears physically and mentally exhausted. Days before, she had confided in him that she rarely slept anymore because her heart raced with anticipation and adrenaline. Yet Lavender now displays more than normal apprehension and general fatigue. She is downright terrified.

Antboy needs to calm her down. It's evident that she no longer feels physically comfortable, her belly heaving with the toll of her emotional flood. Nor is she at ease in his dome, because she's concerned that Scouts are looking for her. As Antboy holds her close, his thoughts wander to nearly five months prior, when Lavender was the only one to awaken on the shuttle. Perhaps he should take her there. They can speak freely, without Lavender worrying about a Scout patrol. Then she can tell him what happened after she retired from his fit of anger yesterday. Not only is the shuttle hidden, secured in its docking bay, set directly upon the planet's surface, surrounded only by the oxygen-deprived nothingness of space, but it may also be nostalgic and bring her back to a serene state.

Motioning that he will be right back, Antboy crosses to a hiding space where he keeps the lanyard, which holds the key to the shuttle door. When he returns, she's doubled over in pain, and he lifts her up, supporting her, and leads her to the dome exit. They slowly traverse the short distance, and Antboy veers Lavender toward the most direct access tunnel, bearing eight false panels, which he removes hastily. From the cavernous docking bay, they proceed into the shuttle.

She rubs her hand along the metal of the shuttle door's exterior and she gasps from the cold metal against her outstretched palm. But she cannot take her hand away and she draws some form of inner calm and outward tranquility from the smooth metallic surface. Then they're inside and he shuts the door. They sit in the pilot seats at the front of the shuttle. For fear he might misplace the key, he drapes the lanyard over her neck, in plain view. By doing so he won't forget this precious item, which he seldom handles, always keeping it securely hidden.

For a moment, her panic and anxiety are replaced with adrenaline, a boost of chaotic, frenzied energy, when she realizes that what hangs from her neck is a key, a key to leave this world. For a brief radiant, bitter moment, she's overcome with a manic desire to flee. Frantically looking around the docked shuttle, she pleads, "Can we leave here? Please, I want to leave. Please. We must leave this place."

Unprepared, unplanned, unemotionally, almost unintelligibly, Antboy unforgivably utters, "No, we can't. Not now, not yet. Oh, Lavender, I'm so sorry, maybe not ever."

As her fingers caress the metal key around her neck, Lavender's expression turns peaceful and her voice and body relax. Dispassionately, she tells him that she had been disciplined in front of the tribe, endlessly it seemed, for questioning Siren's interpretation of the Codex. No longer fearful, Lavender instead resolves to recount Siren's reaction to her queries, and she relays the terrible events that befell her the evening before.

Lavender's grave mistake, questioning Siren regarding the Codex's prescribed treatment of males, was something Siren deemed unforgivable. Siren understood that the underlying source of these questions was Antboy, the Beast. She explained to Lavender that dissent is intolerable, as well as frolicking with a Beast. She reiterated that Antboy, the Beast, had been expressly denied the privilege of commenting and reflecting on their society by the HSI code that comprised the Codex.

Siren conveyed her thoughts to Lavender. She explained that what starts with an innocent question can lead to open questioning of their entire society. Siren espoused that she will never permit the sin of inquiry, from any colonist under any circumstance. Siren adamantly advised Lavender to brace herself for immediate repercussions for her haughty transgressions.

Siren pressed her Codex against Lavender's abdomen, and gazed at her. Siren recognized the emotional and unruly attachment that was growing between the Beast and Lavender. Siren felt threatened by this outside influence. Her insecurity, though, was masked by a dominant, livid, almost dictatorial stare. Her eyes glowed and dots of black began to form. Her pupils diminished in size and Lavender grew afraid, but she was unable to avert Siren's stare.

They continued to look into each other's eyes. Lavender felt her thoughts were being pierced. It felt like Siren was reviewing every one of Lavender's actions, thoughts, and emotions since they first landed on the planet, almost as if Siren were turning the pages of a book within Lavender's mind. As Siren examined Lavender, Lavender scrutinized Siren. Lavender recognized that she would no longer be allowed to visit the Beast.

The extent of Siren's power allowed her to thoroughly invade Lavender's mind, and Lavender perceived Siren's strength and succumbed to this intrusion. Siren was the dominant female, she held the power over the clan, and it was her right to probe, but it was painful for Lavender.

Siren was certain that Lavender had learned enough about the workings of their domes and structures to bypass their dependency on the Beast. She was confident Lavender could convey this knowledge, and pass it on to the other females.

Lavender knew what she had to do, for her own safety and Antboy's. With an indirect communication of body movement, she accepted her banishment from contact with the Beast. Accepting that this was intrinsic to the colony's survival, as well as for Antboy's safety, she humbly, gracefully, gratefully sublimated herself. But she was not prepared for what befell her.

With a twitch of Siren's eyelid, Lavender was swiftly commanded to leave the Queen and report to the Dome of Council. Lavender departed, her stomach fluttering and her hands trembling. She had never been so scared.

Within minutes, the females began to file in, and formed a circle around Lavender. Siren motioned to Isis who approached Lavender and helped her to remove her tunic. Soon Lavender stood naked in the middle of the circle, facing the standing women who clasped hands in unity, and she felt very alone.

The women sat in unison, looked balefully at Lavender, and then snarled and grunted, piercing her with their stares. Their sounds were grotesque, shredding her insides by the strength of their guttural, aggressive moans of utter abhorrence. Stabbed by the intensity of their eyes, Lavender so much wanted to die, for them to push her, cut her, choke her, or do something other than gawk at her, snarling.

Hours passed and her knees weakened, but Lavender was not permitted to sit or kneel. When her balance wavered, Siren held one palm upward and elevated it slightly and Lavender knew her penance was far from over. Tears streamed down her face uncontrollably. When she made a movement to wipe them, she was again motioned to remain standing, at attention, no movement allowed to garner pity, and then they began to spit.

Not in unison, but in solitary fashion did each woman reach within her throat and hurl their disdainful saliva at Lavender's face, her breasts, her child, her heart, her eyes, and she was expected to rotate. She turned to face each one as they spit on her from the perimeter of the circle. The females grew tired but continued to show their contempt by completing many rounds of discipline. Lavender completely lost her balance and stumbled to the ground. While on her knees, she struggled to rise but could not and she lay there.

Then she heard the rustling of tunics, and the circle of punishers rose. Lavender knew her remaining penance was due. Everyone stood, except the Queen and the fatigued Lavender. The colonists resumed spitting on her, no longer in rounds but all at once. Instead of holding hands, they stood with arms defensively crossed over their chests, and the hours passed interminably.

The females grew fatigued and many knees buckled after hours of standing. It was finally morning, and before the circle of unity could collapse in exhaustion, Siren dismissed the settlers. Filing out, they left Lavender naked, soaked and dripping with the excretions of their expelled disdain.

Lavender could not find her clothes anywhere. However, a tunic had been set aside by the door, unlike anything the others wore, made of a course fabric, much longer and bulkier, and marred by large brown stains, reeking of excrement. She realized that she was expected to wear this outfit to mark her trespasses and to display her guilt, to be replaced by the colony's traditional tunic when and if her status was to be restored. In the meantime, the feel, look, and smell of her new tunic, her badge of shame, immediately nauseated her.

Prohibited from seeing Antboy, Lavender realized that a single infraction would result in one month's banishment to the distant Dome of Darkness, away from the population of the colony. She innately knew what this represented. Colonists banned from social contact are at grave risk of developing lunacy, dementia, or general psychosis.

But Lavender knew that she could not possibly abandon Antboy, without at least telling him what had happened. Although she felt the imminent approach of her baby, she resolved to wash up and go to him. Unaware that she was dilating so rapidly, she went to him one last time.

Her eyes laden with tears, Lavender bids farewell to her love, not as a temporary departure but as an end to their relationship. Despite her solemn words, Antboy cannot believe that their brief intimate association is over. He finds it impossible to respond to the magnitude and gravity of her statement.

Unlike Antboy, Lavender accepts her fate. She realizes that their fragile association cannot compare to the bond of the colony, a feminine bond. Regardless of right or wrong, correct or incorrect, the colony is united, and Antboy is an outcast.

Denying that their farewell is definitive, Antboy is deeply determined to save Lavender from torment. He carries her to the shuttle, and he stubbornly, regrettably refuses her request to flee their dreaded planet. Aware that the full impact will not hit him until later, she kisses him, and he kisses her and they do not speak, for they hold each other close, and the words that each had struggled to learn are unnecessary. Their spirits speak for them and their bodies are close, very close, and they love one another. And then Atum tumbles into the world.

XXV

After saving precious, little Atum, Antboy allowed the colony to drift far, far away from his awareness. Antboy revolved around Atum; Atum was his world. Infant Atum became Antboy's drug, and nothing else mattered. The addiction overcame Antboy and his every move, breath, and thought surrounded the security and health of baby Atum. It was difficult and consuming in those first days and weeks.

Although Atum slept well, Antboy did not. His fear of Atum's jaundiced condition kept him on constant watch. At first Atum lost several ounces, but after many wakeful nights of timed feedings, Antboy trembled with joy when he finally saw evidence of his growing baby.

Antboy experimented with the dome's temperature and adjusted newborn Atum's swaddling to insure he was warm but not too warm. Despite the distorted foundation that underlay their society, Antboy regained hope by protecting and providing for the new life he called Atum. His theories, philosophies, and beliefs were meaningless in the face of this little green-eyed beauty that needed him, so desperately required him. Not a day went by without constant attention and care paid from father to son.

When Atum soiled his blanketed diaper, Antboy changed him immediately so that the infant was rarely in discomfort, with minimal rashes. With every hour and day that passed, Atum grew stronger and healthier, his color morphing from a yellowish brown to a pinkish peach. The attention that was continually lavished and endowed upon Atum by his doting, anxious, and protective father, matched or exceeded that of most natural parents.

Antboy had not known how helpless a little baby could be. Birds, dogs, horses, fish, and even ants all cared for themselves much sooner than did a baby human. So fragile, unable to feed, walk or speak, Atum depended upon Antboy. Caring for Atum was special, so uniquely important, and Antboy finally felt essential, and thrived due to this little boy's need for a father.

After Atum's deselection, and Antboy's banishment, the colony paid no heed to Antboy's whereabouts. His daily treks to the Dome of Nursery for milk, well after the expectant mothers were entombed in their nighttime reverie, went unnoticed. The females were busy making constant preparations for the incoming herd of newborns that were due to stampede into the world. No one noticed nor cared where the solitary, reclusive Beast roamed.

On these nocturnal expeditions to secure Atum's food, Antboy would sometimes witness storms of light that had fascinated him since his arrival on the satellite planet six months earlier. It wasn't until Atum turned ten that Antboy shared his knowledge of these storms of light. It was only Atum's persistence that led Antboy to finally share the mysterious and mystical, perhaps mythical knowledge that he had gained. What he shared, Antboy had learned on an ordinary evening during Atum's infancy, as he traveled the tunnels to get the boy's milk. It was a momentous day for father and son, when ten-year old Atum asked, "Father, I want to know more about metal."

Without responding to Atum's question, he instead tells Atum he's sorry for what he's done. He takes responsibility for his observations and research, which he so thoroughly documented and poignantly interpreted. His findings deserve merit, but only in theory, in a vacuum, or textbook. Adopted by the government as the template for a new human social order, his interpretations, though, were implemented on their planet in a most extreme manner, encoded into the Codex, despicable and perversely inflexible. He's certain that the colony's rigid structure shouldn't exist in reality. Nevertheless, his vehement protests of the Codex and its laws were disregarded.

Father tells Atum that he never doubted his decision to save him. He regularly reminds Atum to hide in the secure place if the Queen or her Scouts or Workers make rounds to their dome. It must never be discovered that Father saved Atum and hid him all these years.

He reiterates that Atum will be killed if he's found. The Queen, as supreme leader of the colony, interprets the Codex. Each Queen has found its prescription to be very clear. Its mandate, verbatim, is that certain children be "deselected for survival, unfit for various reasons, a risk to propagation, a drain on the colony's resources, and a scar on the genetic perfection required by the Colony."

And then he tells Atum about metal, the sacred, yet complex substance that shaped his world. "So you want to know about metal, is that right?"

"Yes, I do."

"Then, listen closely. Soon after we landed here, I saw balls of light spiraling to their distant, unique destinations. I was amazed by these beautiful storms of light. Although the light was heading straight for us, the storm consciously veered to avoid our colony. My curiosity was intense.

"Eventually, though, I no longer questioned the meaning behind the storms of light and instead looked forward to seeing them. They offered me comfort, comfort because I grew calm when I watched the serene, ephemeral, almost esoteric, whimsical nature of these multicolored, individual refractions of luminance. I became addicted.

"From the adjoining corridor to our dome, I would marvel at the spirited, growing balls of light as they sped to their destinations. They served as my counselors, my advisors, my mentors, my guardians, my parents, my judge and jury, my overseers and onlookers, and I would hold conversations with them. Most nights, while walking toward the Dome of Nursing to steal your sacred milk, I would glance upward through the translucent roof and, if my timing was right, I could catch the beauty and energy of a passing light storm.

"On one particular night I was admiring a light storm in wonderment, and I felt very open and warm. I noticed how each ball of light was different from every other one that passed overhead. I watched as they seemed to shift their gaseous, fiery, amorphous shape into an almost impercepti-ble curvature of a smile, some nodding, some waving, but all seeming to be at peace, and their salutations warmed my body and soothed my soul.

"As I was basking in their glow, I nearly jumped through the impregnable tunnel's roof when a shrill voice declared harshly, 'You don't even have a clue, not a clue.'

"I spun around anxiously seeking the voice, sensing dan-ger. My concern was that I had broken curfew and that our dome would be subject to search. I was afraid of what they would do to you if they found out I had saved you. But no one was there, not even an approaching or retreating shadow. Then I heard the voice again."

"Yoo hoo, down here, down here, come on, it's not like you haven't spoken to one of us before. Hello, Mr. Antboy. No, a little to your right, no, you've gone too far, just a little back to your left, that's right. You can see me better if you look really closely. Perhaps you can bend down a little and squint, yeah, yeah, right here, see me? That's right.

"Hi, I'm Lucy. Lucy Lips is what they used to call me, nice to meet you. I figured we'd meet some day, but it's been awfully hard to get your attention and, of course, I keep my family far away from the path of any wandering boots. That's because those boots are meant for walking, and they won't walk all over me, or my family for that matter. Hey, by the way, nice brood. Seems like you have a male in your clan.

"That's where I'm so different from my brethren. I'm balanced in my beliefs and that's why they couldn't stand me any more, pushing me to leave the colony. Well, anyway, that's why I'm here, to get away from it all, start my own family, and in my family the males and females are given equal treatment. How can we survive as a whole if not for the important roles that both sexes play in society? I mean, really, how can anyone see it any other way?

"Well, it's too hard to change certain predetermined beliefs that have existed for millions of years, so that's why I made the journey. Some ants that were housed in your top secret intelligence buildings rumored that there was a craft due to leave, bringing humans to another planet, a man-made satellite planet. I knew right away that I had to get on that ship. The naysayers said it couldn't be done, that the distance was too far, that there would be no food here, and that it was pure foolishness to make such a trip. But that didn't stop me; in fact, it inspired me, and I finally made it.

"I had no babies yet, so I was as free as could be. Once we bear children our lives change deeply within the colony. In fact, our movements, minds, and bodies are not the same. So, not only did I make the launch, the only ant by the way, but I was also the first one to board, and I was the last to depart, which was my hedge against stray boots.

"I'm so sorry. I haven't come up for air. I tend to talk so much, and that's one of the reasons I think my clan was happy to see me go. Just to shut me up, I guess. Well, they don't know what they're missing. I mean, you can't get much closer to heaven than this, can you?"

"Well, I," I began, but was interrupted by Lucy. She went on to tell me about herself. Lucy was quite different, admitting her ideas were a bit strange, and she didn't fit into the ant culture of her world. Pregnant upon entering the shuttle, she needed a break from the world. A break because she had become a pariah among her peers. None of her colleagues had heard of an ant wanting nothing to do with its colony. Ants were to function purely for propagation and had adopted a communal society. Ants, she explained, were given no rights to act alone or to venture forth on individual endeavors. Nevertheless, soon after arriving she made her home in a miniscule niche, just meters away from the shuttle dock where she gave birth to her first brood."

"Do you want to know what those balls of light are?" Lucy inquired a bit impatiently.

"Yes, do you know?" I asked.

"Of course I know. Humans sure are dense, and clumsy for that matter, stepping here, stepping there, and paying no heed to the rest of the living creatures in the world. I'm surprised I've even survived this long with all of your traipsing around. I told the father of my children to be careful and watch out for you folks, but he didn't listen. He was stubborn; aren't all males?

"We had hatched the perfect plan for him to avoid self-immolation and live a free life. Instead of waiting until dark, he just rushed right out into the daylight to live his newly emancipated life and, voila, just like that he was squashed. Never saw it coming.

"Sure wish we turn into balls of light like you guys but c'est la vie, or maybe I should say c'est la mort. You're the chosen ones, the ones with a soul, a spirit, free will, and all that jazz. So you get a few more benefits, heaven and all, than the rest of us lowly creatures. The funny thing is, we don't need heaven to live a fulfilled life, do good things unto others, and the rest of the stuff on the list. We just act according to ant nature, and that works just fine for us.

"Anyway, Nelson, as I called the father of my children, was always campaigning for equal rights and the like. He was imprisoned for much of his early life, before he was freed as a result of several large, unruly demonstrations that protested his imprisonment on the basis of habeas antus and other violated statutes. The conservative, older ants that ran our colony always considered me a radical liberal because I traveled in dissident circles. Due to my reputation, it was natural that I would eventually meet him at a protest.

"When I met Nelson picking up crumbs at that popcorn strewn, trashy bowling alley, it was procreation at first sight. What a night it was! I was a virgin until that night and I'd never imagined just how many positions an ant could be bent into. Nor did I realize just how many hours a male ant takes during the process, and how many times he takes his pleasure in the same night. Whew, I'm blushing just thinking about poor, brilliant, tragic Nelson.

"Well, on the night of our blessed union, after nothing was said but much was done, we lay on the bed and discussed so many things, even points of contention that we had with ant culture. Then we had a heyday ripping on the whole ridiculous human saga. We gleefully jumped around our cavern playing childhood games like ants in the pants, and my favorite, this little anty went to market.

"Suddenly he rushed over to the far wall and found a small crevice and stuck his head in there. Then he put all six of his legs perpendicular to the wall and began pushing outward. In an instant I was there pushing against his body to stop him from popping his head off. I realized that this was the sacred act of sacrifice that all males perform after the great act of fertilization.

"When I was just a wee antling, I first saw the ritual. I remember peering into one of the great chambers so that I could watch a grand ball. After everyone had finished dancing, the pairing off began and I watched the orgy with intense fascination. Even though I was still small, my hormones raged with desire.

"I can still taste the vomit, however, that convulsed through my body for what seemed like days, spewing forth when I saw the males jump from their partners and begin to claw and pinch and crush their own heads until they lay motionless, oozing the blood of an incomplete, wasted life. I was sickened with shame that I was part of the species.

"So I saved Nelson from his own destruction, and sternly reminded him what he stood for and what I believed in. Then I eloquently praised him for his essential work as a rebel of our times. I chastised him for adhering and conforming to the standards imposed on him by our society and made him promise not to commit the sacrificial act.

"He said he had no idea what drove him to want to pull his head off. He told me he must have blacked out, because an uncontrollable desire to end everything overtook him, and that's when the horrible, angry cursed voices started. All he wanted was to make them stop, and to rid himself of the pain, and his only thought was to rip his head off to end the wretched voices.

"I lectured him for hours on how necessary it was for him to remain alive, healthy, and safe so that he could fight for what we together believed in. We were both firmly against the self-destruction of males after fertilization. What he realized, though, was that there was an evolved, innate male ant desire to destroy oneself immediately after sex.

"I begged him to leave our colony and seek out another colony that was without a dream interpreter, since our colony already had one. I told him to immediately apply for a position, even if he never received any visions of how to interpret female dreams. I told him that he could pretend and invent advice so that he could live his life campaigning for equal rights.

"He was so excited about his prospects for success that, acting on complete impulse, he immediately raced out of our cavern without so much as a pinch goodbye. The next thing I knew he was squished between the ridges of a passing sneaker.

"So, like all antlings, my children are destined not to know their father. Did he turn into one of those balls of light? No way, not him."

Then, Lucy Lips enlightened me and told me what she knew. "Visualize a fluid-like substance, such as the mercury in a thermometer. Then envision this substance within a large sphere encompassing all that is known and unknown in the universe. Imagine that the life of this metal is boundless such that it universally envelops all shapes and forms, a multidimensional sphere. This sphere pushes ever outward and continues to expand its infinite greatness. Picture the substance within the sphere outlasting the flesh and blood of a human, or any living or inanimate thing for that matter. Like mercury, it shapes and molds itself, combining elements within itself to create the metallic cores that form the center of smaller spheres, or planets.

"These metals are the elements that comprise the planets and stars, and appear in different states, some gaseous, some liquids, and some solids. Metals create magnetism and gravitational pull, which form solar systems where one or more planets circle a star. If a planet receives the proper warmth and light from a star, fragile life is created and evolves, and is sustained and nourished.

"On the surface of a planet, and even within the planet's interior, life can take on many forms which are fragile, compared to the life of the metal that formed the planet. On some planets certain forms of life evolve into beings far more intelligent than others, but they are all partially derived from metal. Humans are that form on your planet.

"Your blood contains iron, a metal, which you depend upon to live, and there are electrical currents within your body. Upon death, those with positive accumulated energy travel great distances and become sources of light, stars. This illumination allows the universe to view itself and its magnificent creations. Over eons, luminosity from stars nurtures additional life to evolve within and throughout darker parts of the universe. However, those with negative accumulated energy enter the unlit space between planets and stars, known as dark matter.

217

"Biological life is dependent on planetary formation and the presence of a star. The formation of a core made of metal and the light provided by a star may, as on earth, provide a suitable environment for life to evolve and sustain itself. Humans, intelligent life with a soul, are a bi-product of the planet's formation. They rely on earth's metallic core for support and to offer the nutrients required for survival. Planets, if their metallic cores have matured properly for billions of years, attempt to produce and reproduce these bi-products, intelligent beings such as humans.

"Those that have positive accumulated energy, when deemed necessary, are recycled to become stars. Then they light the way for more life among the many elemental cores, throughout the infinite greatness of the universe, which comprises the circle of life. Do not fear death; it is part of the circular cycle of life.

"The circle is the eternal symbol. Life and death meet in one point on the circle. Its length is measured using a symbol that you call *pi*, which you recognize has no end. Therefore the circle has no end. It is constantly expanding. In fact, circles actually form in the shape of spirals, due to *pi's* constant expansion. When *pi* enters a predictable pattern, or actually ends so does time and space as you perceive them. At that point, the universe begins to retract, to later expand again, like the circle, or spiral of life and death. The universe is a macrocosm of your life, and you are a microcosm of hers.

"There are species, including the ants, whose senses of perception are heightened and more advanced than those of humans. This is why we accept life and death so easily, while humans continue to struggle with these changes in state. Humans dedicate so much of their lives to understanding life and death and to the battle between good and evil, which is really darkness versus light. It is a terrific shame that there have been thousands of years of disputes concerning religious and scientific explanations for creation and evolution. They all tell a similar story with different versions about the stars, the planets, the solar systems, and the universe which is itself both male and female, the union of life, death, and what follows, everlasting darkness and light."

"Stop, please stop," I begged, my hands firmly squeezing my ears, almost trying to pop my head off like Nelson did. All I could think of was that if every female ant was like Lucy Lips, then I totally understood why male ants would want to pop their heads off, to ease the pain. The agonizing years of future oratorical torture far outweighed the absolute, horrendous brutality of ripping one's head off. But for some reason, I felt I needed to hear more, even though what I'd already heard was far beyond my comprehension. Why couldn't the light storms that I marveled at be simply that, just balls of light? "First of all, Lucy Lips, how do you know all this?" I asked.

"It's absurd to think that you don't know this. Sorry to sound condescending, but..."

"Then don't."

"All right. Listen, just listen, and I will try to spell it out for you in terms that will hopefully make sense. We till the soil, and oxygenate it. That's our role.

"Earth, at its core, is a ball of metal. This ball of metal, an amalgamate of elements and compounds, is within the expanding sphere, which encompasses everything. Every star you see, every planet, everything you have eaten, every animal you have seen, every car you have driven, and book you have read, is within the body of the sphere, which you call the universe.

"The universe is dark, but much of it is lit as well. The light comes from stars. That is the key point here. A planet starts out as a loose collection of elements that forms a metal core in its infant stages, and then congregates into a sphere. With proper care and love from a star that provides light and warmth, the sphere of elements might grow and mature enough to form a planet. Over billions of years, a planet may eventually provide and support many layers of multiple life forms. However, sometimes certain require-ments are unfulfilled and a planet does not evolve to support intelligent life.

"It requires tremendous intelligence for a species to sur-vive the changing conditions of the earth's surface and its atmosphere. Many of earth's earlier species were not able to intelligently adapt, and they became extinct. Certain species lived and died for millions of years to provide the proper environment and balance of elements necessary to incubate, birth, and support younger species, like humans.

"Ants only grow on planets that are evolved enough to need our services. Our role is essential to your continued survival, because every living species on an evolved planet is key to the successful survival of every other species. It is this balance that must be maintained and if it isn't, a planet will fail. As ants, our role is to reproduce massively. We must have huge hordes ready to do the work necessary, living right beneath your feet.

"We cannot afford to feed and house our males, so they sacrifice themselves. But the males know they must provide the required seed and then let the females run the show. We females are great workers and mothers, very organized, highly motivated, and some birth the antlings necessary to till the soil so it can receive oxygen. Without the soil oxygenated, the planet will not breathe, and then it cannot support the food and other species that humans depend upon. It seems so complicated but yet it's so simple."

"I guess."

"Don't guess. Just be grateful. Some planets never form a stable surface. Without the many layers of earth beneath your feet, and the millions of species and elements that support this upper layer of crust, you would not survive. Humans do not recognize how dependent they are on this layer. Instead, because they are selfishly absorbed, they destroy it.

"You dig and dig and drill until you extract, ever expeditiously, the lifeblood of the earth. But this lifeblood, oil and metal from the interior, is as necessary for the planet's continued life as blood is for the pulsing of your heart. The extraction of metal, the blood, from the nucleus of the planet remains an act of danger and disrespect.

"Yet, you continue to invent and extract which disturbs the fragile balance of the earth's weight, threatening planetary destabilization. As a matter of fact, your inventions require a continuous flow of blood from the planet to fuel the ever-increasing desire for new technology. Human fascination with technology is a tremendous gamble and is increasingly addictive. Humans love to gamble, with their money, with their lives, a highly intelligent species that unfortunately thrives on risk. We ants believe that you not only depend upon but are also obsessed with conveniences derived from your metallurgical technology.

"I will never understand why you cannot see the damage that metal has wrought upon your world. To tamper with the metal within the earth is to ignore the effect that this metal core has on the position of the planet in the solar system, its distance from the sun, and weather patterns, particularly storms. The result is ominous: torrential rains, relentless snow, flooding in temperate zones, earthquakes and tsunamis in areas previously considered stable, drought where water had been plentiful, and tornados of great depth and breadth.

"In your quest to make your lives more comfortable and convenient you instead complicate, burden and risk your survival mercilessly. This isn't the path that the planet envisioned for you. You weren't supposed to invade and exploit the planet. Well, I'm ready."

"Ready for what?"

"A simple thank you would be nice. I mean, really. Come on. After what I just said, don't you want to thank me for an eternity of toil that our species has had to endure to support your lifestyles? And not only are we unappreciated, as is evident from the lack of a thank you after my whole speech, but you actively try to annihilate us. You even form corporations to make chemicals, and bottle, market, and distribute them just to kill us because we inconveniently stumble into your homes. So, obviously, if you don't know why the ants are around, then you couldn't possibly have a single clue as to why you're here."

Then, for whatever reason, she just stopped. Lucy Lips just shut her ant mouth and stared at me, almost belligerently. She was highly disappointed in the toil of her brethren and the years of slavery for an ungrateful master. So she began to stare me down. The stare was alive with passion and disappointment and it pierced my soul. I felt obligated to say something, to respond, so I said, "I'm sorry Lucy, but now I'm more confused than before."

Lucy's glare dissipated and she smiled benevolently at me and said, "If I could, I'd wrap my six legs around you and give you a big hug. You're a pitiable species, yet you hold such great power in your spirit. It's the strength of your spirit, which produces the intense energy of your soul. You've been empowered with a soul. This is how you differ from other species. You are both blessed and cursed with this soul. You have choices, unlike other species that are predestined by the natural order to follow certain laws thereby reducing choice. But because of the various options from which you may choose, humans are entitled to not only the glory but also the burdens of everlasting life. The whole thing is so simple."

"Then please explain it simply. I can't stand here much longer."

"Well, if you're so tired of standing, then just sit down, after all, I'm getting a pain in my neck, craning my ant brain up to look you in the eye."

With this rebuke I sat down, although I was disgruntled by her superior tone.

Lucy continued, "When you die, the energy that you have accumulated in your soul is the only asset you take with you. This energy, upon your death, transforms into heat, and light, and travels upward through the heavens, so to speak, attracting matter and gaining in mass and speed, easily piercing through the dark matter.

"Every human is born to accumulate positive energy, and to ultimately bring this energy into the far reaches of the unlit universe, growing along the journey to eventually become a star. As a star, one provides the warmth and light needed to nurture a planet.

"Humans with a negative spirit lack the energy necessary to travel through the dark matter. They do not become stars. Instead they find themselves stuck in the dark matter, empty space, trapped for eternity in the lifeless void, alone.

"So it's a continuous life cycle, filled with good and bad, life and death, rebirth, and the white light and the dark matter. From our vantage on this satellite, you get to see the balls of light on their way to becoming stars. Those are the storms of light that you marvel at."

The stunned silence was deafening to my ears. What she had spoken so altered my perceptions that the soundless corridor continued to echo her last words, again and again.

After a few moments, Lucy continued, "However, your planet and your sun may regret their decision, their mutual resolution to select your species for life. In your planet's history, other species have become extinct due to unlivable conditions caused by the earth and the sun. The earth or the sun may turn against you, especially if you threaten the survival of either one of them. Actually, you might alter the planet in such a permanent way that makes it impossible for your species to survive. This could perhaps force the earth and sun to choose another species to evolve toward a higher consciousness than yours, and replace you."

"Replace us?" I asked, but Lucy Lips had left.

"Son, after Lucy Lips left, I made my way to the Dome of Nursing and then returned to feed you. You were asleep with drying tears upon your cheek. You must have been wailing for quite a while, waiting for me.

"What she had told me was mesmerizing, overwhelming, and startling, but it made little sense to me. She taught me about the power and importance of metal, and tried to explain certain things that remain a mystery to me. In those early days of the colony, I was more concerned with securing your survival than the complex things on which she lectured. You were only a month old when the birthing rituals began, and I needed to make sure you were properly nourished and remained undetected by the colony."

XXVI

The colony was united, a single being with a sole purpose, birthing a new generation, on our satellite planet. A noble and inherently necessary meaning for existence pervaded and permeated the daily routines of the females. Certain hierarchal stratifications began to become evident in the days before the swarms of births were due. The largest women, possibly hosting as many as six newborns, now intuitively rested, allowing the other, smaller women, to do their share of the preparations. There was no dissent to this practice.

Before the journey to this planet, within a sterile, scientific environment, these women had been educated and infused with knowledge directed to achieve one sole aim, the continuation of the species. The Colony had been designed for the benefit of the species, to put the needs of the whole above the needs of the one. Therefore, the HSI code was planned around this fundamental concept, which placed survival of the species as a whole as the highest priority, disregarding the individual needs of any one colonist. Human rights did not exist under this code, only the rights of the entire species. At all costs, the species needed to survive and eventually flourish.

Governments supported the Human Survival Initiative, which permitted science to tamper with creation. Ants were studied, and then defined. Plans were made, and then executed. Humans were saved, but humanity was destroyed. Actions and emotional responses once considered inhuman were somehow deemed appropriately humane.

The colonists had been exposed to the concept of the ocean. The ocean ebbed and flowed as a whole. Individual drops did not affect the ocean's strength and depth. In fact, some drops of water in the ocean were lost upon the sands of the shore, pushed outward by the ocean herself. Others evaporated into the atmosphere, sometimes to be returned in the form of precipitation. Some were swallowed by the very life that the ocean supports. But the ocean as a whole was unaffected, and was not concerned with its individual drops so long as it flourished. Thus the females of the colony were just drops in the ocean; the colony was the ocean herself.

There was no resentment, no misunderstanding of the personal sacrifice necessary to sustain and benefit this ocean, with the exception of one salty droplet, Lavender. She had been affected deeply by her treatment at the hands of the other colonists. Yet Lavender knew that she could bring no attention unto herself. If she did, then it would show the ocean that a drop of water desired to elevate its importance higher than the entire body of water, which is unacceptable.

So Lavender smiled, and worked more diligently than anyone could have expected. She hid her anger, buried her disappointment, and masked the feeling of betrayal that pervaded her every breath, movement, and thought. Slowly plotting her rise to power, Lavender undoubtedly appeared to be the most unselfish of all drops of water. But in her denial, stemmed immense power.

As Lavender suppressed her desires, and strove to achieve the goals of the group, she grew in strength, almighty strength, and her intense patience fueled that might. Unwearyingly, she healed her wounds but allowed some, invisible to the naked eye, very deep, emotional, internal damages, to fester and grow. Lavender did not want those injuries to heal.

Lavender had experienced emotions that she did not know she possessed, yet could no longer deny. For her own survival she had no choice but to suppress her ceaseless desire for revenge, adding salt to her unhealed wounds. She believed that eventually she would no longer be considered the outcast of this group, an embarrassment, and its example of failure. However, Lavender wanted much more than that. Only time would tell what she could achieve. For better or for worse, she would quench her quest for vengeance.

Lavender gained the trust and confidence of the colony in the month between her doomed birth and the wave of expected births. No longer the victim, she was instead the survivor, a true inspiration to the colony, and she busied herself tending to every expectant mother, especially the Queen. They observed a penitent, dutiful, thoughtful colonist, doing her civic duty to the colony, and she was praised for her good work.

Burying her feelings so deep within her soul, Lavender sometimes forgot where she had hidden them. This helped her to forget, momentarily, that which caused her the greatest pain, the source of her bitterness, the leader of their tribe, her nemesis, Queen Siren. Doting upon the Queen, massaging Siren's swelling stomach, Lavender smiled, raising a cup to give Siren the fluids that she needed. Sometimes Lavender forgot about her own stomach, filling incessantly with the acidic lifeblood that pervaded her, the innate meal of hatred, jealousy, and anger tempered with patience and insight, which fueled absolute, necessary revenge.

"Would you like another cool, damp cloth for your warm forehead, my beautiful Queen?"

"Yes, dear, dear Lavender. What would I do without you, my Lavender?"

"Never you worry about that, my Queen, never you worry for I shall never leave you alone." *As long as you take breath within those lungs, I shall never leave you alone, never, never,* Lavender thought.

Birth became contagious, and Mother Sekhmet was the first to deliver. Nearly every four hours thereafter a female was ushered to the Dome of Birth. Lavender and the original three birth attendants worked day and night.

Within four weeks over one hundred sixty babies had arrived. Babies were separated according to their gender. Delivering Mothers were attended by nurse Workers, a group comprised of colonists who had miscarried or had birthed only male children. News spread throughout the colony about the health and quantity of each Mother's litter.

Workers retrieved the newborn baby girls from the Dome of Nursing every few hours, so that they could feed directly with their Mothers. Baby boys were immediately removed from the Dome of Birth and were delivered directly to the Dome of Beasts, to be placed in very small box-like cribs that prohibited nearly all movement. In this manner, the newborns could not accidentally roll over and suffocate. But they cried incessantly due to their cramped conditions. Their isolated dome was far removed from the colony's center, on the outer fringes. These infant boys were as distant from the Village as Antboy's Dome of Maintenance, but on the planet's opposite pole.

The HSI code was exceedingly clear that males were unnecessary to human survival, notwithstanding their seed. Since a single, strong genetic specimen was all that was needed to fertilize multiple females, few males were needed. Those surviving with the least food, attention, and medical care were deemed to be the strongest of the lot. Still, it was in the colony's best interests not to completely neglect this part of the brood. The colonists believed that these males were beasts, a subspecies whose necessity to the females' survival was considered a black mark, an embarrassment representing true weakness in human evolution. Nevertheless, they were needed, and these little, crying beasts were awarded the bare minimum to survive.

While the baby girls were held tight to their mothers' bosoms, covered in blankets that comforted them and provided them warmth, the baby boys knew not what comforts they lacked. Most adapted quickly, acclimatizing to the cold, and adjusting to the hunger, discomfort, and filth, surviving only due to their innate, intense desire to truly live, and they were strong. Some tried, but failed to become accustomed to their environment and expired.

The order of the women was soon established. Siren, as expected, carried six children, and five survived the removal from her surgically sliced abdomen. Four were healthy girls, with one surviving boy. Her female reproductive organs were unblemished in the process. Her recovery was immediate, and she regained her strength quickly.

Others also delivered five healthy babies, but no one other than Siren carried four girls. A few colonists witnessed none of their children survive, or they bore only boys, so they were deemed Workers. They underwent HSI's required surgical procedures, which dismantled their abilities to reproduce.

Workers were coordinated by Lavender to help Mothers, by lifting, carrying, comforting, and even nursing the new babies. In fact, the milk of the colony became an ocean and it flowed wherever it was needed, some here, some there. None went without this very vital, natural food. Though sparsely rationed in bottles to the boys, even they received their sustenance.

Lavender was essential to their success. She reviewed the needs of the colony daily. Lavender helped Queen Siren rule in the weeks following the waves of births, paving the way for Siren to hold supreme power and to command grateful respect. When needed, Lavender was soon at Siren's side. The colony utilized Lavender more than previously expected because she was the only female to understand how the domes worked. When the Mothers were assigned four to a dome, according to fertility ranking, Lavender attended to the domes, their maintenance, food, temperature, and other environmental controls. She did so lovingly and with care.

Lavender accumulated all the data necessary to stratify the colony into its different categories of Workers and Mothers. In marginal cases she decided the fate between Worker, Mother, and Queen's Council, and she did so unmercifully and intuitively, without premeditation. Though assigned the status of Worker, below all the Mothers, Lavender was the Chief Worker and therefore attended the Queen's Council meetings. All Workers regularly reported to

Lavender, they respected her orders, and the colony ran smoothly.

While Lavender continued to care for the children of other Mothers, she internally mourned the loss of her one and only child. Meanwhile, Antboy continued to care for Atum, his precious secret, her consuming grief. Lavender watched and waited, and so did Antboy.

He furtively watched the settlement grow strong, and with this strength he secretly watched Siren grow stalwart. Surreptitiously, he spied Lavender by Siren's side quite often, and it was obvious that his one and only love had adopted all the ways of the HSI code. Lavender was a model citizen, a true follower, a Worker by destiny, and at times a leader. She appeared content and carefree, never looking upon the past, casting not even an occasional stare in the direction of Antboy's dome.

Antboy remained on the fringes of this culture, banned from the colony. He was assigned to attend only certain distant common areas, strictly for the purposes of major dome maintenance. Since Lavender was too busy to handle every maintenance task, Antboy picked up the slack, which allowed him to visit the Dome of Beasts where he was instantly sickened by the decay and mistreatment.

While making his daily trek to the remote Dome of Beasts, Antboy wondered how their outpost could have been allowed, by the propaganda that was the HSI code, to become so inhuman. He realized that these colonists had been ingrained with a completely radical philosophy never before imposed. They followed a roadmap of incorporated regulations contrived to prevent man from ruling again. Distorted from his originally constructive master plan, this deformation was disturbing and sickly twisted. However,

Antboy quelled his disgust and focused solely on caring for Atum and helping the other boys settle in.

Antboy's daily goal was to obtain milk and clean clothing, so he brought Atum to the dome of horrors, the Dome of Beasts where both were available, however sparsely. Unable to ignore the neglected boys, he tended not only to Atum but also to the many hungry, filthy, needy babies. He took several at a time from their cribs, placing them upon blankets on the floor. Removing their swaddled blankets, he scrubbed and scraped the filth from their little bodies. The infants began to calm down, almost contagiously, and as their panic subsided their crying ceased in all corners of the dome. Grabbing spare blankets and cloths, he fashioned diapers and clothing for each newborn. Heaping the dirty laundry in a pile, he rinsed and soaked their clothing.

Manipulating the food generator, Antboy concocted a mild liquid formula that would replace the limited breast milk that was being meagerly doled out to the tots. From unused tubing that flanked the far side of the dome's interior wall, he strung the tubing from crib to crib and then to the food generator providing a liquid food source. He showed each infant how to turn his head slightly and purse his lips to suck the milk. To avoid choking and suffocation each child needed to burp, without which there would be great risk. Antboy shoved cloth under the top legs of each crib to elevate the head and chest of each little one, essentially limiting the risk of crib death.

Because he could not stay long, he did the bare minimum for each newborn. If he were discovered, the consequences could be tragic. Sponge bath, clean clothing, swaddle blankets, on-demand feeding, and eye contact were his routine.

Looking each neglected baby in the eyes, Antboy spoke to their souls. He told the infants that they would be fine, not to worry, not to cry, that tears would do nothing, only dehydrate them. Antboy reassured the boys that he would come back each day, every day, and to calm down and be strong. He told them they would have gas, and sometimes pain or fear, but that he would return as promised. His communicative eye contact was as effective as any word ever spoken, any poem possibly written, or any love song once sung, and the children believed, they really had faith and trusted the kind eyes of Antboy. They saw deep into his soul, having no other method of communication to honor, or to respect than his eyes and voice. They grew assured and gained confidence that he would arrive each and every day as pledged.

The changes he had made to the dome were drastic. Whoever was to attend to these babies would be astounded at the radical improvements to their living conditions. Antboy hoped they would assume that a Worker, upon orders from the Queen or Lavender, had made these changes. Perhaps the attending Worker nurse would not question the modifications, and instead would maintain the sanitation, comfort, and nourishment essential to each child's survival.

One night, very late, during a time when the boys were usually unattended, Antboy was holding Atum in his arms when he heard a rustling somewhere within the Dome of Beasts. Turning instantly, fear and anxiety gripped him. He had taken too long and had been discovered.

"Who's there? Who are you?" Antboy asked. A form shot toward the door, but Antboy ran quickly and stealthily, cutting the woman off before she could flee.

She trembled, and dropped several bottles of milk and a few clean blankets on the floor. Tears streamed down the young woman's face, her knees buckled in fear and she stumbled to the floor, tightly clutching a newborn baby girl to her bosom, defensively and protectively. Clutching his own child, he stood a short distance from her. They stared at each other, while Antboy stroked his son's forehead.

Antboy noticed her thin stature. Low on the hierarchy level, this woman had been assigned the task of tending the little Beasts, as these babies were deemed.

After a few moments, one of the babies near the rear of the dome began to cry and she instantly, intuitively, rose to tend to the child. Antboy's wide smile registered not upon his face but instead was revealed within his core, an internal smile as broad as the largest chasm of the most extensive mountain range in planetary history, and his body grew limp with relief.

Offering his assistance, Antboy approached the woman, but she needed no help. He pointed to the basket of dirty blankets and diapers. Acknowledging the need for sanitation, she began to settle in for the long evening ahead.

Before departing, he lifted his baby to eye level and said, "Atum." Pointing to her resting infant she said, "Ava," and to herself, "Constance," the name Antboy had allocated to her months earlier. With a fluid motion, Antboy formulated a symbol that said he would return the next day.

Childcare was Antboy's only concern, his only duty, a fitting role for one inclined to save humankind. He realized that nothing in the past could be changed. The surreal situation that had befallen him could not be evaluated, contemplated, or understood. Glorious days and nights turned into exhausted weeks that transformed into neces-sary months.

So needy, these little lives were sustained by Antboy and their benefactor Constance. She rarely communicated with Antboy and still feared him. After all, he was a Beast, a heathen, who could contaminate her, as he had done with Lavender. However, she always placed Ava in a crib adjacent to Atum, and the babies soon learned to turn their heads to stare, coo, and smile at each other.

XXVII

Meticulous and methodical, Lavender performed her daily tasks without joy, devoid of emotion, and raw. She was the heartiest of the colonists and was relied upon by every member. Ingratiated and dependent, the colonists and Queen turned to this pariah, this disgraced member of their group, elevating her to the status of martyr. For Lavender had sacrificed much and was consistently dedicated.

Lavender was fundamentally ardent concerning their adherence to the principles of the HSI code, almost a zealot with regard to its interpretation. Every evening in the Dome of Study, Mothers and Workers, and sometimes the Queen and her Council, would attend Lavender's sessions of Codex study. Everyone marveled at her command of its language. When the evening discussion opened to analysis and evaluation, Lavender offered guidance and was trusted by all. Her immense sacrifice, miraculous recovery, and full reinstatement into the settlement only affirmed that she was the strongest believer and representative of all that HSI purported.

Lavender let no one down, taking care of everyone, except herself. She wept inwardly, suppressing all emotions and desires for the benefit of the colony. Yet her tears were oceans of torment captured in the body of a strong, though broken woman. Bereft of her only child, never again to experience the force and spirit of carrying and providing life, Lavender was solely a caregiver to the other Mothers. Tirelessly, she served those who had unanimously chosen to destroy the precious life that was her son, the same colonists who had marked her as a shameful example.

Lavender set her individual value far below those of the other settlers. Her example to the others was one of transformation and triumph, and she subordinated her needs to the whole, just a drop of water that understood its irrelevance in the vast ocean.

However, Lavender knew that this drop of water would one day become the ocean. She watched and waited, the epitome of patience, but when alone, she cried, sobbing convulsively for her lost little boy. Through her pain she grew strong, for she recognized that her day would come.

Thoughts of Antboy diminished entirely for Lavender as the months passed. Primarily banished to his isolated Dome of Maintenance, Antboy rarely crossed her path, and he was quite occupied. For nearly a year, he generally spent his time tending to Atum and the other boys in the Dome of Beasts.

One night, triggered by the familiar cries of his charges, he reminisced to an event in his distant military past.

Antboy was in the dark for what must have been several days before he heard the cries. They were distant and muted, at times terrific wails, calling for needed attention.

He was certain that all combatants had completely left the mountainous region, now his imprisoned home. Yet, he still faced great anxiety, this time from the desperate weeping, ever close, yet very far from the enclosure confining him.

Antboy's meals consisted of anything slimy or moving that made its way into his dank kitchen. His liquids were derived from the occasional drips that fell from the roof of his dungeon confinement. His pillows were rocks, his bed a slab of slate, his light nonexistent, and his domain so small that he could not lie down head to toe without brushing against the narrow walls.

Wedged solidly into the boundary of this enclosure was the barrier to his passage, an immense boulder that had been dislodged, imprisoning Antboy in this obscure nook. He was not willing to rot, to die, or to reap the harvest that his adventure had sown. All that was left were his thoughts, the darkness, and now, probably just a trick of his malnourished mind, a baby's cry.

For hours Antboy listened to the wails, absolutely certain that he was dying. He was certain that his ears, which had begun ringing after a few days of tormented, doomed silence, had concocted this new manifestation of insanity, which was slowly creeping upon him. So he tested his theory, and shouted out to the baby. The infant responded by growing silent for a few brief seconds, and then, upon further consideration, howled more hysterically, now panicked. Seeking the attention it hoped to receive, the child's cries grew more desperate, almost frenzied, its natural desire and attempt to establish a homing signal.

Antboy's heart beat rapidly, having not anticipated such a dilemma. If the baby were real, his own torture would be that much worse. Listening to its distressed cries to get help, Antboy wanted nothing more than to pierce his own wretched eardrums. Its instinct for survival was desperate. If the baby's wails were strictly a hallucinatory fantasy, then his misery was unrelieved, and his fate sealed, because dementia was fast approaching.

Antboy sang out to calm the baby, trying to soothe and pacify the abandoned child. The newborn listened, and responded, quelling its heaving lungs momentarily, believing that someone would help him. But every few moments the baby lost control. Then Antboy attempted to appease the infant again, and this routine continued for many hours.

While calming the child, Antboy was still unable to free himself, and he was attacked by waves of panic. He felt like he was dying, and he began to capitulate. His spirit and soul were readying for his demise and lifting him into another place, a heavenly realm, where death would release him. He knew that death was imminent. He had tried every possible avenue of escape. While death beckoned him, he still sought release.

Antboy threw himself at every portion of his cell, but the rocks incarcerating him did not acquiesce. With renewed vigor he shook and pounded at the wedged barrier, but all that remained was his pain, his bones unable to withstand the brunt of these impacts, his thinning muscles and fat giving way to painful bruising, perhaps fractures.

Still the baby's cacophonous cries persisted and every few moments Antboy's lullabies soothed the infant, this pattern repeating for a day, a night, and then most of another day. The sobbing was too loud, a crashing crescendo heaped upon his battered, abandoned mind. Time was fleeting, and he would not last much longer in these caves.

Antboy could no longer soothe the petrified child. He was unable to sit by and continue listening to the anxious moans. His time had come; the end was fast approaching, and he could endure no more pain. It was certain that no one would come for him, and there was no possible escape.

There was no food to sustain him and his body and mind were starving. His thoughts were incoherent and did not follow linear reasoning. In fact, there was no reason left, and his only desire was to end the pain. Not soothe it, not ease it, but terminate it, for good. The wailing would not stop; it was incessant.

Screaming, shrieking his death cry, trying to scream louder than the howls of the starving, abandoned child, Antboy knew his time was diminishing. He grew angry, so very infuriated, almost boiling, and adrenaline pulsed through his brain and body. It was thick, very profuse adrenaline, powerful, strong in its dosage.

There was nothing that could stop him; he would succeed. He put his head against the bordering barrier of the boulder and he pushed. He shoved his head until it squeezed and ground through to the other side of the cave. From the inside, Antboy grabbed the great rock with his two hands and he raised his feet flat against it, using the leverage to push, to thrust with all his might. He turned his head so that his chin and the back of his head made it impossible for his head to come back inside the pen. He rammed as hard as possible with both of his feet and both of his hands. His head hurt so much it felt like his neck was stretching, stretching impossibly, and the vertebrae in his neck and back were elongating and stretching. It would be just a few more moments until his neck would break or his head would tear off. If only he could endure this tormented, excruciating pain for a few more seconds or minutes. He felt like he was about to pass out, from the pain, the horrific ache. Then he thought, *No more, no more pain,* and with all of his might and strength he gathered his energy for one more grand shove and then, with a pop, it came right off, and began rolling along the floor. No more pain, no more suffering, it was over and the sole giant rock that had supported his captivity, stood at his mercy. With sore neck and bruised soul, Antboy was freed.

In the ruckus, the baby had stopped crying, perhaps terrified by Antboy and his yelps of pain. Stifled sobs could be heard in the distance and Antboy called out to the tot, trying to determine its whereabouts. When the infant heard him approaching, its wails reached a new crescendo of terrified apprehension, worried that it would never be found.

It was because of this child, and this child alone, that Antboy was free. He was determined to rescue the infant. They were interdependent, and a debt of equal gratitude needed to be repaid. He had to find the child, immediately.

Naked and exposed to the elements, a little boy covered in his own fecal matter, thin as a board, appeared in a distant crevice. Crying without tears, dehydrated as a desert rose, illuminated by a glimmer of light that peeked through an aperture in the rocks, the tot stared unfocused as Antboy grabbed him.

Then he ran aimlessly, child wedged between his elbow and chest, cradled in his hand, and he hurried down pathways that he hoped led toward the distant light. The light that was just a glint became a shimmer, then a sparkle, an illumination, then a swath of sunlight. He ran toward the glow and it was bright, so very intensely brilliant. He placed his remaining free hand protectively over the child's eyes, though Antboy himself was quickly blinded by the piercing rays of sunlight, and soon they were doused by its warmth.

Falling to his knees and lowering his head to the ground, Antboy opened his eyes after a few, brief moments. He focused on the dry, smooth earth pressing against his cheek and eyes, poking into his left temple. He saw a colony of ants busy at work. The ants noticed nothing out of the ordinary about this filthy, starving man, bent over with his filthy, starving child. Then he was vastly sick. The ants rapidly scattered, but soon festively feasted upon the upheaval of his billowing bile.

He picked himself up and moved steadily along the ridge of caves that, for days, had housed him and this poor, lost child. He sat and rested and cradled the now sleeping infant in his arms. He vaguely remembered the maps he had been given prior to insertion into this desolate area. His forces had cut off the enemy combatants and trapped them in this mountainous region. Antboy supposed that their village was somewhere to the northwest.

He knew that the child would soon die without necessary nourishment and shelter. There was no suitable shelter, food, or water to be found, and they were both extensively dehydrated. Northwest was the only choice. Right into the hands of the enemy, the lion's den, but the child would be saved, and hopefully Antboy's life spared.

Onward he plodded, across the sun scorched, dry earth, in search of the village, which bordered a river. He knew that if he could stay utterly and intensely focused, that he would make it. A drink of water, cool, crisp, refreshing hydration, was all he wanted, and he was determined to get it, even if it took miles, hours, days. If his knees would not buckle, his arms not tire holding the child, and his bare feet not give up he would get there.

Because his clothing had been shredded in his attempt to escape the cave, his half-naked torso burned in the strong desert sun. The sweat stung his wounded, bruised body.

Alone in the vacuum of the desolate desert, he wondered if they would survive. The newborn gave him impetus to continue his seemingly endless quest. The infant needed Antboy's feet to keep walking, and so he did, with a renewed purpose. One step, two steps, save the child, three steps, four steps, must rest, no, must keep going, getting closer, much closer. He convinced himself that the little water remaining in his body, rapidly leaving his porous skin, would soon be vitally replaced.

Reports said that combatants flourished in the region but there were none to be found. No water, food, or suitable shelter appeared on the horizon, and the heat was utterly oppressive. For a brief instant Antboy thought he spied a structure ahead and he picked up his pace and proceeded directly toward it. As he bridged the gap, Antboy realized he was approaching nothing more than a monstrous boulder, just a big ominous rock. There was shade and a good place to rest, maybe even sleep. No, he should not sleep; he should only rest. He needed a slight break from the exorbitant exposure that plagued him. Closing his eyes for a few minutes, Antboy knew everything would be...

The pain of his cheekbone being crushed startled him. Holding his hand to his face, he was unable to comprehend anything. In front of his unfocused face were blurred shapes and he kept opening and closing his eyes but to no avail. He heard some shouting and something poked him in his already throbbing rib cage. Trying to rise, first moving on his hands and knees to elevate himself into a standing position, he realized he could not see.

His vision was blurred and his equilibrium was off, and he kept falling. Every time he fell, he heard strange, guttural laughter. As he stood upright and steadied himself, something, perhaps a rifle, smashed the weak areas behind his knees, buckling his legs, collapsing his body backwards and he thudded heavily to the ground. Again, laughter, and then he heard a baby cry, so familiar the sound.

Antboy reached out his hands to the sound, and then his whole body was kicked in many places simultaneously. Curling into a ball, protecting his face and head, he hoped it would soon stop. The infant kept wailing, and Antboy so badly wanted to hold him, and protect him. Then there was a shrieking woman, and the kicking stopped, followed by utter silence.

His mind was foggy, due to dehydration and high fever, and he attained an unsettling delirium. Strange faces hovered. Damp cloths were being placed upon his forehead and his chest. He was spoon fed a hot broth and other faces peered at him, within what he determined was a tent. Then things went dark.

In his dreams he was in a cage, and he was screaming, screaming, but no one could hear. Then he was naked. He was being scrubbed and salve was being rubbed into his wounds and he flinched from the stinging sensation.

He bolted upright, and then fell forward, his legs unable to support himself. Someone fled through the closed flap of the tent. Moments later, he stared at the boots of several men. Behind these men could be heard the voices of what seemed like many frantic women, trying to break through the line of men. He instinctively curled into a fetal ball to protect himself from the impending attack. He heard a rustling between the men, and then he felt the presence of someone nearby. He peeked through his fingers to spot a man kneeling prostrate before him.

Two men approached Antboy, pulling him upright, each supporting one of his arms, his legs too weak to support himself. The man before him was dressed in a flowing robe of tan and green silk, and he uttered something unintelligible. A young boy was asked to come forward who bowed low before speaking.

"The Prince of this land asks for your permission so that he may rise."

Antboy shakes his head to clear the dream. Unable to find the use of his tongue, to enunciate a single syllable, he indicates with an upward movement of his palm for the kneeling man to rise.

A flock of women enter the tent and lay out a long red carpet. They dress it with plates of silver and chalices of gold and then ladle heaps of food and pour goblets of wine. Men in fine clothing sit along the longer edges of the royal carpet. When all the spots along the length are filled, the Prince sits directly opposite Antboy, taking the head position of the feast.

Bowing his head, the Prince chants. The other men join him. Antboy bows his head in turn befuddled and slightly amused at what he is certain is his unstable imagination. He assumes he's been drugged with some form of tonic, perhaps to ease his concerns while they try to access his intelligence. The feast before him might be his last.

Raising his wine goblet, the Prince shouts something to the heavens above. Others follow suit, and long drafts are taken from the goblets. The boy interpreter, kneeling next to Antboy, explains the Prince's very significant benediction, "Our Prince has just thanked the Great One for sending you with his son. He is grateful to you for bringing his son back from the dead."

Then a woman appears in the doorway holding a barely visible little baby. Antboy instinctively holds out his arms toward the child, but the nurse instead brings the sleeping infant to his father, the Prince.

"Tell me about the child. Why was he abandoned?"

The boy translator is pensive, and responds patiently to Antboy. "The child wasn't abandoned, he was dead. We had to flee after the mortar shells ripped through the caverns."

"But he wasn't dead."

"He was definitely dead. The Prince would never have left him otherwise. You brought him back to life. You created a miracle for our people."

"What happened to his mother?"

"She was sitting by the Prince, nursing the Lost Child, when a mortar shell ripped her in half. Right in front of the Prince's eyes his wife was shredded into several pieces and the boy, his only son, was sent hurtling and plummeting several caverns below.

"As the smallest boy, I was lowered into the dark abyss, and I checked the infant. He was deceased, cold as ice. No breath, no heartbeat, no pulse, even his tongue was icy. I waited quite a while. I made several attempts to resuscitate him, but he was gone. There was no way that I could carry him and also maintain the footholds, while holding the rope to return to the top. The bombing was getting more vigorous, so I had no choice but to leave the dead child, the youngest of the lifeline of our great Prince.

"When I reached the ledge of the cave empty handed, the Prince collapsed. We carried him from those caverns, bereft of his one love and his newborn. He had been broken and incoherent, hopelessly forlorn for almost four days, until a villager witnessed your horrific, near fatal beating by our patrol, and she recognized the baby. She demanded you be saved, and personally carried the infant directly to our grateful Prince. Then she delivered you into the hands of our most revered healers," the boy concluded.

Then goblets were raised, and the rest of the evening became a blur of inebriated, divine, inexplicable destiny.

The Prince sent his most trusted messengers to spread word of Antboy's recovery throughout the neighboring, yet distant villages, intending for news of his rescue to reach the Army. Recuperating steadily, Antboy lived with the Prince and his family while his mind and body healed. The Prince attended to Antboy personally, and took great lengths to help him heal during the weeks that followed. He introduced a fast from solid food, with a series of liquids that Antboy was to take at prescribed hours of the day and night.

News of Antboy's whereabouts traveled a meandering route through the fringes of disconnected civilization and eventually it reached the Army. The Prince was aware that when the Army received intelligence on Antboy's location, it would initiate an extensive verification process. Then the Army would form an extraction plan to insure his safe return. The Prince knew that he had ample time to bestow a treasured gift upon Antboy. So he endowed Antboy with the sacred art of Shakthura.

The Prince practiced Shakthura in Antboy's tent, inviting the recovering Antboy to accompany him in the initial meditative phase, since little physical exertion was required. The Prince wanted him to experience the transcendent physical and emotional curative effects of Shakthura, from which generations of his royal family had benefitted.

Originally brought to the nobles of his land by a select warrior class of swordsmen, Shakthura became a preserved doctrine taught by masters who traveled incessantly to spread its therapeutic power. Shakthura cleared the mind of all thought, focusing on both the infinite and infinitesimal simultaneously and disparately.

The Prince soon noted a subtle transformation in Antboy. He observed a pristine translucence to Antboy's gaze and a diminished sense of wariness in his demeanor. By introducing the symmetric art of balancing in moderately uncomfortable positions, the Prince diverted Antboy's unremitting pain by accompanying him in maintaining unfamiliar poses and stretches. The healthful effects, from the release of stress and tension in the tendons and muscles, were soon evident in Antboy's regained ability to rise early with vigor.

Soon the Prince introduced the physical stages of Shakthura, particularly grappling, where opponents face eye to eye, and strategically try to take down their adversary, even one with greater physical prowess. As Antboy and the Prince wrestled in a locked Shakthura position of defensive aggression, Antboy was ultimately able to overcome their ceaseless deadlock knocking the Prince to the ground.

Then one morning the Prince came to Antboy and told him the news. Antboy would be retrieved that night, about a mile from their camp, a distance that would prevent retaliatory attacks. The Prince was to create a massive bonfire, so that Antboy could be easily spotted from the air.

They walked to the extraction zone, and exchanged somber farewells along the way. When the helicopter arrived it hesitated for several minutes before touching down about sixty meters from the vast conflagration, where Antboy sat, the Prince to his right, holding the infant.

As Antboy reached out to hold the child one last time, there was not just one, but instead there were dozens of male babies staring at him, needing him. No longer residing within the fleeting memories of his brief, yet enlightening journey into the realm of his captors, he had returned to caring for the forsaken babies in the Dome of Beasts. Atum had not been the first child he had saved, and from the look of these desperate little faces, he wouldn't be the last.

XXVIII

Atum grew and crawled and toddled and walked and ran, as did the rest of the boys, who were no longer as dependent, and they grew up faster than any children Antboy had ever witnessed. Their desire to survive was strong. In their first two years, they learned how and when to feed themselves, clean their bodies and clothing, and how to walk and talk. They knew when it was appropriate and necessary to seek help from Ava's mother, Constance.

Toward the end of the second year, Antboy asked Constance to assume his duties in the Dome of Beasts completely, since the toddlers had become less needy and more self-sufficient. It was now best for Atum to remain within the confines of their Dome of Maintenance.

Antboy wrote at length in the journals he had brought from his faraway home. Consistently, he recorded his observations on disks and assigned Atum daily listening assignments. In this manner, Atum learned about the world he could not witness, from which they were banned.

Atum was a good student and asked many questions of Antboy. Throughout the years that followed, within their haven, Antboy diligently taught Atum, knowing that one day Atum would inevitably venture from the safety of their shelter. He firmly believed that in Atum, and the story that Atum would one day tell, would unfold the future of mankind, a brighter future than ever imagined.

My memory is keen and I have memorized the map of the colony. Disobeying Father, I am finally putting my knowledge into action by venturing forth from the sanctuary of our dome to find my mother. I will avoid the path that Father will take to Queen Lavender. I will take a parallel route toward the same vicinity of the Village center.

I have to be careful. I can't jeopardize anything, yet I'm endangering everything that Father has provided, our safety and security. But, I'm compelled to seek her. It's absolutely necessary for me to find my mother, who believes I'm dead.

When I was young and quite impressionable Father would speak to me about things that were complex. He said that everything was in some type of code, even down to the genetics that control our very existence. He said that no one can escape this code, and it is this very code that, however deciphered, always repeats itself, inexplicably, undeniably. Father always said that we cannot escape our history, our heritage, and now he knows for certain that history, regardless of intense scrutiny and discussion, will always repeat itself like a never-ending code. No matter what we try to change, most things are beyond our control; we are bound to the code.

As I approach the Dome of the Queen, I carefully scan my surroundings to avoid contact, and barely, incandescently, I can see Father's silhouette just ahead, kneeling before the dais of Queen Lavender. When Father speaks to me about his love for Queen Lavender, it makes me angry, and I cannot understand his feelings. He always refers to love as a living thing. Father once told me about a conversation he had with Lucy Lips regarding love, which confuses me. Lucy was a renegade ant, and she defied convention.

"We ants do not love, except me, of course, for I am a passionate, liberated ant, but I am an anomaly. One cannot control love. Once the heart has loved, it is forever. Even if it is an impossible love, the heart will always remember love and the hurt that is love lost. It truly never forgets that which it has loved.

"It is love that controls, that dictates actions and thoughts, which have no basis in rationality, practicality, or predictability. It is love that gives rise to all the other dangerous emotions. Love can destroy what one strives to create, and she is very dangerous, yet exceptionally vital. Love lives invisibly and is fleeting, floating just beyond perception. One cannot see love as she approaches, but once she has pierced the heart, the most vital of organs, it is too late. When her unavoidable arrow has been flung, beware of what she strikes, for she is merciless, unrelenting, utterly human and therefore flawed.

"Love is a very funny thing because she defies reason. She does not feed on logic and rationality; she has no defined formula and follows no pattern but instead randomness, even chaos. Love cannot be touched but she can touch, she can even thrust herself upon one, even launch herself to fall upon unsuspecting prey. She is not predictable and should be feared and welcomed, simultaneously, for she is whimsical, sometimes eternal, sometimes transitory.

"But love that is forbidden is the most dangerous, because she is taboo, and she must hide. The consequences of her discovery can alter the life and body that houses her, that feeds her, that supports her very existence. And this love can strike like a snake, a deadly snake, if cornered, and can often turn quickly on that which she loves or that which she fears, in an instant.

"Love that brews within, in deep, hidden, inner recesses, is sedate and complacent in her hibernation, yet innately violent and tumultuous. She knows not what she will become, especially if she is banned. From banishment, love faces an uncertain, tortured, perhaps incarcerated future. Beware of the power of love, for masked within her beauty can roar an angry beast within whose belly gives rise to the destructive force called hate."

"Are you Atum?" a voice quietly asks.

"Who are you?" I ask apprehensively, searching the shadows.

"I am Constance, and this is my daughter, Ava. I've known your Father since you were born. He saved you, and I helped him."

"Father has mentioned you. Why are you here?"

"He told me to keep my eye out for you. He came to me, before coming here, to the Dome of the Queen."

"Why?"

"You're at great risk. You must return to your dome immediately."

"I won't. I came here to find my mother."

"Don't be foolish, Atum. It's too risky."

"It's my choice."

"Atum, you are putting your Father's life in danger, as well as your own. Not to mention Ava and mine, by being here with you. Now go!"

Back home, I try to piece together what had just happened. I sprinted through tunnel after connecting tunnel, that I know. I retraced the steps that I had finally taken, having envisioned them for so long, after years catching glimpses of the colony's map. But something occurred after Constance commanded me to go, that caused me to flee, not in terror, though terrifying nevertheless.

Ava had taken my hand and pressed it against her smooth, warm cheek, and she placed her hand on mine. Her lips kissed my palm, and the tip of her tongue glided across my fingers. I put my other hand over hers and felt her delicate fingers on my cheek, and then on my lips.

As I pulled Ava toward me, the essence of an ephemeral smile crossed her lips, and then she turned away, saying, "Go!" and I ran, confused, trembling in fear, afraid of the strange sensation that rumbled within me.

I put a disk in the reader, as I do whenever Father leaves me, and I try to bury my thoughts within the history of our imprisonment. Father claims that his people walked earth in an unconscious state. People were unaware of their presence, oblivious to their meaning, and uninformed of their importance to all that comprises the cosmos, and they became poisoned.

Father insists that all it takes is one, a single individual with the desire to save the world, to affect great change. At this point, he feels he can do nothing more than to pass on his knowledge to me. Father says that I must find where his footsteps have ended and place my feet just ahead of his, so that the journey may continue. I have no idea, though, where to even look for his footsteps, but I continue to study the disks for clues.

Father was guided by the smallest, ancient species that he calls ants. Passionately, he describes them. He's adamant that without man's respect for the tiniest forms of life, and without understanding how and why ants exist, that man reveals his inherent weakness, his belief in his superiority.

Though the soft, warm brush of Ava's lips still haunts me, I try to distract myself with the knowledge that Father has recorded. I feign interest in his description of the colony's origination.

XXIX

All domes were the same, opaque and bland white with just a hint of yellow. Worn by all were ivory tunics bordering on light tan. Color alterations were explicitly prohibited by HSI code. Mothers were permitted to wear more flowing, larger, and longer robes that trailed them. These robes were more luxurious, representing their role as reproducers, and would interfere with the lifestyle of a Worker, but not with a Mother, since her manual work was minimal. The Queen's robe was to be no longer than any other Mother's robe. Upon laundering, Mothers' robes were distributed daily and randomly. Workers' robes did not trail and adorned each woman in a very form-fitting manner, cuffs falling some-where between elbow and wrist, and the pant hem falling in the region between the knee and ankle, allowing less friction between the bodice and the cloth during daily tasks.

Uniformity dominated. Everyone was like everyone else. No one stood out; none wanted to. There was no reward for uniqueness, nothing to gain. No one complained; all felt necessary yet worthless, essential yet inconsequential, which kept the balance in check. Praise was neither expected nor given; complaints were neither considered nor issued. One existed for the benefit of all, and all benefitted every one. Antboy had never seen a city operate so smoothly. Eating, sleeping, sanitizing, caring for and educating the young, preserving and increasing fertility, and studying the Codex were the essential activities that sustained the colony.

HSI code established that the supreme goal and purpose was to maximize the number of female births per cycle. This remained the mission of their settlement. Upon the results of each birthing season, the Queen would step down and designate the most fertile prospect to replace her, unless her own fertility was superior, which would allow her to retain the crown. A retiring Queen is expected to live a life of inner stillness and relaxation in a dome of her choosing.

Every Mother desired to be Queen. That was the driving force of the entire colony, to be Queen. This mantra was to be integrated, at every Queen's demand, even pounded, into the minds of the child Breeders at the earliest of early ages.

Birthing cycles became known as races and each dome competed as a unit, taking its bid for victory seriously. Upon review of each race's verified birth results, fertility ranks were then determined, compiled from several factors. Mothers were re-ranked receiving either upgrades or downgrades in their status, and their housing. The dome with the highest number of female births in one birthing cycle would be listed in the historic annals of the Codex.

Mothers avidly prepared for every upcoming race, and Workers served them well. Each dome contained four Mothers, and one Worker was exclusively assigned to them. Workers were fed less than Mothers, as they needed less fat and more muscle. Their bodies adapted accordingly. Workers were assigned to prepare and serve meals, maintain the Dome, launder clothing and linens, remove waste matter, give daily massages and sustain each Mother's personal hygiene. They also cared for the male Beasts, carried things, repaired and manufactured items that were broken or needed, made clothing, and cleaned. They provided childcare for the Mothers by bringing their girls from the nursery to be fed, and then sanitizing them. Workers returned to the Worker Village each evening, upon completion of their duties and dismissal by the Mothers they served.

Mothers were pampered, and naturally benefitted from their relationships with Workers. Workers, conversely, derived benefits from their stints of superior service. Workers were afforded slightly more food at mealtimes when they met and exceeded expectations. Food was motivation enough for the extra effort each Worker put forth to exceptionally maintain her assigned Mothers.

Colonists were not permitted to criticize that which was written in the Codex. With the Queen's full approbation, in support of the community, Lavender brought clarity to the practical applications of the Codex. The Queen allowed Lavender to lead the colony in spiritual matters, every seventh day, the Day of the Spirit, when she read from and interpreted the Codex. Everyone praised Lavender, for she had the insight to understand its implicit contents.

With each passing week, the colony grew more dependent on Lavender's knowledge. Their absolute and essential dependence on her, deeply frightened Antboy. The settlers could not recognize the destructive force manifesting within the thoughts of a betrayed, vindictive woman with a highly developed brain, able to derail even a master plan designed

257

by the greatest architect of the universe. No one could fathom the vengeance that Lavender planned.

Mothers rarely studied the HSI code, instead expecting Workers to do so. Workers were responsible for reviewing the daily, brief excerpts that Lavender selected. Workers reveled in their faith, bringing glorious stories to the ears of Mothers, and were reverent in their service to their respective Mothers. Mothers loved the stories relayed to them by Workers, especially the specific chronicles that Lavender initially recounted to the Workers. These narratives were simple yet filled with deep, hidden meanings that reveal the true order of things. Anecdotal accounts of community and suffering, equal treatment and respect, too little and too much food, sometimes complete fantasies, were told daily.

In some stories there is an evil leader that does not want equality for her people. In others there is a Mother who finds more to life than fertility. One story is about a baby who can talk from birth, and also feed herself. The story of a Worker that refuses to go to work often is left unfinished and the Mothers are asked to provide their own endings to the parable. The tale of a Mother who loves and misses her one deformed and deselected male child, is condemned by all.

While Workers praised the order that had been established, they occasionally prompted interactive discussions about scenarios that reversed the roles firmly established and condoned by HSI code. Mothers preferred stories about the comfortable bliss and uniformity of their daily lives.

Particularly they loved the tale of a Mother who had been housed in a lower fertility district, but worked hard, religiously attending, even twice daily, the ceremonies held at the Dome of Fertility. Quest, as she is known, wants nothing more than to increase her fertility rank, and takes every step advised to do so. She cares for her body, and believes both deeply in the HSI code, and herself. She works hard to live a life that every Mother would consider worthy, that every Worker would revere, that even the Queen would extol. At the next birthing cycle, she receives the injected seed with love, and she has faith that she has done all that she can do to provide the world with the next generation of children. To the Mothers' delight, the story ends well, with Quest moving up two fertility ranks as a result of her good birthing numbers and strong devotion and desire.

Another story that is told over the course of three nights is rarely prescribed by Lavender, only after certain events, or signs, as she calls them, and it is not well received. It involves another Mother, Desiree, who wants the same thing, to increase her fertility rank. She firmly believes that the higher ranking Mothers, since they live in larger domes, with higher food allotments, have many more privileges than the lower ranks, and this is her driving force, her desire. However, Desiree delivers no children, and is designated a Worker.

Desiree struggles with her new rank and provides her service in a lackluster manner, unaccustomed to the physical requirements of her new duties. After several assignments, Desiree finally finds true understanding in the service of others. Realizing that when she was a Mother she had previously mistreated Workers, Desiree now strives to change the order of things. As a Worker she outwardly proclaims that her class be treated better, afforded more time off, given more food, and offered better housing.

Desiree does not stop until she gains the council of the Queen. At a Council meeting, Desiree voices her beliefs and desires and sympathy for the plight of the Workers, only to be banned to the Dome of Darkness by the Queen. It is in the complete isolation of the Dome of Darkness, that

Desiree reaches the pit of human suffering, and then rises in triumph, developing a new system of beliefs, a philosophy to end injustice and achieve equality for all. After her banishment, Desiree sets forth to overthrow the colony, and is unequivocally defeated.

Mothers chuckle at the fable, then burst into hysterical laughter. Such is their disassociation from the purpose of this disarming story. But the spark of the Worker Revolt is lit. Thoughts have been planted, not yet ready for harvest.

The Dome of Fertility is a spiritual temple, filled with positive energy. Within, Mothers take care of their bodies to achieve greater fertility. The predominant symbol that greets every entrant into the sacred dome is a huge sculpture of a beautiful, vibrant, extraordinary set of ovaries that hangs just above the entryway. Additionally, various paintings and carvings represent the mysterious, immense power that flourishes in their bodies. They serve as constant reminders that each Mother's sole objective is to assume the role of host to this divine inner presence. Morning and evening prayers are offered consistently to these symbols of genesis, and tests of faith are constant and meaningful.

Candles burn at all hours of the day and night. Fountains are placed along the walls of the dome and Mothers kneel to sip the eternal nectar of life. At the door to the inner courtyard, each female bows deeply toward the tapestry of birth, adding one more link in the necessary chain of continuous life. The tapestry shows a montage of pictures which display the holiest of events, the entire cycle of life: the capture of seed from a fettered Beast, the insertion of seed into the wet, warmly welcoming enclave, the dome-shaped curve of the abdomen of expectation, the exceptionally impossible swelling and widening of the pink canal of birth, and, finally, release of new life into the hands of faith.

Then they line up according to fertility rank, the highest in the front, the lowest in the back, all forming the pose of the sacred egg, clothing discarded, flat on their backs, legs spread wide, toes touching ears, right arms directly out to the side with outstretched, upward facing palm, left hands hugging the left breast and areola drawing energy from the heart, designed to harness the humming, inward purring and to vibrate the entire body from the vocal chords up to the cerebrum down to the now exposed, stimulated moist lips of infinite desire. This energy ultimately connects each woman with her inner faith, a complex and complicated divine structure, which releases eggs that, upon fertilization, will hatch the new generation. Through concentrating on the energy within, and focusing on this positive energy, Mothers achieve immense inner calm and an initial quiet that merges with these ovarian structures of immense power.

Those that concentrate most on the messages of the Codex, and are most apt in performing the rituals, achieve the greatest pleasure, the release of healthy eggs. Eggs that prepare, compete, and capture internal beauty to meet their mate, the mate of impatient seeds, seeds that seek this most beautiful and frantic union of pure ecstasy.

Upon deep contemplation and concentration, the women begin to twitch and convulse and many groan sighs of hidden desire and struggle. Deep guttural evoked moans erupt from their primal exploration, and some thrash their heads back and forth. Open outstretched hands clench involuntarily, while some hold their breasts delicately. Many find their centers of internal vibrations and frictional excitement, and they often bounce up and down, even side to side, the movement nothing more than a catalyst for an unpredictably erotic and somewhat passionate, at times even, frighteningly violent reaction, forming patterns of deeper consciousness and unbridled sensuality. Some shriek loudly, panting between short breaths and bursts of ecstasy, then calming to a somnolent state, to return again to an even deeper and stronger, higher apex of pure emotional and physical pleasure.

Some release nectar, stimulating more flow. Their groans and shrieks of absolute inner freedom are contagions of primitive fulfillment. In their honeyed pools of selfish abandon, in their vortex of frenzied sensuality, drip healthy juices and essential daily purification of their tunnels of life, yielding fluids of oozing desire and necessary eggs of life.

On only one occasion, Antboy witnesses this ritual, and he is disturbed. He realizes that these women need no man; man has all but completely been eliminated from the equation of intimacy, relationships, and reproduction. He sees exactly what he had seen in the ants, but wishes it were not so.

Father suddenly storms in. "Is everything, all right, Father?"

"No. It isn't."

"What did the Queen say, Father?"

"Never mind that. I met Constance and she told me that you were right outside the Dome of the Queen, while I was meeting with Queen Lavender."

"I'm sorry. I was, but then I got scared, so I came right back."

"Atum, with all that I've taught you, why do you want to get yourself killed?"

"I don't. I just couldn't stop myself."

"Don't leave home again, son. Promise me you won't."

"Ok, I won't. I promise. I've been studying, though."

"That's good. What parts?"

"Mainly Foundations."

"Insert the disk titled Worker Revolt and deal with that material. In the meantime, I'm drawing up plans to get you off this satellite."

"Off the planet? How?"

"I discovered some important things today when I met with Queen Lavender. I learned why she has scheduled the Endeavors to begin in two days, rather than waiting another six months, which she's permitted to do by the Codex."

"What did you learn?"

"That things may be getting very dangerous, very quickly when she commences the opening ceremonies. I'm thoroughly opposed to what she's doing."

"Is there any way of getting her to change her mind?"

"No. I tried, but she won't listen. She's misinterpreted things terribly, tragically. Now that I see what she's capable of, I have to ready the shuttle for launch. There'll be great chaos in the next two weeks, and the confusion will provide cover for the launch back to earth."

"Back to earth!? Really!? Can I help you with the plans?"

"Not right now. Just keep listening to the disks."

"Ok, I will. I met someone else besides Constance today. Father, I have some questions."

"I know. She told me you met her daughter, Ava. No time for questions now, son. We both have work to do. Let's get to it. Play the disk called 'Origins of the Worker Revolt'."

XXX

It had been several birthing cycles after the colony's foundation, long after Queen Siren had retired, when Antboy spotted Lavender leaving Queen Isis' dome, wearing the robe of a Mother, freshly ripped, shreds hanging from her nearly naked form. This Queen wouldn't allow anyone, even a Worker as important as Lavender, to act like someone she wasn't. Queen Isis would not permit Lavender to assume a privilege that had not been granted. She would not allow anyone, notwithstanding Lavender, to defy the law.

From that day forward, Queen Isis began to lead the colony in a new direction, dividing and devising class systems. She reminded the colony about Lavender's actions during the early stages of the settlement, and what had befallen her child. She set forth conditions. Workers, numbering fourteen, and Mothers, comprising fifty-six, were no longer considered equally important to the success of the colony. She proclaimed that Workers were solely necessary to serve Mothers. There was no other reason for them to exist. Any Worker that stepped out of line would face grave punishment. Struggle ensued. It was a quiet struggle, which was not outwardly evident, but grew with time. It was the Worker Revolt that Father wants me to learn about.

"Please rise, the Queen approaches," the Scouts announced in unison.

The Queen's gown trailed far behind her, as she swept through the dome in a semicircular arc until she found her way to the head of the royal mat. While Queen Isis looked up from her oversized, fluffy cushion, with her prominent nose originating from bushy eyebrows atop brilliantly large brown, troubled eyes, the Council members sat cross-legged upon their cushioned bottoms.

Statistics were discussed at each Council meeting. Numbers were of primary importance to every Queen and were always evaluated. Each week measurements were taken of the Mothers' expanding bellies. These, in turn, helped to calculate future birth projections. Meetings usually focused on determining the specific Mothers that were to be highest ranked, how many Breeders versus Beasts were to be born, and proper dome placement of Mothers. Of great importance was the reevaluation and charting of the specific day and time as to when the next birthing cycle, and the injections of seed to initiate it, would commence. Queen Isis was very precise, and took comfort in her obsession with precision. Unfortunately, she was very disappointed with the numbers that were projected.

At the Queen's Council meetings, Lavender mainly listened, no longer providing much input. It was rare that the Queen asked Lavender for her views. But this time, Queen Isis engaged Lavender in every discussion, and the Dome of

Council resounded with the Queen's unusual requests for Lavender's opinions. "Lavender, dear, how are you?"

"I am well, my Queen, and how have you been?"

"As always, very well. However, we are not projected to make numbers this season. Are you aware of this? Do you have any ideas as to why we might be facing a shortfall?"

"I've heard rumors that we will have a possible shortfall, my Queen. I do not know the reasons, though. We appear to be on schedule to *match* last season, but it doesn't look like we will meet our quota this season, and *exceed* those numbers. I'm not aware of any contributing factors that are causing a shortfall, your Majesty."

"You have always been a loyal friend and ally to our colony, have you not?"

"My Queen, you, of course, must be the judge of that. I believe I have only brought good tidings to our colony and I will continue to do what is right so that we may all benefit."

"Yes, Lavender, I knew I could rely on you. But Lavender, how do your people feel? What are their thoughts about the structure of our now thriving colony? Are they content?"

"My Queen, I have seen nothing that would lead me to believe that Workers are anything but content. We take great pride in our work and look forward to a continuation of the prosperity that has graced our colony. We are humble and accept the way things are as the way they are meant to be. We have always felt this way and always will. We serve you eternally, my Queen."

"Well said, my eternal friend. Should I pay any heed to the extraordinary stories of late?"

"I am not sure, my Queen, of what you speak. Please enlighten me about these tales."

"I don't know if they're relevant right now, considering your loyalty to the Mothers. Maybe we should discuss this at another Council meeting."

"If you so choose, my Queen. But if there is anything that concerns you, this is your forum, and I'm sure everyone here, and the entire colony, will rest much more easily if these issues are discussed and resolved. We only have today, my Queen. The past cannot be changed and the future is uncertain, so my philosophy is to deal with the present. I suspect that there are things still left unsaid. But it is your choice, my Queen. Your word is final here."

Queen Isis looked at her Council Mothers for support in the matter. Gesturing for her to get on with it, one of the Mothers lost patience and blurted out, "Lavender, how do Workers feel about the way they are treated by Mothers? It is essential that we know exactly how they feel."

"I'm not sure we feel anything at all. We've been well trained to care for Mothers and Breeders and we believe we've lived up to your expectations of us as Workers. Have we not?"

Queen Isis responded, "You certainly have. And we expect that this assiduous dedication continue uninterrupted, unaffected by any changes in treatment that may unexpectedly evolve, unchanged by things that cannot be controlled, particularly human nature."

"I'm not sure what you mean, my Queen, about changes in treatment that may 'evolve'. Is there something I should be aware of, something I should communicate to the Workers? We are quite adaptable. Advance notice of changes, though, would be greatly appreciated. If we have time to prepare, we can adapt expediently, without any interruption in the service we so aptly provide. Please speak freely, my Queen."

"Well, Lavender, to be frank, as guardian of the Colony, and with the full approval of our Mothers certain changes are imminent."

"Very good, my Queen, please do let me know so that I may, with your permission, broach these subjects right away, to make sure Workers prepare immediately. We, as you well know, are here, by our designated name 'Worker', strictly to work and provide for the needs of the colony. This is our chosen path, and we accept this without emotion, thought, or consideration. We are a very studious and dedicated people and we reflect rather than react. In this way, the colony will always benefit from our most necessary contributions."

"Lavender, thank you. You do speak so wisely. I will no longer hesitate in what I must say." With this, Queen Isis turned to the Council Mothers, who in turn echoed her deep sigh of relief. One of them approached Lavender and deftly tore to shreds the gown she wore, a Mother's gown, and shoved the traditional Worker tunic into the crook of Lavender's trembling arm.

Queen Isis rose and declared, "Certain changes will occur immediately and you must be the liaison. These new regulations, or proclamations, if you will, must go into effect immediately. No Worker is allowed within the central district of our colony, including the Dome of Study, Dome of Council, or Dome of Fertility, unless specifically requested. Workers, upon completion of each assignment, must return immediately to the Worker Village, and must take the remote path in their travels. There are to be no unnecessary exchanges or communications between Workers and Mothers, no more stories or casual communication.

"Mothers cannot afford for their fertility to be tainted by Workers, especially since Workers hold the lowest fertility rank. Mothers must be prevented from being poisoned by the diluted energy forces of Workers. No other objective is more important than revitalizing the colony's fertility, especially since our recent birth numbers have fallen short of expected projections.

"If a Worker should accidentally encounter a Mother, she must bow to the ground, completely to the ground, until that Mother should pass, or until told by that Mother to perform some form of duty. Mothers are no longer to be addressed by name, only by title, and Workers may be called anything at anytime by a Mother's discretion. There will be no limits to what may be asked of a Worker during her assignment. Workers may be asked to relinquish their own personal linens, blankets, garments, cushions, food rations or other belongings to any Mother that requests. Things may be asked of a Worker that have no correlation to a specific need, and, in fact, may be commanded strictly for the personal amusement and entertainment of a Mother or group of Mothers. Any Worker that does not comply with these new rules will be sentenced to a term in the Dome of Darkness, a length to be determined at the Council's discretion. What say you to all this, Lavender?"

"My Queen, your word has been heard and it will be obeyed. Unquestionably and unswervingly, Workers will follow your commands. You know what is best for this colony and what is best for all the people, Workers, Mothers, Breeders, and Beasts that live here. For that we are grateful and for that we will show you just how dedicated we are to the improvement of our sacred home. We will not disappoint you, of that I am certain. You will find that we are a stronger people than you could ever have imagined and we will endure what we must for the benefit of all." And with that,

Lavender clasped her hands in front of her lap and bowed deeply.

Some miscellaneous items were discussed amongst Queen Isis and the Mothers. Then the Council was adjourned. As Lavender left, her face studied by all, she was stoic, pacifying those that watched. But when Lavender turned away, toward the remote path of the Worker village, she smiled widely, broadly, unexpectedly and her cheeks flushed with the energy of the moment. She would never return to the Dome of Council as Lavender, the servant.

Even if it took years, she would return as someone quite different, someone that all would respect, and all would serve. In this knowledge, she found the comfort she needed to return to her fellow Workers, compounded by the fact that all was going according to plan, almost too well.

It was as if the Codex foretold the motion and movement of her every step along the remote path toward her people. And each step now brought a deeper, more resonant smile to her lips, and she whiffed an aroma she hadn't inhaled in so very many years. It was her own scent, the smell of lavender, and for a fleeting moment she thought about Antboy, whose shadow she had just unsuspectingly passed.

Within days, the new rules of the colony took effect, permeating even the stadium sized Dome of Girls. Breeders were quite a social bunch, generally forming circles and conducting games of Mother and Worker. The girls switched between roles often and got quite a kick out of the game. Most preferred to be Mothers in this ritual, but all were taught the important value of Workers to society. Breeders were instructed that the primary role of a female was to increase her fertility to provide the most births for the colony. Discussion flourished among these girls, who spent most of their time together in the Dome of Girls.

They discussed the customs of the society, the differences between classes, and the HSI code, the Codex. It was a fascinating and repetitive process for the Breeders because they always wanted to know just how they fit into the order of things and what divine purpose they served. They also loved to brush each other's hair and tell each other how beautiful they looked. Then there was their favorite game of Queen for a day.

"Well, now, who is the Queen today, children?" Asked Cactus, a slender, lithe, very tall Worker with sandy brown, straight, shoulder-length hair, assigned to supervise the Breeders.

"Cleopatra is the Queen today," the children chorused. "She is a very good Queen and she leads the colony well."

"I see, I see," said Cactus. "So, children, why are we here, what purpose do we serve?"

"We are not children," the children declared.

"Oh, no, my mistake, did I say you were children? What a mistake. I meant to ask you, the gracious colonists of our beloved planet, how you are doing today?"

The girls chorused, some playing Workers, some playing Mothers, all unified in their response, "We are doing very well, very well indeed."

One girl said nothing, and only sighed. All turned to her, Queen Cleopatra, who seemed very unsettled, even somewhat irate in her jerky movements, sitting upon the raised dais. The most impatient of the Breeders, Cleopatra was generally considered a bit precocious by the attending Worker overseers. Worker Cactus held and eventually released a deep, cleansing breath and prepared for Breeder Cleopatra's dysfunctional role-play.

"You call this well?" Queen Cleopatra retorted.

Cactus felt prickly and suddenly darted out of the dome, scanning for signs of additional Workers that could assist. She pulled aside a bustling Worker and engaged her to help out at the Dome of Girls, and recruited another Worker to summon Lavender. Cactus turned to reenter the dome and stared into the cold, dark eyes of two of the taller, larger girls, barring her entrance.

"Who wishes to see the Queen?" One of the mock Scouts queried.

"Enough of this nonsense, I must return to monitor and teach the girls," Cactus weakly responded. Her ability to guide the Breeders, as was her Worker responsibility, was evaporating.

"I will ask the Queen if she is taking visitors at this time. But I doubt she has the desire to see one of the lowly Workers." The pretend Scout disappeared within the dome to ask the Queen.

Cactus waited. The girl returned shortly to say, "Queen Cleopatra requests that you return tomorrow and she may permit your entrance then."

Cactus grew furious. She skirted the wide entrance, hurriedly pushing and shoving her way past both of the pretend Queen's imaginary Scouts, back into the large arena.

Usually, daily Breeder tasks were imaginatively performed which mimicked the essential roles of their civilization, with nearly four hundred girls in various stages of play. Food preparation, birthing, hygiene, fertility rituals, essential daily tasks, Council meetings, Scout duty, study of the Codex, storytelling, prayer, child care, deselection, celebrations of birth and colonization, and even bedtime were all levels of acceptable children's play that were encouraged and mentored by the chaperone Workers.

But this atrocity could not have been predicted nor could it be condoned under any circumstances. Cactus observed an unnatural evolution of their social order under an extremist ruler, Cleopatra, and the scene was quite unsettling. Cactus witnessed the horrific manifestation of a mutated human society under despotic rule. The magnitude of their game's didactic impact transcended great consternation and bordered on manic panic. Cleopatra had learned about the new rules proclaimed by Queen Isis, and to her, the fun was just beginning.

Feigning Queen, Cleopatra was terse in her words and sharp in her tone. Simulated Workers were sent here and there, some sharply scolded for this, others physically abused for that. Pretend Mothers taunted and mocked their counterparts, those unfortunate play Workers, who they forced to stoop, and crawl from one place to another. Occasionally a child Mother would prohibit a child Worker from wandering here or walking there, exclaiming that a particular space was reserved for Mothers only.

Cleopatra was being massaged by a Scout while pretending to indolently receive food into her gaping mouth from a hunched Worker. Some Workers were ordered to act as if they carried a baby to its Mother and were forced to bow in a terribly contorted submissive position during nursing. Snickers and then shrieks of uncontrollable laughter could be heard from the role-playing Mothers who forced their make-believe Workers to disrobe and dance repetitively.

One little girl, Lilac, was whimpering and tears flowed down her cheek. "I don't want to be a Worker anymore. Please, please let me be a Mother now. I would rather die than be a Worker for one more minute."

Queen Cleopatra responded, "Why, Lilac? You know that it is just as valuable to the Colony to be a Worker, as it is to be a Mother. Remember, my friends, respect the fertility rules and you will not have to complain like poor Lilac here." The child Mothers broke into hysterical laughter and Lilac was assigned to even more strenuous invented tasks than before.

Then Lavender appeared and witnessed the spectacle that appeared before her disbelieving eyes. Years later, after the Worker Revolt had run its course and put Queen Lavender on the throne, she occasionally carved pieces of dried jerky meat, only at special celebrations, into her soup. This seasoned delight gave Lavender much pleasure and a curious sort of wicked smile appeared on her lips when she tasted the strangely misshapen, chewy meat. No adults, neither Mothers nor Workers, quite knew why Lavender held this dried meat in such high regard.

But in the Dome of Girls, Breeders requested only to play the roles of Workers in their future games, as a result of Lavender's visit during the fake tyrant Cleopatra's brief reign. Those that were relegated to play Mothers did so with much complaining and whining to follow.

And Cleopatra, the mute, wished she had never wagged her tongue that day, preferring that she had held her tongue in order to still possess one.

XXXI

"Father, I have completed 'Origins of the Worker Revolt' as you asked."

"Good. Do you have any questions?"

"Yes. I have some questions about Ava."

"Son, it's late, and we can talk about her in the morning. You need to get your mind off her for now. The Endeavors start the day after tomorrow, so I need my rest and so do you. Let's get ready for bed."

"Yes, Father." But I will be long gone before Father wakes up. I must see Ava again.

"Ava?"

"What are you doing here, Atum? You can get in serious trouble for being here."

"Come outside with me," I plead.

"I will, but you have to leave here first, right away, and please don't wake anyone up."

Having finished nine birthing seasons, the Dome of Girls Primary is packed, and I slink my way through their huddled sleeping bodies, toward one of the side exits. It had taken me almost an hour to find Ava among nearly five hundred girls ranging in age from six years to nearly mine, thirteen and a half, soundly sleeping in this massive dome.

In the shadows I hide, between Ava's dome and the Dome of Girls Secondary, where another two hundred fifty girls from the three previous birthing seasons rest, ages one and a half to four and a half. Attempting to stifle the sound of my movements, I realize that the girls' contented snoring masks my already muffled noise. By dawn I must make the four-hour return journey, and deal with Father's wrath.

Where's Ava? I shouldn't enter her dome again because it's far too risky for both of us. I'm already too close to such an enormity of lightly sleeping girls, more than seven hundred fifty, out of what Father tells me are nearly twelve hundred people on our planet. He projects that our satellite will reach its capacity of ten thousand inhabitants upon completion of the seventeenth birthing cycle. He says I'll be twenty-five earth years old at that time.

Father says that our satellite planet is programmed to return to earth at that juncture, and he will have fulfilled his commitment to live here for a generation. He has always promised that he and I will be on the shuttle back to earth, while HSI determines the next phase for our returning satellite.

If successful, Father will have established the first human "backup", securing the survival of our species in the event of a cataclysmic disaster on earth. This is why he says the Endeavors are an important event, where the first babies born here will conceive new babies, allowing the original pioneering Mothers and Workers to guide younger Mothers and Workers to great fertility.

When Father patiently struggles to teach me exponential math, he tries to show me how seventy-two pregnant women have multiplied to become twelve hundred, and how, in the next twelve years, as long as the Endeavors are fruitful, that twelve hundred will swell to ten thousand. Trying to take my impatient mind off Ava, I perform some mental calculations to see if I'm ready for Father's upcoming math challenge.

"Atum, follow me." Ava finally appears and leads me away from the colony's core, through a very dark corridor, until we reach a dome marked Eleven. "I have to get back before I'm missed. Why are you here? You shouldn't be looking for your Mother again. It's too dangerous, especially with so many people working odd, long hours preparing for the Endeavors."

"I know. I'm not looking for my Mother right now. I came to see you, Ava."

"But, Atum, it's unsafe. Why are you risking your life, and maybe mine too?"

"I don't know, exactly. I just had to see you. After yesterday, I just, I really can't explain it, Ava. It's just a feeling I have, I guess, and I had to come back to see you, and to, maybe to-"

"Atum, it's an early call this morning. There are eighty-two of us, the first Breeders born here, and we're receiving our final preparations for the Endeavors. We'll be cleansing most of the day, and fasting. So if you don't get out of here soon, they'll throw you in with the other Beasts. They could harm you. And if I'm caught, I'll bring great shame upon Mother for being with you."

"But, Ava, it was your touch, that I came back for." And she caresses his cheek, his lips.

"I felt the same thing, Atum." And their lips brush against each other, and she dances her tongue lazily along the inside of his upper lip, and then slowly loops it around his tongue. Suddenly moving away, breathing heavily she says, "We have to stop, Atum. I have to go."

"Why not stay with me a little longer, Ava? No one will find us here."

"I want to, Atum, but they tell us we won't get much rest during the fourteen days of the Endeavors. If I don't get enough sleep now, I may end up with a low fertility rank, or maybe not conceive at all. I don't think I'm cut out to be a Worker, Atum. They still have a hard life, even with Queen Lavender on the throne. She couldn't change much. The Codex is the Codex."

"Father says that if I'd been brought to the Dome of Beasts, rather than deselected, that I would be added to the registry to compete in the first Endeavors."

"That's if you were fortunate enough to have survived. Mother has told me that nearly half of the first eighty Beasts born have perished since their birth. Out of those remaining, another half won't make it through the Endeavors is what Queen Lavender projects."

"What? What do you mean, 'won't make it'?"

"They'll die, Atum."

"Die? But Father told me the first Endeavors would be games and competitions, of strength, agility, and mental strategic preparedness. He used to prepare me, and test me."

"That's what we all thought too, Atum. We didn't think the Endeavors would take place for another half year. The Codex said the colony could prepare for an extra six months, increasing our current birthing cycle to two years instead of eighteen months."

"That's exactly what Father told me. He was shocked when the Scouts came to our door with the announcement."

"We were shocked as well. Suddenly, Queen Lavender announced the changes. Apparently, there's a section of the Codex called the Coda, which specifies that an alternate format of the Endeavors needs to be implemented if certain criteria warrant the change. Atum, I'm just very scared now. I don't get it at all."

"Me neither, no wonder Father looked so grim when he came back from his meeting with Queen Lavender. He said that circumstances have changed, but he didn't tell me what that meant."

"They've changed, overnight. Queen Lavender says she finally cracked the Coda, and it revealed that the Beasts will compete to the death, and only half will survive. It says something about this being the best means of selecting the top genetic specimens for reproduction. It's horrific! The Endeavors will be completely different than anything we had previously imagined. Soon my torture will begin. Our whole Breeder class is terrified. Some of us don't think we can survive the ordeal."

"This is horrible. It must be stopped."

"Atum, no one can go up against the Colony, especially now that Queen Lavender rules."

"I'm going to talk to Father as soon as I get back. He wants to get me off the planet, as soon as the Endeavors start. That's why I came here, Ava, because I want you to come with me."

"Atum, that's impossible. There's nowhere to go. This is my home, and it's all I know."

"Father says there's an entire world, where he grew up, and he wants me to go there."

"Mother's here, Atum. I could never leave her. We're very close, unlike the other Mothers or the low fertility ranked Workers, who rarely see their children. I must stay here."

"Ava, we can bring Constance. I promise that if you come with me, so will she."

"Atum, it's almost dawn. By tomorrow, midday, the entire colony will be at the Dome of Endeavors. I'm thirteen, like you, and part of the first Breeder class, so they won't allow us out until the closing ceremonies. I will live there for fourteen days. The Scouts will keep us in."

"Why?"

"Atum, after the Beasts compete, the best of them, the survivors, fertilize us with seed."

"Fertilize you? Father told me that there were extraction devices, purely humane, painless and with minimal contact. That's what the harvesting tools are for. Reaping the seeds of life."

"Well, Queen Lavender says she has interpreted the postscript to the Codex, the Coda. She says Beasts are a drain on our resources, and that only some of them are needed. The best will thrive and pass on their genes. She said the numbers were too low from the ninth, and final, administration of the fertility vials. She believes that this will boost our numbers."

"I still don't get it."

"She said she had a revelation, and that we need to have something she calls 'natural fertilization' for this cycle. She predicts a surge in our rates, which she says are lagging."

"But Father explained to me that the only method of fertilization allowed on our planet, is when the harvesting tools of extraction are used to painlessly remove the seed."

"No, Atum, the Queen says that 'natural fertilization' is when the Beasts compete for survival and then use their man thing on us."

"Their man thing? But that's primitive, and prohibited, dangerous and unsanitary."

"That's not how Queen Lavender has interpreted this addendum, this new Coda."

"I think she's wrong about this. I'm sure. This is not how Father said things would be."

"But Atum, there's no way to change things now. Even if we wanted to, which I do."

"Ava, um, I felt something change inside me yesterday."

"Me too, Atum. I felt very different yesterday, especially when you pressed against me."

"Yes, I remember." Ava and Atum blush brightly, and squeeze each other's hands.

"But Ava, Father says that it's only during the diversion of the Endeavors that he can get the shuttle launched without being observed. So, you have to come with me now, please Ava."

"I can't. This is your chance, Atum. You can get free of here. If I were you, I'd leave instantly. Better to leave, than to live here as a slave to the Codex. Please, you must go."

A long series of notes can be heard, blown from a horn by a Worker atop the Dome of Gathering. Ava recognizes the pattern of notes, which signal that the Dome of Girls Primary must rise up quickly, and immediately assemble at the Dome of Study.

"Go, Atum." Ava scampers off to her dome.

Atum flees in the opposite direction, speaking tightly, distraught, between clenched jaws, words just out of earshot, "I will return for you, Ava, I promise."

Atum fears Father's reprimand.

XXXII

Antboy is completely furious that Atum had left again. Now that Atum is roaming at will, a Scout will find him eventually, and then Atum will face severe repercussions. Antboy must get Atum off the planet, away from the horrors of the imminent Endeavors. He did not envision being apart from Atum, as he now intended. Antboy had to honor his word, and stay with the colony. Antboy could not leave, but Atum could no longer remain. It was time to help Atum escape.

Manually overriding the program that holds the shuttle fast and solid to the satellite planet will take the better part of a day. Then the craft will follow the twenty-six hour pre-programmed flight path back to earth, to arrive twelve years earlier than planned. Better that Antboy break the HSI schedule and send Atum. The alternative of keeping Atum here, where he might not survive the satellite's harsh life of a Beast, nor the dreaded Endeavors, is no longer an option. Antboy decided that he would not let Atum know, until the last minute, that they would be separated.

Antboy's frustration at Atum's disappearance quickly twisted, contorted, and festered into disdain for Queen Lavender, especially after what he had learned the day before in the Dome of the Queen.

Lavender's back was to him. Hearing Antboy's footsteps she flinched slightly, in fear and recognition. His scent was too familiar and reminiscent of a distant past, a former life, conjuring up prior feelings that she had buried so long ago: love, betrayal, disappointment, and passion.

"Get up from that ridiculous position." Queen Lavender commanded.

"Yes, my Queen," Antboy responded mechanically. He struggled out of his accustomed subservient contortion to sit cross-legged before her.

"Stop with the 'my Queen'. I've sought your counsel perhaps eight or nine times, since the colony's Foundation, three since I've been Queen, and you're well aware that I don't enforce the Rules of Beast Conduct with you."

"I know, your Majesty. It's a habit ingrained in me, by those that came before you, Queen Siren, Queen Isis, and Queen Blue. It's still the law. You know I follow the law to the letter."

"I know you do. All too well, I know you follow the letter of the law. We have a long history together, Antboy. As always, the Queen asks for your counsel with regard to each fertility season. And on its eve, each Queen has asked you to interpret her dreams. I have summoned you once again to be my dream interpreter, since our first Endeavors are just two days away."

Lavender flung her legs around the side of her body and lay down, propping her head up, supported by her hand and elbow. She appeared comfortable, and looked rested. Her expression was pensive, somewhat quizzical. "Speak freely, Antboy, and tell me what you see."

"It's been a very long time since I've been permitted to speak freely. Please forgive me."

Neither spoke for many, silent moments, each of them deep in thought. He could not find the courage to share his feelings with her. All he wanted was to hold her, to kiss her, to make things right between them, perhaps even, at this point, to take her and Atum and a half dozen children to the shuttle and leave this desolate, destructive wasteland of an experimental society.

Queen Lavender sat patiently waiting for Antboy's wise words, remembering a time, during the Worker Revolt, when she had closely heeded his sage and prophetic advice. He helped propel her to victory during that strategic and subliminal battle. Now, the colony faced another momentous turning point. Perhaps Antboy's advice will assist Lavender in making the difficult decisions required to lead their colony. Meanwhile, while Antboy pondered his response, Lavender waited.

But her thoughts began to wander to an earlier time. It was a time when Antboy's words and his interpretations helped her gain the strength and assume the power to wrest control and become Queen. Lavender recalled the critical day she was frantically informed of Queen Blue's immoral treatment of Worker Ethica.

Regardless of retired Queen Isis' stringent class modifications, equilibrium between the parties was eventually reestablished. The traditional style of Mothers remained nothing short of courteous, and patronizingly kind. Workers performed consistently, both loyally and unconditionally for several fertility cycles.

Although Queen Isis initiated the repression of Workers, Queen Blue disrespected them thoroughly, and degraded their status to a new level of insignificance. The manner in which Queen Blue spoke to Workers was a radical departure from polite. Queen Blue's furious and demeaning outbursts reached an intolerable crescendo, and her actions spawned Lavender's Worker Revolt. "Get that right now!" Queen Blue shouted at Ethica, pointing to a blanket, which she had obviously and deliberately tossed onto the floor.

At first Ethica did nothing but jump back a little, involuntarily reacting in fear. Her heartbeat was fast, her blood raced in her veins and her ears pounded. She had never felt this way and had never heard such a tone, hoping she never again would. So she did nothing, pretending she had not heard. But there it was again.

"Ethica, did you lose your ears, or are you ignoring me? Get that right now!"

Ethica did as she was told; she was terrified and could do nothing else. After all, Blue was Queen. Even though Lavender, the Worker, preached equal rights, Ethica knew better. It was true that the colony depended equally on both Workers and Mothers, but Mothers outnumbered Workers almost four to one, and they controlled most of the food producing domes. Even though Mothers were weak, having built very little muscle mass during their birthing years, their sheer numbers spoke volumes. Ethica, always one to follow directions, complied, donning her smile.

Blue was very creative in her torture. She wanted better treatment than any previous Queen, complaining ceaselessly, "The linens you brought are not clean enough, fetch more. The dome is rather dirty, sweep the floor and wash down the entire inside of my home. Your comrades before you did a poor job in their maintenance duties. Oh, and don't forget, I want my food piping hot tonight. I can't stand a lukewarm meal. Now get to it, and after the meal, we need to have a serious talk."

"Yes, your Majesty, I will get right to it," Ethica weakly responded. She rapidly disappeared attending to her chores, shaking off the paralyzing panic that wracked her brain.

Upon completion of all that Queen Blue had demanded, and after the evening meal was finished and the dishes were clean, Ethica hesitantly approached the Queen, who rested indolently on her regal mat.

"My Queen, everything is done, and prepared for bedtime. You wanted to speak to me?"

Queen Blue's tirade defied reasonable boundaries that had existed since the settlement of the colony. Ethica impassively sat before the Queen, taking note of every uttered word to relay them verbatim to Lavender, who she hoped would emancipate the officially oppressed Workers.

Queen Blue spewed, "You are nothing more than a Worker. You may have been taught that you are important but you are meaningless, a simple peasant, a poor slave. Your sole existence is to benefit me and the other Mothers. We do not symbiotically coexist here.

"You must disregard whatever Lavender may be feeding your infertile, worthless brains. We rule, you serve, that is the law of the Codex. We produce babies and you care for them. We prepare for more births, you maintain and support our preparations. It's all about us, not you.

"You are assigned the hard work because you are not fit to be a Mother. Not because it is a noble and divine profession as Lavender's irreverent proclamation of the Codex falsifies, nor a revered role as she espouses. It is your punishment for being unfit to fertilize and it is your doomed fate. That is why Mothers no longer listen to your parables nor to Lavender's divine preaching anymore. That vermin Lavender only seeks to control your minds with such ridiculous garbage. Now, Worker, prepare my resting place for bedtime."

Every few days, word spread back to the Worker Village that more and more Mothers were abusing Workers. The impact of Blue's contempt and degradation was toxically infectious. Workers pleaded with Lavender to take some form of action, to do something, anything, just to regain some form of respect for Wokers, because none existed. A chasm had formed between the two classes and reconciliation seemed improbable.

Lavender was adamant and declared that no action be taken. Emphasizing that the plight of Workers was a temporary state, and that Workers were truly the stronger and more deserving of the two classes, Lavender promised change. She predicted the emergence of a day that loomed near on the horizon, and her rhetoric resounded throughout the Worker village. She requested that Workers be patient. Lavender's preaching specified that all previous, harmful actions of persecution would be rectified in one sudden moment of glorious upheaval, in which the order of things would be drastically altered.

Then Lavender sought Antboy's advice. He taught her how to establish a mental advantage in her quest to usurp Queen Blue. He coached her thoroughly, drawing upon his vast and complex life experiences, particularly his special forces training. "When something is expected, deliver the unexpected. When asked to give, deny. When asked to take, refuse. Show no gratitude when shown kindness, reflect only harmony when there is discord. When asked to approve, disagree. Randomly act out of character, change moods often, and move suddenly. When one expects to relax, create unease, and when unease is warranted, allow the enemy to relax. Great leaders are feared and respected equally. It was not really a war," Antboy stipulated. But then he scratched his head and pondered, and said, "Well, yes, it actually was a war."

But it was a war like none before. It was a battle unlike those conducted by men, for this conflict killed no one. It was waged and it was won, with the eventual Queen Lavender, the first Worker Queen, killing not a soul.

Queen Blue's dome unexpectedly malfunctioned entombing her in the darkness with no food and thinning air. Mothers sent for Lavender but she could not be found.

Scouts interrogated Workers for information. Some claimed Lavender was busy educating Breeders at the Dome of Girls, while others said she was meeting with Constance at the Dome of Beasts. Still others insisted that she was supervising some Workers on the outskirts of the colony. One Worker was certain that she had overheard Lavender preparing to meet with Queen Blue regarding essential dome maintenance and technological upgrades.

Mothers scattered in all directions seeking Lavender, trying desperately to silence the terrified screams of the trapped Queen Blue. It was hinted that Lavender was on a spiritual retreat in the Dome of Darkness, enmeshed in deep study of the Codex, something that she did from time to time. Her annual ritual involved seclusion and fasting for a full day. She credited this practice as the impetus for new revelations about the future, through deeper interpretations of her Codex. Scouts were sent to scour the planet and to search every dome and tunnel for signs of Lavender.

Nearly two days later, Lavender appeared and was brought to the Dome of the Queen immediately. The swarm of Mothers who had unflinchingly stood vigil returned to their domes, hesitant and fearful, sadly accepting the unfortunate Queen Blue's inevitable fate. Lavender circled the dome seeking the control panel with which she had previously tampered.

After a few minutes of fiddling with certain buttons and codes, Lavender allowed the supply of oxygen to the dome to return to its normal levels. The air within Queen Blue's dome had been diluted with a mixture of elements, which had slowly induced Queen Blue to sleep fitfully. But only after extended sensations of suffocation, followed by hours of intense panic, did Queen Blue gratefully lapse into a coma-like trance.

Lavender entered the dome and eventually woke Queen Blue as both her captor and savior. But she did not allow the Queen to rise until she applied the psychologically innovative strategies that Antboy had unwittingly prescribed. She zealously whispered into the wretched Queen's semiconscious ears, permanently disarming her. She kneeled over the helpless Queen Blue for an entire day, a night, and the better part of the next day, chattering ceaselessly, hypnotically. She responded to the periodic knocks upon the Queen's door with, "Let the Queen rest!"

Hovering over the temporarily paralyzed and comatose Queen, she concluded, "Blue, you have been deep asleep, very deep. I am now going to wake you. It is I, Lavender. I am the one responsible for what has happened to your dome. When you awake, you will remember only that the Workers may be few but we are strong. We will no longer allow Mothers to mistreat us. If you again take any action against a Worker, your punishment will be even more severe. Let the Codex never again be defiled, nor blasphemed. It is now time to wake."

Lavender took the symbolic key, worn by every Queen since Siren, that lay upon Queen Blue's, nearly lifeless, sapphire complexion, and put it around her own neck. With that, Blue groggily, hungrily, weakly awoke from her trance-like state. Lavender carried the deposed Queen Blue from the Dome of the Queen, deposited her outside of its door, and closed it behind the slumped Queen Blue. Lavender ascended the dais, sat upon the throne and made herself comfortable in her new home. She twirled the key within her fingers, slightly surprised by the coldness of the metal, thinking back to the time when Antboy had placed it upon her neck. She vowed to never part with it again.

The Colony was grateful and celebrated the inauguration of Queen Lavender. There was immediate restoration of peace and harmony among both Workers and Mothers. The Worker Revolt had ended.

Sitting cross-legged before Queen Lavender, Antboy was silent. He placed his chin in his palms, pontificating. Antboy hoped his words would endow Lavender with courage to change her mind, and to disavow the Endeavors, at least for a while. His words had inspired her years before, and she had listened to him, and he prayed she would do so again.

"Lavender, please do not do this. Postpone the Endeavors. It is too soon."

"I will not."

His last chance to reach her, to convince her to abandon her plans, loomed. "Your Majesty, I beg you to reconsider your position."

"If that is all you have to offer me, Antboy, after I have taken the time to summon you, and you have traveled far from your home to meet me, then you must leave." She stared icily into his eyes.

Antboy summoned his words carefully, choosing an approach he hoped would be subliminally effective, "Great people are not born; they are formed. Created from complex situations that require major change. No one is born with the guts to alter things. This courage derives from inner strength and extraordinary faith.

"A belief so strong that change must occur forces a great person, alone, to take the first steps to transform things. You have already taken these fledgling steps. Now, if you are certain in your beliefs, then you will finish the walk that guides your feet. But if you are not absolutely willing to face the ramifications of your actions, then this path should not be traveled at this time."

Antboy wished she was still simply Lavender, the woman that woke up first, all those years ago, the girl with the aromatic scent of lavender, who had loved him and whom he had loved. Wafts of her scent undulated through his nostrils, and he was overtaken by a lustful, passionate impulse. She was feared and respected now, but not long ago she was abused and humiliated, and deeply scarred. Wounded, she had not run away; instead she vowed revenge.

And it was this revenge that had consumed Lavender. What he strove to know was whether every essence of her being had been burnt to ash in that furious fire that seized her soul. If he looked into the pit of her heart, was there anything left of what once was, or what could have been? There had to be. If he sifted through the ashes he was sure that he would find a piece of Lavender's heart that survived the bitter conflagration that had become her daily breath.

Lavender was still so very beautiful, so utterly, gloriously lovely. Although her motivations had been self-serving, desiring only vengeance, she had actually saved the colony, which had teetered on the brink of calamitous consequences. Lavender had struggled, inherently resisting the use of unnecessary force.

Reconciling her personal desires with those of the colony, Lavender restored the mutually beneficial and symbiotic relationship between Workers and Mothers, a peaceful and cohesive existence within the colony. There was no longer strife, or struggle, but still she was not healed.

Long ago, Antboy had given up on Lavender and abandoned hope for her salvation, but his emotions and passion for her were momentarily resurrected. Something stirred in him that he hadn't felt since the earliest days of their arrival, seemingly a lifetime ago. Feelings undefined, irrepressible, and incomprehensible overcame him, and his desire to share his feelings for her, and his coveted secret could not be suppressed.

He felt the need to tell her what he had done. Lavender had a right to raise her son, and know what an amazement Atum had become. He was certain she would hear him out. Overwhelmed with emotion, Antboy lost the control that he had maintained for so long. So he said, "Lavender, I have something to tell you. I did something a long time ago that..."

Lavender held up her hand to silence Antboy. It was not the time, nor would it ever be.

"Please, Lavender," he pleaded, but two Scouts approached Antboy to enforce the Queen's command for silence. "I love you," his wrenching soul shouted unheard in the stillness. His now impossible opportunity had slid away, a drowning victim slipping from his rescuer into the dark, unforgiving waters below.

Queen Lavender stood majestically and militantly, and pronouncedly told him what she had interpreted from the Coda. Then she resolutely proclaimed, "We are ready for the

Endeavors. The colonists have already been informed. Arrangements have been made for this essential event. The first born Beasts shall vie to spread their seed, by competing to the death!"

Antboy was aghast at what he heard. "No, please, for love of the Codex, do not do this, your Majesty! Radical change causes radical results, and you may risk the balance of the order you strove so long to establish. Something else can be done, must be done. You cannot commit this atrocity, you mustn't!"

Lavender quickly signaled for her Scouts to advance and escort Antboy swiftly from her chamber. Tossed boorishly from the Dome of the Queen, and barred from reentry, Antboy regained his balance and sullenly retreated home, traveling the abandoned tunnels along the outskirts of the colony. Antboy was again alone, eternally alone, and he returned forlornly to Atum.

XXXIII

"Hello, Father. I know you're upset." Atum sheepishly strides into their dome.

"Atum, come here and sit down. Where have you been?"

"I went to see Ava. I think I love her."

"Atum, things are getting complicated right now. What you think you feel for Ava is going to confuse things even further. Queen Lavender told me that the Endeavors will begin midday tomorrow, less than thirty hours from now."

"Yes, Father, Ava told me about them, and about the addendum that Queen Lavender has interpreted from the Codex."

"That's just it, Atum. I don't even know if there is an addendum, because you know I haven't been able to crack their language completely. What I've deciphered from my copy of the Codex doesn't speak at all about the horrors that she claims have now been revealed. I have no Coda in my version. Either she's made it up, or someone back on earth sent us with a single, revised Codex that was surely written by a madman."

"But, Father, I know the Codex was supposed to be based upon your research."

"It was, Atum, but then my work was taken, and I was never able to document my conclusions. This alleged Codex is a deformed, deviously distorted version of my work."

"Why, Father, and how? Who did this?"

"I don't know if HSI is behind this manipulation, or another entity, or a rogue individual. Possibly it's been corrupted by Queen Lavender's delusions, but somehow I doubt that. Boarding the shuttle on Departure Day, I saw seventy-two females, in some type of trance or maybe under sedation, each one with a copy of an encrypted book, the Codex. That's the first time I saw it."

"Isn't there a way to stop the Endeavors, Father?"

"Not now, son. I must stay and make sure they never occur again. I need to get you off the planet immediately, Atum. You'll return to the launch site on the Peninsula, where we departed in '16, thirteen years ago."

"I'm not leaving without you, Father."

"Don't argue. We're out of time."

"I'm not going to leave here, without you. I won't."

"That's impossible. I have to finish what I started here. We'll be separated for a short time. Don't be unreasonable."

"I'm not leaving without Ava either."

"Atum, if I send you with Ava, there will be severe penalties imposed on Constance, and others. I'm going to make it look like the shuttle broke away from the planet. With only you on board, no one will be missed. If Ava goes missing, they will suspect something."

"I'm not leaving without you or Ava."

"Son, you and Ava can be together once you let the right people know exactly what's going on here. Then you and I will be reunited. There are people that won't allow this to continue, but they need to be notified."

"Father, I'm not sure I'm ready to leave. I'm scared. I think I should stay. I can hide."

"Atum, this is the most difficult thing for me to say to you. I need you to leave. I must make sure that what will happen here tomorrow, will never occur again. By staying, your life and many others are in peril. Son, I've never risked showing you the shuttle, but it's time now."

"All right, Father, but my mind is made up. We all leave together, even Constance."

"Ok, Atum, let's talk about that while we walk to the shuttle. Let's go. I'm sending you back to earth with a copy of the Codex. I'll give you names of people that I knew from HSI and the International Coalition. I began working with them when I left the military in early '12."

"The year the world was supposed to end."

"Yes, Atum, the year it was predicted the world would end."

"But it didn't."

"No, it didn't. When we launched it was right before the election of '16, in fact, Election Day, November 1, was exactly one week away."

"You told me it was a historic election."

"Yes, Atum, it was. All the elections during those years were historic. It was certain that the nation would have a female Vice President, because both Presidential candidates had chosen a female running mate. Beyond the significance of that breakthrough, there were rumors that whichever party won also planned to make history again, at the next election. Apparently both pairs of candidates had come to a cooperative arrangement. Each party internally agreed, if they were victorious, that they would reverse the ticket when the time came to run for reelection. Basically the female Vice President would run as President and the male President would be on the ticket as VP. The nation was trying to break gender and racial barriers in those days."

"But you don't know who won, right Father?"

"No, I don't. Communication was lost as soon as we got here. Either way, a female Vice President was going to be elected in '16. Once this was certain to happen, HSI lobbied for our satellite launch, and each pair of candidates met separately with HSI. Neither party wanted our launch to look like a female-based initiative. Everyone agreed that the project should be pushed earlier to avoid gender politics, with a scheduled launch date before the election. It was timed well and our launch date of October 25 was drowned out by the media blitz that predictably surrounded the election. The coverage easily dwarfed news of our launch, which was considered best, considering the controversy that surrounded HSI."

Father and I traverse foreign territory, comprised of involved twists and turns. He's studying a map that I've never seen him produce before. He keeps getting frustrated, saying, "It's a needle in a haystack," and he counts steps as we take them. I'm memorizing as I go, as always.

I will not leave here without Ava and I'll get her as soon as Father shows me what I need to know for the launch. I have to get her before the Endeavors start. I have about twelve hours to spare, which is all the time that I can afford to stay with Father. Then I'll slip away.

"Father, there is so much metal in this area."

"Yes, Atum, that's because we're getting closer. We're approaching the outer perimeter of our planet, and the entire outside is made of metal."

"It's so cold around here."

"The closer we get, the colder it gets."

"All of this metal is contraband, Father, right?"

"Yes, that's right, Atum, it's illegal for a settler to take or remove any of this metal. The planet will become imbalanced and destabilize if too much metal is shifted around. We depend on this metal to protect us. It's precious metal from earth herself. We're getting closer."

"It's strange. On your planet people took metal out of the inside to help them live on top, but here the metal is on top, which helps us live inside."

"That is kind of strange. Here, this is the section that we need to manually remove, and behind it is the shuttle." They struggle to pull down the panels that Antboy had used to camouflage the craft, just after their arrival, five months before Atum's birth.

Before them lies their immaculate craft of escape, the shuttle *Endeavour*.

"There she is, Atum."

"Wow. She's awesome, Father. But she's too big for me to fly her."

"Atum, you won't need to. She'll fly herself. You just need to be aboard."

"But the key, Father, you don't have the key."

"Atum, the key was just used for the door, and I jimmied that a long time ago. The ignition is completely electronic, and I have the passwords for the launch sequence. I know how to override the system to manually liftoff, which will occur exactly twenty-four hours after I commence the launch procedures. It may not be '41, when the entire satellite is due to return, but when we launched in '16, there were many that bet against us lasting more than a couple of years. They were wrong. For you it's Birthing Cycle Nine, but where you're going, it's '29."

"I want to see the inside, Father."

"You will. First I need to get the door to release." Father begins fiddling and poking.

"When was she first launched?"

" In '92."

"She's old, Father. Are you sure she'll still fly?"

"She's not as old as me, son, and I'm still working. I was eight years old when she was first launched. She's also the last and youngest of all five shuttles that were built. Throughout your life, I couldn't risk bringing you here, but I've kept up annual maintenance on her. Let's go inside now, and begin the power up procedures. We have a lot of preparation to do and I'll be giving you very specific instructions. I have important things to explain to you."

We board the enormous, beautiful craft. Father motions for me to watch him as he plays with certain switches and dials, and he flips through a manual, pointing at numbered diagrams.

Father continues explaining the events surrounding Departure Day. "Several powerful women were heavily involved with the process of bringing a female Vice President into office. Two were former First Ladies. Another was a powerful iconic media figure that had launched her own television network. There were a couple of former female Secretaries of State. One woman had survived an assassination attempt while serving in Congress. Some former Governors, as well as CEO's were also active. All were determined to advance their gender's role and rule in the third millennium. These powerful women avidly followed the General's advice, to first run alongside the men, and to defer their own pursuit of the Presidency until the subsequent election. The ubiquitous General lured and maneuvered them into the controversial, yet appealing objectives of the newly reconfigured IC."

"Your world seems so complicated, Father."

"Yes it was, and most probably still is. Unfortunately, I'm going to make things even more complicated for you, son."

"How?"

"I'm going to turn on a video recorder and explain some things to you, which I thought I had another twelve years to tell you. That's when our satellite is scheduled to orbit back into earth's atmosphere and glide downward to gently splash into the ocean. Much of what I will say may not make sense now, but I'm recording it for you to watch again."

"All right, Father, I'm ready."

"Atum, I told you I retired from the military at age twenty-eight. I served ten years, and had been deployed four times. After Target One was eliminated, I decided to finish my tour of duty and return to civilian life. There were things that were unresolved from my childhood, and it was time to address them. There was the cryptic discussion that I had with Hiawatha about saving the bees and drilling down to the mantle. I needed to figure out if that was truly possible, and see if it could be achieved. I wanted to see the General, who I hadn't seen since I went into basic training. Most importantly, I hoped to reconcile and form a stronger connection with my parents, who had taken a new assignment at ADX Supermax.

"I went first to my parents. They were working on a classified project at the nation's only federal supermax prison. It housed four hundred of the most dangerous convicted male criminals in the world. Within that prison was a much smaller and most heinous set of offenders, which were the most perfidious on the planet.

"There were six-dozen men who were considered too dangerous or high profile to be in any other prison. They were so menacing that they were not allowed contact with any other inmates, ever. Most of them were sentenced to life, with no possibility of parole. Some were issued release dates two hundred years in the future. They were cartel leaders, organized crime bosses, gang founders, mafia heads, mass murderers, international spies, and the group that my parents were studying, the bombers.

"The bombers were supremely dangerous because they were highly intelligent, and had no guilt about killing for their causes. They also knew how to kill from a distance without harming themselves. A few were suicide bombers whose plans went awry, killing no one but forever incarcerating themselves as a result of their failed attempts.

"My parents sought to find patterns among the bombers, and they had received a sizable grant and approval to perform psychiatric evaluations. The bombers had been incarcerated for years without being allowed visitors, so they opened up easily during analysis. I saw things on their tapes that no one else was privy to see. In these sessions, the bombers sought to rationalize their actions and their life choices, and also to figure out why things went wrong for them.

"It was chilling watching those tapes in my parents' living room. The people throughout the years that I had heard about, the most feared and deadliest were housed under one roof. Many of them met with my parents. Still others were in the pipeline to see them when I left my parents to visit the General."

"Father, it sounds terrible there. It seems safer here."

"To some degree you're right, but there weren't that many of these guys. They were a slim minority of the population. They were essentially bad people, doing evil things. The work my parents did substantially helped to understand the mind of a bomber. Bombers were methodical and meticulous planners. They were angry at something in their own lives. Then they directed that anger outward, wanting to be heard, to be loud, to go off like a bomb, to get attention, possibly to get back at someone, or to prove something to someone. It was personal with these bombers. They felt they had a right to take lives to make their point. These guys felt that they had been victimized at some point, and they held the masses responsible for their victimization. So, no one was an innocent bystander in their calculations, in fact, anyone was fair game. The suicidal ones blamed the world as well and wanted to make their mark by taking out themselves and as many others as possible.

"Hearing them pour out their thoughts and emotions was sickening and surreal. They readily admitted that they were capable of committing the same crimes if released, and if angry enough, they would. I brought some of their tapes and they're in the digital library of this craft.

"One of the bombers, an offender named Rednose, came up with an idea called Bombertown. He casually, possibly humorously, proposed that bombers like him shouldn't cost the country millions to cage him and feed him for the rest of his natural life. Instead, Rednose suggested that it would better serve the public if these offenders were dropped off in a remote, designated spot where they couldn't get out, and then be given the means to battle and blow each other up until there was no one left. When I heard this absurdly compelling idea of Bombertown, I knew I would eventually relay it to the General, upon my next visit to him. So I did.

The General grew obsessed with the concept. By Departure Day he was heavily promoting the idea.

"The disks are all here for you, including the data analysis I completed during those four years between my military retirement and Departure Day. You'll learn about the work that I started on the underground colonies, work that I left unfinished when I boarded this craft before your birth. Watch them while the shuttle fulfills its pre-flight checklist, during the time I'm at the Endeavors. I'll be back before you finish watching them. Sit down, here in the Commander's seat."

I sit in the Commander's seat and feel empowered. Father tells me to relax and puts the seat into a reclining position, nearly horizontal, which he says is utilized when the flight crew rotates their sleeping shifts.

Then he tells me about the meeting he had with the General, which he arranged, right after leaving his parents.

XXXIV

"Atum, I had spent ten years in the military, for the most part separated from my homeland, in tribal, border desert regions hunting terrorists. I was glad to be home. Then, while spending time with my parents, I realized I had some unfinished business.

"Hiawatha's complex advice about bees, honey, drills, and underground colonization had been beyond my conception as an eleven year old boy. Yet in the emptiness of my recently departed career, her words rang out and echoed clearly. I vowed to work on preserving the bees and studying them, and to research methods of designing and building the world's largest drill. I planned on doing this after visiting my parents.

"Before I could set out to research the process of establishing underground colonies, which was next on my agenda, I knew that the General expected me to visit him for a military exit interview and to be personally debriefed by him. I said farewell to my parents, and set out for the Capitol, to report to the General. I had important things to tell him, but first I wanted to hear what he had to say."

The two military men salute, and share a hug. "Sir, what threats are we now facing?" It was as if no time had passed.

"Son, walk with me." The General and Antboy make their way into the adjoining room and face a wall of paintings displaying the country's greatest military leaders.

The General pontificates, "As a nation, we have successfully faced the deadliest threats the world has ever known. There are consistent threats of international and domestic terrorism. There is increased potential for chemical, biological, or nuclear warfare. There has always been the grim possibility of poisoned water supplies. The release of highly communicable deadly viruses is something we still defend against. Most of our resources are devoted to fighting global threats to our political and economic systems. However, the threats that plague us now, are different.

"Nations throughout the world face destructive trends that endanger our species. Our experts have compiled and studied statistics for decades. They say these threats are invisible, irreversible, inexorable, and insurmountable. Immune systems have been weakened. There are higher fatality rates from viruses such as common influenza. Other diseases that had been previously eliminated now flourish unchecked. Infant mortality is rising. Fertility rates are severely down. Prospective parents face a higher probability that one or both of them will be infertile. We have extinguished many species and, alternately, have brought back others from the brink of extinction. But we are the species that now faces such a cataclysmic fate.

"That's why I traveled to the Patent Office so long ago, to meet you, and to intervene. A boy with a box, they told me, and I was on my way. As a result of your invention, and your discoveries, a pact was formed among an international coalition of nations. This agreement formed HSI, the Human Survival Initiative, whose sole mission was to prevent human extinction. We are the lead country of the International Coalition, and we hold worldwide patents on the technologies involved, and maintain control of the timeline for the initiative's implementation."

"Sir, you know I've thought long and hard about our prospects for survival as a species."

"Son, you are prophetic, a visionary at the very least. What is it that you see?"

"Father, what did you reveal to the General?" Atum listens intently as Antboy tells him.

"The insight I shared with the General was gleaned the day I saw our world from an ant's perspective. I imparted my perceptions and predictions, straight from the day I lived as an ant."

Father laughed and so did I. It felt good.

"So you don't believe I was an ant for a day?"

"No, I don't."

"Well, Atum, I don't really know what to believe either anymore. I obviously didn't share that I was an ant with the General because he would have had me committed. I left out everything about me being an ant, but I shared with him what I learned from little Benazir and the open door. It was my twenty-third birthday, and when I woke up I was an ant. I can't really explain it, but I think they gave me a sort of present, an unimaginable gift. The ants must have known that if I could see the world from their perspective I would achieve true enlightenment.

"As I was leaning over to get out of bed I started running and it seemed to take forever just to reach the edge of my foam military mat. All six of my legs were frenziedly busy propelling me to what looked like a cliff drop at the edge. When I reached the precipice, I thought I would fall off but instead my legs stuck to the makeshift mattress and I moved at a ninety-degree angle directly toward the ground until I fell off and hurtled downward, plunging, unmercifully landing on my back. As I wriggled my limbs to roll over on my front I realized I was indeed an ant.

"Soon I encountered what looked like herds of strange creatures that were approaching. One of them was carrying a bright torch and she announced that she was Benazir, their leader. The rest gathered in a circle around me."

"'Antboy, today you will see from our eyes,' they chanted. They signaled for me to open any one of forty doors that suddenly appeared before us. Randomly, I picked one and entered, and so did the herds of ants behind me. Then they swarmed me, lifting me above them and I rode a tidal wave, passing back and forth, back and forth, and I was lulled into some type of reverie.

"Through the random door I had chosen, I saw and perceived more clearly what I had only witnessed on television and had read in periodicals. Woven into my dreamlike trance was spun an intuitive interpretation of the past, present, and future. I saw a medicated world, a world where most were taking prescription medicines, taken freely to combat basic ailments. Depression rose and populations were pervaded by rampant drug use. Minds and bodies grew dependent on drugs, and immune systems suffered, creating susceptibility and vulnerability to bacterial and viral attack. Viruses and bacteria became stronger and resisted medications. Epidemics abounded. Computer viruses knocked out power grids. Nations were sublimated and paralyzed by lack of electricity. There was no energy to power the machines that purified water, and rampant, deadly viruses bred easily. Factors caused fertility rates to decrease precipitously in some areas and rise unpredictably in others. Exposure to toxins in food, additives, preservatives, dyes, traces of metal and plastics from packaging, and low levels of radiation caused epidemic proportions of infertility in both men and women. Contraception predominated. Women produced fewer healthy eggs and birth defects rose. Waves permeated. Microwaves mutated the molecular structure of food. Waves of cellular communication spread through the air, invisible to the naked eye, traveling through our bodies and particularly through our brains. Autism flourished. Technology was affixed to our ears, bodies, and brains. Cancer was commonplace.

"I slammed the door shut, and stood in front of Benazir critically, demanding to know why she chose to ruin my birthday. She ignored me and began reading a prepared lecture."

"We ants have the desire to live, to continue as a species, and this desire is part of our collective consciousness. This awareness has allowed us to proliferate throughout the universe, like the infrared rays you cannot see, throughout time and space. We burrow, plan, hunt food, build, and take only that which is provided, nothing more, living solely within our natural environs, that which was provided to us by the original source of all life.

"Your desire to live is countered by your collective longing to accumulate. Your information technology spreads throughout the world. Your species is enamored with things that it cannot afford, so it slavishly works, without thought, hopelessly living day to day, wanting and yearning. For you, knowledge is no longer power, it is the power to purchase.

"Life will become a much greater struggle. Food quality will rapidly deteriorate. The reliability of goods and services will greatly diminish. Health care will be unreliable. Mass genocides will exterminate those that want to slow the bureaucracy and machinery of progress. You will no longer be able to sustain the elderly. Infant death rates will increase, fertility will decrease, and resources like clean air and water will be obtained only at high cost."

Antboy absorbed Benazir's words for several moments, before responding, "Most people believe that what you're telling me is purely myth. They argue that statistics are rubbish."

"They are wrong. This planet is finite, with limited resources. Your spacecraft can circle the globe in less two hours, so earth is not as large as you may think."

"Can you tell me what we're supposed to do?"

"From a practical perspective you need to hedge your bets. Bring your species elsewhere and colonize under very strict rules. Establish a permanent society, or systems of societies, run by the power that was created for you to use, the star you call the sun. This power is free. Store solar energy and abandon all other forms of power. Connect with the sun, because it was provided for you. Preserve the immense knowledge that you have accumulated. Build a computer that stores all the knowledge necessary for survival, along with the history of this planet. Launch it, to be powered solely by the sun."

"Benazir, you don't understand us at all. That's too radical and will never happen."

"You must expand your thinking by removing the skepticism and barriers that you project upon yourselves. Your species has accumulated a vast wealth of knowledge. You are too intelligent to annihilate yourselves. You were not created simply to disappear without a trace."

With that Benazir scurried away without a trace. The wave stopped and the amassed ants disseminated. Antboy scuttled back to bed and fell asleep, awakening to find that he had recovered his two arms and two legs.

"Atum, I told the General about all of my visions and prophecies, shared everything that I had learned from both Hiawatha and Benazir, and discussed the convict interviews and Bombertown.

"He listened to everything that I said, and motioned for me to continue, so I did. I shared my belief that specific plans must be made to appropriately back up the human species and its knowledge. Supercomputers should be created and located off planet, set in space as satellites, storing all knowledge of mankind, and run completely by solar energy, engineered to be adaptable to various environments. I emphasized that man must settle outside the earth and deep within it. To better insure human survival, a satellite planet should be sent up as a birthing machine, readily able to provide new life that can settle in diversified locations. Underground colonies should also be established within the earth's mantle as a hedge against living on the crust and off the earth.

"I took several deep breaths and stared at the General. The General said nothing for quite some time. He somberly looked off into the distance, thinking about my words. Then he said, 'Antboy, you are the voice of the future casting a stern warning that the reckoning is near. You are also the voice of the past, disdain and disillusionment, colored by the recognition of disobedient transgressions, and finally the voice of the present, which is hope.'

"I asked him, 'Sir, what are we going to do?'
"He acknowledged, 'Son, I'm not sure yet.'"

Antboy departed to research and draw up plans for the underground colonies.

Dismissing Antboy, the General knew exactly what *he* needed to do. Setting off a chain of events in order to preempt the extinction, was what needed to be done, he mused. Attempting to control the inevitable by accelerating it, from a military standpoint, was extraordinarily practical, tactically precise and expedient. He began to draw up plans for Bombertown.

XXXV

I stretch and yawn, and realize I drifted off. I glance up to see a video of Father in a white beekeeper suit, which looks very similar to the space suits hanging here in the shuttle. He's talking about pesticides, honey production, feeding schedules, and failed hives.

Where's Father? I need him with me. I'm certainly not prepared to go to his world alone. Craning my neck to find him, I pull myself upward but I'm restrained, harnessed to the reclined seat, by some type of secured belt. There's a display above the screen with numbers that are counting down, less than nineteen hours until launch.

Father tricked me. I should have known. He had me lie back in the chair, and knew that his voice would eventually put me to sleep, like it did so many nights, for over nine birthing cycles, here on this place I call home, a day's journey to his.

I'll get out. Then I'll get Ava, Father, and Constance, and we'll be back here before liftoff. I can do this. I'll figure this out. I strain and strain, pulling muscles throughout my body. There has to be a way out of this.

Father and some men are laughing on the screen above me. They're looking at a jar of honey and remarking on the color, congratulating each other for some accomplishment. There's footage of a bee preserve, with miles and miles of hives.

Then there's footage of some men who are talking about a huge drill, a drill used to rescue what looks like trapped miners, coming up a metal tube to the surface. Then there's a picture of thirty-three men, very happy to be alive, having been trapped for over two months. The drill that was used to rescue them was almost a half-mile long.

Father and several men are huddled over a drafting table looking at design plans for a massive drilling system. Then they are looking at a wall high computer screen and they're touching portions of the monitor. They are tracing a long line from the top to the bottom, and performing calculations on the upper right portion of the display. Father and the men are animated. They're working on Father's big plan to colonize the mantle, to preserve humans by creating a new place for them to live. Unfortunately, Father never found out what happened to his plans for underground human colonization, because he was called into duty to launch here.

"Open! Detach! Unfasten! Open seat belt! Remove! Unlock! Let me out!" Every word that Father has taught me that means "open" is hollered from my lips. When Father was showing me the control systems he was issuing commands through voice activation, as he did with some components of the dome maintenance system. Nothing is working.

"Release! Undo! Unbolt! Help! Get me out of here! Stop!" The screen above me goes blank. There must be an instruction manual here, or some automatic command that will release this locking mechanism. "Display Procedures!" I yell at the screen. A menu of options for me to choose from appears on the screen, replacing its empty display. "Cabin!" A picture of the cabin appears. "Commander's Chair!" A blueprint of the chair upon which I sit is shown. The chair is labeled J-41. "J-41!" I shout, but nothing happens. Then I see there's a list of technical specifications for the chair, with a line that says Release Command: Open Sesame.

"Open Sesame!" I scream and the buckles unfasten and belts retract. I bolt upright from the seat and head to the door, looking back to catch a glimpse of the digital display which registers the eighteen hour mark. Five hours to get to the Dome of Endeavors and another five back, gives me eight hours to find Ava and Father and get them here safely. I run at full speed, twisting and turning my way through the labyrinthine tunnels to rescue Ava from the dreaded Endeavors. Stopping briefly to catch my breath, I resume, for thirty minutes at a stretch, alternating with rest breaks.

I must reach Constance at the Dome of Beasts. I will convince her to find Ava for me, because it's too risky for me to approach the Dome of Girls myself, with everyone sure to be awake. Father has trusted her all these years, and I must, because she's the mother of Ava, the girl I love.

Through my covert studies of Father's copy of the concealed Codex, during those nights when he slept soundly and I did not, I have learned the colonial language well. But I had never put it into practice until days ago. I hope that Constance understands me now, and the urgency of the situation, because even Ava is at risk during the fourteen days of Endeavors ahead.

Constance trusts Father implicitly, so once she believes that this is his plan, I think she'll help me find Ava. Ava won't leave without her Mother so I must convince Constance that she must also come with us. If Ava leaves without her Mother, Constance will face a bleak life here, possibly to be banished to the Dome of Darkness with former Queen Blue, or maybe worse. Through the dim entrance to the Dome of Beasts, I vaguely see Constance tending the youngest boys. There are no other Workers.

"Constance."

"Atum, what are you doing here? You should be waiting for your Father at the Dome of Maintenance, and you should be hiding."

"I know. I need to find Ava."

"What do you want with Ava, Atum?"

I tell Constance about the shuttle and our plans to return to the planet where she herself was born. Though I realize that her remembrance of earth is nearly void, having been raised in experimental isolation with the other original colonists, I try to create a sense of nostalgia in her. I appeal to Constance using every method I've ever used with Father to get my way, and then I fall to my knees and beg. She eyes me warily and then bluntly, simply refuses my request.

"I can't get Ava. By now she's in the Dome of Endeavors, preparing for the opening ceremonies due to begin in a few hours. As soon as I finish here, I'm going there. It's mandatory that we all attend."

"Please, Constance, you must tell her I came back and that I'm going to rescue her."

"It's impossible for you to rescue her. How can you? Even so, I won't be allowed to contact her while final details for the competitions are being made. I'm sorry, Atum."

"But Father has made all the arrangements. I'm going to take you and Ava away from here, to a better place."

"What better place? Better for you? This is our home and we don't know anything else. It's tough for Beasts here, but not for us."

"Constance, you can bring children, some of the boys here, and some girls. They'll have a better life. I know how much you care for the children. You know that half of the boys here in this dome won't even make it to my age now. And then, they'll face the Endeavors. You can round up some of them and meet us at a rendezvous spot where I'll return with Ava and Father."

"It won't work. Besides, it's too risky. If they catch us, the punishment will be severe."

"No matter what, the shuttle is launching. It's better for us to be on it, than not."

"This sounds crazy, Atum, and so do you. You're just like your Father."

"I'm sorry, Constance, but the shuttle will launch in fifteen hours, so I must leave right now to get Ava and Father."

"Atum, if I don't show up at the Dome of Endeavors, the Scouts will look for me."

"No, they won't notice that you're missing. They'll be very busy with the opening ceremonies for hours. I can trace the path to the shuttle on the wall, and you can meet us there. It's a complicated path but I can direct you to a safe, remote tunnel near the launch site and we'll find you there."

"Atum, you'll get yourself killed, and Ava too, and my heart will be broken."

"I swear to you, I will not fail. It will take several hours, but we'll be there."

"How many children should I bring? You know that I'll be risking their lives as well."

"As many as you can handle, without drawing attention. A small group is best."

I trace the path for Constance, and review it with her several times. She memorizes it.

"Travel swiftly and safely, Atum. Be careful with Ava."

"I will, I promise, and you as well, Constance. Thank you for believing in me."

"Atum, I don't believe in you, but I wish I did. I just can't argue with you, that's all."

"Goodbye, Constance."

"See you soon, Atum."

XXXVI

Two more grueling hours of sprinting and navigating the tortuous tunnels, and then I see the palatial, awesome dome that towers over all others, the frightful Dome of Endeavors. There are four Scouts blocking the dome's entrance ahead. I watch them meticulously from the hidden recesses of an adjacent, vacant dome. Periodically, two disappear inside the dome, and then return, trading places with the others. One of them leaves their post, heading away from me, leaving only one Scout as sentinel, and two on the inside.

This is my chance. I can get past the sentry at the entrance, find Ava and Father, create a diversion, and depart. They won't be able to track us easily. I have the map memorized and can lose anyone easily in the winding tunnels.

I perceive a slight movement in my peripheral vision. My eyes dart left to look, then something crashes brutally into my temple, and I fall to the ground. I cannot rise. Darkness descends upon my aching skull. The still silence of my capture reigns painfully as I'm dragged away, alternating in and out of consciousness. I try to regain focus, yet every blink of my eyes deeply and agonizingly blurs my surroundings, although I know exactly where they've put me.

Blinding light surrounds and pierces the arena, filtering through the large dome's massive ceiling. Mothers enter the dome in linear formation, the highest fertility rankings entering first, followed by Mothers in descending order of rank. Then Queen Lavender enters the pavilion, in a regal ivory robe unworn until this moment, originally designed for this event by Queen Siren, during the first birthing cycle of the colony. Immediately following the Queen are Workers.

Queen Lavender connects Mothers and Workers. She had ascended the throne to lead and uphold the laws of the colony, which still favored Mothers, but she still maintained strong ties with her constituents of Workers without whom she would not be Queen.

They formally file into an ascended region of the dome where benches have been placed in concentric circles for spectator viewing. Queen Lavender sits in the middle, and Mothers fill the first concentric circles, and then Workers sit in the circle furthest from the Queen. All turn to face Queen Lavender, while preparations continue for the competitions, several levels below on the busy floor.

Lavender explains that the event they will behold marks the beginning of the Tenth Birthing Cycle. She clarifies that without these Endeavors the colony will fail to meet appropriately established fertility goals. If that happens, she solemnly warns, then their colony will no longer flourish and instead will enter a period of decadence preceding eventual collapse and ruination. By virtue of this event's structure, to be held every eighteen months, the birth of a new generation of Mothers and Workers is assured. She reminds them that all Workers and Mothers have been granted leave from their normal duties to attend any or all fourteen days of Endeavors.

Lavender cautions Mothers and Workers to feel no sorrow for what they will see, for both Breeders and Beasts must undergo this transformation. She explains that the Beasts competing are the best genetic specimens. Only the winning Beasts will be allowed to participate in the Aftermath, at which point Breeders will receive them, and reward them gloriously. Lavender advises them that those Breeders most fit to bear children will begin their journey to Motherhood during these fourteen days. Breeders not deemed worthy of that honor, will hold the precious title of Worker, a most valued group without which the colony would perish.

Lavender predicts that half of the forty-one Beasts competing will survive the Endeavors. She will not stay for the Aftermath, which will begin when the scorching midday sun directly over them reaches the outer boundary of the dome's exterior. She will take a sabbatical to plan the new housing configurations. Soon, she must situate these courageous Breeders within their new domiciles, having graduated from their residence in the overpopulated Dome of Girls Primary.

Asking everyone to turn their attention to the scene below, she spots her four Scouts busily making final preparations. In the distance Lavender perceives the hunched figure of Antboy, who is being led by a Scout to the Queen's position, far removed from the violent dangers below. Although he begged not to attend, Antboy was paid no heed by Queen Lavender, who required his presence.

When she sent for him just two days before, he was reluctant to be present. He reasoned that he could be of no assistance at the Endeavors, and instead cautioned that his animosity toward the event might even hinder its successful completion. She dismissed his feeble attempt to protest, quoting from the Codex that his specific attendance was required at all colony wide events. To disobey, would be viewed by any Queen as an act of disloyalty and subversion.

To put an end to Antboy's argument, Queen Lavender expressly forewarned that his absence would bring severe repercussions onto all ages of Beasts, even the babies. Knowing that she had hit upon a sensitive area, she was certain he would promptly arrive, ready to take the seat next to her, and hear the opening proclamation. Ever punctual, Antboy, bearing gloomy demeanor, follows the Scout to Queen Lavender's side. She notes his walk of condemnation. He is a prisoner of his own creation.

Workers and Mothers surrounding the Queen shirk Antboy as he moves between them to reach the inner circle of the circles. He is still shunned by them, as forever he will be. They hiss and hurl unfathomable phrases of irate scorn in his direction, but Queen Lavender silences them with a dismissive gesture from one hand. "He must be here for it is written in the Codex. Show the respect that he deserves. Discontinue your disapproval, or you will face dire punishment," Queen Lavender solemnly advises her loyal attendants. Antboy meekly sits by her side, resigned to witness the loathsome occasion. Lavender and Antboy survey the massive pavilion.

The eldest Breeders, the firstborn girls of the colony are in a high-fenced pen on the left side of the dome. A massive rock sits in the center of the dome and two Scouts surround it. The remaining two Scouts stand in front of a large cage at the far end of the dome. Occasionally they jab the enclosed Beasts with javelins to be used in the Endeavors.

Howls of pain can be heard, followed by fearful whimpers. The Beasts are in tattered clothing, some hairy, some hairless, all dirty, and a few smell of fecal matter.

Atum lies in a corner, apart from his peers, neatly groomed in comparison, his ripped clothes covered in blood, body bruised, rubbing his eyes, attempting to soothe his throbbing, and pounding head. He is with the first males born to the colony, the first Beasts to participate in the Endeavors, and he is the eldest, by one month, an alien to them, a survivor of deselection. The other Beasts distrust him; they do not like his smell. These are the smartest Beasts. They had used their brains to survive, to feed themselves, to stay healthy, and to learn the rules. They had fought for their lives, every day of their lives.

The Scouts assume Atum had escaped from the Dome of Beasts when the boys were being herded and assembled for the Endeavors, and they don't know or care how he escaped. Afraid to report him to Queen Lavender, they feared that they would be punished rigorously for his escape, let alone for the savage beating they inflicted upon him. So they did not tell her anything, instead deeply relishing their barbaric attack upon his cowering form.

The strong midday sun directly overhead signals readiness for the Queen's impending call to action. From Antboy's view, only indistinct shapes appear throughout the massive dome, since he, the Queen, and the original colonial founders are seated far from the melee about to commence.

A tinge of nervous energy surrounds Lavender, Antboy, and all the spectators and participants in the Dome of Endeavors. They watch and wait. Chatter can be heard in every portion of the Dome of Endeavors. The Scouts signal to Queen Lavender that all is ready.

"Your Majesty, none of them have to die," Antboy firmly suggests.

"True, Antboy, none of them do have to die," Lavender replies.

"Then why are the Scouts rolling that boulder back and forth?"

"Antboy, our colony does not have the resources to care for the injured. I am more concerned with how the winning Beasts will treat the Breeders during the Aftermath, than I am about this first stage. My Scouts will be on duty from opening to closing and will eliminate any Beasts that harm a Breeder, which I am certain will occur."

"How many of them will survive?"

"We need at least half, but when the sun gets to the far end of this dome, in six hours, everyone alive is a winner. Or when only half of them are left, whichever comes first. Let them all live if they are perfect specimens. Every survivor will live in comfort, away from the Dome of Beasts, to compete again in eighteen months with the next Beasts."

"This is not right, Lavender. This is wrong."

"Who are you to tell me what is right or wrong? I've got a colony to feed. I'm a Worker Queen who still repairs the food generators when they're down. I'm still the one who knows the system better than any, except you. I cannot afford to feed and sustain the weak. You, more than anyone, certainly know that I cannot afford to bring any weakness into being. Have you forgotten so quickly, Antboy?"

"I don't forget anything, your Majesty."

"Neither do I. Without my technical knowledge, that which you bestowed upon me, I would never have been able to overthrow Queen Blue. I owe that to you. I have protected you, making sure every Queen understands that we may need your technical knowledge. You have obviously forgotten your place in this colony. You have forgotten much."

"My Queen, I have not forgotten."

"You act as if you have. Have you forgotten that you volunteered to deselect my child when Queen Siren and the Council deemed him weak? You barely protested, and then offered to destroy him. I have lived by the Codex, since the day that precious life was taken from me."

"I'm sorry, your Majesty, but there is something I need to tell you."

"There's nothing you can say that will repair the tear in my heart, and the worst part is that I've faced my suffering in silent, internal mourning. Don't ever pretend you can mend me."

"But, Lavender." She cuts him off, taking a long tube from an outstretched hand of a nearby Mother. She sees forty or so Beasts in a cage at the far end of the dome, and caddy corner she views at least eighty Breeders in a pen. The attentive Scouts await Lavender's call to action.

Lavender continues, "No one will ever face that pain again, now that I have banned deselection, irrevocably. No mother will ever face the tear of her heart, a tear beyond repair. To humiliate me, Queen Siren propagated a rumor that you poisoned my son and me. The ignominious stigma that befell me, and that I lived with, was torture, even worse than my occasional relegation to the Dome of Darkness."

"I saved your son, Lavender. I saved him. I swear to you I saved him."

"Even now you mock me. You saved him from what? From the harshness of life as a Beast on this colony, you saved him? From today's Endeavors he was spared? By killing him, you think you've saved him? He would have been out there today, now, alive!" She spits in Antboy's face, and then defiantly spits again. She raises and waves a long, curved horn. "These Beasts have had it good. They've had their entire lives to prepare for this day, so let them compete, and live, or die!"

Lavender inaugurates the first Endeavors, by putting her lips to the horn, which augments her voice to reverberate throughout the arena. "Today we celebrate an important ritual, that will now be a tradition for our colony. Today marks a milestone, that we have made it this far, and that we have fertilized, conceived, and birthed well. Today it is time to reap what we have sown. Let the competitions commence! Let the seed be spread! Let the Endeavors begin!"

Queen Lavender hurls a javelin with all her might and it lands, just short of the caged Beasts, impaling the sandy layers of the floor below. Roars can be heard from the cage. Workers and Mothers, comfortably seated along the circles surrounding the Queen jeer, whistle, and scream in anticipation, passing several long spying tubes among their ranks. They appear to be selecting favorites. Breeders, enclosed in their separated, remote pen, pace nervously, some cry, others laugh hysterically, and a few lie unconscious upon the ground.

XXXVII

And then the cage is open, and everyone rushes to the door. Someone's pulling me upward, shoving me out the door. *Ouch*, a javelin is jabbed into my thigh, and it hurts, it really, really hurts. I am in a herd. I am following. We are circling the perimeter of the dome, and constant jabs keep us running along the perimeter of the stands. To the right, as I gallop with the others, I can see screaming, manic Mothers and Workers cheering and jeering, insulting us. To the left, as we circle, we can see another pen, filled with the eldest Breeders. I trip and fall. I get up. We are circling and circling, maybe in a race. I better run faster, something makes me think I should be up in the front, not here in the back. I sprint faster, but my thigh just hurts so much.

Some of the Beasts grow agitated by this strenuous activity. The one just ahead of me falls, he has twisted his ankle and he is clutching it, rolling left and right, whimpering in immense pain. Most run around him, some step on top of him, others kick him out of the way as they pass. When I get there I will help him up. One of the leaders slows for a moment, only to deliberately trip a Beast who had just overtaken him. The unfortunate boy flies headlong, cracking his head into the wall separating the perimeter from the benches where Mothers and Workers sit. And the others pay no heed and just keep running, fearing the spears.

I throw the arm of the injured boy over my shoulder, but he cannot stand. He tries to put his weight on the ankle and then I see a piece of white bone, jagged, protruding from his foot. I drape his arm over my shoulder, to try to help him to a safe place where he can get assistance. As we hobble toward the perimeter, some runners tackle us, get up, and then leave us. He's yelping now, in excruciating pain. He's so heavy, but I lift him again.

Then I see the Scouts doing something odd. They are, no, no, no, it can't, no, stop, you can't, oh, how terrible, I've got to get out of here. I drop him and run, and the rock, the boulder crushes his skull, and I can't get the popping sound, the crushed, bone splitting sound out of my head. I am running and running and I get it now, if you fall, you die. There are too many of us; they don't need us all.

A few vomit as they pass the crumpled figure. Then the Scouts are again rolling the boulder, picking up speed. It's headed straight for the one who was tripped. His head was hurt badly, blood streaming down his cheek from a deep gash. He tries to get up, holding the wall for support, but the boulder smothers him. When they push it back to the center, his flattened, broken, gushing body slowly slides down the wall that had tossed him a temporary lifeline.

I have to keep running. A few of us stop and are resting toward the other side of the dome. That's it. Rest, when possible. I have to rest. Rest when the boulder is far. So I slow down a little and notice that some of us are walking.

The Scouts are working the crowd, jabbing this Beast, rolling the boulder toward that one, and now we're all running again. Everyone looks slightly healthier and stronger after our brief rest. But now we have to keep running.

"Atum!"

"Who's there!?"

"Atum it's me."

"Who?"

"Look over here. It's me."

"I can't turn around. I have to keep running."

"Keep running Atum, you have to live, live, please live. I can't bear to watch you die."

"I can't see you. Who are you?"

"It's me, Ava."

"Ava?"

"Yes Atum, look, look at my face, the next time you pass me, look at me. I want you to live. Just use your brain Atum, and you will live. Try! Don't give up!"

"But I'm in so much pain, and I'm so tired. I don't think I can do it."

"You must."

"I'll try."

One of the runners falls and they roll the boulder over him. He's convulsing, his arms and legs flailing from underneath the massive rock. He's not dead yet. How disgusting! Most of us are walking, resting for a moment, far from the big rock. They back up the boulder to the middle and roll it to crush him again. He just won't die, how horrible!

"Ava, where are you?"

"Here, Atum. Look, you can find me, over here, over here. See me? I'm in this pen. Atum I'm so scared."

"Don't be scared Ava."

"But Atum it's so horrible."

"I know, but how can they do this? They're killing us."

"If I were born male I would be with you, Atum. Just try. Try to live, and we will be all right, you and I. But I'm just so scared. Keep running!"

"I'm trying, Ava. I'm getting tired, but I'll keep running!"

The boulder is rolling here, rolling there, and threatening all. Some try to resume running and can't. They just can't. A few are walking and others have their hands on their knees and they are bent over, trying to catch their breath. They are so tired and no longer wish to resist their fate.

I catch up to them and make them move, push them, carry them, slap them, and yell at them to keep going. They will die if they don't keep moving. They're running again, perhaps I can save them, maybe a few. We stay together in a pack, running for our lives, occasionally looking at the three bodies, all horribly mutilated, one still dying, how great their pain.

"Oh Father, I think I see you. Is that you? Are you up there, with the Queen? Yes, it's you. How much I want to see you. I want to go home. I can't even signal you. You can't see me. I want to see you again. I want to hear your stories. I want you to protect me, help me, but if I show them I know you, or if you try to save me, they might kill us both. This problem is mine! I'll do it; I'll make you proud."

The Scouts are rolling the boulder like a game, crushing a runner's legs, then returning to crush his chest and skull. Stop, stop, we are signaled to stop, and we form into a bunch. The group is collapsing, resting, trying to catch our breath, and the boulder rests dormant, with the four sentinels of death ready to roll it.

Before we were released from the cage, the Scouts wanted our attention. They poked us repeatedly with the pointed blades of their javelins. They told us that the

Endeavors end when the sun reaches the outer edge of the grand pavilion. Those of us still standing at that time are the winners. I won't let them kill me. I'll save as many of my fearful companions as I can.

The sun is moving steadily across the sky. It looks like we have completed the first quarter of our torment!

Two Scouts stay with the boulder, while two stay with their spears. They herd us to a portion where there is a long rectangular area filled with sand. I know this event well. Father would set up this game in our dome, but not very often. It was rare when Father would let me have run of our entire home, the Dome of Maintenance. In fact, only at the height of birthing season, every eighteen months, was he certain that no Scouts patrolled our remote region. There was a four-week period when nearly six babies were born each day and all colonists were needed to help with birthing and nursing.

Only then would he allow me to roam the full extent of our massive dome, giving me a much needed break from academics. Ours was as big as the largest domes on our planet, the Dome of Darkness, Dome of Beasts, and Dome of Endeavors, which were all symmetrically balanced, located at four different poles of our sphere. For that reason, I always looked forward to birthing season, when Father trained me athletically in events that were common on his planet. At the close of each birthing season, Father again restricted me to a smaller, yet cozy area that housed us comfortably. Whenever Scout patrols were active, Father would alert me to hide in the Alcove adjacent to our home.

Father said I was always good at jumping far, so this challenge should be no problem for me. One Scout draws a line in the sand, and then quite a distance away draws another line. A tall lithe Scout demonstrates the object of this contest, and I signal to everyone in our group to make sure to land with knees bent, leaning forward. Then I show them that if they tilt backward they'll fall and they will lose.

The Scout goes to the first line and takes a few steps backward and draws another line. She pounds her chest and we watch her. She is standing just inside the first of the three lines and she takes a few running steps. Just before her foot hits the second line she is in the air, running in the air, her arms and legs continuing their movement, and she lands well beyond the third line. Mothers and Workers cheer. She draws another set of three lines and we are separated into two groups.

The first Beast in line is immediately jabbed by the spears and he sprints quickly and glides through the air, landing in the safety zone just outside the third line. A few more clear the line. Then one lands on the line, teetering backward, then forward, then backward again, trying to maintain his balance, faltering, now in control, now falling backward, landing between the second and third lines, and the gigantic rock quickly crushes him. Two Scouts drag him out of the way, pulling him by his floppy broken neck.

It's all in the run. I have to run at full speed, and lean, inclining forward. I can't take a chance on falling backward. One lanky contender trips and falls headlong not even making it to the jump's starting point. He quickly recovers and starts again, but the boulder is already rolling, and he runs. He's fast. He runs away, and two Scouts chase him, taking aim. They both launch their javelins, and he's pierced not once, but twice, through the chest. He is impaled completely, and the javelin is midway through him, but he is still standing, in disbelief as he looks at the two sticks that have gone through him. He tries to pull one out, falls over, but the javelins prop him up at an angle, and he struggles,

331

until blood gurgles up from his mouth. As the Scouts catch up to the condemned boy, his body goes limp, instants before they withdraw the javelins and return to the long jump. I run, I fly, I land, and I make it. We stand, the survivors, the winners, and then we sit and wait.

I ignore the observers whose frenzied shouts permeate the dome. I no longer watch, I no longer hear, I am numb.

Many of us will not lose, will not fail, and are immensely capable and strong physically. How many more games will we need to win to stay alive? The sun has conquered a third of the dome's breadth, and six of us have been eliminated. The exertion has left me spent, but I'm thinking more clearly now and catching my breath.

We are told to assemble in a straight line along some stones that lie at our feet. One Scout, standing near us, hurls a rock with all her might, trying to achieve a great distance. Father and I loved this game. One at a time, we hurl the rock and we wait, for thirty-five stones to come to a rest in the distance ahead. Two competitors, with the shortest throws, one to my far left, and the other kneeling just off to my right, are pushed forward by a Scout to retrieve their rocks. When they see the boulder they begin to run, but they have nowhere to go. The Scouts enjoy the challenge, taunting them, first letting them get away, and then pretending to give up. The Scouts signal for both to return to the line, to prepare for the next event.

But then one of them is ambushed, struck in the back of the head by a Scout's pounding fists, to be kicked repeatedly, and then a signal is given, and the boulder rushes in. I stand defiantly in front of the other losing contestant. The Scouts approach but we dodge them for a while until they notice the sun hitting the middle of the roof above. Our stall

332

works and they resume preparations for the next endeavor, letting my companion live, but taking notice of me.

The remaining competitors line up for a pole vault. The Scout makes it look effortless. Running with a long pole, then digging it into the sand, pushing up, letting go, and then flying over an elevated, horizontal stick. If we get over the stick without causing it to fall, we live. Those that are clumsy, inept at the game won't see it coming. The Scouts are standing with a boulder right next to the landing area. Father explained how this sport required technical finesse, and he was a taskmaster during my practices.

Fortunately the Scouts display three fingers, showing that we will each get three attempts, due the complications of using the pole. The bar is not set terribly high, for fear of knocking too many of us out too soon. They give us poles of four different sizes, which we allocate according to our weight, and they allow us to practice.

It's all about timing. Running with the pole horizontal, knowing where and at what angle to place the pole into the ground, and understanding when to release and fly over the bar in one continuous mechanical motion, is difficult. It's an unnatural motion, requiring strength, superior speed, and immense dexterity. If anyone lets go too early, he will fall headfirst into the box. Then the enormous rock will crush him, and his body will be removed, pulled away barbarously.

I take a pole and swing it around me in a circle so everyone knows I will go first. I want them to see I hold the pole toward the top, and that my right arm is fully extended vertically. My left foot is placed directly below my left hand, which is my take off point. I maintain upright and forward posture. I start from a standing position and take about ten to twelve steps, keeping my hips high and lowering the pole gradually. With just two steps left to reach my objective, I plant the pole as vertical as possible and extend my body at maximum forward speed and hurl myself over the bar.

Even Mothers and Workers are impressed, and whistle their approval. I do not need my two extra attempts but I return to take them anyway, not only to offer more visual examples to my companions, but also to see if the Scouts will exempt two of the more portly competitors due to my extra exertions. They agree. I choose two boys that couldn't possibly launch themselves over the bar. They stand aside, appreciative, marveling at my beneficence. When everyone has finished, one more body has been dragged to the side.

More than four hours have passed, and we are numb to our plight and to the misfortunes of our comrades. The next challenge looks excessively harsh. It requires two distinctly different simultaneous skills. We must run and hurdle over four objects while a partner runs parallel. We must also hurl a disk between us a total of four times before we reach the final hurdle. If we drop the disk twice, both are eliminated. Many drop the disk once, and bobble it anxiously, but no team drops it twice. Nervously joyous, we revel briefly.

The sun is more than three quarters across the dome. I think eight are gone, but I've lost count. Hopefully the next event is the last. The Scouts announce that this event is the battle to reach the cage. Rush the cage. The object of this one is clear to all. Get around the boulder safely back to the cage in an hour, before the sun sets on the far side of the dome, and we are winners. I try to gather the remaining competitors in a huddle, but some are impatient, and charge the immense rock, which directly blocks the doorway.

One lean, speedy, eager contender convinces others to join him, feeling safety in numbers. He dodges left, another right, several go straight at it, and the boulder rolls here, rolls there, catching an arm here, a leg there. Two have made it in, two have not and lay lifeless, mouths gaping, asphyxiated by their crushed rib cages, their impaled lungs, their smashed windpipes. A group diverts the boulder out of the doorway, and it rolls directly at the mob. Most escape, but two don't, yet sustain only minor blows to their hips.

Most of us have yet to attempt the rush, while some have rejoined us, having failed in their serendipitous journey to freedom. We pace and strategize, watching the sun, aware that if we don't make it inside the cage without delay, it will lock, and we are doomed. Full speed, we all charge the doorway, but too many too fast are trying to get in and bodies are tangled. Others still charge, trampling, pushing, and pulling limbs that are enmeshed in the narrow entry.

I'm in a wave of pushing bodies and I can't breathe. My chest is being squeezed. I'm pushing. We must get through the cage's entrance, which is unattended. The Scouts are getting closer, cursing us, and the boulder is coming. It's rolling so fast, right at the doorway, right at the huddle of us trying to force our way in, directly at the ones that are stuck, physically unable to pass through the threshold, their bodies squeezed awkwardly between the metal of the cage and various compressed parts of different bodies.

Struggling to remain conscious, we push and push. I am pushing the one ahead of me with my elbows, in his back, but he is unresponsive and terribly heavy. Others push me. Again the boulder is upon us. With a loud thud it hits the furthest of the competitors, and the entire line collapses, the force literally breaking the cluster of bodies that were blocking the doorway.

Then I'm atop so many bodies and so many are atop me. I slither from the pile, and my chest and head are now free, but my legs are stuck. The boulder's final impact pushed us mercilessly within the cage, our safety zone. We have won.

The top layer of boys are the most injured, but they are still alive and slowly drop from the peak of the pile, falling to the ground, in pain. Then I fall, and get up quickly resuscitating two critically injured brethren from unconsciousness. The door to the cage abruptly slams shut. Thirty-one of us have won our lives. Ten bodies on the perimeter somberly remind us of our fortune, their misfortune, and the fate we narrowly avoided. The sun has completed her journey.

Father, it's me, Atum, but you can't hear me. I made it. I'm so sorry. Will you forgive me? I should have listened to you. Tell me another story, about the way things used to be. You were so good to me. I would have died so long ago. I know why you saved me. You saved me so that I can change things, but now I've failed you.

Tell me about love. Tell me a story about love. I see Ava crying in the distance. I love her. Try to look after her. The cage is shaking horrendously, and we'll soon be free. They are shaking the cage and it's going to collapse. We are almost free, but I'm terrified.

XXXVIII

"Finally, the winners," speaks an impassive, stoic Lavender.

"Winners, yes, the winners," methodically repeats a shocked, distant, detached Antboy.

"Three quarters of the competitors made it."

"Three quarters, yes, three quarters." Antboy refuses to wipe away the flowing tears he had disallowed for so long.

With a depressed and dour expression, Lavender twists to face Antboy, and she attempts to bring closure to the day, "They have earned a precious victory. We have only you to thank, Antboy. Your masterpiece, the HSI code, the Codex has allowed this prophecy to be fulfilled."

"Your Majesty, you know I didn't write this horrid mess."

"I know. How often you told me that others twisted your studies, your work, into this new society. Their creatively devious and genius minds made this, what we have witnessed today, which was undeniably planned by men."

"This is just horrible, truly horrible," Antboy sputters and vomits again, but this time he uncontrollably heaves, and his body convulses; no more can be expelled, nothing remains. "My work was distorted, undeniably altered."

Queen Lavender completely loses patience with him. "What does it matter? This satellite will return to your home one day. Ten thousand of us will come home, but to what kind of world? Is it really better than here? Granted, it's probably better for Beasts there than here. However, my colonists are protected here. So do not judge me, Antboy.

"Today is the worst of it, a monstrous, horrific, required solution to limited resources and necessary rebirth. One brief day of violence, is all that we will tolerate. It's a small sacrifice to reinforce our belief system, and remind us that conserving our resources is important.

"Even if these domes are designed to prevent us from shortages, one day we will face limitations and tough choices. Our system ensures that our species persists and thrives during adversity, allowing a whole new population to exist, one that could not have had a chance otherwise. Females breed, males impregnate, that is the way things have always been, and that is how they will remain."

"Lavender, there is so much more to it; you never had a chance to understand that."

"What more could there be?"

"Much, much more." The eyes of Antboy are glazed, unfocused.

Queen Lavender authoritatively rises, saying, "We must leave. They will open the cage and chaos will reign. For fourteen days the Beasts will strive to fulfill their quest. I'm leaving before the Beasts realize that they can, as a whole, break out of that cage. We must go. I refuse to participate in the Aftermath. I'll return for the Closing Ceremonies on the fourteenth day. All is secure now. We have fulfilled the prophecy. Now, get up, we must go!"

With that, Lavender, and the trembling, distraught Antboy, head down to the Scouts to give the order to open the cage. Some Workers and Mothers rapidly file toward the doorway, to distance themselves from the imminent melee, while others stay and gawk at the spectacle. Two Scouts await the Queen, between the cage and the doorway, ready to escort her out, while two anticipate her order to release the winners.

Antboy and Queen Lavender reach the Scouts at the cage. Lavender commands the Scouts to open the cage, but first she will leave the dome. Antboy hesitates near the cage. Averting his eyes as he passes the cage, trying not to look, Antboy knows he must. He sees bruised, filthy bodies, but then leafy green eyes, impossibly green eyes.

"Atum?" In disbelief, Antboy stares at the cage. It is being shaken to its core by the impatient Beasts. The door bursts opens and the champions pile out. Frozen in his tracks, Antboy cannot move. He is utterly paralyzed. Two Scouts urgently usher Lavender out of the dome to safety.

"Atum! Atum!" Antboy's agonized screams fall muted against the cacophonous commotion. Roars of ecstatic relief are heard from the survivors who tumble from captivity.

Realizing that Antboy did not follow her, Lavender breaks free of the Scouts, and rushes back inside to retrieve Antboy, rebuking him, "You fool, we must go. Don't be stupid, this is no sight to see!" Antboy points, and Lavender looks at the scene. The victors approach the Breeder pen.

Some intrepidly, others warily, but all of us jubilantly thread our way through the event-lined stadium, gaining speed on our trek toward the circular pen where the Breeders await. I lead the pack by a few strides, but two Scouts are far ahead of me. The Scouts had taken off as soon as the cage door flew open, to preserve order and to soften the boisterous and raucous approach of the Beasts.

Past the point of exhaustion, the last dredges of desperate energy having been sapped by our triumphant squeeze into the cage, we plod forward. We anxiously approach the Scouts, who stand elevated on thick supportive poles, holding javelins poised to strike. We are signaled to assume the prostrate position of respectful submission, and in seeming synchronicity, we flop to the ground, bowing low. Breeders filter out of their enclosure and approach us.

I peer through an opening in our mass of leveled bodies to see Father and Queen Lavender standing in observance, midway between our cage and the dome's entrance. I look up to see Ava walking toward us. She immediately spots me and blinks nervously, a tear strolling down her cheek.

We're signaled to rise slowly. Then one of our crew, a gargantuan youth, the mammoth among us, pushes his way to the front and charges at the approaching girls. One Scout heaves herself from the pillar and tackles the offender, while the other Scout shouts and focuses our attention on the menacing spears that her arms project pointedly.

None of us move or cast a glance in the rogue's direction. Knocking the Scout sideways, he lumbers indecisively then centers his powerful strength and runs full speed, darting past us, toward the exit. The Scout guarding us throws a javelin, which spirals toward the runner, only to glance off the outer layer of his sinewy, muscular thigh.

I edge toward Ava unnoticed, and she runs to me. Our hands clasp gratefully. The injured Scout regains her footing, recovering quickly, and swiftly tosses a javelin toward the fleeing figure. As all eyes turn to witness the massive, clearly focused launch of the javelin, Ava and I make our exodus, our feet plowing the sand beneath us, toward Father, Queen Lavender, and the arched door to freedom.

The precision of the missile is astounding as we see the broad figure lurch forward, pierced in the center of his back. The sheer momentum of his gallop keeps him upright. The javelin's powerful thrust pushed the sharp blade to pass completely through his body, its midpoint immersing itself and resting in his chest. Miraculously, he mechanically bolts forward, blood spurting from his wound.

Ava and I weave to the side, hastily circumnavigating the dome's perimeter, cautiously withdrawing from the keen peripheral vision of the watchful Scouts, who focus on the desperately departing goliath. The Scouts hurl spears, but then withdraw as the Beast gets closer to Queen Lavender, who is standing adjacent to Father. Both are directly in the path of the charging form, who races toward them with the pointed javelin firmly entrenched in his body. Aiming to immobilize the threat, one of the Queen's escort Scouts rushes to block the menacing approach, and she braces for impact. Her body crumples from the crushing collision, the lodged spear ripping an artery near her collarbone.

Ava and I run faster, veering from our circuitous route, directly toward Father, as he moves in front of Queen Lavender, to fend off the imminent blunt force. Father is knocked down and trampled underfoot, tangling the massive legs of the frenzied frame, who loses his footing, stumbles forward, and falls upon the panicked, cowering Queen.

We race onward, heading to Father, who springs upright and jets to Lavender, adrenaline pulsing through his bruised body. He finds the large limp Beast, with spear enmeshed, hovering dead atop the Queen, in an eerily awkward position. Father pushes the colossal corpse with all his might until the deceased slides off the piercing javelin, which has impaled the Queen's abdomen.

Father kneels by Lavender, holding her close, whispering into her ear. He raises her slightly and points in our direction, and her eyelids flutter, but regain focus, acknowledging our approach. When we reach them, Father is on the ground, desperately, gently holding the bleeding Queen. She whimpers slightly, her eyes wide with terror, convulsing in agony.

"Father!" I shout at him to break the sad reverie into which he has fallen. I notice that Queen Lavender is straining to see me, far beyond what her injured, limited capabilities should allow. Yet she is intent on viewing me.

Antboy beckons me to kneel at his side, "Atum, I'm here. Come here, son."

Lavender wheezes, "Atum? Is that his name? Oh, how I wish I knew. Atum, come here." Blood gurgles from her parched lips, trailing down her mouth. Father cradles the perspiring Queen, caressing her blistering, beaded forehead.

She has a strange look, a puzzled expression of recognition, and also of shock and pain. The spear is deep inside her abdomen. I see her profound eyes, grassy green, so pretty, in pain, but so calm, trying to tell me something in her circular language. She is impossible to comprehend, spiraling infinitely, in randomly associated indecipherable syllables.

"Father? We have to go. The Scouts will be here any second," I urge him.

I look at her. She looks deeply into my eyes. With her weakened, shaking hand, she takes a key from around her neck and presses it into my palm.

"Father, we must go. Look, the Scouts, they're coming. Father, take my hand, Ava, run!"

Antboy breaks Atum's grip. "Son, go to the shuttle. Take Ava. I will follow soon. Go!"

Ava is pulling me, "We must go! We must go!"

"Father, we must go. Let's go, Father!" I implore.

"Atum, leave now! I must help her. I'll meet you. Go!"

Lavender reaches toward me. Respectfully, I take her hand and spontaneously kiss it. Oddly, my being resounds with pity for her unintentional misfortune, and I wish there was something I could do to ease her pain. Gratefully, she reaches further, to touch my face. Then, a strangely warm sensation tenderly and unexpectedly permeates my body.

"Atum, we must go! We must go!" Ava's insistent voice breaks the spell that holds me transfixed. I gently place Queen Lavender's hand in Father's. She smiles faintly and a slight rosy glow returns to her pallid complexion. Her short, shallow breathing resumes a normal pattern and her body relaxes into restful unconsciousness, slightly retreating from the tragic tumult.

"Father, meet us soon!" I demand. Father grips my hand, then releases. Ava pulls me and we run headlong for the door. I barrel forward, tackling a Scout guarding the exit, momentarily breaking Ava's grip. We run faster, into a nearby tunnel, turning left, left again, another left, completing a meandering circle that the Scouts would not predict. Certain that we haven't been followed, we stop to rest.

XXXIX

"Ava, Constance is meeting us near the shuttle, but we have a long path ahead," I pant.

"Atum, I know you're weary, but we can't wait long. The Scouts can track us easily."

"Then we better put more distance between us and them." Ava offers her outstretched arm. Leaning on it for support, I regain my equilibrium.

Jogging at a steady clip, we exert ourselves, pushing beyond what we thought possible. Having traced this path for years, with my fingers along the fading, lightly sketched parchment of the colony map, the twists and turns come easily, familiar in the deep recesses of my memory. We are soon out of reach of the Scouts.

Father needs to come immediately. He started the twenty-four hour launch sequence nearly twenty-one hours ago. If necessary, I'll abort but with severe consequences. The new countdown cycle will need another twenty-four hours. We'll surely be found, and face horrific ramifications.

I reach for Ava's hand, and she reaches for mine. We reach the end of a branched tunnel and we stop to rest. I see she is not yet comfortable with her flowing hair. She had faithfully worn it according to the standards prescribed by the Codex, which prohibited her from wearing it down. Only during culmination, at dawn this morning, when her class graduated, was she permitted to release her bundled hair. She took down the traditional hairstyle mandated to be worn up and about the head, in braids, as required of all Breeders. Now that she was of age for the Endeavors, she could freely choose the style of hair she wanted.

As we weave through tunnels for another hour, I notice that she is wearing the customary large rectangular linen tunic wrapped, but the formerly required sectional piece of wool is missing. Having graduated, she no longer needs to carry an attached blanket, as the younger girls do. I will keep her warm when we reach the cold metallic shuttle region.

She is challenging me, goading me to run faster, but my energy is spent. Struggling to catch up to her, I dig deep, focusing on the etched symbol on the back of her garment, the word for Constance. Ava's status was displayed while asleep and awake, by that one name, relegating her to a low ranking, having come from a female who birthed only one female child, unable to list a single sibling. Soon we will find Constance, donning a similar tunic, as usual showing just Ava's name. Seven more tunnels, six, five, four, three, two, at the end I see Constance, surrounded by four girls with their hair up, braided around their foreheads and temples, most bearing one or two names on their fresh attire.

Ava hails Constance, and shouts of joy ring forth. As we arrive I see four boys sitting to the side, Constance's favorite adolescent ragamuffins, with close-cropped hair, who she hurriedly scooped out of the Dome of Beasts. She

345

had taken them directly to the Dome of Girls Secondary, where she gathered her most complicit younger girls, of lower fertility ranking like Ava. No one took notice, since everyone was in another quadrant, at the Endeavors.

Within minutes we all arrive at the strikingly stark shuttle dock. With Father's arrival, we will be twelve. Bypassing the tedious procedures that Father had taken to reopen the shuttle door, I insert the electronic key that Queen Lavender had inexplicably taken from her neck and puzzlingly pressed into my hand. The door swings open, we rush in and I leave it open for Father to close later. Soon we settle into our protective suits and headgear. Constance adjusts and bunches up the extra material around the smaller children.

I glance at Ava's placid face and quickly look back at the excitement and energy spread across the faces of the children aboard the craft. I know how much depends on me. I quell the panic that again attempts to overtake me. I think about Father and the courage he has shown me and taught me. Nearly one hour to lift off. *Where's Father?* Above us, the bay door yawns open. Our craft methodically rotates to its vertical launch position.

"Where is Father?" I ask no one, everyone. I have no choice. I must abort our escape. I lean over the command control system and push the button. There is no response and the countdown continues. I push it again, and again, and still nothing happens. We are seconds away from the one-hour mark, when the door will shut irrevocably, and the final departure phase will commence. Ava sees my distress and my troubled demeanor as I pound and pummel the abort button, bashing it.

"Atum, Father wanted you off the planet. You know this was his plan for you, for us."

346

"I know Ava, but I need him with me!" The door retracts shut, loudly and definitively.

"You can do it, Atum. I believe in you. We are depending on you. Focus on us, Atum."

The engines begin to grow more confident and the next step is for me to simply push the autopilot button. I am calm, I am focused, and I have resumed breathing normally. The display asks if the shuttle should return to its point of origin. I answer affirmatively and we rock, pitch, yawl, and then we are completely vertical, and every membrane in our bodies is shaking violently.

Incredibly, the craft lifts, and then jolts upward in a steady ascent, and rolls, shooting impossibly outward. Our three main engines and two solid rocket boosters steadily overcome the gravitational force exerted on the craft, and propel us skyward to our destination.

Our bodies are pressed backwards into our seats for nearly eight unfeasible minutes, until we suddenly feel the strange, unexpected sensation of buoyancy. The shuttle flies fluidly as we break from the sun's orbit, and somehow I feel motionless, yet the view proves we are airborne. Heading toward the atmosphere of the unknown planet where Father was born, I vastly miss him already, and my inordinate pain progresses.

I turn toward the children. The boys, dressed in ragged clothing covering grimy bodies, are on one side and the girls, wearing their traditional apparel, the off-white robes of girls in waiting, are opposite them, each group staring distrustfully at the other. I explain to them wordlessly, with my eyes and my thoughts, that we are going on a journey to a place where we will live as a family and that both boys and girls will equally share the same freedoms and responsibilities. They stare at me, quizzically, without comprehension but their brows furrow not with apprehension but instead with trust and willingness to learn and obey.

Ava reaches for my hand and I feel at ease and settle in for what Father said is a twenty-six hour journey. While the children sleep, some fitfully, others peacefully, Constance does not rest, keeping her watchful, wakeful eyes on them, and I sense she is also wary of me. She knew me as Father's boy, deselected Atum, and she insured my survival, as she did with so many of the Beasts throughout the years.

To her, though, I am still a Beast, and I have convinced her daughter to leave her birth planet, and head with me to a foreign place. I will honor Constance. Father would want nothing less. As Ava and I stare at each other, through each other, into each other, we are equally as conscious of the uncertainties and dangers that lie ahead as to the hazards we left behind. In the stillness of that momentous median, our eyelids droop and sleep overwhelms us.

When I awake, Ava and Constance are sitting toward the back of the cabin, speaking with the children, comforting them, feeding them food from the sacks Father had hauled on board in preparation for our flight. The boys are hungrily inhaling anything put in front of them, this feast far out-weighing their normally meager rations. The girls keep their distance from the boys, and are jittery, mostly excited and sometimes giggle. A sense of mirth pervades everyone.

I don't know what to expect. Father says our shuttle is programmed to land in the Peninsula where most every shuttle departed and landed before the fleet was retired in '11. He said our shuttle had been decommissioned and sent to a museum as part of its permanent collection. Then, when the green light was given for launch five years later, it was pulled and readied for Departure Day. But our shuttle was not meant to return alone. It was scheduled to be the precursor vehicle, and was due to launch just ahead of the entire satellite planet, in twelve more years.

With the remote control I flip through some of the things Father has recorded for me. "Atum, seek out my parents and the General, who will be in their seventies, if still alive."

"What are you doing, Atum?" Ava asks, having returned to a nearby seat.

"I'm trying to figure out what we're supposed to do when we get there. Father has left me some specific instructions, and I'm reviewing them."

"It seems like a very different place where we're headed, strange and dangerous."

"It sure does, Ava, and complicated too."

Gracefully, our hunk of metal intuitively heads toward the planet. It flies with miraculous and effortless ease. As we continue to circle the beautiful planet below, our craft gains momentum and alters its trajectory angle, making the necessary adjustments to enter the atmosphere. The colors of the approaching planet outweigh every imaginable spectrum of color that Father taught me to envision. It is a spectacle that I could not have possibly anticipated, even in the most bizarre dreams of my subconscious. The surreal, mystical view fantastically casts its hypnotic spell upon us, and the children fall fast asleep, while Ava, Constance and I remain awake and mesmerized. The serenity of the shuttle allows me to be soothed by the steady hum of the thrusters, although Father has warned me that reentry can be quite unsettling.

I no longer fear what is ahead of us. I will return to Father as soon as humanly possible. I gape at the sphere incomprehensively, its magnitude more immense than my synapses had fathomed. I signal for everyone to brace for imminent reentry.

XXXX

As the shuttle shakes and rattles, emitting ghastly sounds, I focus on the video screen's new images. Two political pundits are debating Bombertown, the brainchild of convicted bomber Rednose. The ominous idea, which Father condemned, yet forever fascinated the General, had won its first legislative victory. Rednose had particularly opened up to Father's parents and their video camera in the next video clip, leading them on an egocentric expedition into the maniacal mind of a bomber.

Rednose explained that a bomber has issues with rage, but is able to contain and repress his irrepressible anger for great lengths, in order to time its explosion when he chooses. The bomber usually feels controlled by others, alienated, deemed a failure by someone important in his life, and often has been rejected by a lover. The greatest threat is the suicidal bomber who no longer wants to live. Ultimately the bomber wants attention, and is angry at the way the world has treated him. By creating a large explosion, instilling fear, and causing bodily harm and death, the bomber feels his statement is finally heard. After detonating a bomb, Rednose would simply vanish. For years he lived off the land, hiding in the vast outback woods, where he eluded capture for years. Periodically, he resumed bombing. Intermittently, Rednose bombed methodically, indiscriminately maiming and killing, evading detection, and frustrating authorities and international security experts. The furious public demanded his apprehension, and wanted improved security measures and enhanced containment protocol. The government responded vociferously by pledging reform, but it took many years to capture Rednose.

In the next video sequence that Father had arranged for our flight, he introduces it as a momentous press conference where the General speaks to the news media. The General displays architectural drawings of a two-mile by two-mile region in the desert, where he plans to build Bombertown. He recommends that his proposed facility be used for anyone convicted of detonating a bomb, making a bomb, possessing a bomb, or owning materials used to make bombs.

He asserts that projected infrastructure and maintenance expenses will cost taxpayers less long term than the accelerating budgets required to run the nation's maximum-security facilities. When fully funded and developed, Bombertown would never present a possibility for escape. He proposes that the world's bombers be dropped directly into Bombertown, and any previous threat that they had posed will be eliminated.

His plans called for convicts to be dropped, parachuted into his four square mile haven. Bombertown would restrict bombers to a place where they would essentially blow each other up. For those that wanted to kill, and those that

351

wanted to die, Bombertown would meet both their homicidal and suicidal needs, boasting an impressive array of explosive devices.

The General claims that the appeal of Bombertown would draw psychopaths and sociopaths to voluntarily visit the site. Once allowed in, they would not be let out. They would live and die by the mechanisms that appeased their fury. Rather than killing innocent victims, and destroying families, dangerous psychotics would be given an outlet. Bombertown would corral them so that they could harm only others sharing their illness.

Suddenly, the screen turns black. The ship quakes and violently rocks us against the harnesses that fasten us securely. We hurtle toward earth at breakneck speed. The children scream in fright. Constance and Ava are powerless to quell their anxiety. Fear tempestuously bubbles from clenched jaws, grinding teeth, and pursed, bitten, bleeding lips.

Several terrifying jolts shake us to the core. Our shuttle descends from the bleak exosphere, through the thermosphere, mesosphere, stratosphere, and finally to the temperate troposphere, where we cruise high above the planet's vast pool of reflective liquid.

The computer announces that we are T-minus twelve minutes from our destination. Anxiously scanning the horizon on both sides of the ship, I observe the immensity of the planet's watery surface, which Father described as the ocean. He explained that oceans covered seventy percent of the earth, and he predicted that the percentage had likely risen since his departure.

There is no land in sight. At T-minus six minutes, I spot a land formation, which fades illusively into the deceptive mirage from which it was conceived. At T-minus three minutes, I am growing concerned that our ship might just land in the ocean.

Father explained that our craft was equipped with multiple flotation devices, designed for what he called an inevitable ocean splashdown. Shrieking for everyone to hold tight and prepare for a crash landing, I clench the armrests of the Commander's chair firmly. As our shuttle descends, I scan the region, hoping to find the Peninsula. One minute is announced through the speaker. At T-minus thirty seconds, I panic and abort, which prompts the computer to search for, and select, an alternate landing base.

Unsure if the computer has understood my command, Ava, Constance, and I grimly watch the shuttle's shadow as it cruises the ocean below us. We're suddenly relieved when our craft begins to increase elevation, no longer descending. I quickly ascertain that we remain over water. The shuttle redirects toward new coordinates at a steady clip.

The dials displaying our energy reserves, markedly full at the inception of our journey, now read just under half capacity. I see a land mass ahead, and we're suddenly flying over miles of dusty, vacant land. An involuntary sigh escapes my lips; I am overwhelmed with relief.

A booming voice suddenly belches from the sound console, directly between the flight control panel and the video screen above, "This is IC-3366. We have intercepted your flight pattern, and request that you redirect. I repeat, this is IC-3366, and you are flying in restricted airspace. Please identify. Over."

"I am Atum. We were programmed to land at the Peninsula. There was no landing strip, just water. Over!"

"This is IC-3366. This is restricted airspace. You must depart this sector, within sixty seconds, or you will be shot down. Immediately change your quadrant coordinates. Over."

"Sir, listen! Do not fire on us! I repeat, do not fire on us! We're not hostile! Over!"

"This is IC-3366. Change your settings immediately. You are in violation of a no-fly zone, patrolled by the International Coalition. You have forty-five seconds. Over."

"I don't know how to redirect. Please, help us land! Over!"

"This is IC-3366. I have IC approval to shoot bogies in this region. I have a lock on you. T-minus thirty seconds. Over."

"I am under orders to contact the General at Central Command. Antboy sent me. We need help! Over!"

A few seconds tick away. "There is no General at Central Command. T-minus fifteen seconds. Over."

"HSI, we were launched by HSI! Over!"

The seconds churn, and heartbeats pound, and then, "This is IC-3366. We have confirmation. You've been acknowledged to land. Stand by for reprogramming. Over."

"Affirmative. Over!"

"This is IC-3366. Your alternate landing site has been programmed. Stand by, T-minus fourteen minutes. Over."

"Where are we landing? Over."

"White Sands Test Facility. I am turning you over to flight control. Over and out." The jets that had flanked the shuttle sharply veer away, and are swiftly out of sight.

The shuttle ascends again, and continues toward its destination. Indistinguishable voices can be heard from the flight command station, and every minute is read off as it ticks away. The panel shows that we are cruising at about ten thousand feet. Then our speed decreases and we descend toward a narrow landing strip in the sandy, dusty distance of desert ahead. The landing gear automatically deploys, and soon we touch down on the back wheels, the nose of the shuttle dips forward, and I feel a chute dragging behind the shuttle, helping to pull us to a stop.

Father had described the landing procedures as he remembered them, and I watch them through my portal window. No one approaches the orbiter for several minutes while we cool down. Small teams at the front and back of the orbiter test for hydrogen, hydrazine, nitrogen tetroxide, and ammonia, and we're cleared. The shuttle begins to power down. More than a hundred specially trained technicians and exigent engineers in protective outfits approach, riding in a convoy of two-dozen specialized vehicles. They surround our shuttle and flush and spray it with foam. Purge and vent lines are attached to our fuel lines and cargo bay. We wait an hour as toxic gases are removed. Thick foam drapes our windows, eliminating our view of the desolate surroundings, blocking the methodical, yet urgent preparations outside, careful measures executed swiftly throughout our unexpected arrival.

Barking commands are heard, then silence. Something bothers me about this reception. Then loud, blaring sounds erupt vibrantly from outside, forming a cadent march, repeating violently and warlike. An austere voice orders, bellowing above the cacophonous roar, "Open the door, and prepare to be boarded!"

Seeing my look of consternation, Ava states calmly, "It will be all right, Atum."

The controls beckon me to lift off. It is fight or flight for us. "I know, Ava. Go to the back and strap in the children, please."

XXXXI

Puffing effortlessly on the slimy stub of his favorite and most revered brand of cigar, freshly picked from his vast inherited collection of still banned tobacco, the retired General inevitably annoys those sitting around him eating ice cream. He pays no heed to the querulous comments, and poignant looks of disdain. Sitting in front of his favorite place for rumination, the ice cream bar decorated in superhero colors, he belches intuitively, pleased with his accomplishments, yet somehow discontent in his retirement. In response to the vibration of his phone, the recently retired General sees that he has a video message waiting.

Flipping open the screen, he sticks the smoky stub in his mouth and wonders if it will be a two-cigar day. The message is brief. A boy named Atum has arrived on a shuttle dispatched from an unknown source, and he's asking to speak with the General at Central Command. His orders are to fly to White Sands to meet with the boy. Momentarily stunned, he looks at the ice cream gobblers surrounding him, and they're surprised by his irregular look of astonishment. Realizing he's no longer a civilian, and that he has just been recalled to active duty, the General responds with mechanical military acumen and accesses a secure line to White Sands. Reacting quickly, he relays specialized instructions for detaining Atum and those accompanying him.

The newly unretired General relishes the thought of another cigar. This momentous occasion absolutely warrants a two cigar day. Atum has arrived!

Flagging down the two officers permanently assigned as his military escort, he is just getting used to the convenience afforded by this lifetime security fixture. They will swing the car around to pick him up rapidly, so that he can go home and pack.

The General is briefed on his ride home. Atum had landed at the nation's lead military testing facility, adjacent to the General's beloved Bombertown. Atum had been hesitant to get off the shuttle, actually refusing, until he was granted a meeting with someone that knew his father, Antboy. The standoff lasted for hours until someone ran a search and the General's name appeared, at which time Atum was reassured that he and his passengers would not be harmed. He agreed to leave the shuttle voluntarily in exchange for a guaranteed meeting with the General.

There could be no better news for the General than this unexpected visit from the satellite colony. Retirement had grown mundane, compared to the life he had led, but that was destined to change. These days, the General led a civilian life of regularity, rarely missing his usual television shows, particularly his favorite and most personal show, *The Colony*. While establishing his itinerary and packing his valise, he catches up on the past week's episodes. He had obviously missed some major events, given that Atum had somehow gotten off the satellite.

Scanning the missed shows in fast-forward, he realizes that Queen Lavender had escalated the commencement of the Endeavors. He didn't see this coming, having expected that they would begin in six months, as planned. Things had changed suddenly.

As he sits patiently for several hours, awaiting his ride to the air base, he views episode after episode. He watches the spectacle he never thought he would see. Antboy is nursing the comatose Queen Lavender, and the colonists remain respectfully distant, praying that their Queen will recover consciousness to lead them again. The General knows that Antboy's inferno of love for the Queen will never be consented to by the colonists. When they discover that there has been a breach, and that Constance and some children have fled, Antboy will be held accountable. The General could do nothing for Antboy, except pray that they would be merciful with him. Hopefully Antboy's life will be spared.

Now that Atum has arrived, the General ponders what will happen when he informs Atum of his parentage. Atum had sought the identity of his mother for so long, only to watch her nearly killed, and he still had not discovered that Lavender is his mother. The General surmises that Atum will gladly welcome an overdue introduction to one of his natural parents.

Never thinking that he would meet the only child he ever conceived, the General had not emotionally prepared himself for this possibility. When he had selected one of the colonists to receive his specimen of seed in the first vial, he was dubious that anyone would ever return, let alone during his lifetime. Known for his ability to choose future leaders, the General had picked well again. The colonist that had received his vial prior to Departure Day, the one bearing his genetic code, was later named Lavender, the outpost's first Worker Queen.

The General knows he cannot readily reveal to anyone that he is connected to Atum, nor that they are related in any way. The most important thing is to ensure that the media neither locate Atum, nor Ava, nor any of the refugees. Atum is the first child, in the history of mankind, to be born off the planet. To return more than a dozen years later, bringing others with him, is historic, yet embedded with great risk. Should the networks get word of these events, vital plans laid long ago could be ruined. Fortunately, there is a thirty-six hour delay on the video feed from the satellite. He will pull rank and postpone, then censor, certain upcoming broadcasts. There will be no broadcast of their exodus, exciting and dramatic as it would be, a guaranteed ratings sweep. He will make sure that international security trumps public awareness of this knowledge.

He must adequately seclude Atum and his clan before the blitz to pinpoint their position commences. He'll detain them for a while in the isolated, secure desert facility where they're being held. This way Atum will not discover the television coverage of his homeland. Without access to technology there, Atum will have no contact with the world, nor will he be able to attempt contact with Antboy. Of course, the General will make sure Atum and the other colonists are comfortable, and secure, as he had done with Antboy at the old Governor's mansion so long ago.

In a few months, he'll extradite them all to the underground colony, down where no one can ask them questions. He'll send Atum and the other refugees down, perhaps after five or six more consecutive monthly shuttles arrive at the mantle successfully. After eight years of failed monthly attempts, transport to the first underground colony had grown quite stable during the past eighteen months. Pioneering citizens, who signed waivers, were now allowed to make the formerly deadly journey, previously only assigned to Bombertown detainees. Bombertown, minutes from White Sands, was the place where the General selected his original test subjects, those convicts who incinerated during attempted transport to the mantle. Better there, than here on earth, the General always espoused. But now, people actually lived there, and before long, the General surmised, a spin-off will air, and break all ratings records.

Atum will be fascinated to see what his father, Antboy, had envisioned. Conjured from his imagination, Antboy's evolutionary dream had been executed successfully, and the mantle project was daring and revolutionary.

"Son, I am the General and I am pleased to meet you. Welcome home, son. It's good to have you home, son," practices the General, yet he realizes the insufficiency of these platitudes. "Welcome, son. I knew your father, Antboy, when he was just a couple of years younger than you. There is much to share with you, Atum. Let's get you settled," rehearses the General, satisfied with this greeting. Puffing gracefully in anticipation of the imminent encounter, he hears the car arrive to deliver him to his expectant son.

Ava seems almost transcendental in her visage, her composure enlightened, ever since we left the shuttle and took up residence in our large, vacant military warehouse. When I refused to open the shuttle, and things grew tense, I confided in Ava that I was deeply concerned, and afraid for our lives. I wanted to liftoff and return to Father and our home, but there was not enough fuel. She helped me reason through our options. I cannot reconcile the fact that she has such strong confidence in me. All that she utters calms me, and her demeanor reflects the love that I feel for her emanating from my heart.

"Atum, we have nothing to fear now, because we can build a future together. We can create our own destiny and make it anything we want it to be. We never had that choice before, but now we do. So, my dearest love, there is nothing to fear. And if you feel the fear, then think about what we have now, and what we left behind, and what we could have lost if we'd stayed. Never fear, never fear again, Atum, for I'm here with you, and together we'll be fine."

"Yes, Ava, we will be fine. I've been so afraid, because I didn't want to lose you. But right now I am no longer fearful, because you are here with me. I love you, Ava."

"I love you too, Atum," she whispers into my ear.

My will is strong and I know we will survive and prosper, regardless of our plight. Soon, I'll meet the General and tell him about our home and the Endeavors. While awaiting his arrival, I venture outside to experience the oppressive heat of the desert that surrounds us. Due to our vulnerability and limited exposure to this strange environment, our guardians insist that we wear protective clothing when we're outside the designated, sanitized shelter.

As I move my gloved, protected hand over an abandoned anthill, and the surrounding dirt, I spot something unusual and then I discern another and another. My finger sweeps playfully along one blade and the next and I see that the entire area is just budding with these little blades. Quickly, I pull one up and run excitedly toward our new home. I must ask Ava if this blade is actually the color of my eyes as Father had insisted. Beholding this bloom of green grass, the essence of life, I hurry to Ava with love and renewed hope.

ABOUT THE AUTHOR

Scott Pauker, author of *The Colony Chronicles*, was born in Philadelphia, Pennsylvania in 1968, and studied at the University of California, Los Angeles. His collection of short stories, *Eight Tales from the Loony Bin,* has been translated into four languages. He resides in Los Angeles, California with his two children.